Totally Bound Publishing books by Tracy St. John

Clans of Kalquor

Alien Embrace
Alien Rule
Alien Conquest
Alien Salvation
Alien Slave
Alien Redemption
Alien Refuge
Alien Caged
Alien Indiscretions
Alien Hostage

Clans of Kalquor

ALIEN INDISCRETIONS

TRACY ST. JOHN

Alien Indiscretions
ISBN # 978-1-78686-358-4
©Copyright Tracy St. John 2018
Cover Art by Posh Gosh ©Copyright May 2018
Interior text design by Claire Siemaszkiewicz
Totally Bound Publishing

This is a work of fiction. All characters, places and events are from the author's imagination and should not be confused with fact. Any resemblance to persons, living or dead, events or places is purely coincidental.

All rights reserved. No part of this publication may be reproduced in any material form, whether by printing, photocopying, scanning or otherwise without the written permission of the publisher, Totally Bound Publishing.

Applications should be addressed in the first instance, in writing, to Totally Bound Publishing. Unauthorised or restricted acts in relation to this publication may result in civil proceedings and/or criminal prosecution.

The author and illustrator have asserted their respective rights under the Copyright Designs and Patents Acts 1988 (as amended) to be identified as the author of this book and illustrator of the artwork.

Published in 2018 by Totally Bound Publishing, United Kingdom.

No part of this book may be reproduced, scanned, or distributed in any printed or electronic form without permission. Please do not participate in or encourage piracy of copyrighted materials in violation of the authors' rights. Purchase only authorised copies.

Totally Bound Publishing is an imprint of Totally Entwined Group Limited.

If you purchased this book without a cover you should be aware that this book is stolen property. It was reported as "unsold and destroyed" to the publisher and neither the author nor the publisher has received any payment for this "stripped book".

ALIEN INDISCRETIONS

Prologue

The Kalquorian Empire was and still is a civilisation of great importance to the Galactic Council of Planets. The fierce but intelligent species has been at the forefront of technological, medical and scientific breakthroughs for millennia. Their military might has never been in question—even their ancient enemy, the opportunistic race of Tragooms, hesitates to attack a Kalquorian force half its size.

However, Kalquor's survival is in jeopardy. The force that threatened this mighty race was not one that wielded weaponry. It could not even be seen with the naked eye. It was a virus.

Centuries ago, this virus struck the home world of Kalquor, wiping out a substantial number of its people, particularly the females. Symptoms included massive bleeding of the body's major organs, along with those of the female reproductive tract. Damaging the X-chromosome of the Kalquorians, the virus's effects went beyond death. The majority of women not killed outright were rendered infertile and daughters born to those who could bear children were not guaranteed the ability to do the same. The virus altered the very DNA of the entire race.

In an effort to keep their race from going extinct and prevent fighting amongst the men, family groups called clans were formed. Each clan was made up of one female known as the Matara (childbearer or 'lifebringer') and representatives of each of the three breeds of male—the Dramok (leader), Imdiko (caregiver) and Nobek (protector).

Despite their efforts, the numbers of Kalquorians continued to decline. So few children were born that many thought extinction to be inevitable. The Kalquorian culture seemed destined to disappear despite all their medical expertise and attempts to find compatible species to mate with.

A little over a decade ago, a scout ship from a small, isolated planet no one knew of flew into the Galactic Council of Planets' space. These newcomers, searching for a new planet to house the overflow of their ever-growing population, called their home planet Earth. It was immediately remarked upon how similar they were to Kalquorians. The doomed race took note at once and hope was restored. It was theorised that perhaps the Earthers were the fabled Lost Tribe of Kalquor's ancient ancestors.

Earth, however, was not as enthralled with their potential distant cousins. Ruled by a government based on fanatical religious beliefs, Earthers were taught they were God's Chosen, made in his wondrous image. They looked upon Kalquor with hostility and outrage, particularly since the beleaguered inhabitants of that empire suggested compatibility testing for purposes of interbreeding.

The leaders of the Kalquorian Empire, feeling they had no other recourse, decided the time had come to seduce Earther females and convince them to come to Kalquor. Women on Earth were treated as lesser creatures and second-class citizens by their government and religion and the Kalquorians, with their near-worship of women, hoped they could entice these lifebringers to join their clans. And if the women would not be seduced, Kalquor was no longer above the distasteful necessity of abducting them outright.

Almost two thousand Earther women went to Kalquor, putting the Empire and Earth at each other's throats. Then the unthinkable happened—an Earther woman joined the aliens' ruling clan, making her Kalquor's empress. Earth immediately declared war.

The fighting was horrific, with Earth's greater numbers slowly overwhelming Kalquor's more advanced technology. With its already dwindling numbers reaching crisis stage, the Empire was desperate to find a way to win the war and secure its future. It staged an invasion of Earth itself. Earth's answer was to set off nuclear explosions beneath its own major cities, devastating the population and dooming the planet.

Kalquor has rescued most of the survivors. Some women, traumatised by their experiences under Earth's tyranny, have dared to start anew with the Kalquorians. There are still too few to guarantee Kalquor's survival and most of the alien men hold these Mataras in the highest regard.

But not all Kalquorians are happy to have the Earthers amongst them. Some are determined to see Kalquor go extinct rather than mix the species. Many who have not attracted women to their clans feel they have been unjustly denied. Those with a political axe to grind ask the question, who exactly ordered the abductions of the first Earther Mataras? Who should answer for the deaths of billions and the destruction of an entire planet?

A revolt, led by a shadowy figure known only as 'the Basma', is brewing amongst the disaffected Kalquorians. Those in power know it won't take much to widen the rift between those clans who have won lifebringing females and those who have not. A wrong word, a thoughtless gesture or a long-held secret is all that is needed to shake the foundations of an Empire…and finish the existence of two cultures already teetering on the brink of extinction.

Prelude to a Scandal

Imperial Father Nobek Yuder wandered his home set in the cliffs overlooking the ocean. The Imperial Fathers' Suite felt cavernous with emptiness. He thought about calling out for his Imdiko Tidro but did not dare. He had the suspicion that his long-time clanmate would not answer. For the first time in his life, Yuder felt alone, as if everyone he'd ever loved had been erased from the world.

It was a ridiculous fancy, certainly one beneath a Nobek of his strength and standing. Yuder had faced many enemies over the years. He had been threatened with death and killed a number of men during his long life as a warrior and protector. He'd loved and lost before. He'd survived. Yet the former emperor couldn't shake the sensation of having been utterly forsaken. The ball of fear lodged in his throat, the one that kept him from calling Tidro's name, would not budge.

He found his clanmate standing on the balcony outside the sleeping room that had been used solely by their Dramok for the last few years. Imperial Father

Zarl's poor crippled body had degenerated to the point that no one could sleep on the same mat with him without causing him considerable pain. Tidro had taken over one of the guest suites in their apartments, with Yuder and his Earther lover Tara occupying another.

The bed was now empty. Yuder did his best to keep from looking at it as he passed.

Yuder paused in the archway that led out to the balcony. His Imdiko stared out at the snarling ocean. The elder man's long, bone-white hair flew wild in the wind. Tidro still wore the mourning robes of brown along with a thick black cape, the hems of both flapping in the stiff breeze. It was cold out there, especially with that wind coming off the sea. Tidro had no business standing in the blustery elements.

His Imdiko clanmate looked so very alone out there. The balcony had been stripped of all its furnishings at the beginning of winter. It remained bare, as the soon-to-arrive spring had not yet put in an appearance.

Seeing Tidro like that made something in Yuder's throat ache. How would they continue on without Zarl? What was their clan without its Dramok?

He tried to concentrate on the fact that he still had Tidro. He also had Tara McInness, the beautiful Earther woman he'd made his lover. A Nobek didn't often like to think he needed others for strength. Still, he was willing to admit privately to himself that Tidro and Tara had been the rocks he'd clung to in the last few stormy days of Zarl's final illness and passing.

Unfortunately, those storms would only build in strength in the coming weeks. Yuder had a duty to his Imdiko. He had to keep Tidro safe against the trouble that awaited them. He didn't know if his placid but stubborn clanmate would allow it.

Squaring his shoulders, Yuder stepped through the home's temperature-control shield to join his clanmate in the bitter wind of the night. The cold seemed to slide straight through him despite his heavy cloak.

He made his steps loud enough to be heard over the moaning wind. He didn't want to startle the other man by suddenly speaking in his ear. Tidro tilted his head in his direction, but he didn't turn around.

Yuder chastised him as he drew near. "My Imdiko, you shouldn't be out here in this cold." Acting like a nurturing Imdiko himself, he tugged Tidro's hood up over his head.

He got a slight smile for his efforts. Tidro leaned back against his chest when Yuder circled his arms about him.

The Imdiko asked, "Where is Tara?"

Yuder couldn't help but smile at the sound of his beloved's name. "She's with her daughters and the grandchildren. The little ones do not quite get the concept of where their grandfather Zarl has gone."

"Lucky younglings." Tidro sighed. A single tear tracked down his creased cheek. "I miss him already, my Nobek. My heart cries for my Dramok. Yet at the same time I am relieved he has died."

Yuder nodded his understanding. "He had suffered too damned long. There was no quality left to his life. Even the pleasures of his grandchildren offered little joy in the end."

It made Yuder angry that a good man had died in such needless pain. Those who had cursed Zarl with a crippled, weakened body had died years ago in terrible ways. Still, their executions had not spared the clan leader any agony in the end.

As gentle as Tidro was, his voice nonetheless shook with the same fury that Yuder felt. The Nobek also detected an unhealthy dose of guilt lying beneath it. "Damn it, Yuder. There was no glory in Zarl wasting away as he did, wracked with pain. He deserved a better end."

Yuder spoke in his ear as consolingly as one of his fierce breed could. "You did all you could to give him comfort. I know he was grateful."

"I can't stop thinking I should be attending him. I catch myself wondering, did I take Zarl his latest round of medicines? Should I check to see if he requires something to eat or drink? Then I remember he doesn't need any of that anymore."

Yuder's grip on him tightened. "The pain is over for him. Now it is time for you to do something for yourself, my Imdiko. You have sacrificed your own needs these last years to serve his."

Tidro laughed, but there was no humour in the sound. It sounded more like sobbing to Yuder. "I have no idea what to do with myself anymore, my Nobek. I'm no longer an emperor. I'm no longer needed as a nursemaid. You have your lovely Tara to see to you. What do I do?"

It was the opening Yuder had hoped for. He said, "I think a retreat for you to rest and recover from your grief is in order. Perhaps the Temple of Life on Alirsu would be a good place."

"But that moon is so remote, Yuder." Tidro considered and added, "Though the thought of quiet and contemplation is appealing at this stage. Hiding away from my cares and getting out of this place where I see Zarl everywhere would be good."

Yuder insisted, "It would be healing. You can figure out what it is you wish to do now that you have time to be selfish."

Tidro twisted around in his arms to face him. His eyes narrowed with suspicion, driving deep creases in the corners. "You may think you're fooling me, but after nearly two hundred years, I know better. Why are you trying to get rid of me?"

Yuder scowled to be caught, though he wasn't surprised. Tidro was nobody's fool, not by a long shot. Just because he had always been the quietest member of Clan Zarl didn't mean he didn't see everything going on around him.

He said, "The Royal Council will be going through Zarl's official records soon."

Tidro shrugged. "Of course. That's what always happens when a monarch or former monarch dies."

"They will learn the truth of the Earthers being brought here to Kalquor."

The Imdiko rolled his eyes. "So?"

"It will give them the proof some have searched for. With this threatened rebellion, it could lead to more trouble. Open revolt is not out of the question."

Tidro snorted. "Rebellion. Revolt. The Basma and his fools with their ridiculous defence of the 'pure' Kalquorian. We are dying out, Yuder. The Kalquorian Empire was coming to an end. What choice did we have?"

Of them all, Tidro had always been convinced that they'd done the right thing. Zarl and Yuder had held reservations about kidnapping the Earther females that now gave the Empire hope. In the end, for better or worse, desperation had won out.

To his Imdiko, Yuder said, "Why we made the decision we did doesn't matter to those who oppose mixing Kalquorians and Earthers. The fact remains that we took women away against Earth's wishes—and sometimes against the women's wishes—which led to war with Earth. Many of our own died and Earth is a dead world now."

Tidro's tone turned hot. "Due to the crazy religious faction that ruled that planet."

"Due to us taking their females in order to continue our culture," Yuder corrected firmly. "Let's not pretty this up, my Imdiko. No matter how desperate we were, we did something that resulted in billions of deaths. Billions, Tidro."

Tidro still wouldn't accept any of it as their doing. "We had no idea how mad their leaders were. How could we know they would destroy themselves like that? It's not like we triggered the explosives ourselves. The last thing we wanted was to see Earth destroyed!"

It was easy to be patient with his Imdiko, since Yuder had long given up on changing his mind about the matter. "It doesn't matter what we did or didn't know at the time. What matters is it happened and the likelihood is great that Zarl's records will show our complicity. The disaffected will flock to the Basma's rebellion once it comes out. There will be many shouting for justice for the dead. I want you out of here before that happens."

Tidro stared at him. "What are you saying, Yuder? That you will take the blame on my behalf? Am I to blithely go off to contemplation while you are dragged into an enquiry? Maybe even a trial?" He shoved at Yuder and the Nobek let himself be driven back as Tidro vented. "By the ancestors, the Galactic Council of Planets has been after us for these last three years to allow them to open an investigation of their own. What if they drag you out of the Empire to face those charges?"

Yuder kept his tone even. "My fate was predetermined from the moment I was born a Nobek and a prince. I am Empire and clan protector. My function is to see to it that my people remain safe from all threats. Failing that, I see to my clan. Zarl is now beyond the reach of those who would harm him, but I can still shield you."

Tidro scowled. "Don't be a fool. I supported our decision. I argued with you and Zarl for that decision."

"You did what you thought best for the Empire. We all did. It still remains that some women were brought here against their will. The charges that will be brought are valid."

The Imdiko clenched his fists. "I regret none of it. Those poor Earther women lived under such oppression…charged for lewdness when they were raped. They were even executed for it. Executed, Yuder! For the crimes committed against them!"

He paced now, storming up and down the balcony as he dealt with guilt he refused to acknowledge. "We saved some of them. Most have been made happy since coming here."

Yuder had let Tidro enjoy his illusions all these years. The idea that they had done the Earther women a service had kept his Imdiko's mind at an uneasy peace. Yet the time had come for Tidro to face the consequences of their actions. Hard truths were bound to come out now, truths that could put his elderly clanmate in a prison camp…or worse. Yuder couldn't let that happen.

He told Tidro, "More Earthers died than were saved."

Tidro halted in his tracks. He stared at Yuder for an instant, his expression one of great misery. He bowed his head. "Damn you."

Yuder sighed. He was not nearly as old as Tidro, but he felt the weight of too many years on his shoulders nonetheless.

He told the Imdiko, "My clanmate, my greatest concern now is you."

Tidro shook his head. "If they need a scapegoat so badly, they can do as they like. Put me on trial. Sentence me. It makes no difference any longer."

"It makes a difference to me. You are nearing your two hundred and fortieth year. I will not have you sentenced to a penal facility at your age."

Tidro looked up at Yuder, his expression startled. "Clajak would never allow it."

"Our son is an emperor. To maintain the stability of the Empire, he and the rest of the Imperial Clan may have no choice but to let justice be served." Yuder took Tidro in his arms. He tried not to think how frail the aged body felt against his. "My Imdiko, you are all that is left of my clan. You must let me protect you."

Tidro wasn't quite ready to give up the fight. "What of Tara? You have found love with a woman again, one that makes you happier than I've seen you in decades. What of her?"

Yuder kept the throb of regret and pain to himself. "She is strong and able to bear what I may have to go through."

"And you think I can't?"

Yuder had to chuckle despite the trouble in his heart. "I have come to believe that Mataras and Imdikos are the strongest of us all. You would be my strength in the times ahead, as you have been so many times before. As you were Zarl's." His grip on Tidro tightened. "It is I who cannot bear to see your pain. I am the one who is weak."

The other man frowned at him, but Yuder felt how his clanmate's body softened. Thank the ancestors, Tidro was beginning to see reason.

Pressing his advantage, Yuder pleaded, "Go to Alirsu, Tidro. Do it for my sake. I cannot watch you dragged before an enquiry and interrogated like some common criminal. I cannot remain strong when people call for you to pay the price of our short-sightedness."

Tidro bowed his head. Tears dripped from his eyes to the stone balcony beneath their feet. Yuder prayed to the ancestors that his Imdiko would do as he was asked. He had already vowed to himself that if Tidro refused to go on retreat, Yuder would force him into hiding. He would not watch his clanmate face the coming controversy, not so soon after coping with their Dramok's death.

"All right. If it is what you truly wish, I will go." The aged man's voice came out in a sob.

"Thank you, my Imdiko." Yuder's grip tightened around Tidro.

Tidro returned the embrace, holding fast to Yuder. They clung to each other, as if the other man were all that kept them from being taken away.

Yuder had never felt as fragile as he did now. He felt like a hot-air balloon that was held to the earth by one last straining mooring. The storm lashing the balcony only intensified that feeling. Zarl's death had torn his clanmates' world apart.

The wind continued to blow hard. Even if it had been calm, Yuder would have felt adrift without the anchor of his Dramok.

Chapter One

Cissy gripped hands with her identical twin sister, Tasha. She tried to appear cool and calm for the Kalquorian shuttle attendants. They didn't need to know how her heart raced or that her palm sweated as freely as Tasha's. She prided herself on always looking in control, even when control seemed well out of reach.

They'd left the doomed Earth nine months ago on a large transport, now in orbit around the planet of Kalquor. Most of the other women on board had been taken to the complex that would house them until they found clans to join. Though Cissy and Tasha also planned to live in the complex, they were regarded as a special case. They had gotten a shuttle all to themselves and it had just landed within a cliff. They stood now before the hatch, waiting for it to open.

To Cissy's surprise, the bay did not look like it was within a great rock jutting onto the pink-sanded shore on the planet Kalquor. The vid viewer to the left of the Salter twins showed them a thoroughly modern landing area with soft illumination glowing from the walls and ceiling. Other shuttles and transports dotted the large area.

The vid also showed them a number of people waiting for their arrival. There were easily fifty individuals out there, if one didn't count the red-formsuited guards at attention all over the place. Most of those outside the shuttle were the dark-skinned, black-haired Kalquorian race. They were almost all male…unabashedly masculine and muscular men. Judging from the blue robes worn by many in the group, they were also politically powerful men, the ruling elite of the Kalquorian Empire.

Cissy swallowed against the rush of nervousness that flooded her. Her cousin Jessica had clanned with the emperors of Kalquor. As a member of the empress's family, Cissy herself had been treated with deference throughout her journey here, deference that bordered on embarrassing. Still, the status she'd gained hadn't made a real impression until this moment.

Tasha sounded just as breathless as Cissy felt. "Wow. It looks like half the Royal Council showed up along with the Imperial Family. You'd think we were important."

Cissy was glad she wasn't the only one feeling a bit off-balance. She whispered, "Who would have ever guessed we'd end up related to royalty? I am so underdressed for this."

Tasha emitted a nervous giggle as her long-lashed hazel eyes took in Cissy's denim trousers and black T-shirt. At least she'd also thrown on a nice turquoise button-down blouse, which Cissy wore unbuttoned over the tee. "Better than flaunting all your wares like you've been doing on the transport." Tasha winked. "Everyone knows you hate pretension. No sense dressing like someone you're not, Cis."

Cissy eyed her twin. Tasha liked pretty clothes, so she looked perfectly presentable in her purple wraparound dress. She'd put her dark brown waves into a tidy bun, except for the few tendrils that had artfully escaped from it.

Except for their clothing, they were nearly impossible to tell apart. They'd even gained the same amount of weight during their nine-month trip from Earth to Kalquor. Close to starved to death before finally admitting there was no choice but to turn themselves in to their former enemies, the petite pair had resembled children at first glance. It had been hard to convince their rescuers they were in their early thirties.

Discovering that Cissy and Tasha were also first cousins to the Earther Empress of Kalquor had caused quite the sensation amongst the aliens. Though supplies in those last days of evacuating the dying Earth had dwindled, the Kalquorians had made sure the women had everything they could give them. That included copious amounts of delicious food, which the sisters had availed themselves of without restrictions.

Cissy had laughingly referred to Tasha and herself as Chub One and Chub Two for the last couple of months. Tasha hated hearing that. She constantly insisted she was going to eat less and take up an exercise regimen. Yet the men on the transport that brought them from Earth to Kalquor had discovered how much the pair loved chocolate…and pizza…and pie…and many, many other things. Edible gifts from those wishing to enjoy the twins' favours had abounded.

'Stop fretting,' Cissy had told her twin more than once as they'd walked the corridors of the huge Kalquorian ship. 'So we're curvy gals now. None of the Kalquorians are complaining. In fact, I keep hearing how soft I am.'

'These men do seem to appreciate the extra cushion,' Tasha had agreed. 'But I'm logging another mile before I take it easy this evening. Those fried mozzarella balls Dramok Niot brought me this afternoon are not adding another inch to my ass!'

'Didn't he already help you work them off?' Cissy had teased.

'A lady doesn't discuss such things.'

'A lady also doesn't yell "Harder, you beast" at the top of her lungs for all the Matara section of the ship to hear.'

'Pig.'

'Prude.'

Thinking about all the eating they'd done following weeks of starvation made Cissy feel nauseated as she waited for the shuttle's hatch to open. If the Kalquorians on board the transport hadn't been devoted to showing her how much they approved of cuddly girls, she'd be even more nervous. Especially since her space-pale porcelain skin contributed to what she thought of as the doughy look.

I hope the Earthers who got here before me convinced the Kalquorians to stock up on tanning spray. I'm not walking around like a living marshmallow.

Tasha drew a deep breath. "Well, here we go. It's time to greet Empress Jessica. Are we supposed to curtsey or something?"

Cissy laughed harder than the statement warranted. She told her twin, "Jessica will break both your legs if you dare. You know that girl. No way living on an alien planet has changed her that much…even if she is royalty now."

Cissy checked the vid to reassure herself. Their youngest cousin, standing in the bay on the other side of the hatch, looked impatient as only Jessica could. No, she couldn't have changed much…right?

Jessica's mother, Tara, had been the sister of the twins' father. While Jessica and her older sister, Lindsey, had lived in Fort Lauderdale, Florida, the twins had lived in Lower Matecumbe Key. Frequent visits had made them all fast friends…and had gotten Cissy and Tasha detained by authorities when Jessica had been proclaimed Kalquor's empress.

None of that was important now. Cissy and Tasha would have given their lives for their cousin. Fortunately, it hadn't come to that. Now they would be reunited with the last living members of their family. Excitement made itself the equal partner to anxiety.

The Imdiko flight attendant on the shuttle stepped up to one side of the hatch and bowed to them. "Are you ready to greet your family, Mataras?"

"As ready as we'll ever be."

The young, handsome Kalquorian smiled encouragingly. Though he'd kept in the background during the flight from the transport except to offer them refreshments, Cissy was pretty sure he'd listened in on their conversations. His breed was dedicated to nurturing others. He'd have eavesdropped to make sure they had everything they needed. The Kalquorians Cissy had met, whether the solicitous Imdikos, the protective Nobeks or the guiding Dramoks, were always kind to a fault to Earther women. A number of the aliens rejected the need for Earthers to breed with, but so far she'd not run across those people.

The attendant issued the open command and the hatch slid away. Stairs descended beneath the opening, waiting for the women to disembark.

Tasha balked at the last moment. Since she was dressed nicer than Cissy, she was to have stepped out first, but panic asserted itself and she hesitated. Her hazel eyes wide, she told Cissy, "You're the brave one. You go first."

Cissy's heart thundered and she attempted to cover her sudden terror with humour. "The brave one? I thought you said I'm the twin with no sense."

"That too. That's what makes you so brave." Tasha gave her a little push.

"Twit."

"Moron."

The women grinned shakily at each other. Then Cissy squared her shoulders and took a step forward. She'd always been the tough one of the pair. She'd protected her sweeter-natured sister when situations had called for it. She didn't like to think about some of the things she'd done to make sure Tasha would not be hurt.

Cissy led the way off the hatch, holding Tasha's hand at the small of her back as she might a small child. To keep her cool, she refused to look at the crowd of huge, muscled Kalquorians, members of royalty and the elite. Instead, she looked at her cousins and aunt, seeking the old warmth of family thought long-lost.

Cissy needn't have worried about their reception or greeting Jessica with regal decorum. Like the exuberant children they had been, Jessica and Lindsey shrieked with delight at the twins' appearance. Cissy yelled back in a wordless shout of happy greeting.

The four women didn't run across the space separating them, but they didn't precisely walk, either. Within moments they were in a knot of embracing arms, laughter and joyful tears. Cissy thought they all spoke, saying one another's names and talking over one another, but she wasn't sure of anything that was said. The glee of full hearts overrode everything else, making words meaningless. Emotion ruled for several minutes.

At last the four women began to talk sense to one another, the first burst of exhilaration easing enough to do so. Jessica wasted no time in chortling and tugging on one of the belt loops of Cissy's jeans.

"There's my rough and ready tomboy cousin! You haven't changed one bit, Cissy!"

"Well, you have. When did you get so fat and ugly?"

Jessica shrieked with laughter, knowing the joke for what it was. In truth, she looked spectacular. The years since Cissy had last seen her cousin had been more than kind. Jessica was almost thirty now. Maturity, along with a few extra pounds, had softened her once too-stark elfin features. Jessica was still tiny, especially compared to the Kalquorians standing nearby, but at least now a breeze had no chance of blowing her away.

Elder sister Lindsey planted a kiss on Cissy's cheek. Bigger boned with classically lovely features, Lindsey appeared just the same as when Cissy had last seen her. "We've missed you two so much!" she exclaimed. "I can hardly believe you're here."

"Can I join in?" came a melodious and calm voice.

Cissy and Tasha turned at once to see an older, shorter version of Jessica beaming at them. "Auntie Tara!" they simultaneously cried. They wrapped their father's sister in a hug between them, kissing and exclaiming with abandon once again.

When they'd calmed once more, Tara jerked her chin towards the three men heading their way. "Here are the rest of us. They've been almost as excited for your arrival as we have."

One of the three emperors did not have the typical black hair of the Kalquorians. Instead, his shoulder-length locks were the colour of dark steel. Cissy was amused to have an emperor bow before her and her sister before he shook a warning finger at them.

Blue-robed Dramok Emperor Clajak gave them a mischievous grin. The expression lit his broad, handsome face and crinkled the skin at the corners of his eyes. "Don't you dare bow to us, you two. I am glad you made it here safely, my cousins. Welcome home."

The heart-stoppingly gorgeous Nobek Emperor Bevau also bowed to them, his red robes doing little to hide the perfect body beneath them. "And if half the stories Jessica and Lindsey tell us are true, the Empire will never be the same."

His comment brought laughter from everyone, including the often aloof Imdiko Emperor Egilka. As staid as the eldest member of the Imperial Clan often was, his smile offered pure warmth as he added his welcome. Cissy thought Egilka should smile more often. It softened his sharp features.

Apparently, he was loosening up these days. He even hugged the twins, wrapping them in his emerald-green robes. Leaner than his clanmates, Egilka still felt like muscled granite to Cissy. Nice. Very nice. She had to remind herself not to grope her cousin's Imdiko.

When he released her and stepped back, Cissy fixed Jessica with a glare. "Oh, so you're telling stories on us, are you? I think we might have a few of our own to share about the empress and the Imperial Sister."

Jessica and Lindsey shook their fists. "Put them in chains and throw them in the dungeons!" Jessica cried.

Clajak gave her one of his naughty grins. In a voice kept low so only their family could hear, he said, "We don't have dungeons, my love. As for the chains, you know they are reserved for you."

Cissy guffawed with the emperors and Lindsey as Jessica turned pink. The small empress punched her Dramok none too gently in the stomach. He laughed harder, not reacting with the slightest hint of pain.

Tasha set about rescuing Jessica from being the centre of attention. "Clajak, I am so sorry about the loss of your father Zarl. Jessica always had the highest regard for him, so I can only imagine how it's affected you."

Clajak's hilarity fled, but his smile stayed steady as he bowed to Cissy's twin. "Thank you. I miss him more than I can tell, but at the same time, I am glad his pain is over. His life might have been cut short, but it was full and he was much loved. For that, I am grateful."

Jessica waved her hands as her eyes filled with tears. "Oh, don't get me started crying. I wish you could have met Father Zarl. He was wonderful."

That started off a fresh round of hugs between the cousins and Aunt Tara. Cissy was sorry for Jessica's pain, but at the same time it was good to see her cousin still had a tender heart beneath her fiery personality.

Clajak stroked Jessica's hair with a gentle hand. "All right now, my love. Zarl would hate to see you crying over him again. Especially at this happy occasion. More of our family has come home and we must be glad."

He bowed once more to Cissy and Tasha, deeper than before. As if given a signal, his male clanmates and the other male Kalquorians in the bay followed suit. In a strong voice that filled the space, Clajak announced, "Cecilia and Natasha Salter, cousins to our empress, welcome to your new home of Kalquor."

Chapter Two

Dramok Ospar made his way through the greeting line. Now that the initial reunion between Empress Jessica, her mother and sister and the recently arrived cousins had occurred, many important men of Kalquor queued up to meet the lovely newcomers. As a man who was not only a governor to one of Kalquor's colonies but also counted himself as a friend to the Imperial Clan, Ospar had been one of the first in line to offer his welcome.

His famously charming smile appeared as he introduced himself with a bow to twins Cecilia and Natasha Salter. The joyful family brought together gave plenty of reason to smile. The quiet strength of the one referred to as Tasha, along with the obvious spirit of the woman nicknamed Cissy, helped Ospar's mood.

Now that formal duty had been attended to, the governor of the Kalquorian/Earther colony of Haven felt concern worming its way into his thoughts. Worry and fatigue had become Ospar's constant companions of late. Ever since Imperial Father Zarl's death, he'd had plenty of past misdeeds to ruminate over.

Ospar had been on his home planet of Kalquor, attending the former Emperor's funeral when the Salter twins had arrived. The wily Dramok had hoped to return to Haven and his own clan once the last rites for Zarl had been performed. However, Empress Jessica had asked him to be a part of the official contingent that would herald the safe arrival of her cousins. Ospar had never been able to refuse his monarchs anything. He delayed returning to Haven, though it grated on his nerves to be away from his Imdiko, Nobek, Matara and son. Suspecting how little time he might have left as colony governor—perhaps even as a free man—had made honouring Jessica's innocent request difficult.

He greeted men he'd known from his tenure on the Royal Council and when he'd been Kalquor's ambassador to the Galactic Council of Planets. Ospar had been a mover and shaker amongst those who controlled the Empire's destiny for many years now. Even newer councilmen who'd had little contact with him bowed in respectful acknowledgement.

Those old friends and former colleagues who hadn't spoken to him before and after Zarl's funeral now took the opportunity to do so. Ospar concealed his impatience with practised ease. In truth, he wished to have a word with only one man. Navigating his way to a small knot of councilman took forever, but his quarry was among them.

Dramok Rajhir saw him coming. Ospar knew his old friend had been on a well-deserved vacation when Zarl's death occurred. Rajhir's clan had rushed home to attend the final rites, but there had been no opportunity for Ospar to meet with his closest confidant in private.

Rajhir returned Ospar's smile as his former mentor approached. The younger Dramok's eyes were watchful, letting Ospar know Rajhir was as tense as he was. It was a bad sign. Even back when Rajhir had been a raw youngling, serving as Ospar's aide when he was a councilman, he had been good at disguising his emotions.

Rajhir bowed to the men he conversed with. His voice carried to Ospar, still several feet away. "Please excuse me, everyone. I wish to have a few words with my old friend here before he runs off to his colony."

The others turned and the air filled with knowing chuckles when they saw Ospar. They offered him bows, which he returned as Rajhir approached him.

"Watch out for those crazy Earther revolts!" someone called.

"I worry more about the Basma's followers," Ospar answered. That shut up the teasing in a hurry.

Rajhir reached him and the pair turned away from the rest. They walked to an empty part of the shuttle bay. Ospar made no effort to hide his assessment of Rajhir. The younger Dramok arched an eyebrow at him but said nothing.

Rajhir was taller than Ospar by about five inches. His frame was leaner, too, a sleek version of the muscular Kalquorian race. He'd been handsome and dashing when Ospar first met him so many years ago and maturity had only added to his good looks. Rajhir appeared every inch the noble Kalquorian—dedicated to honour and Empire with every fibre of his being. It wasn't an air he put on—Rajhir had always been about duty to Kalquor.

They wandered to an area well away from the rest of those who had come to greet the empress's cousins.

Here, they could speak with some measure of privacy. Ospar kept his ready smile in place, though he felt no cheer.

In a low voice, he asked his former aide, "Have you received any word on Zarl's records yet?"

Rajhir nodded, his gaze moving over the rest of the councilmen in the bay. "The Royal Oversight Committee has narrowed the choices for reviewer down to two men—Councilmen Maf and Diltan, both who serve on the Ethics Committee."

"Maf, huh?" Ospar eyed the councilman, who stood on the fringes of the crowd with another man he didn't recognise. Both wore the blue robes of the Royal Council.

Sadly, Dramok Maf did not wear his well. Severely deformed from birth, the man's body was a twisted, painful prison. Surgeries performed by the best doctors in the Empire had been unable to do much for the warped skeleton and distorted muscles. All they could manage was to give Maf mobility. Despite his having a strong, if not precisely attractive, face and a brilliant mind, people tended to be repulsed by the sight of Maf. Some had even made the mistake of dismissing him as little more than a freak to be shunned or, even worse, pitied. Ospar, who had met the man and enjoyed something of a friendly sparring acquaintance, had better sense.

He narrowed his gaze at Maf. He was surprised to see the councilman amongst those present to greet the Salter twins. Maf had never hidden his dislike for the mixing of the Earther and Kalquorian races, not even to preserve the Empire's culture in face of extinction. It was the one thing Ospar found himself hard-pressed to forgive.

He told Rajhir, "I respect the man, but I don't like what he stands for. He will be the first to cry foul if Zarl kept records of our arrangement. He might even pursue it to litigation."

Rajhir's expression was equally grim. "I have no doubt the Imperial Father did keep an account of everything he decided as emperor. He was devoted to transparency, even if it was to happen in the future rather than the present. It will come out, Ospar."

Ospar drew a deep breath. He had done things in his long career that he regretted, things that he'd known might eventually bite him in the ass. Until a year ago, he'd not had so much at stake.

With the faces of his Matara Iris and his son Thomas in his mind, Ospar said, "I wonder how long after I return to Haven Colony before I am brought back here to face charges."

Rajhir mused for a few seconds before answering. "It could be months. Zarl was almost as meticulous as you when it came to details."

"You've never forgiven me all those files you had to organise back when you first came to work for me."

Rajhir chuckled, finding a touch of real humour at last. "There is knowing your potential opponents and then madness, my friend. Who cares what a man eats for his breakfast every day?"

Ospar would have liked to join the other Dramok in the brief moment of amusement, but their current predicament was too heavy on his mind. "Zarl was a great man, Rajhir. His legacy and how others perceive it will go far in determining the Empire's future."

Rajhir immediately sobered. "Don't I know it. Honour and Empire."

"Always. The rebellion would seize on what we did as a means to swell its ranks."

Rajhir nodded without the slightest hesitation. "Much is at stake."

Ospar eyed his friend, knowing his next observation would not be welcome. "I would prefer to see you emerge from this unscathed. You kidnapped the first Earther under my orders."

Rajhir's eyes narrowed and his lips thinned. "Don't you dare, Ospar. I was well aware of what you were asking me to do when I went to Plasius to test Amelia for breeding compatibility. I know the difference between right and wrong. I'm every bit as much to blame as you."

Ospar shook his head. He'd rehearsed this conversation a million times over and his words came with ease. "As my Matara would say, you're an angel compared to me. I sent in over a thousand clans to claim Earther mates. You took only one woman and managed to make her love you and celebrate her clanning in the process. I am the chief architect in this matter and I am ready to assume full responsibility."

Rajhir stared at him. "Are you to be our martyr, Ospar? Don't be a fool. No one will believe one man was behind all those abductions."

Ospar went for the proverbial throat with his next point. "Your twins are young yet. Your clan needs you at home, not on trial. Have you considered this could land us on a penal colony?"

Rajhir's hiss was angry. "And what of your clan? You claimed your Matara less than a year ago. Your son needs extra support. Little Thomas depends on you. You are no more dispensable than I when it comes to our families."

Ospar tried not to think of his adopted son. Thomas was a smart, engaging child. However, it was true that the boy's autism made changes in his family life difficult to cope with. Despite the nightly coms Ospar had made during his trip, Thomas demanded his Dramok father come home right away. Iris had confirmed the boy cried each night that only three of his four parents put him to bed.

The thought that he caused Thomas any pain devastated Ospar as nothing else could. That he might have to cause the boy more hurt had kept him from sleeping these past nights.

Ospar had the weight of an empire on his shoulders. In the end, his clan and Thomas would persevere. It still made his guts twist to know they would pay with him for his crimes.

He could keep the others out of trouble, however. Men like Rajhir need never damage their clans the way Ospar was forced to damage his.

With this in mind, he told his friend, "If the Ethics Committee goes after you, it'll have to indict over half the council, too. Trust me, plenty of men lost their concerns over coerced clannings when I called on them to do so. There is no reason you should sacrifice yourself and your clan's well-being."

"The more of us there are to shoulder the blame, the less gets shifted to the Imperial Clans, present and past. The rebellion loses traction that way."

"No. The Basma's new tactic is pointing out how it's the high-ranking clans getting most of the Mataras. He's claiming elite privilege now."

"Ridiculous. The lottery is random. Clans from all walks of success are getting their chance to attract female mates," Rajhir fumed.

"The ones with money and prestige aren't afraid to wave that in the women's faces. They pull out all the stops to dazzle the Mataras with gifts and promises of gilded futures. Out of all the clans, they are almost certain to win lifebringers. Then there are the men without clans, the ones with no hope at all of winning Mataras. Jealousy is driving them to answer the Basma's call."

"They are traitors, then. There is no excuse for such nonsense." Rajhir's purple eyes sparked with fury. "Honour and Empire. For that, I will defend Kalquor no matter what the cost to me."

Ospar sighed. Rajhir was being stubborn. However, he thought, given time to consider the situation properly, his friend would be reasonable.

If they had time.

Ospar asked, "What of this Councilman Diltan? What can we expect from him should he be chosen over Maf to examine the records?"

Rajhir looked at the blue-robed men still waiting in line to greet the empress's cousins. "I can't be sure. With him we might have a slightly better chance. He's loyal to the current Imperial Clan."

"How loyal?"

"There was a time when he went to great lengths to curry favour. When Diltan first came to the council, it was almost embarrassing how determined he was to get close to them. He wore ambition like a badge on his chest."

Rajhir's assessment gave Ospar a glimpse of hope. "That could help us."

"Don't bet on it. These days, Diltan is a competent councilman. He's settled into duty in the last couple of years. He has issued challenges to a few things the royals have wanted. The empress can't shout him down when they disagree, something many can't claim."

"So he went from sycophant to honourable."

"To the point that his appointment to the Ethics Committee last year did not receive one single challenge."

The dim hope died. Nominations to important committees like the one that policed government ethics were always challenged. That Dramok Diltan had assumed his duties without dispute spoke volumes for a principled reputation…and trouble for Zarl's legacy, along with Ospar's future.

"Such moral standing is good for the Empire, not so good for us." Ospar managed a wry chuckle that hinted only slightly of the nausea in his belly. "I could soon be choking on the folly of my ways, old friend. There are a great many people who will enjoy seeing that."

Rajhir gave him bleak eyes. "I won't be one of them, Ospar. I guess we'll just have to wait and see how it all pans out."

They looked at each other, their grimaces mirror images.

* * * *

Half an hour ticked by. Cissy got bored with the reception in the shuttle bay. One robed councilman or dignitary after another stepped before her, bowed, told her his name and said pretty much the same thing: "Welcome to Kalquor. We are delighted to have more members of our empress's family among us. Let me congratulate you on escaping Earth. If you need anything, do not hesitate to call on me."

They were all nice and some men were fodder for naughty fantasy. Yet the process dragged on and on. Cissy would not remember more than half a dozen names of these men who made the Empire function. She wanted the infernally long greetings to be done with.

Tasha was as polite as ever, taking the time to exchange a few words beyond pleasantries. Cissy, however, had no qualms about showing how bored she had become and tried to rush the proceedings along. She pasted a stiff, insincere smile on her face and muttered 'thank you' in the most ungrateful tone she could come up with that wouldn't cause outright offence. The men's brows drew together at her performance, but they didn't speak of her lack of courtesy. They bowed and moved on.

Cissy could have shouted her relief when the last man in the long line stood before her. It was yet another councilman in blue robes who bowed before her, his face in a smile a little more eager than most.

He was fabulous. The tall Kalquorian was almost as handsome as Emperor Bevau. Despite her impatience with the tedium, Cissy couldn't help but admire the councilman. His bone structure was model perfect while still masculine. His hair was a little shorter than the norm for Kalquorian men, barely brushing his shoulders. He wore it swept back from that flawless visage. His smile showed straight white teeth that gleamed from his bronze god face. The slight creases at the corners of his purple eyes added character rather than detracting from his looks.

As he straightened from his bow, his silky robe settled about his body. The loose folds did nothing to hide that his frame was as perfectly made as his face.

Cissy liked that she only got a hint of the muscular beauty concealed within the robes rather than a blatant exhibition of the package. Sometimes a tease was more alluring than getting to see everything.

The delicious morsel before her was a good way to end this whole ridiculous, formal mess. Her return smile to the Kalquorian councilman was close to sincere.

She thought, *One last quick hello, thank you and goodbye. Then maybe I can finally get the hell out of here. Maybe I can get this one to go with me. Welcome to Kalquor with a bang.*

The man spoke, his deep voice delivering yet another version of the same thing Cissy had heard for what she thought must be the thousandth time. "Matara Cecilia, welcome to Kalquor. I am Councilman Dramok Diltan. We are most delighted that more of our beloved empress's family has been found."

His voice was made for speeches, beautifully modulated, deep without sounding thunderous, spoken with an air of the educated man. It tickled Cissy's eardrums, sending a shiver of pleasure down her spine. Cissy wanted to hear that voice say dirty words while he did dirty things to her.

Forget it. He's too damned handsome. I know the type. This Diltan knows he's hot and probably uses it to get whatever he wants. I bet I'd see the arrogance within one minute of conversation.

Deep down, Cissy knew she was intimidated. More than ever, she regretted her casual outfit of jeans and T-shirt. The rest of her clothing had been too wild to greet her family and dignitaries in, however. Cissy had shaken off Earth's repression with a vengeance in the last few months. Tasha had once called her Miss Cleavage and not in a joking manner.

So she'd gone a little outrageous lately. The outfits she owned that weren't tomboyish were a bit on the showy side. Okay, extremely showy, leaving no doubt that she was very much a woman.

Cissy hated pretension, but she could have at least bought a nice, demure outfit. That or borrowed something of Tasha's. Something that might have impressed the gorgeous Kalquorian in front of her long enough to get him naked. Oh well, too late now.

Keeping her tone offhand so Councilman Eye Candy wouldn't think she'd been affected by his insane amount of gorgeousness, Cissy said, "It's nice to meet you. Thanks for taking the time to say hello."

As she spoke, a movement behind Diltan caught Cissy's eye. She glanced past him to see Lindsey standing several feet away. Her cousin was shaking her head, a note of warning in her eyes as she surreptitiously pointed at Diltan.

Meanwhile, the councilman regarded Cissy with a slight frown. He started to turn his head, noting her distraction. Lindsey moved away, walking behind a group of conversing councilmen so Diltan couldn't spot her.

He turned back to Cissy, clearly puzzled. His ingratiating smile returned as he spoke to her again. "If there is anything at all—"

"That you can do on our behalf, just let you know," Cissy interrupted, her tone going cold. "Thanks, Diltan. Tasha, this is Diltan, another councilman. Say hello so he can go do something important."

Tasha scowled at her as the councilman gaped in shock. In her most disapproving tone, her twin said, "Cissy, stop being so grumpy. Just because you're tired is no excuse for bad manners."

With that verbal spanking, Tasha switched her sweet smile on, bestowing it on the speechless Diltan. "Thank you so much for coming to greet us, Dramok. We are delighted to be a part of your empire."

Diltan didn't respond immediately. Instead, he looked at Cissy. This time, his eyes roamed over her trousers and T-shirt. His lips pursed in an expression that verged on disapproval.

Cissy glared. So he found her clothes wanting, did he? Just as she'd figured, Diltan was an arrogant jerk. He didn't have to say anything to verify that assessment. The look said it all.

He bowed to her sister, as he took in the other woman's much more appropriate attire. Real pleasure lit his stupid-perfect face.

Diltan said, "The honour is all mine, Matara Natasha."

"Tasha, please." She returned the dazzling smile with interest.

"Yes. Tasha, please," Cissy parroted, her tone oozing sarcasm.

At her twin's warning glare, Cissy decided it was high time she wandered off. Talking to Lindsey suddenly seemed like a wonderful idea. At the same time, she would keep a close eye on Tasha, since Lindsey had given her that warning look.

Moving away from Tasha and the councilman, Cissy went in search of her oldest cousin. She wanted the lowdown on Diltan and the sooner, the better. On the surface, he seemed okay, just uptight.

I've known people who seemed perfectly fine and turned out to be anything but. Never judge a book by its cover…even one as nice as Dramok Diltan's. Especially *one as nice as his.*

Fortunately, Lindsey wanted to talk to Cissy as much as Cissy wanted to talk to her. Lindsey intercepted her cousin and motioned that they should stand a little apart from the rest of the gathering.

Side by side, they walked towards the emptiest spot in the crowded bay. Two Kalquorian men were leaving that section and the one in council robes nodded and smiled at Lindsey with recognition. She returned the smile.

"Hello, Dramok Rajhir. You're looking well. How are the twins?" she said.

"Thank you for asking, Imperial Sister. Everyone is well."

"Please give Amelia my best wishes. Let her know I'll com her soon."

"I will. How are you? Ready for your own younglings yet?"

There was a teasing note to Rajhir's tone, though Cissy saw his smile seemed a little strained. The other man chuckled, as if in on a private joke.

Lindsey glared at them both. "I hear enough of doing my 'duty' from my clanmates' mothers. Don't you and Ospar start in on me, too."

The two men laughed outright that time. Ospar nudged Rajhir.

"I wonder who else I've heard say such things?"

The men moved off. Cissy followed a chuckling Lindsey to where they could talk in relative privacy.

"Spill the beans," she urged her cousin. "What's up with that Dramok Diltan?"

Lindsey wrinkled her nose as she eyed the councilman still chatting up Tasha. "I'm not at liberty to go into details, but know he's something of a status-seeker."

"Not at liberty?" Cissy frowned at the other woman.

Lindsey shrugged. "I made a promise that I would not discuss my specific objections to the man, not to anyone. I want to keep peace anyway. He invested the bulk of the capital that got my clan's businesses started."

Cissy looked at the devastatingly handsome Dramok with narrowed eyes. "Uh-oh. You owe money to a guy you don't like?"

Lindsey waved a dismissive hand. "Oh, he made back his investment. We don't owe him a thing now." She made a face. "In truth, I should let bygones be bygones. He didn't charge us interest or keep any profit he was entitled to. I'm not a good Buddhist when it comes to Diltan."

"Having trouble unloading past grudges? That's one of my stumbling blocks, too." Cissy recited the lesson her late father had done his best to get her to heed. "Holding on to grievances only extends the harm done. Forgiveness cures the heart."

"Still, you know how it is when someone pulls a stunt that you pretty much regard as unforgiveable."

Cissy knew that feeling all too well. "Do I need to drag Tasha away from Diltan?"

"Still protective of her, I see." Lindsey chuckled.

"She doesn't need it. You should have seen how tough she was when we were hauled in by the authorities to answer for Jessica becoming Empress. Then after Armageddon, she got tougher still."

"I can imagine." Lindsey's gaze went distant, as if remembering her own trials back on Earth. "It's amazing the strength you discover you have when the chips are down."

"Tasha doesn't need me to keep her safe, but she's all I have left. It's hard not to go back to those old patterns."

Lindsey's brow rose as she regarded Cissy. "She's not all you have left."

Cissy leaned into her cousin's embrace when Lindsey put her arm around her shoulders. For a moment, she thought she would cry. It was hard to believe she was back amongst those she loved.

"It is so good to be with family again," she said, not caring about the husky emotion in her voice.

"There is nothing more important," Lindsey agreed.

Chapter Three

Dramok Diltan lived close to the Government House where the Royal Council chambers were located. When the weather was good, he walked to and from work. However, the weather was blustery cold with winter's last gasp, the kind of cold that stole a man's breath the first second he was in it. Diltan had taken his shuttle to work. It barely took a minute to travel home that night.

Like the Government House, Diltan's home was cut out of the seaside cliffs of the Eastern Seaboard Territory. He owned the top two levels of the cliff dwelling, high above where the waves crashed upon the shore. It was prime real estate on Kalquor, perhaps the most expensive that could be bought since the Royal House where the Imperial Clan and their family lived could not be sold. Even so, buying the dwelling decades earlier had barely made an impression on Clan Diltan's financial well-being.

Diltan's clanmates had come from prosperous families, just as he had. Yet it was his eye for business that had made them ridiculously wealthy. Diltan's ability to spot a lucrative start-up was a gift, one he wielded for the rush of achievement rather than for the financial rewards. Getting a new company on its feet, watching it grow and succeed just as he'd foreseen, the excitement of knowing he'd proved himself again… It was what kept Diltan in the game long after it ceased to make financial sense to continue investing.

Diltan's expansive home, complete with guest suites that were better and more comfortable than most people's dwellings, was a testament to his success. The hollowed-out cliff boasted an indoor pool, an art collection that resembled a mini museum and a music hall in which concerts were played for Clan Diltan's friends. The only trapping of success that he lacked was a full-time household staff. His clanmates preferred to not have cleaning and cooking personnel underfoot all the time. Unless they had guests for a lengthy stay, janitorial services showed up once a week. The complex's kitchen sent up their meals when they chose not to cook for themselves.

Diltan stepped into the opulent greeting room where the clan hosted formal parties. He strode past comfortable but luxurious conversation areas, the full-size bar that would have been at home in an upscale restaurant, the entertainment vid system where friends often gathered to watch kurble championships and other sports-related events and a collection of gaming tables. Diltan didn't see the vast room empty of people. His memories of wonderful gatherings played out around him as he moved on to the formal dining room with its long table, and down the hall.

As the Dramok wandered towards the clan's private common room, he swept his council robes off and dumped them into the laundry intake that was conveniently secreted within one wall. Such intakes were scattered throughout the home. It kept things simple, a must for men who dealt with more than enough complexities in the outside world.

As Diltan had expected, he found his clanmates in the common room, playing a round of akmag at the gaming table. Wal was tossing the stones as Diltan walked in. Rolat groaned and flung a card at the grinning Imdiko as one of the vid tokens moved across the holoboard.

The entertainment vid system, slightly smaller than the one in the greeting room, was predictably off. While Diltan found it necessary to keep up to date on the news once a day, no one in his clan was a fan of the teleplays on the broadcasts. Documentaries, educational lessons and the occasional concert were more to their tastes. The three men saw more than enough news and drama in their everyday lives.

Wal's smirk turned gentle as he glanced at Diltan. Warmth pulsed through the Dramok's heart at the welcoming expression from his clanmate. It was hard to believe that Wal had once despised him with all of his being.

Diltan loved the expression that transformed the quietly handsome Imdiko into a beautiful man. Nothing about Wal stood out as noteworthy until he smiled. His features were well-formed but not memorable. His hair was the typical Kalquorian black—wildly curly, slightly below shoulder-length, usually pulled back off his face at the temples. He was toned but not overly muscled, his frame long and more elegantly shaped than either of his clanmates'.

He had a tendency to look serious or worried, no surprise for a judge who sat on the most important cases that affected the Empire. It was not the typical career for an Imdiko, but having been raised by a family steeped in law enforcement, Wal had found a niche. Still, it was a tough vocation for the nurturing breed. The corners of Wal's mouth were slightly lined because he found too many reasons to frown. He had sentenced men to life imprisonment and even execution. It wore on his conscience to do so, to the point that his clanmates had found it necessary to monitor his drinking when sensational cases came Wal's way. Without supervision, the Imdiko tended to find more solace in the bottle than was wise.

Diltan was delighted to see his clanmate in good spirits. Even after decades of clanship, the sight of Wal's smile was enough to thrill the Dramok.

Rolat beamed at Diltan, too, the cheerful countenance at odds with his bestial, heavy-browed face. His good humour was something of an oddity for one of the warrior Nobek breed. The easy-going attitude was even more a rarity since he was the Empire's Head of Penal Colonies. Diltan often wondered if Rolat kept that side of himself secret from everyone but those closest to him. The eldest of their clan, Rolat often acted the part of a wise uncle, particularly when Wal and Diltan weren't making the best of decisions.

"Did the cousins of our empress make it here safe and sound?" Rolat asked by way of greeting.

Diltan nodded at his Nobek. "They did. Empress Jessica is beside herself with joy to have them here."

Wal wanted to know, "Are they really identical? Could you tell them apart?"

Twins were a rarity on Kalquor. Only a few of the Earther-Kalquorian hybrid pregnancies had resulted in such remarkable births. As far as Diltan knew, none of those had been identical.

He told his Imdiko, "You can tell one from the other, though they appear the same on the outside. They dress differently, plus their attitudes are completely at odds. The one they call Tasha has a sweet, open personality. She's got wonderful manners and a proper carriage."

Rolat shook one muscled arm as he rolled the stones. "And the other twin?"

Diltan grimaced. He wasn't sure how to describe Cecilia Salter. The brief encounter he'd had with the woman defied easy explanation.

He tried. "She's…I don't know. I hate to use the word 'provincial'—"

Wal choked back laughter. "Careful, my Dramok. Your rank is showing."

Diltan scowled as hard as Rolat, who was not doing well in the game. "I'm not trying to be a snob. She's beautiful. Spirited, too. But I'm sure the clothing she wore was more suited to an Earther male than a woman. She has an aggressive way about her that I can only describe as rude."

Rolat brightened, his brow lifting with interest. "Aggressive? Really? That sounds like fun."

Diltan flopped down on a nearby seating cushion. "Fun for you, maybe. I've heard some refer to Empress Jessica as a female version of a Nobek. Well, this one was even more so. Maybe more ill-natured than a Nobek."

"Hopefully, she's prettier than me, too," Rolat teased. He didn't mind not being conventionally handsome.

Diltan didn't mind, either. Rolat was brute masculinity personified and that suited the Dramok fine. He liked his Nobek's strength.

He also liked Rolat's tendency towards lightheartedness, something he hadn't seen much of in Cissy. He told his clanmates, "Matara Cecilia seemed more interested in confrontation than accepting the well wishes of us councilmen. She was damned near insulting. Others I spoke to remarked on it."

Wal shrugged as he shook the stones and let them fly. He snickered at Rolat's curse before telling Diltan, "Maybe she just wanted to be with her family. Who can be bothered with a bunch of strangers when you've just landed on your new home?"

As usual, the Imdiko had seen to the heart of things. Diltan had to agree with Wal's take on the matter. "You're probably right. Yet her sister showed all the signs of gentle breeding. Matara Natasha displayed manners and patience. Plus, she knows how to dress. Those clothes Cecilia wore…ugh. Such a pretty girl shouldn't wear ugly things."

"Clothes do not make a person good or bad," Rolat opined. He arched a brow at Wal.

Diltan chuckled as the Imdiko made a face. Wal's closets overflowed with clothing. The man had a fetish for the latest fashions.

Wal said, "So the sisters are pretty?"

The Dramok said, "Quite lovely. Pleasing figures that make a man think illicit thoughts." That spark in Cissy's eyes had given Diltan some thoughts as well, but her sarcastic tone had been enough to turn him off. Almost.

Barely aware he spoke aloud, Diltan added, "Cecilia should take more care with her appearance. Maybe she thinks her rank as cousin to the Imperial Clan is all she needs to attract good mates."

Wal rolled his eyes. "Believe it or not, Diltan, some people could care less about rank."

It was an offhand remark, yet Diltan's face heated at the words. He had never told his clanmates about the time he'd tried to lure the Imperial Sister Lindsey into de-clanning her young, low-status mates for his clan. The memory of being shamed by Lindsey and the mothers of her clanmates made his stomach twist in a sickened loop. He'd never been so humiliated in all his life.

At least the four women had stuck to their promise to not disclose his ill-conceived attempt. Diltan was more than ready to admit to himself he'd been an ass to try to worm his way into the Imperial Family. He just didn't want anyone else to know about it.

To his Imdiko, he grouched, "I know rank isn't everything, damn it. I fight the urge to chase further accolades and symbols of success. Why do you insist that I still put prestige first?"

It was Rolat who answered. "Because, though you are a good man and a good Dramok, you remain ambitious as hell. You still feel the need to prove your worth to everyone else." He rolled the stones and yelled in wordless anger. He picked them up and tossed them at Wal, conceding defeat.

Ducking the flying game pieces, Wal added, "You also remain a bit of a snob, though I agree you are fighting that tendency." He beamed at Diltan. It wasn't clear whether his victory over Rolat or giving Diltan hell made him happier.

Diltan grumbled, "At least you acknowledge I try."

His clanmates chuckled. Wal came over to sit next to him. The Imdiko wrapped his arms around Diltan in an effort to make amends. "It's that effort that makes you so endearing, my Dramok. You do have a good heart. It's not your fault you were born to such advantageous circumstances."

Diltan uttered a rude noise, but he didn't push Wal away. He'd been born into an affluent family, then he'd made himself ridiculously rich then obscenely wealthy. He knew he didn't understand many of the issues that the common man faced. Yet he did his best to have empathy for others' problems.

Rolat winked at him. "Don't worry, my Dramok. We'll keep working on you, despite your many faults."

Diltan scowled. "You two didn't grow up in diminished circumstances yourselves."

Wal squeezed tighter and let him go. "No, we didn't. More is the pity. I see plenty of men in my court who think they're entitled to special treatment simply because they've always been given such. Sometimes I think too much money is as bad a condition as too little."

The Imdiko had apparently decided Diltan had been teased enough, because he changed the subject. "So…the well-behaved twin. Natasha? Is she worth our suit?"

Diltan brightened. Being picked on for his ambition had made him worry his clanmates would poke fun at him for wanting to pursue the cousin of the empress. "I believe she is. She and her sister have decided to enter the lottery rather than rely on Empress Jessica to introduce them to suitors."

Rolat seemed impressed. "That's interesting. A sign they're well grounded. What's the other one's name again? The spitfire?"

Diltan answered with impatience, since he wanted to talk about Tasha and not her dismissive sister. "Cecilia. I believe they call her Cissy. Anyway, I mentioned to Tasha that our clan had been selected by the lottery to present ourselves to interested Mataras. After speaking with her for a few minutes, she offered to see if our profiles had come up as a potential compatible match—with no prompting on my part."

He glared at his clanmates as if to dare them to challenge his assertion. They snickered at him but said nothing.

Mollified that they at least were amiable enough to go along with his account—which was true—Diltan continued. "Tasha said I seemed nice. If our profiles are a decent match, she'd put our clan as her first choice to interview."

Wal looked delighted. "Wonderful. I can't wait to meet her, my Dramok. I know you made a good impression."

Though he also appeared pleased, Rolat wasn't as quick to congratulate Diltan. "Just don't push us to clan her simply because she's got links to the royals. Your standing as a councilman has given us plenty of interest from other Mataras. Personality and compatibility are more important than connections. We need to choose our potential mates on that."

Diltan's tone was dry. "Thank you, my father."

Wal laughed hard at that. Rolat gave them both a glare.

The Imdiko said, "Well, you did sound terribly paternal just now, my Nobek."

Rolat considered before joining in with their snickers. “I guess I did. But you two need a minder.”

Diltan slapped his hand on his clanmate’s shoulder. “I promise you’ll like Tasha, my Nobek. She’s smart, well-spoken and nice.”

Much nicer than that rambunctious Cissy, he thought. Tasha wasn’t as lively, not by far…but that was sure to be a good thing.

Chapter Four

Cissy and Tasha spent the night in guest suites in the Royal House. Jessica had not been subtle in the least as she went over all the amenities that came with living just two levels below her grand home in the cliff.

"A kitchen open twenty-seven hours a day every day, ready to whip up whatever your hearts and stomachs desire," she gushed. "They've gotten really good at preparing Earther food, which our colony on Haven supplies. We've got chocolate. Fresh-roasted coffee. Vax himself taught them how to cook the best dishes, a kind of Kalquorian-Earther fusion that will make you fat and happy."

Imdiko Vax was one of Lindsey's clanmates, a celebrated chef who owned three restaurants on Kalquor. To hear Lindsey and Jessica tell it, most people needed reservations months in advance to hope to eat in one of his establishments.

"Look in the entertainment room," Jessica went on, tugging the twins all over the guest suite. "The latest in vid technology. You'd swear you're in the middle of every program you watch. Just listen to that sound system!"

She instructed the entertainment to play some rimnastin, a newer form of music that was all the rage throughout the various worlds. It had grown out of the thunder of Kalquorian lemanthev, crossed improbably with sounds similar to dance-friendly Plasian sleshirin. It had been created by young Earthers who had taken the minor-key-heavy lemanthev and incorporated swirling tones of Earther sonic guitars and keyboards. It was music Cissy herself had grown partial to. Her head bobbed in time with the thudding beat.

The bathing facility was no less impressive with its shower built big enough for an entire Kalquorian clan to use at once (or a football team, as Cissy whispered to Tasha), a sauna, a whirlpool and a bathing pool the size of a small pond. The bedrooms were even more immense, with balconies that looked over the ocean and sleeping mats every bit as large as the bathing pool.

The opulence was mind-boggling, beguiling even. Cissy wondered if she'd made a mistake in planning to live in modest Matara Complex quarters. The Matara Complex was where women from Earth stayed as they courted likely clans for lifemates. She'd never been one for fancy things, but she thought she might be able to get used to such luxury…not that she'd ever admit to it for fear of sounding obnoxious.

However, she and Tasha both found the suite far too big after their cousins left for the night. With just two of them knocking about, the huge space felt like a mausoleum, echoing and devoid of life no matter how loud the women cranked up the rimnastin music.

After a somewhat restless night during which Cissy drowned in the immense sleeping mat, she found Tasha eager to quit the grand suite of rooms. "It would be one thing to live here with a clan and children," Tasha mused. "It's ridiculous for us, though."

Cissy agreed. They had their storage bins by the door when Lindsey and Jessica arrived at sunrise.

"Overkill, huh?" Lindsey laughed as she handed them each a mug of coffee. "Now you see why my clan lives in a much more modest setting."

Cissy sipped from her steaming cup, moaning with pleasure as she did so. First thing in the morning and after every meal, she was grateful that the Kalquorians had seen fit to import coffee from the Earther colonies that grew the beans. Coffee had become a big hit in the Empire, she'd discovered.

Tasha smiled apologetically at Jessica. "It's beautiful here, but I feel lost in so much space. I guess I got used to ship's quarters on the transport."

Jessica sighed, but she didn't seem insulted. "You'll appreciate being able to get lost once you have a clan and kids. I love my brood and lifemates beyond all sense, but sometimes escape is a wonderful thing."

"So says the woman trying for another child." Lindsey smirked.

"Are you?" Cissy grinned. "Two isn't enough?"

"Not even close," Jessica asserted. "I want lots of kids. After all, I have plenty of home in which to hide from them."

"There is logic somewhere in there," Tasha mused. "I'm sure of it."

Laughing, the four women headed for the shuttle bay, where they were joined by a contingent of the Royal

Guard. A pilot was quickly located to take them to the Matara Complex.

Cissy and Tasha's new home was in an underground cavern, created by the mining that was the Kalquorian Empire's greatest asset. Cissy hadn't been too sure about living underground, but she'd been told she would never know the difference. *We'll see about that,* she thought as the small Imperial shuttle left the cliff to perform a steep banking manoeuvre that took them into a tunnel within the cliff face.

Jessica said, "Usually only emergency vehicles are allowed in the underground. You have to walk or run everywhere otherwise."

"I guess being royal has its advantages, Your Grace?" Cissy teased.

"Be nice or I'll shove my silver spoon up your nose," Jessica said in a snotty tone. The effect was ruined as she broke down in giggles.

Lindsey didn't join in the humour. "Jessica has to be careful, as little as she wants to admit it. This rebellion issue has meant abduction attempts. It's scary how close we've come to losing her."

"But you haven't and you won't." The young woman tried to wave off everyone's concern. "The Basma doesn't have enough followers to make his revolt a true threat."

"Yet." Lindsey was dogged in her determination to give them the full story. "There are signs that more Kalquorians are swayed to his cause every day. He damned near cost us Haven Colony a few months ago."

"You're being dramatic," Jessica complained. It was funny for her to ascribe that to Lindsey, since Jessica's stormy temper was legendary in their family.

"I heard what Governor Ospar told you. Earthers and Kalquorians on that colony banding together under the common cause of keeping the races separate? Even though it could drive us both into extinction? That's unheard of."

"Ospar loves to be dramatic. He thrives on the hint of conspiracies and mayhem. I suspect he's behind quite a few such things himself. I love that guy, but he's not happy unless he's in the middle of trouble." Jessica waved her hand dismissively. "Enough talk of rebellions. Full vid on."

Cissy and Tasha yelped as the entire shuttle seemed to disappear from around them. Except for the doorway that opened into the vessel's cockpit and the lushly cushioned seats they sat upon, there was nothing but a lit tunnel rushing past them.

"You ass," Cissy said, shoving her cousin. Out of the corner of her eye, she saw the Royal Guards stiffen, coming to alert attention.

Oops. I didn't think of how Jessica's security would take an 'attack' on her royal person. It's a good thing she's laughing at me or I might be a spot on the nonexistent floor.

Lindsey wasn't worried about the Royal Guards, either, aiming a kick at Jessica's shin. "You are such a brat. I think Tasha wet herself."

"No, it was a good trick." Agreeable as always, Tasha smiled at Jessica. "It's amazing to see everything like this."

Jessica blew a raspberry at her. "Damn it, I forgot how good you are at making me feel guilty. When are you going to get an ugly side like Cissy?"

Cissy had heard enough. "That's it. Hold her down, Lindsey. I'm going to tickle her until she pees her royal panties."

Before she could make a move towards her chortling cousin, they flew out of the tunnel. Cissy froze and stared all around at the scenery.

They'd told her the underground area didn't look like it was underground, but she was in no way prepared for the brilliant blue sky overhead and the distant sun streaming from it. There were walls of craggy rock in the distance, showing the immense size of the now defunct mine, but there was also a rich landscape of trees and shrubs leading up to those walls.

The ceiling of the former mine was one vast vid screen, programmed to show the sky outside. Today was a gorgeous early spring day, the weather warming nicely after yesterday's brutally cold blast. It looked as if they were within a small, verdant canyon. Cissy had the impression that if she were to stand outside, she'd even feel the sun on her shoulders, left bare by the tank top she wore. She wondered if the Kalquorians manufactured breezes down here to further fool the senses.

Beyond the tunnel were two wide paths, just large enough for a medium-size shuttle to navigate. One went to the left and was bordered by newly blooming flowers and colourful shrubs. With spring arriving at the Eastern Seaboard Territory, the underground's landscapers had wasted no time in celebrating. Cissy appreciated that they'd managed to make the foliage seem like naturally occurring growth as in the wild. Kalquorians loved nature and abhorred anything that appeared too planned.

The shuttle took the right-hand path, the way that was more wooded. The shuttle flew well off the gravel-packed ground, over the heads of pedestrians travelling the trail. They stared up in interest as the vessel passed—after all, Jessica had said only emergency vehicles were allowed in the habitat.

"I love the trees on this planet," Tasha murmured, gazing at the forest on either side. The foliage was splendid, with the trees sporting rainbow-hued colours like a crazy quilt. Blue, red, gold and green leaves against branches as white as ivory made the landscape seem almost magical.

Jessica and Lindsey looked, too. "It sucks to get used to it," the young empress said. "I forget how stunning this planet is until someone new shows up and reminds me of it."

"It's amazing all over again when you get to see it through someone else's eyes," Lindsey agreed.

Cissy frowned to see something not so natural on one side of the path. A utilitarian building, metal and somehow forbidding, sat there. Three Kalquorians in black-armoured formsuits stood outside its door, watching the shuttle pass overhead. They had percussion blasters on their belts, as well as sheathed knives. One man had a laser rifle slung over one shoulder.

"Do you get much trouble out here?" she asked.

Jessica frowned when she followed Cissy's gaze. "Not lately. We had a serial killer who targeted Earth women run amok about a year ago. It was the same Nobek who instigated the Slaughter of the Innocents on New Bethlehem."

"No shit." Cissy was suddenly glad to have the grim-faced Royal Guards on board. "I thought it was two men involved, though?"

"It was just the one on New Bethlehem. He was a high-ranking soldier there and lost his mind. He came back here and started killing women. His Dramok discovered what was happening but didn't tell anyone. They were both executed for their crimes."

Tasha bit her lip. "Executed? But if the killer was unstable, shouldn't he have been allowed some mercy?"

There was a shadow in Jessica's eyes as she shook her head. "He was mentally ill, but the guy still knew right from wrong. The doctors who examined him said he acted on compulsions rather than a complete lack of control." She drew herself up. "Either way, there was no excusing his Dramok. He knowingly let his Nobek continue to torture then murder innocent victims."

The four women fell silent as they considered the matter. All had been secretly raised as Buddhists despite Earth's police state that dictated how people could worship. Their belief was based on non-violence and execution was usually an anathema to that.

Especially generate compassion for those whose ill deeds are horrible, the great scholar Nagarjuna had said. Their faith taught that karma would deliver the consequences of a person's actions without fail, whether in this life or the next. People who had committed unthinkable crimes were to be pitied and prayed for because they would suffer horribly for them.

"But in self-defence, it's not so bad," Cissy whispered to herself. "Or defending someone else's life."

"What?" Tasha asked.

"Nothing. Just talking to myself."

Lindsey gave her a wicked smile. "You know what that's a sign of, right?"

Cissy's grin was equally evil. "That I appreciate intellectual conversation with the brightest person in the room."

That got her a mixture of groans, gagging sounds and hoots of derision.

The women went back to watching their surroundings and commenting on them. In the distance were the first free-standing buildings Cissy had seen on Kalquor. They dotted between the trees, none too close to others, leaving plenty of room for whoever lived there. Despite being houses that had been built rather than carved out of the landscape, they still had an organic feel to them, almost melting into the environment. They boasted curves and rounded shapes.

"Like large, abstract sculptures that have been worn by the elements over time," Tasha opined.

Cissy's attention focused on a great structure rising in the distance as the wooded area ended and the landscape opened up. It was similar to the free-standing homes except for its size.

"Home sweet home," Jessica announced, confirming that this was the long-awaited Matara Complex.

Cissy recognised it from vids. Like everything else to do with the Empire, it was more impressive in person.

Curved and flowing in shape, it looked like granite that had not been so much carved as poured into a mould. It was impossible to tell from the outside where in the building one would find the administrative offices, the recreational areas or the apartments where the Earther women resided. The structure was rounded, much like the Roman Coliseum, enclosing the interior. The exterior, with its undulating top, appeared downright sensual to Cissy. She wondered if that had been the intent of its architects.

There were openings here and there near the top, and the shuttle flew through one. For a moment darkness reigned. Then they were through and back in the sunshine. The vid sunshine, Cissy reminded herself. Jessica had been right when she'd said they would forget they were underground. Already it was hard for Cissy to believe she wasn't in the real outdoors.

They'd emerged over a landing area for emergency vehicles. Their shuttle floated down and settled without the slightest bump.

Two Kalquorian men and an Earther woman waited for them as they disembarked. The men bowed deeply. The woman, an older female, smiled her welcome.

"It is an honour to see you again, Empress, along with your esteemed family," the shorter of the two men said. "I am Chief Administrator Besat. This is my assistant Imdiko Garlel and Head of Liaisons, Matara Anna."

Besat was an older man, with thick threads of grey streaking through his shoulder-length hair. His eyes nested in deep creases, more of which bracketed his mouth. Despite the advancing years, Cissy thought he was a rather handsome fellow. His body still retained its strength if the wide shoulders and tree-trunk thighs filling out his simple grey formsuit were any indication. She had no doubt Besat had been a striking man in his youth.

Imdiko Garlel was younger but still on the mature side of life. Cissy guessed he was middle-aged, which for a Kalquorian would be about one hundred and twenty-five years. His hair was dusted with a touch of grey, too, making it appear similar to Emperor Clajak's distinctive steel-coloured shade. Garlel's smile was the sunny sweetness Cissy had come to expect from the Imdiko breed. He'd given outright cuteness a near miss, his features settling for pleasant. He was lean for a Kalquorian. He too wore a grey formsuit. Cissy supposed it was the uniform for those who worked at the complex.

Liaison Anna was a cheerful-looking lady, the kind of woman Cissy thought should be hosting neighbourhood parties. Her smile was welcoming in her round, slightly lined face. Her dark blond hair was caught back in a ponytail. She was as cuddly as Cissy and Tasha with the soft roundness that Kalquorians seemed to enjoy.

She shook hands Earther-style with everyone. "Hello, ladies, Empress and Imperial Sister," Anna said in a delighted tone. "What an honour. Can I interest any of you in refreshment before we take the tour? I know I have to have some coffee drinkers here. I also have tea and warm mela, if you prefer."

Cissy said with all the drama she could muster, "I've found my first clanmate! Be my Matara, Anna, and bring all your coffee as a dowry."

Besat and Garlel blinked uncertainly, but the other women laughed. "Add some chocolate and I'll play for the home team, too." Tasha giggled.

Anna's laugh was a wonderful belly-shaking guffaw. "Oh, you girls. You all love me for those two things. Plus ice cream. When will I find someone who wants me for me?"

Just like that, Cissy adored Anna. When she tasted the coffee the liaison brought, she liked her even more.

"As long as there is caffeine in the universe, everything else will work itself out. I can't tell you how grateful I am that the Empire buys this stuff from the Earther colonies," she proclaimed. "Tell me, Anna, is a liaison here the same as what we had on the transport that brought us to Kalquor?"

Anna nodded. "Pretty much. Tilda will be your liaison, but today is her day off. If you have any questions or concerns about anything at all while you're here, she'll be glad to help you."

"We all will." Imdiko Garlel offered one of his sweet smiles. "Don't be afraid to approach any of us at any time."

"Thank you," Tasha said.

Besat gestured towards a closed door. "Shall we begin the tour?"

They followed the chief administrator through the tunnel behind the door and out into the complex's courtyard.

Cissy had known what to expect, but that didn't keep her from whistling in appreciation. The courtyard was beautiful, a vision of Eden.

Banks of flowerbeds separated the courtyard into sections. Each bed was a profusion of colour, as if the flowers were fireworks caught at the moment of full explosion. Heady scents came from them, sweeter than any perfume Cissy had ever smelled. She inhaled with pleasure.

Also separating each pie-shaped section was the use of different-coloured marble tiles that made up the courtyard floor. The section the little group had entered through was lemon yellow, as bright and cheerful as the sunlight beaming down on them. Firepits dotted throughout the vast area, sending even lovelier smells from the burning scentwood wafting in their direction. Cushions scattered around the pits. Women relaxed at about half a dozen of the pits, and the hum of conversation and easy laughter floated on the aromatic air. One woman sat in an area off in the corner, attended by three Kalquorian men.

"Our outdoor lounge," Besat told them. "This is a good place to relax with friends and potential clanmates. Some take their meals here and even throw parties."

They moved on to the section with sky-blue tiles. Small, sunken pools bubbled and steamed. Women in bathing suits both modest and revealing relaxed in them.

"Whirlpools," Anna said, smirking a little to see her male companions looking everywhere but the glistening skin of the scantily clad brunette they'd stopped beside. "Very relaxing, aren't they, Bridgette?"

The girl in the shallow basin smiled lazily up at them. "Welcome to paradise," she sighed. She blinked at Jessica. "Has anyone ever told you that you look just like the empress?"

Chuckling, the group moved on. The next section featured grass-green tiles and raised platforms upon which billowy mats rested. Most were taken up by more nearly naked women, all lying on their stomachs. Again, Besat and Garlel found gazing in the distance to be a noble pursuit.

Cissy grimaced to see tentacle-waving Tratsods moving over the reclining women's bodies. The aliens' coloration landed in a hideous zone somewhere between orange and pink. They slid along the Earthers' backs, shoulders and thighs, their many tentacles playing over the oil-glistened skin, rubbing all. Eyes attached to the lumpy circular bodies on thin stalks blinked at Cissy's group. A droning hum emitted from the creatures, soft and hypnotic.

"Once you get used to their appearance, you'll love their massages," Anna assured Cissy and Tasha. "They're gentle, sweet creatures."

"Don't judge a book by its cover, huh?" Cissy said. Tratsods weren't pretty by any means, but the face of every woman under their care was rapturous. It might be worth the squick to feel that good.

A large pool took up another section of the courtyard. Its blue-green depths shimmered with silvery ripples birthed by the women swimming its length. The final area, tiled in lilac purple, was filled with laughing women dancing to exotic Middle Eastern–sounding music with a quick beat. Cissy and Tasha both stopped to gape as at least two dozen women attempted to follow the instructor, an Earther woman as dark-skinned as the Kalquorians. Her brilliant smile flashed white as she called out instructions and encouragement.

"Once a week, Matara Michaela teaches a form of outlawed Earth dancing called Raqs Sharqi," Besat told them. "I believe you are acquainted with her, my Empress?"

"You would be right. She's my best friend." Jessica snickered. "By the way, I'm not a half-bad belly dancer myself. Michaela taught me."

Tasha's eyes went wide. "You dance like that?"

Jessica laughed. "After the babies, I wouldn't be in this good of shape without it. Trust me, you want to take her class. If you're good enough, she'll put you in her exhibition company and you can make a lot of potential clans lay at your feet."

Cissy eyed the class. The moves were astoundingly sexy, she thought. "I'm in," she said.

"There are other classes, too," Anna said. "Stretching, meditation, other forms of dance…too many to mention. You'll be given the schedules and can choose whatever you like."

The tour continued inside the complex. There were workout machines to tone the body, which Cissy immediately dismissed by blowing a raspberry. They didn't look nearly as fun as the belly dancing. The heated indoor pool was more to her liking as well. The vid gaming section, in which one could interact with any number of sporting, music or instruction scenarios, was enticing. They peeked into one room in which two women practised their golf swings. In another, a woman took lessons on how to play a Plasian eflan pipe.

"We have one-on-one classes on things such as Kalquorian language, history and the like," Garlel said. "You may wish to request live lessons in subjects, hobbies and careers that interest you. We've had cooking courses, computer sciences, childcare…pretty much anything you can imagine."

"Plus there are off-site options," Anna enthused. "Kestarsh riding—they're similar to horses—sailing, mountain climbing…oh, everything."

Cissy gave Jessica a mock glare. "And you wanted us to stay in your piddling Royal House. Sheesh."

"Hell, I might run away from home and move in here. Do you think anyone would notice?"

"Only the entire Empire," Lindsey said.

The women were ushered to the in-house transport to go to the twins' private rooms. Jessica, Lindsey, Besat and four of the Royal Guards went to the seventh floor in one, while Cissy, Tasha, Anna, Garlel and the other two guards went up in the other.

"Pretty spiffy digs," Cissy told Anna. "Somehow, I didn't expect so much."

"Your apartments are modest," the liaison told her. "Most women don't mind the smaller quarters since there is so much otherwise to enjoy, though."

"It's like those illegal spas that were uncovered on Earth from time to time," Tasha said. "Except this is a million times nicer."

Garlel smiled to hear her say that. "I am glad you are not disappointed so far."

"Not one bit." Tasha grinned at Cissy. "It's like being at one of those resorts the rich always got to go to."

The transport door opened onto their floor. The two Royal Guards stepped out first and peered around. The four that had gone up with Jessica and Lindsey were already in the hallway, also checking their surroundings.

"Clear," the one Jessica had identified as the captain said.

Cissy and Tasha disembarked as the other transport emptied out. "We're going to Rooms 623 and 624," Besat told the captain.

The head of the guards bowed to Jessica before accompanying half the square at the front of their group. The other half fell in at the back. Cissy wondered how her cousin could stand being watched all the time. It would drive her crazy to be surrounded every time she stepped out of her home.

The rooms assigned to the twins were side by side at the far end of the hall. Cissy's was closest to the outer wall. "Of course, you are free to exchange places, but the rooms are mirror images of each other. You even have a connecting door between the two. They are exactly the same," Besat informed them as he waved a coded card before the admittance pad embedded in one of the doors. When it opened, two of the guards went in to sweep the apartment's interior and Besat let two more of the red-formsuited Nobeks into the other room.

Besat handed the two cards he'd used to open the doors to Tasha and Cissy. "These are your keys while you live here," he told them. "They will activate all doors and machines the tenants have access to, so you'll want to keep them handy."

It took the Royal Guards no time to go through the apartments. The captain bowed to Jessica when he rejoined the group in the hall.

"The quarters are clear, my empress."

She smiled up at him. "Thank you, Captain Kel. Well, let's see your new digs, girls."

Tasha led the way into the apartment that her key card was coded to. Cissy was impatient enough to push her twin a little, which only made Tasha drag her feet more in revenge. She giggled as Cissy huffed with impatience.

"Come on, come on! I want to see."

Tussling and laughing, the sisters stumbled into the quarters. Once inside, they stopped and turned in circles, having a good look around.

The room was what the Kalquorians termed a greeting room. Back on Earth, Cissy would have called it a living room. It was small and plain, with an oval table in the middle and seating cushions surrounding it. Its only decoration was a vid monitor hanging on the wall and a basket full of blue-plumed fronds.

Jessica looked askance at their surroundings and snorted. "Blessed Buddha, there's barely enough room for the four of us in here. Are you sure you don't want to stay in the Royal House? We've got scads of room. Plus you'll be close to me."

"Ew, not you," Cissy cried out with mock horror. Then she spoke seriously. "We're close to you here, sweetie. It took all of, what, five minutes to get here?"

She appreciated the cosiness after the huge guest suite they'd spent the night in. The way that place had echoed… She shuddered at the thought of spending her days and nights there.

Tasha must have felt the same way because she said, "Seriously, Jess, we appreciate the offer but you know we're not into all that pomp. Besides, you saw the amenities here. It's like living life on vacation."

Cissy nodded. "I can't believe I'm saying this given how the Tratsods look, but I can't wait to get one of those massages. I want to be that blissed out."

Tasha was not on the same page on that account. "Eek. Those squishy aliens aren't laying a tentacle on me. I know they're okay but I don't want something so squid-y crawling across my back."

Lindsey and Jessica laughed. The elder sister said, "Close your eyes and think happy thoughts. I've had the Tratsod massage and it is heavenly. You won't want to move a muscle for an hour afterwards."

Cissy said, "I'm going to have a go at it. Besides, the apartment may just as well be small because I plan to spend as little time as possible in it. I already have a date."

Tasha knew about the meetings Cissy had lined up. The other two women squealed. Jessica yanked on her arm in excitement. "You brat! Who did you pick? I want to have Bevau check them out."

Cissy chuckled. "Clan Mocnoz. They're a little young and not the most compatible according to my questionnaire results, but they seem like they'd be fun."

Lindsey pretended shock. "How young, you rowdy girl?"

"Only ten years older than me. The oldest isn't even forty-five yet. They barely qualified for the lottery as Dramok Mocnoz just opened his own law practice."

Lindsey giggled. "Scandalous!"

Lindsey's clanmates were young to have clanned a Matara. Cissy had heard some Kalquorians, particularly those with status, had called the match between the empress's sister and Clan Bacoj outrageous. When they'd met Lindsey, Bacoj, Japohn and Vax had acquired no rank at all. Only in their thirties, the three men had been hard pressed to prove to Kalquorian society that they deserved Lindsey. Fortunately, the four had loved one another with such devotion that they refused to let anything tear them apart.

Jessica threw her hands up as if giving up all hope. "All right, live here and be wild and free. But know I'm going to want every naughty detail."

Tasha fixed her with a shrewd look. "I know you don't regret joining the first available clan you found, Jess."

"Not for one second. What I envy is your appalling lack of duty to the Empire and the ability to play like a Plasian. What I wouldn't give to have no responsibilities!"

Lindsey rolled her eyes. "Oh, go put on a pretty dress that would cost me my entire year's worth of earnings and get over it, Your Highness."

The four women laughed again. Jessica said, "Do I have to talk to your clanmates about giving you a raise? Handling the accounts of successful businesses like your clan's does mean a lot of work. You should be handsomely rewarded."

"Trust me. I get my rewards." Lindsey arched a brow to make sure they all got her meaning. The red faces of Besat and Garlel, who stood in the background as they chattered, made Cissy laugh even harder.

Lindsey sighed when the hilarity calmed. "Speaking of business—"

Jessica made a face. "Yes, we working types need to get where we're supposed to be. We can't all be ladies of leisure." She wrapped her arms around Tasha. "Com me if you need anything at all, though."

Tasha returned the embrace with interest. "Thanks, Jess."

Lindsey and Cissy shared a hug of their own. "Don't forget, a girls-only dinner tonight. Keep your boy toys for later, Cissy."

The twins switched cousins for another round of hugs. Jessica added, "We'll pick you up."

Cissy told her, "We'll be waiting. I might even put on a skirt in honour of the occasion."

Lindsey pretended to faint. "Did you hit your head?"

More hugs and kisses on the cheeks ensued. After having been separated from one another for years, Cissy sensed her cousins were every bit as loath to break away as she was. It didn't matter that they'd be able to see one another every day if they wished. Having family nearby once more was a precious thing.

Jessica and Lindsey departed, surrounded by the dispassionate Royal Guards. It took only five more minutes for Besat, Garlel and Anna to tour the twins about the remainder of Tasha's quarters. The kitchenette was miniscule with a cooling unit filled with pre-prepared meals and a warmer. There was a mix of the Kalquorian and Earther foods Tasha preferred. Cissy was assured her preferences were stocked in her apartment.

"You can eat in the complex's dining room or out in the courtyard as well," Besat informed them. "Also, your potential clans will be taking you to various dining establishments."

"You can call the kitchen for something special to be sent to your room," Garlel assured. "Do not be shy about what you want."

Tasha turned to Cissy. "Sweetie, do you remember the meaning of the word 'shy'?"

"No, but I remember how to kick your rear." Cissy smiled at Besat. "What else do you have to show us?"

The chuckling administrator showed them the bath facility and the single bedroom. "Again, Matara Cissy's quarters are exactly the same," he said as they looked at the tiny space that was just big enough for the sleeping mat, a table and a desk. At least the closet was large, Cissy noted. Not that either woman had much in the way of clothing.

That wrapped up the tour. After a few more instructions, Besat, Garlel and Anna took their leave. Tasha and Cissy trooped over to the other twin's apartment and confirmed it was indeed as identical as they were.

Their few belongings were delivered—their clothes, some makeup, treasured photo vids and other small items.

Cissy grimaced at the two tiny piles of all they owned. "I'm feeling that I've been downsized too far," she told her sister.

Tasha nodded. "Me too. Shall we take a walk to the marketplace and remedy the matter?"

Cissy pretended to contemplate the wisdom of such action. "Let's see. We each have a full account granted by the Kalquorian government and deplorably empty closets. I thought you'd never ask."

No further conversation was required. In perfect accord, they linked arms and left their new home.

Chapter Five

The twins' shopping excursion was a roaring success in that they managed to spend all of their carefully saved government allowances in one day. They agreed they loved the vast market area of the underground with its many stores, eating options and entertainments. By the end of the jaunt, they were exhausted, but at least their closets were no longer empty.

Cissy spent the rest of the day arranging her apartment to her liking. Personal mementos went up everywhere, making the tiny quarters seem more like home. She and Tasha bounced between their connected abodes, talking about this and that and musing over what classes they wanted to sample in the days ahead.

The day was late when Cissy wandered into her sister's apartment again. They'd decided the connecting door would remain unlocked unless one of them was 'vetting' potential clanmates. A locked door meant private playtime. Cissy thought she wouldn't need the locked door to dissuade her from entering Tasha's quarters at the wrong time. Her sister was a screamer.

Cissy was vaguely uncomfortable as she came into Tasha's greeting room and not because she thought she'd stumble upon her sister being wild…at least not on their first night in their new home. Cissy had dressed for that night's dinner. Being 'all dolled up', as she called it, felt funny to her. Tonight, she looked almost as sedate as Tasha tended to appear.

The light blue slacks she'd bought that afternoon, while cut to flatter her rounded hips, didn't bind. The fabric was light and airy. The patterned light blue, gold and white blouse embraced her curves while giving the impression of modesty. Cissy had to admit she looked pretty good in the ensemble, especially with the strappy gold sandals and her hair falling in waves to her shoulders.

She was too respectable for her own liking. Cissy had bought wilder outfits during her shopping spree, clothing that told the universe how happy she was to shed the restrictions Earth had once imposed on its women. However, this was her first night out on Kalquor and she was going to be in Empress Jessica's company. She thought she'd behave and not cause a scandal for her cousin…just this once.

She found her twin sitting at the low table in her greeting room, tapping away at the keyboard on the computer Tasha and Cissy had bought together. Thus far, the machine only responded to Kalquorian speech. Though Tasha had mastered the written form of the language, she struggled with speaking it. It was easier for her to type her commands since she refused to install the crutch of English interpretation software.

Lovely as always, Tasha had put her hair in a bun with artful bits straggling loose to frame her made-up face. Her blouse and skirt matched in a blushing pink. The hue made her skin appear to glow despite the paleness that came from months of space travel. She looked at ease in her sedate clothing, while Cissy felt as prickly as a cactus. It was hard not to be jealous.

Trying to embrace her dive into Tasha ness, Cissy twirled in front of her sister. "Here I am, ready to not embarrass everyone for a change."

Tasha applauded her with a grin. "You actually appear suitable. No one will be able to tell us apart."

Cissy snorted her disbelief on that notion. She flopped down on the seating cushion across the table from her sister, doing it in the most unladylike fashion she could manage. She snickered as Tasha shook her head.

"There. Now there can be no mistaking who I am."

"Only if you spend the evening tossing yourself onto the ground like a landed fish."

"Everyone will know it's me within five seconds of opening my mouth." Cissy frowned as Tasha went back to her keyboard. "We've only got a couple of minutes before the cuzzies pick us up. What are you doing?"

Tasha wiggled her perfectly trimmed eyebrows. "I'm confirming my date with a clan tomorrow."

"Oh, you're getting busy right away, too. Shall we double?"

"I doubt it." Tasha made her snooty face, the one she used when she played at being above Cissy's antics. "This is a more mature clan than the one you picked for a first date. My guess is their tastes would run more operatic than that lemanthev concert you're going to. We're doing dinner and a live theatre show."

Cissy yawned. "How very exciting. Are they at least cute?" She waved to forestall Tasha's answer. "No, you wouldn't want cute. Adorable isn't your thing. Are they handsome, I mean?"

Tasha closed out the computer program. "Does it matter? Looks aren't as important as what's inside."

"No, it doesn't matter. I was just curious."

Tasha touched her hair, making sure it was still in its bun. "Actually, the Dramok is insanely handsome, almost the equal of Jessica's Bevau. He was at the reception last night. The one you were so rude to…Councilman Diltan."

Cissy bit her lower lip. Of course she remembered Diltan, the gorgeous jerk. She thought of his smile when he'd first approached her, how warm it appeared on his face. Then that voice…a voice that trembled her bones.

She also remembered his dismissive attitude as he eyed her clothing. *I bet he'd be impressed with how I look now, the shallow jerk.*

She said, "Oh boy. Tasha, Lindsey told me we should be careful of that one."

Tasha shrugged. "I thought he was nice. Besides, I checked with Jessica and she thinks Diltan is wonderful. He often supports the measures the Imperial Clan wants, but when he doesn't, he lets them know under no uncertain terms."

That didn't sound much like the man Lindsey had described. But then, Lindsey had also admitted Diltan had changed lately and that she held a grudge she shouldn't.

He still has a thing for outward appearances. Heaven forbid he check beyond the packaging like Tasha prefers to do.

Cissy knew she didn't present herself as well as her twin. Most of the time, she didn't care. However, something about Diltan rankled, the way he almost seemed pained by her clothing. If she cared one whit about his opinion, it would have hurt. She didn't know the man, though, so of course his view of her appearance didn't matter. Not one bit.

She didn't share any of her thoughts with her twin. Instead, she said, "I don't know. You and a smarmy politician? What do his clanmates do?"

"The Nobek is the head of their prison system. He's a fierce-looking one, downright scary, in fact. Not pretty like his Dramok. The Imdiko is a judge of Kalquor's highest court."

It was the kind of match Jessica might have wrangled for Tasha, had they given her the chance. Cissy rolled her eyes and stuck her pinkie out in a pseudo-sophisticated pose. "Well, lah-dee-dah."

Tasha made her own snobbish face. "Lah-dee-dah is right. While I dine on caviar and champagne or whatever the Kalquorian equivalent is, you can have the alien version of chicken wings and beer. Let me hear you grunt, you animal."

The women snickered at each other. They never truly butted heads over their differences most of the time. They enjoyed being unique in personality while nearly identical in looks.

A low beep sounded from the large vid on the wall. An electronic male voice said, "This is your reminder that you have a dinner appointment this evening."

Both jumped to their feet. Cissy's gaze went to the chronometer on the vid and she yelped, "Shit! Look at the time. We've got to get moving!"

They hurried to the door and jostled to be first out, rushing to meet their cousins.

* * * *

Early the next morning, a Royal Council closed meeting was held. Diltan could hardly contain his excitement, though the anticipation had nothing to do with the meeting.

Several measures had been introduced and argued on the council floor. Now members of the council were standing in turn, publicly voicing their support for various pieces of legislation and on the matter of a peer review—the official examination of the late Dramok Zarl's papers. Diltan had made his vote for the latest matter known. Now he fidgeted on the seating step where the councilmen gathered. He was a bundle of nerves, a fact that his friend Councilman Oiteil picked up on.

"This Matara Natasha must be quite the lovely lady. You can barely keep still," the elder Oiteil observed as they sat in a far corner of the room. "You've hardly paid attention to the vote as to who will review Imperial Father Zarl's records."

Diltan waved his friend and occasional mentor off. "Oh, that honour will fall to Maf. Everyone knows that."

Oiteil raised a bushy eyebrow at him. For the mild-mannered Dramok, such an expression was akin to a shout, though there was the note of a chuckle in his tone. "With all the wheeling and dealing going on to give you the job?"

That got Diltan's attention, ending his ruminations on how best to impress Tasha Salter. "What wheeling and dealing? What are you talking about?"

Oiteil's grin faded. His eyes widened in astonishment. "You really don't know? You didn't recruit our allies to get the undecided to vote for you?"

"Why would I? I don't stand a chance, not with Maf head of the Ethics Committee."

"You're on that committee as well. Most see you as much more objective than Maf on matters to do with the Imperial Family."

"Well, that much is good to know."

Diltan looked about the council floor and noted Dramok Weslo was on his feet. The vote was drawing to a close if he was casting his. With solemn majesty, the white-bearded councilman intoned, "I cast my vote for Councilman Diltan."

Diltan's brow wrinkled. Weslo was conservative in his views and usually set against the younger councilmen. More than once, he'd voiced displeasure over some of Diltan's past proposals and arguments.

Thinking about that, Diltan told Oiteil, "I'm still marked by many as being enraptured with the Imperial Clan. These men don't tend to forget such things easily."

His friend quirked a knowing smile. "It's a good thing you've kept your appointment with the empress's cousin under wraps. In a few minutes, the voting will be done, however, and who you attract for a Matara will no longer be a factor—until the next time you want a piece of legislation passed."

Diltan shrugged. "My choice for a lifemate is my business. A Matara lasts longer and is of more importance than my political career. Her connection to the Imperial Clan notwithstanding, Matara Tasha is a lovely woman."

"And if she doesn't work out, there is the sister, correct?"

Diltan snorted. "I have no interest in the twin. If Tasha is not compatible with my clan, I will happily move on to a woman with no Imperial connections."

The wry tone he spoke with made Oiteil snicker. "It's like that, is it? Alike in appearance but not in personalities? Is it really impossible to tell the two females apart physically?"

Diltan thought about the rough-around-the-edges twin. The memory of that insolent sparkle in her eye that had first caught his attention made his heart quicken for a moment. Too bad she had such a poor attitude to go with that exciting inner fire. "They are identical physically. After a moment or two of talking to them, you get a good idea of which is which."

Oiteil considered. "Isn't that amazing? Two women, identical in features, brought up in the same household, and yet utterly different in personality."

"Indeed. Matara Cissy is—how can I say this? Spirited. That's a good word for it. Tasha is more, uh, sedate." Diltan frowned. He'd almost described Tasha as 'predictable'. Which she seemed to be and that was a good thing. The last thing he needed was a mate that left him guessing all the time.

Oiteil turned his attention to official concerns. "Listen, we need to discuss more serious matters soon. If you aren't picked to review Zarl's papers, what does your calendar look like for the next week?"

"Nothing I can't shuffle around. What's up?"

"I'm trying to round up our like-minded associates on this matter of Bi'is working with the Basma and Earth's Holy Leader."

"The *supposed* matter of Bi'is' involvement," Diltan said. When Oiteil frowned a little, he added, "Oh, I agree there is something to the story, but it's bad form to assume guilt. I like to approach each case looking at the facts with no rumour attached." He grinned. "That's what I get for having a judge as a clanmate."

Oiteil nodded approvingly. "Your point is well taken. Yet you were there for the deposition. You know trouble is afoot."

Diltan sighed. When it came to disputes with other empires, only outright war could move things at a decent pace. "The Bi'is kingdom will swear up and down that any illegal biological research on our people is being carried out by renegade scientists. They'll refuse to admit to any knowledge about the matter."

Oiteil's lip curled. "It's bullshit and you know it."

"Without hard evidence to the contrary, the Galactic Council will have to side with Bi'is."

Oiteil flung his arms out in an angry gesture. "So what? We don't have a meeting? We don't lodge a protest? We sit back and do nothing?"

"Of course we have a meeting and send out a referendum of protest. As for doing nothing, I have it on good authority that our spyships are actively employed in finding the evidence we need against Bi'is."

"Meanwhile, the Basma and Copeland continue to prey on our ships. Confrontation with Bi'is should happen sooner rather than later."

Diltan regarded him with patient worry. "Do you want to kill off the Empire? We're just four years out of our war with Earth. We took a hell of a beating. The only way we could possibly fight another war is to put younglings not even of clanning age on the front lines."

"The Earthers did it."

"And it was wrong," Diltan insisted.

Oiteil sighed. "I hate the idea of Bi'is getting away with such travesties as using our people as research animals. They used to abduct us on a huge scale for their experiments. It can't be allowed to happen again."

Diltan had to make him see that, warranted or not, opening up another conflict would be too draining on the Empire's resources—namely, its men. "Those abductions were hundreds of years ago, even before the virus. Don't worry. The Galactic Council—"

"Your attention, please."

The deep bass of Head Councilman Fernlen's voice halted Diltan and Oiteil's conversation, as well as all others. The councilmen turned their attention to him.

Dramok Fernlen stood in the middle of the council chamber's floor, looking up at the stepped seats. An introspective man who rarely engaged in heated diatribes against his fellow councilmen or the Imperial Clan, Fernlen was well liked by most.

When everyone had settled into their seats and waited expectantly, the grey-haired head councilman smiled at them all. "Well, that went right to the very end, didn't it? I don't believe I've ever seen a tighter margin in any vote. Congratulations to Councilmen Diltan and Maf for their equal popularity."

As the gathered laughed at Fernlen's light teasing, Diltan blinked. The vote had been that close? Surely this was a joke.

Fernlen continued. "By a margin of only seven votes, you have decided that Councilman Diltan shall assume responsibility for former Emperor Zarl's records. Do you accept this task, Councilman?"

Diltan stared at Fernlen in shock. Dramok Maf, down at the lowest tier of the steps, twisted awkwardly about. The deformed councilman smiled and nodded to him, an acknowledgement of equals.

Diltan still couldn't summon the sense to respond until Oiteil's nudge reminded him that Fernlen waited for an answer. In a voice that didn't entirely sound like his own, Diltan said, "Yes, Head Councilman. I accept the charge of my fellow councilmen to review Imperial Father Zarl's records. I will answer this honour by serving with honour."

Fernlen nodded. "So noted. This was our final vote for the session. I believe that concludes today's full council business unless anyone else has new work to discuss? No? Council dismissed."

Conversation buzzed as men rose from their seats and headed for the chamber's exit. Those who passed Diltan offered their congratulations. He accepted the accolades, feeling numb as he did so. He couldn't believe he'd been offered such a responsibility.

"Well done," Oiteil praised him as they stood. The chamber was nearly empty now.

"I suppose. I can't say that I worked for this opportunity," Diltan said. "Maf seems to be waiting. I'd better speak to him."

Despite the serene way Maf had accepted his defeat, Diltan couldn't be sure how the other councilman was taking the matter. After all, he headed the Ethics Committee. Maf had fought hard against the disabilities that made his life painful and difficult. Even the men who didn't like Maf or his quiet but steady demonstrations against the interbreeding of Earther women and Kalquorian men still respected him.

He's been a thorn in the Imperial Clan's side and more than half the council's over the notion of us dying out pure, Diltan thought as he neared the waiting man. *Could it be that is the reason he was passed over for this? Am I the lesser of two evils?*

So much for being honoured, if that was the case.

Maf's twisted frame didn't allow for the man to manage more than the suggestion of a bow. "Congratulations to you, my dear Diltan. I am sure you will do a fine job."

Still wondering how this had come to pass, Diltan bowed deeper than was warranted. "Thank you, Maf. I hope I am up to such a great task." He couldn't help adding, "It should have gone to you."

Maf chuckled and patted his shoulder with a gnarled hand that looked as if it should belong to a man three times his age. "Not at all. You'll do splendid. If I couldn't be allowed the honour, I am glad the duty falls to a man like you."

"A man like me?"

"Of course." Maf beamed at him, like a proud father might at a successful son. "Smart, loyal to the Empire, bound by duty—and with your wealth, not a man who can be bought if something less than flattering to the former Imperial Clan should come to light."

Suspicion cast a shadow on Diltan's thoughts. "Are you not the same man who once proclaimed me as devoted to the empress as the babe that suckled on her teat? Did you not insinuate that was where my hopes ultimately lay for my future?"

Maf roared with laughter. His face lit in merriment. "And it damned near had the emperors ready to tear out my throat with their fangs! If I was not such a crippled wreck, I believe they would have done so. Fortunately for me, there is no glory in killing a disabled man." He grinned. "You have changed in the last few years, Diltan. I have no doubts when it comes to your honour any longer."

Diltan wasn't sure if he should feel complimented or insulted. Yet Maf was being a good sport about not winning the right to pore over the former emperor's records. Diltan thought it best to be charitable with his response.

Plus there was the matter of the duty itself. Now that it had landed in his lap, Diltan felt overwhelmed. Maf's response meant he could be both conciliatory as well as ask for support, and thus build an affiliation that might aid Diltan in the future. He hoped the waiting Oiteil would not be offended by him reaching out to Maf rather than his usual mentor.

"May I impose on you? I didn't expect this to happen and I'm worried I'll be in over my head. Zarl's reign was a long one, with much legislation passed under his watch. If I have any questions—"

Maf greeted his request with surprised delight. "Thank you for asking, Dramok Diltan. Indeed, do not hesitate to consult with me. My office is open to you at all times."

Diltan bowed. "Thank you."

Maf returned the bow as best his infirmities allowed. He limped off, giving Oiteil a nod as he passed. It was only then that Diltan noted Maf's long-time aide Sitrel, a tall, handsome Dramok who had waited silently for the conversation to end. Sitrel fell in beside Maf as they left the chamber.

Before Diltan could explain himself to Oiteil, the elder councilman gave him a knowing smile. "A stroke of genius to request Maf's assistance with any problems that arise from the review."

Diltan blew out a breath he hadn't realised he'd been holding. "I had hoped you wouldn't take it as a slight. You are always my first choice when it comes to being set straight."

"You made a smart move in diplomacy. When you want to see a piece of legislation passed, Maf will bring many votes to your corner." Oiteil clapped a hand on his shoulder and joked, "There is hope for you yet."

"You keep saying that," Diltan said. They moved out of the chamber into the corridor beyond, heading towards the in-house transport that would take them to their fourth-floor offices. "When will I move beyond hope into realisation?"

"I'd say you're damned close. First the honour of an Imperial review and a lovely Matara to woo. You are a most fortunate man, my friend."

"Indeed I am." Only one thing bothered Diltan in the wake of his unexpected triumph. "I would like to know who was involved in pushing me to be the reviewer?"

"Somebody with excellent sense would be my guess," was Oiteil's breezy reply.

Diltan grinned so hard his face ached.

Chapter Six

Even with their special issue passes, it took fifteen minutes for Clan Diltan to gain admittance to the Matara Complex to collect Tasha for their acquainting date. There were three checkpoints. At each one, the three men had to present credentials and submit to security scans. They put up with the inconvenience with good humour. After all, several women had been targeted by a serial killer in the past and the Basma's rebellion had abducted a few others. Diltan, Rolat and Wal understood the need for the extreme security measures. Even men of their rank were afforded no exceptions.

At last they walked through the complex's main entry. It opened into the huge courtyard in the middle of the complex, surrounded by the lodgings of the Earther women who had come to Kalquor to be wooed by clans like Diltan's.

Women, particularly Earther women, were becoming more commonplace in the capital city of Kalquor. Most days, Diltan saw at least half a dozen of the small females in the marketplace or visiting their Dramok clanmates at the Government House. He had even begun taking the presence of Empress Jessica for granted.

Yet he'd never seen so many females similar to his race all at once. More astonishing still was the sight of several of the beauties not fully clothed. Wal gasped out loud then snapped his jaw shut with embarrassment. Rolat, who might have laughed at his Imdiko's faux pas, stared around at the dazzling sight before him. At least three dozen women sat on loungers, lay on massage beds under the talented tentacles of Tratsods or relaxed in whirlpools. A lot of skin showed. It was a paradise of pale pink, peach, tan, brown and nearly black flesh laid out before the clan.

As Diltan took in the vision of beauty, a familiar face smiled at him from a whirlpool. She waved. Feeling dazed, Diltan led his astounded clan to that part of the courtyard.

As they neared, the woman stood and mounted the steps, stepping out of the hot tub. "Hi, Dramok Diltan. Is it that time already?"

The men stopped in their tracks a few feet away. Judging from the welcoming smile, it had to be Tasha who stood before them, her body gleaming wet and scantily clad. There was more skin than soaksuit, so much more that she might as well have not bothered putting anything on. Triangles of blue fabric hid her areolae and pubic mound and little else. The straps holding those triangles in place were so thin they looked as if they might snap in an instant, especially given the fullness of her breasts and buttocks.

Diltan's heart galloped as he stared. Tasha was lush and rounded, her pale body a dream of soft curves and pliant flesh. His cocks twitched and filled at the arousing vision before him.

Rolat whispered, "By the ancestors and Mother of All. Is that our potential Matara, Diltan?"

Wal made a choked sound in his throat. He seemed incapable of speech at the moment.

Diltan swallowed hard and whispered back, "I guess it is her, though she's not dressed for our meeting."

Seemingly oblivious to the sensation she caused, the young woman sauntered over to a nearby table. She picked up a glass of what appeared to be dlas, a rather potent drink. She took a healthy swallow, set the glass back down and grabbed a folded towel lying by her drink. She rubbed it all over, drying off. Her breasts swayed under her efforts. Diltan's cocks gave another jerk.

The woman smiled ruefully. "How did it get so late in the day? Holy Hannah, I've got to get dressed for my date. Don't worry, Tasha is much more prompt than I am. If I know her, she's dressed and ready to go."

With a strange mixture of relief and disappointment, Diltan realised this was Cissy and not Tasha. He cleared his throat and bowed. "Matara Cecilia, how nice to see you again. These are my clanmates, Nobek Rolat and Imdiko Wal. This is our date's twin sister, Cecilia."

The two men bowed, though they did not speak. They were still overcome by Cissy's lack of clothing. Wal's eyes were almost perfectly round in his amazement.

Cissy grinned and motioned them to follow her. "Come along, gentlemen. I'll take you to Tasha. Where are you all going tonight?"

Diltan tried to talk, but he was almost as tongue-tied as his clanmates. He cleared his throat. "We plan to take her to the Taste of Home eatery."

"Oh yeah, Lindsey's Imdiko's place. We had dinner there last night. You financed that, didn't you, Dramok?"

Cissy gave Diltan an appraising look. It made him wonder if Lindsey had broken their agreement that they never speak of his terrible judgment a couple of years before.

In a stilted tone, he answered, "I am honoured to have helped Imdiko Vax realise his dream of owning his own establishment. He has shown beyond any doubt how greatly he deserved it. I am sorry I won't be the one to introduce his great work to Matara Natasha. It is the best place to eat on all of Kalquor."

Cissy's laugh was a hearty bellow, uttered without the least bit of self-consciousness. The agreeable sound filled Diltan's ears. He couldn't keep from smiling in response.

She told him, "Oh, don't you worry about Tasha already having eaten there. We didn't get to sample but a fraction of what that place serves and as you can see"—Cissy smacked her uncovered ass—"Tasha and I aren't shy about eating!"

Wal moaned low in his throat. His stare was riveted on the handprint appearing on Cissy's well-rounded rump. Diltan nudged him, worried Cissy would catch the Imdiko staring.

Cissy didn't appear to have noticed. "What else are you doing besides dinner? Tasha said something about a show."

Diltan nodded as they walked inside one of the buildings. The room they entered had lovely art vids that he barely noted as they went straight to the in-house transport.

"Sixth floor, north wing," Cissy commanded the conveyance. The door closed them in and the floor beneath their feet shifted.

Diltan tried to not acknowledge how close all that bare flesh was. He had to clear his throat again before answering her enquiry. "We're attending a well-received play about the First Clan. It's a historical drama. "

Cissy yawned. "It sounds stuffy and self-important. I'm sure Tasha will love it." Before Diltan could react to her disparaging remark, she skewered the three men with a sharp look. "After that, you'll bring Tasha straight home?"

Rolat finally broke through his silence. Maybe it was the protective way Cissy grilled them about their plans with her sister for the evening. The big Nobek wore an expression that said he was amused as well as enthralled by the Earther.

"We will escort her back here as soon as she wishes it. We'll let her make the decisions about our evening as we get to know one another."

Cissy looked him over with narrowed eyes. Diltan also gazed at Rolat. He tried to see him not from the viewpoint of a clanmate of many years but as an unknown entity, a stranger.

He had to admit his Nobek was a fearsome specimen. Most of Rolat's scars were covered by his tunic and pants. They were hidden, keeping evidence of past violence from frightening a small Earther woman.

As a long-time prison guard then warden, Rolat had seen his share of vicious, life-threatening struggles. Having moved up to Head of Penal Colonies, he was now removed from most of the danger. He still insisted on frequent in-person inspections of prison facilities and had been present for a riot that had nearly cost him his life. Diltan was grateful such occurrences were increasingly rare.

Only one thin, whitish streak on Rolat's cheek marred his strong features, but he possessed an aura of contained brutality, the hallmark of most Nobeks. His wide shoulders and broad chest spoke of his strength. Big and imposing, Rolat's mere appearance demanded respect.

Cissy might have respected the power that oozed from Diltan's clanmate, but she showed no sign of being intimidated by it. Her next statement underscored that assessment.

"Make sure Tasha does make all the decisions, big boy. Otherwise Kalquor will get three more Mataras come sunrise."

For a moment, Diltan didn't catch on to what Cissy was threatening. When realisation dawned, he was shocked. To suggest she would emasculate them—even in jest, the comment was crude. Rolat's and Wal's mouths hung open as well.

How could Cissy be related to Empress Jessica or her sister, Lindsey? With that mouth, she was more suited to running a brothel.

It's a good thing we are courting the other girl. This one is simply too brazen. If I had to take such an outspoken woman to an official function where diplomacy is needed…

Diltan shook his head at the idea. However, a part of him appreciated how hilarious it would be for a few councilmen and ambassadors he didn't like to get an earful from Cecilia Salter. That might be worth a little humiliation to hear.

He admired her fire and drive to protect her sister. If only she could manage a little tact as well, he might find it possible to like her. But no, she was far too rebellious.

Ancestors help the clan that ends up with her.

Cissy stopped in front of the next to last door in the corridor and thumbed the visitor announce. Before anyone answered, she called out, "Hey, Tasha, your fun bunch is here for your date. Have a good time." She turned away from the door and gave the three men a daring smile. "As for you, Clan Diltan…don't have too good a time with my sister, if you get my drift."

With that final warning, Cissy sashayed off to the last door in the hall. Just as she reached her quarters, the door in front of Diltan opened.

Standing there with an expectant smile, Tasha looked more than presentable in a demure blouse and skirt ensemble. Her hair cascaded to her shoulders in perfect curls—not a hair out of place.

Diltan bowed but was the only one to do so. A glance at his clanmates revealed they stared after Cissy, who was just disappearing into her own quarters.

He spoke in a louder than usual voice to remind Rolat and Wal that their attention was supposed to be on the other twin. "Good evening, Matara. You look lovely."

Their expressions still stunned, his Nobek and Imdiko realised their date stood there. They bowed somewhat clumsily to Tasha, murmuring greetings.

His most pleasant smile plastered on his face, Diltan made the introductions. As he did so, he did his best to see the pretty and more appropriate Salter sister standing before them. However, it was the image of the other, nearly naked twin with spirited eyes that remained seared on his retinas.

* * * *

Imdiko Wal sat in a private booth at A Taste of Home, wearing a set smile that he couldn't feel. He wished it were only a dinner date. That he had to get through a theatre show as well made the night stretch endlessly before him.

It made no sense for him to feel this way. Imdiko Vax's restaurant was perfect, as always. The setting, a semi-private table before the flickering firepit, was pleasant. Romantic, even, as it was meant to be. The strains of a violin wove a sweet spell in the air. The young Earther male playing it coaxed melodies out of the alien instrument that made one think good thoughts. The food was as delicious as ever. Wal had ordered his favourite dish—grilled chicken wrapped in ronka strips with a mozzarella-and-gusasp herb sauce drizzled over it.

The food and atmosphere were a delight. Matara Tasha was beautiful, intelligent and pleasant, a perfectly lovely woman to talk to. Wal knew he should be in heaven right now. And yet…

And yet it was Tasha's twin sister, Cissy, who Wal's mind kept returning to. The brash and sassy twin filled his mind, drawing him away from conversation again and again. That quick wit. Her cocky smile. The cutting sarcasm that let Wal know Cissy was a woman who would excite mind as well as body.

Damn, did she ever excite his body. Wal had a lively libido, but the effect that merely thinking about Cissy had on him was ridiculous. Every time he envisioned her in that daring soaksuit, her handprint emblazoned on her exposed rump, he got hard. He was hard now. If it weren't for the tabletop hiding the erections that insisted on showing up, he'd be humiliated several times over.

At least he knew he wasn't alone in his amorous state. Wal had caught a whiff of his clanmates' spicy arousal scents from time to time. It didn't mitigate his chagrin that he lusted after the wrong woman, however. If Tasha would do or say something that would set off the same sparks that Cissy did, he'd feel a lot better about the night.

Tasha is a good woman. There is not one damned thing wrong with her. Get over this silly infatuation with her sister and count yourself lucky for this opportunity, he told himself.

But damn it, Wal was bored after the shocking encounter with Cissy. If she were here, they wouldn't be discussing mundane things like the men's work. What they would discuss he couldn't imagine, but he was sure it would be riveting.

Stop it, you idiot. You're not out with Cissy. You're courting Tasha and she's a wonderful lady. She even looks just like her twin with that soft, round body and those big, expressive eyes. Pay attention to her and discover that she's just as fascinating as that wild, nearly naked creature you met earlier.

He'd reminded himself to attend to his date just in time. Tasha chose that moment to turn to Wal and ask, "What has been your most outrageous case, Imdiko Wal? Or your funniest one?"

"My funniest case as a judge?" He considered the question. It was a good one. Most people wanted to know about the high-profile lawsuits or the sensational landmark cases that involved Kalquor's elite. No one had ever asked Wal about the outrageous ones.

Thinking of outrageous situations brought the image of that red handprint on Cissy's ass to mind. Wal forced his thoughts away from that.

He came up with an anecdote he thought Tasha would find amusing. "There was one case in which two men broke into someone's home. They stole a couple of computers, an entertainment vid system and a few other items. What they forgot to take with them was the vid recorder they'd spent some time playing with, recording themselves eating the owner's food, soaking in his whirlpool, having sex in his sleeping room and generally enjoying themselves in his nice home before leaving."

Tasha laughed outright at that, reminding Wal once more of Cissy's more exuberant mien. Tasha was every bit as pretty as Cissy, especially when she smiled. So why was it Wal kept wishing he spoke to Cissy and not her sister?

Diltan grinned at him. "You had to go way back for that story, my Imdiko. A judge of your rank doesn't get the petty cases like that."

Wal shrugged. "It was the silliest case I ever had. I still laugh when I think of those two idiots."

Rolat smirked. "Stupidity is always amusing to those of us who don't suffer from it."

Wal couldn't resist the opening his clanmate had given him. "Hmm, I might have another story or twenty about a certain Nobek I know."

Rolat gave him a look that was half amusement and half warning. The gentle kick against Wal's shin only broadened the Imdiko's smile.

He chuckled but said no more. It was too early to be embarrassing his clanmate in front of Tasha. If things worked out, there would be time enough for that. Plus for every humiliating story he could share about Diltan and Rolat, they had just as many about him. Such was the price of a long clanship.

Wal settled for giving Tasha a knowing wink that promised future disclosure. She hid her smile behind her hand, as perfectly demure as ever. The Imdiko squelched the urge to sigh.

Rolat relaxed when he realised Wal wasn't going to tell any tales. That was good, especially since they didn't know if they would end up with Tasha in the long run. The fewer the embarrassing stories floating around the general population, the better.

Rolat paid close attention to everything Tasha did and said. As a Nobek, it was in his nature to be watchful. However, he had a particular interest in catching every nuance from his potential lifemate.

Occasionally he thought he saw some of that amazing spark that had captured his interest earlier…the fire that Tasha's twin, Cissy, had displayed. Such spirit was an instant attraction for the Nobek. If Tasha had any of that, Rolat would be well pleased to be her clanmate. He liked how smart she was. He enjoyed intelligent conversation and there was no doubt Tasha could offer that.

Her attractiveness was another point in her favour. Though Tasha's clothes did not display her body as much as Cissy's soaksuit had displayed hers, Rolat was sure the curves were similar. Such a soft, rounded figure pleased the Nobek to no end, as his twitching cocks kept reminding him.

Yet there was a reticence to Tasha that bothered him. Obviously she would not share her innermost thoughts and secrets on a first date, but he felt she kept herself closed off. She seemed to be holding back more than she should. She answered their questions with short, sometimes meaningless replies then distracted them with questions of her own. Rolat got the feeling Tasha tried to keep them talking about themselves so she didn't have to share much.

She gently grilled Wal even now. "Tell me what kind of cases you deal with if you're not serving justice to the mentally incompetent."

Rolat's Imdiko gave her a bland smile. "I get the ones that involve threats to the Empire or leaders of Kalquor. In recent years, I've sat on a panel that had to decide the fate of a decorated war hero who had become a serial killer, which was most unpleasant."

Rolat let Wal's voice drone into the background. It wasn't that he didn't find his clanmate's work interesting or that he didn't respect what Wal had to say. He already knew the story the Imdiko judge shared, knew it inside and out. If Tasha was going to continue to gloss over her own background, there seemed to be little point in attending the conversation so closely.

He glanced at the Earther male playing the violin. The man was young, his face almost as pretty as a girl's. He was the exact opposite of Kalquorian men—fair-skinned, blond, blue-eyed. The slender youth stood barely taller than Tasha. For the Kalquorian men who couldn't hope to clan or for the clans who preferred males to females, Earther men had become as welcome in the Empire as their female lifebearer counterparts. The homosexual Earthers, as repressed as the women, were finding loving homes in the Empire. No doubt this young man had been courted by some Kalquorian man or men and given a new life away from his own kind's persecution.

Rolat looked at Tasha. Like most Kalquorian men, he was bisexual, enjoying the company of males and females. With his clan's rank, he hoped to attract a Matara to their unit, though Kalquorian women were rare. His clan being picked for the lottery had enhanced their chances greatly, allowing them to compete for the Earther women.

Being in the company of the lovely Tasha was a chance that could not be allowed to pass them by. Yet Rolat's thoughts kept roaming to the lookalike sister, the one who had threatened to turn the Nobek and his clanmates into women if they didn't treat Tasha with respect. Remembering that almost made Rolat laugh out loud right there and then. He contained his amusement with great difficulty.

If only Tasha would show more of that spirit instead of the quiet politeness she'd worn all evening! Rolat wanted to wonder if his dinner companion would be exciting in bed...but instead, he wondered that about Cissy. By the ancestors, he could already imagine her naked after seeing her in that barely there soaksuit. The fantasy of that body beneath his, perhaps struggling against him in an effort to be on top... His mouth went dry and his cocks swelled. Rolat was sure Cissy might try to fight him for superior position. The thrill of gaining the surrender of such a woman was too enticing to dismiss easily. Pinning Cissy down, her bountiful breasts heaving with effort, her eyes wide as she realised she had no choice but to be dominated by him—

Diltan's none-too-gentle kick to his ankle beneath the table brought Rolat out of his fantasy. The Nobek was abruptly aware that his Dramok, Wal and Tasha all looked at him. Tasha's smile was expectant, not that challenging smirk Cissy had worn. She must have asked him one of her many questions.

Rolat cleared his throat, his face heating with embarrassment. "Please excuse me, Matara. I'm afraid Wal bored me to the point that I tuned out. I've heard all his stories, you see."

The Imdiko scowled at him. "That's right, Rolat. Show her what a jerk you are."

The Nobek gave Wal a slow wink to placate his sensitive clanmate. Wal snorted, but the crease between his brows eased, letting Rolat know the slight was forgiven.

Rolat couldn't resist teasing just a little. "If it makes you feel any better, you're not half as boring as Diltan."

"Yes, I know. No one is." Wal's smile filled with devilish delight as he joined in on the fun. The Imdiko never resisted the chance to dig at their Dramok.

As Diltan gave them both a warning frown, Tasha tittered behind her hand. "Boys, boys. Behave yourselves or you get no dessert."

Rolat grinned at her. She might not be the livewire Cissy was, but Tasha was a good sport. He inclined his head in respect. "Please forgive my rudeness, Tasha. What did you ask?"

"I asked how much you have to travel as the head of all the Empire's prisons and work camps."

"Speaking of boring," Diltan snorted.

Rolat agreed, but he ignored his Dramok and politely answered. "I travel for work as much as possible. We Nobeks don't tend to do well behind desks, so any excuse to go to the facilities in person is a good excuse in my book."

Tasha hid her mouth behind her hand to giggle again. Her tendency to do that made Rolat feel she masked more than just her smile. Yet he could hardly imagine what a placid, sweet girl like her could have to hide.

Diltan poured them all another round of bohut, which he was glad Tasha liked to drink. He felt this initial appointment with the Earther was going well. He chalked up the boredom he felt to the painful necessity of getting to know someone for the first time.

Tasha had good breeding written all over her. Quiet and polite, she was as well-mannered as Diltan could hope for in a potential mate. Tasha was nothing like her too-bold sister, thank the ancestors.

Once more Diltan was forced to wonder how two women, raised side by side since birth, could be so monumentally different. He also wondered how outrageously Cissy would have behaved had it been her they'd brought to the restaurant. What would she have replaced that scandalous little soaksuit with for a night out?

Every time Diltan saw Cissy, she wore something inappropriate. First had been the casual and mannish outfit she'd come to Kalquor in. Then all that flesh this evening!

But he couldn't think about that, not when remembering all that luscious flesh got him as hard as a hormonally charged youngling. That Cissy had such an effect on him irritated Diltan to no end.

So she's wonderful to look at. What of it? Doesn't that mean Tasha will be every bit as enticing when she isn't covered so modestly? This is the perfect one – the one who looks so classy in public and possibly erotic in private.

Yet no matter how hard he tried, Diltan couldn't imagine Tasha naked. Every time he tried, he saw fiery-eyed Cissy in the blue soaksuit…with that handprint on her smooth flank and cock-cutting smile on her face.

Diltan felt sure Tasha was witty and strong in her own right. She had to be…all the liveliness Cissy exhibited had to be present in Tasha as well. Right?

Yet his date didn't strike him as daring. There was more than just a hint of caution to Tasha, almost as if she'd erected some invisible barrier between herself and Diltan's clan. She might have the same face as Cissy, but Diltan couldn't visualise her with any of her sister's exuberance or spunk.

Diltan mentally shook his head at himself. What did it matter if Tasha was proper? That was what he wanted anyway. He did not want to clan an outrageous Matara who would balk him at every turn. Certainly he did not want a lifemate who threatened to rip his dicks off.

Tasha was a perfectly nice woman, one who would be an asset to Diltan's public life. Given time, he might even find that she was indeed the woman for his clan.

Chapter Seven

By the time Cissy peeled her eyelids apart the next day, the morning was almost done. Yawning hugely, she made herself get up, throw on a robe and trudge to her tiny kitchen. Minutes later she went through the door connecting her apartment to her sister's, carrying two cups of coffee. She was slow in waking but kept alert for any sign that Tasha had not come home alone.

There were no puddles of clothing thrown off in mad desire as Cissy made the short trip to Tasha's bedroom. The only apparel she had to step over consisted of her sister's skirt and blouse ensemble from the night before, which Tasha had dropped carelessly on the floor. One form huddled under the covers on the sleeping mat. Cissy set the cups down on the bedside shelf next to a silver-framed picture of her parents. She gave their beaming images a sad smile, missing her mother and father even though years had passed since their deaths. The boating accident that had taken the elder Salters' lives had occurred while the twins had been away at college. Jessica and Lindsey, along with their parents, Tara and Aaron, had been their strength during that sad time. The McInness family had taken the weight of funeral arrangements off the shoulders of the grieving twins. Auntie Tara had even identified the bodies, taking on that awful responsibility and sparing Cissy and Tasha any memory that would ruin the one of a happy, lively couple.

Cissy straightened, putting the past where it belonged. Her mother and father would have been devastated to think they ever caused her any pain. It was best to recall the full, joyful lives they had managed to have under the shadow of an often-paranoid government. They had lived well, proving it was the spirit that made for a good existence, more so than the circumstances that surrounded it.

Cissy yawned again. She wrinkled her nose at the window vid that gave the illusion of a flowering garden right outside Tasha's room—even though they were six floors off the ground level. Cissy wished the rooms had real windows, though she understood how well vids conserved energy. The quarters were well-ventilated, but it would be nice to open a window and have a breeze float through the room.

Needing caffeine to improve her mood, Cissy set about bouncing on Tasha's bed. "Wakie, wakie! Rise and shine, give the world your glow, you precious sunbeam!"

"Bitch," the mound under the covers muttered. It curled into a tight ball.

Cissy stopped bouncing. "I brought coffee."

Tasha sat up and reached her hand out with her eyes still closed. "Give me."

Cissy laughed and handed the goods over, careful to not slop hot java. Tasha woke in as good a mood as her sister did. *And looks twice as bad*, Cissy thought, hoping it was true but suspecting otherwise. Tasha's perfect coif from the night before was now a snarled bird's nest, sticking up all over the place. Cissy put her hands to her own head to check on how her mane had fared after the night.

Nope. Her tangles felt as if they were much worse than Tasha's. Cissy patted at the mess in a vain attempt to calm it before reaching for her cup of coffee.

Tasha didn't start drinking right away. As always, she inhaled the steam rising from her cup with pleasure before taking that first glorious sip. She grimaced with semi-happiness and her eyes slitted open. "You may return in an hour and only then if you bring more."

Cissy crossed her legs in a lotus position, getting comfortable on her sister's bed. "Forget it. I'm dying to hear about your date last night."

Tasha's eyes opened a little more, her interest piqued. "Why? Was yours that boring?"

Cissy waved a dismissive hand. "We had a good time. Lemanthev concerts don't allow for much conversation, though. I can't say I got to know the clan I was with, but I do like the raw energy of that tribal-sounding stuff. I went more for the music than the company, in all honesty. So, that's about it from me. What about that Clan Diltan? Were they as stuffy and boring as they looked?"

Actually, none of the three men had looked stuffy to Cissy's eyes, not even Diltan. Nor boring. In particular, the Nobek had caught Cissy's attention. Rolat had been an amazing eyeful of rough and ready. Big, bold and delicious. Cissy had entertained the fantasy of grabbing him by the wonderfully muscled arm and dragging him to her bed. So what if he wasn't the gorgeous equal of his Dramok? Cissy found such men much more fascinating to look at than the handsome ones.

Not that Diltan was conventionally handsome. He was gorgeous, damn the man. Someone needed to break his nose, just to steal some of that perfection away. Cissy thought that if he ever asked for volunteers, she'd be glad to offer her services.

Even quiet Wal had not committed the sin of being one-dimensionally pleasing to the eye. He was attractive, just nice enough to pass the gaze over. However, there had been the flash of a grin once, before the three men had seen Cissy in the pool—then he'd been quite stunning, in an intelligent, nerdy way.

As Cissy mused about her sister's dates, Tasha said, "They were okay. I don't think we connected, but they were nice enough."

Trying to sound unconcerned and believing she pulled it off, Cissy asked, "Do you think you'll see them again?"

Tasha shrugged. She took a deep swallow of her coffee before answering. "I don't know. They aren't bad, but…I don't know. I might give it another shot. They all have that rank and status these Kalquorians are so crazy to show off."

"That's true." A councilman, the director of the Empire's prison system and a judge. *Rank out the wazoo,* Cissy thought. If Tasha joined Clan Diltan, she'd never want for anything. If they could make her sister happy, Cissy would even try to be nice to Diltan on holidays and special occasions.

Thinking this, she told her twin, "You never know, Tash. Dramok Snooty and his boys might be your happily-ever-after."

Tasha made a face. "It makes me feel bad that they only get to try five gals before they get shut out of the lottery. That's not a lot of opportunity, is it? I suppose I should see them again. Maybe."

Tasha was clearly ambivalent about Clan Diltan. Only her typical kindness made her consider seeing them again. It would be a waste of her time.

There's no harm in them coming around one or two more times, though, Cissy thought. So they were uppity. They were still decent eye candy for her to enjoy as long as Tasha remained willing to give them a chance. Unlike the men, Tasha had no limits on the clans she could entertain before making a final decision.

Cissy wondered if a trio like Clan Diltan ever cut loose and had real fun. It was hard to imagine Diltan or his bookish-looking Imdiko attending a lemanthev concert. Rolat probably would like that sort of thing. Or maybe his clanmates had drained all the hedonism out of the big, burly beast.

And why for heaven's sake was she thinking about Clan Diltan so much?

They were not on Cissy's list of potential suitors, at least not that she'd seen. Then again, she hadn't looked at her prospects in about the last month, either. Had Clan Diltan joined the lottery since that time? If they'd been there before, Cissy knew for a fact they weren't on the first screen that held her most compatible choices.

What the hell, even her compatibility score was a joke. The lottery questionnaire had been an hours-long task, one Cissy hadn't taken seriously for an instant. When Tasha discovered Cissy was posting sarcastic answers, she'd taken over her unrepentant twin's profile. There was no telling what responsible Tasha had written about Cissy.

No doubt Tasha would have done her best to represent Cissy in a positive light, one that would attract the best possible clan. Cissy told herself it was for the same reason that she was interested in Clan Diltan on Tasha's behalf. Her twin deserved mates who were successful and could funnel some of their prestige and money into Tasha's dreams for the future. Tasha had been an interior decorator back on Earth, but she'd dreamed of being an architect using sustainable materials. Crowded, polluted Earth had needed people with such skills. Earth was gone, but with Kalquor's insistence on pristine natural settings, their new home seemed the perfect place to study eco-friendly building. Tasha just needed the funds and schooling to pursue that wish. She was too proud to ask Jessica for such assistance, though their cousin would have surely given it to her. Tasha wanted to be a part of a clan to which she could repay any contribution made. Surely the finances of a councilman, judge and head of an entire governmental department would allow for that.

First, Tasha had to get off her duff and be serious about finding a clan. She had been ambivalent about settling down all of her adult life. She was reticent given even the repressive rules on Earth when it came to interactions with the opposite sex. Tasha had never gone on more than one date with the same man. The last five years they'd lived on Earth, she hadn't dated at all. Cissy had wondered if her sister was determined to be an old maid.

However, Tasha had been an absolute beast for sex on the Kalquorian transport—yet just like on Earth, she rarely saw the same men twice. She had shown no real interest in ever marrying. That Tasha had entered the lottery had been a surprise to Cissy. As cousin to the empress, she would have been allowed to stay on Kalquor without searching for clanmates.

If her sister held true to form, Cissy had the feeling Tasha would never see Clan Diltan again. That was too bad given what they could offer her. Plus it was fun to needle those guys. Making Diltan look horrified could have provided no end of amusement for Cissy. However, she couldn't push Tasha to see three men just to provide her with entertainment.

Cissy mentally shrugged, not thinking too hard about the stab of regret she felt. Maybe Tasha would make good on her guilty feelings to allow another date with the councilman's clan. In the end, it came down to one thing—it was Tasha's life and, therefore, her call.

* * * *

Two weeks later

Diltan sighed. His throbbing head sank down to where his arms folded on the surface of his desk.

As with many things men aspired to gain, Diltan's latest reward was nothing like he had hoped. The honour of reviewing the late Imperial Father Zarl's records truly was an honour. It was also sheer drudgery.

Diltan had known the review would have its share of boredom. After all, Zarl had been part of the Empire's ruling clan for over eighty years. Only the months that followed the shuttle crash that claimed Empress Irdis' life and caused Zarl horrific injuries had interrupted his reign. Even then, he had ruled from his bed with his son Clajak speaking on his behalf when needed.

Zarl had been meticulous to the nth degree when it came to keeping notes on governing Kalquor. Every piece of legislation, every memo he'd sent to assistants and councilmen and ambassadors, every query to every committee, every scrap of research—he'd accounted all of it. To call the number of records staggering would be an understatement.

At first Diltan had found the work fascinating. With such detailed records, Diltan got more than a glimpse into how the former emperor's mind worked. Zarl had been just and fair in his dealings with people in public. His kindness was legendary, almost to the point where opponents named him weak. Yet from the private communications Zarl had exchanged, Diltan detected examples of a man impatient with those who didn't see things his way, a crafty persuader who liked to tip the scales in his favour when possible. Slights might be publicly forgiven, but Zarl never forgot them. It was interesting to see how he'd often had to rein in his less-kind impulses. One refrain Diltan saw repeated over and over in Zarl's private messages was, 'It is killing me to agree with these idiots, but they are right on this occasion. I must swallow my pride and do what is best for the Empire.'

He was just a man underneath it all. Few people saw the moments of indecision, the moments of anger. What Kalquor saw was the sage judgment that happened after Zarl privately vented his frustrations to those he trusted. Once he was able to share his angst, he let honour and duty dictate his course—never personal feelings.

Diltan was awed at Zarl's iron control over his feelings.

Two weeks had passed since Diltan had been given the files to review. The Dramok had taken to skimming over the more mundane issues of Zarl's day—budget issues, food and education regulatory matters and other small items that meant nothing to the Empire's current well-being. He'd been more careful when it came to border issues with Bi'is, Empire security against the always opportunistic Tragooms and the first reports of Earther encounters.

Even though Diltan was deep into Zarl's records about early discussions with officials about Earth, his thoughts kept drifting away. Most of it was the same boring thing over and over anyway. *We must keep offering help to Earth, must keep showing them proof we may have a common ancestry, must keep asking to test for breeding compatibility.* On and on it went, Zarl's nonstop hope of coming to a peaceful accord with the other planet. Diltan had to re-read documents because he couldn't keep his mind on the repetitive memos and missives.

He even switched off his com and all other vids from his three computers, save the one showing the current document he reviewed. Diltan listened to music during his workday, especially the new rimnastin music that was coming out due to the fusion of Kalquorian and Earther cultures. He particularly liked to have it playing when those councilmen who protested the mixing of the two races dropped by to negotiate deals. It amused him to see them ask him for help while being forced to hear evidence that they could not stop integration from happening.

Unfortunately, removing all those diversions left more room for the biggest distraction of them all—Tasha Salter's call a few days ago setting up a second date. Clan Diltan was getting another chance to impress her tonight.

Diltan's excitement drew his attention from the files he should have been examining. His hopes of seeing the lovely Tasha again had been growing dimmer as the days passed with no word after their first meeting. Not that he'd expected to hear from her. She'd given no indication that she found his clan enticing. Rolat and Wal had spoken of finding her a bit boring and were more than happy to move on to other potential Mataras. Diltan had to admit he had felt the same way. Still, Tasha had been an acceptable choice of a mate. His urge to gain yet another status symbol signifying his success had wanted things to work out with the empress's cousin.

It irritated Diltan that part of him still chased a higher standing amongst his peers. He knew full well it wasn't others he wanted to prove himself to. He was still grasping for the inner knowledge that he was good enough to warrant the prizes and rank he'd risen to.

Only a fool would not make good on the chance to win Tasha's favour, though. She was all the things Diltan had hoped for in a mate. Surely he could grow to love the woman if given the chance. Her family ties were secondary.

Yet as Diltan stared unseeing at his vid screen once more, Cissy in her scandalous soaksuit kept popping up in his mind's eye. Cissy with that spark in her hazel eyes. Cissy with her crude warnings. Cissy with her handprint blazing on a mouth-wateringly round ass cheek.

Diltan realised he'd lost another five minutes contemplating the wrong woman. He squeezed his eyes shut and muttered between clenched teeth, "You rambunctious rascal. I would not clan you in a million years, not that you'd give me the option. Get out of my head."

The Dramok took a deep breath and opened his eyes to gaze at his small office bar with longing. Lounging on the comfortable seating cushions of the nearby conversation area with a drink in hand would be a wonderful escape from this review drudgery. Enough drinks and he might even be able to drown out thoughts of Cissy. The temptation beckoned.

Instead, Diltan leaned forward in his hover chair and re-read the latest document of the review. Then he perused another file. This time he managed to get through some of the work. He scanned yet another list of Zarl's concerns about proposed legislation that would ban Kalquorian men and clans from taking on AWOL Earther soldiers as live-in companions. Zarl had wanted to give all those Earther men sanctuary since homosexual relations were a death penalty felony on Earth. His wishes had prevailed, thank the ancestors. Who knew how many lives had been saved because of Zarl?

Another document came up, one that concerned a memorial for those killed in past skirmishes with Bi'is. Zarl had signed off on it, probably without a second's hesitation.

Next came notes on the assignment of a new ambassador to Joshada, made seven years ago. Diltan scowled. He thought he'd already cleared out the small stuff like this and the veterans' memorial. These nitpicky documents kept slipping through the cracks, however. *At least they're easy to get through.*

Who knew that being an emperor was so damned boring? Diltan wondered how much more awful it was for the Nobek of the Imperial Clan. If former Emperor Yuder and the present emperor Bevau were forced to deal with so many administrative bits and pieces, it was a wonder they didn't go crazy and murder the entire Royal Council.

Diltan chuckled to himself. His own Nobek often came home grouchy when he'd been stuck in the office all day, meeting with staff and regulators. Fortunately Rolat had a couple of Dramok assistants to foist the most meaningless drivel onto. Emperor Bevau's assistant was also a Dramok. That couldn't be an accident.

Meanwhile, Diltan still had his own endless documents to wade through. He checked the time and groaned. Was it still so long until the end of the day? At least he had a date to look forward to.

Maybe I'll see that scamp Cissy when we pick up Tasha tonight. Maybe for once, I'll be able to put her in her place.

The thought made Diltan smirk. He opened a letter from Zarl to an unknown recipient and began to read:

Greetings my dear young friend,

After careful consideration and conversation, I have come to agree – reluctantly – with your assessment regarding Earther women and their potential to assure the Empire's future. As you have pointed out, we are out of options, especially given the Medical Board's latest findings in regard to the Fertility Research Project. We are going extinct, but our culture does not need to. Therefore, I am giving you permission to move ahead with the assignment of locating and testing an Earther female for breeding compatibility.

Diltan could barely breathe in his shock. Here, right before his eyes, was the smoking gun that opponents of interbreeding with the Earthers had sworn was out there. Laid out as plain as day was Zarl's plan to capture and test a woman in order to save the Empire.

Clan Zarl had disavowed all knowledge of who had ordered the abductions that had ultimately resulted in war and Earth's destruction. Everyone in the Royal Council had done the same. Even those who had clanned the Earther women—most of whom had been Royal Councilmen—had insisted they did not know who was behind the orders to kidnap the alien females. All they knew was that the orders had borne official seals that could have only come from the Imperial Clan, a majority of the council voting in conjunction with territory governors or leading officials from cabinet departments.

The trail had been a byzantine tangle that sometimes led to governmental departments, sometimes led to the Royal Council and sometimes indicated the Imperial Clan. Yet everyone claimed to have had nothing to do with the official order to seduce, coerce and even kidnap Earther women once it had been established that they were breeding compatible with Kalquorian men. With no real evidence linking any specific person or persons to that mandate, there had been only accusations and rumours as to who was ultimately responsible.

By the time the Empire had got around to allowing unhappy Earther Mataras to leave the clans who had taken them in those first weeks, Clan Clajak had assumed rulership. So few women had elected to de-clan that most Kalquorians dismissed the shouts of men like Councilman Maf to launch a full-fledged investigation into the abductions. Likewise, the Galactic Council of Planets' requests for information in the wake of Earth's destruction and the deaths of billions of its inhabitants had been similarly dismissed. With most of the Earther women and their clans happy with their lives, it was hard to prove any victimisation. Most of the first Mataras insisted they'd come to Kalquor of their own volition.

Diltan wondered if that was all about to change, especially since not enough Earther women were coming to Kalquor to meet the demand of clans eager to sire children. In their frustration, some disappointed men had taken up the Basma's cry for a pure Kalquor. What was it Empress Jessica had grumbled one day in regard to those attitudes? Something like, *'They're all saying, "If I can't have a woman, then nobody gets one".'* Diltan agreed with her assessment. Jealous disappointment was winning the revolt its share of followers these days.

His heart thumping hard, Diltan resumed reading Zarl's letter.

If the woman you choose for our other friend and his clan proves to be compatible for our purposes, then you may proceed with the second part of the plan to procure all the Earther women we can. I know you have a few ideas on the best clans to achieve our ends and I trust you to be discerning with your choices. It is also my wish that you send out as many of those on the council as you find agreeable, as having Mataras of their own will mitigate any outcry of our methods within our own government. Of course I don't have to warn you of the need for absolute discretion in this matter. No doubt you already have a plan in place that will confound anyone trying to trace those of us responsible. That will be important beyond the Empire's boundaries as well. The Galactic Council of Planets will take a dim view of the Empire abducting another member planet's citizenry. Not even their need for our precious ores will circumvent an investigation of that body if any evidence is found.

Diltan's horror reached its zenith. One word loomed larger than the rest, searing in its baldness—*abducting*.

Emperor Zarl, probably with the agreement of the rest of the Imperial Clan, had ordered Earther women kidnapped—and not by mercenaries or men of questionable stature. Through some mediator, he'd ordered it of the Royal Council itself.

But who was the mediator? Who was it Zarl had entrusted to carry out such an awful plan?

No matter how Diltan searched and ran programs, he couldn't figure out who the message had gone to or who had sent out the command on the Empire's behalf. Whoever the perpetrator was, Zarl had not wanted to expose him. The former emperor was ready to take on all the blame and let this man go free.

The Earther woman who had been tested and found positive for breeding compatibility with Kalquorians had become the Matara to Councilman Rajhir. Rajhir had to be the 'other friend' Zarl alluded to in his letter. Like the other councilmen who had stolen the first Earther Mataras, had Rajhir been oblivious to who pulled the strings? To a man, they had all protested ignorance over and over.

No matter who knew what, Diltan reeled at the thought of the repercussions for the Empire. Now that there was black-and-white evidence of the Imperial Clan being behind the Earther abductions, abductions that had indirectly led to the destruction of Earth itself, there would be trouble. With a revolt brewing courtesy of the shadowy Basma, this could mean dire consequences indeed.

Chapter Eight

Cissy lay on Tasha's bed, watching her sister put on makeup. The table her sister sat at did double duty as a desk and a vanity. The top of it was so cluttered, it was a wonder Tasha could find anything.

As neat and tidy as she kept her appearance, she tended to be a slob around her living quarters. Tasha had been a whirlwind of activity earlier, trying to get her greeting room neat enough to be seen by Clan Diltan. That she'd made no attempt to do the same with her bedroom told Cissy that Tasha had no intention of inviting them in for a romp.

Maybe she'll go home with them tonight, Cissy thought as Tasha applied powder to her flawless skin. *Even if Diltan is something of a jerk and Wal never talks, it would be hard to resist an invitation to get up close and personal.*

The three men were a temptation. Even she was willing to admit that, at least to herself. Rolat with his brute masculinity. Wal with his kind face and intelligent eyes. Diltan with his sheer beauty and aura of command. She squeezed her thighs together at the thought of them naked.

With determined nonchalance, Cissy hinted, "So, you're giving that councilman and his buds another try at the Tasha sweepstakes, huh?"

Tasha shrugged. She poked through the debris on her table until she found her rouge. "They were nice enough. There was no spark, but I don't see the harm in a second date."

That seemed to sum up Tasha's courting experience thus far. She had been on several dates since the first one with Clan Diltan but had not seen any of the clans twice. She had yet to show excitement about any of them, though the men had run the gamut of ages, professions and levels of attractiveness. Cissy wondered if her sister had the slightest clue of what she wanted from a clan.

Not that she had any right to throw stones at her twin. Cissy's dates thus far had been fun, but there had been little as far as any real connections. It was her own fault. She'd been gravitating to younger clans with rowdy tastes. Cissy had sampled lemanthev and rimnastin concerts by the score, high-speed shuttle races, kurble games and fighting matches. Tasha teased her about being more like a teenage boy tearing loose with his friends than a grown woman looking to settle down.

Cissy had to admit there might be some truth to her sister's assessment. After thirty years of being prim and proper on Earth, who wouldn't revel in her newfound freedom? It was hard to contact the more settled and mature clans, to think of being a boring wife and mother. Life beckoned with too many new experiences never possible before.

Tasha roused her from her ruminations. "Shouldn't you be getting ready for your date? Fixing your hair, putting on makeup?"

Cissy shrugged. It had occurred to her to pull herself together before Clan Diltan showed up. Would they notice? Would they care? Would Diltan be approving for a change?

The fact that she had been tempted to make herself look nice for that snob had been enough to feed Cissy's stubborn resolve to do nothing of the sort. Screw Diltan and his high-ranking clan. She shouldn't care. Until she didn't, she'd pretend not to.

She stood and gathered her sister's clothes from their piles on the floor. "The concert doesn't start for another couple of hours. I've got time. For crying out loud, Tasha, the laundry intake is right here in this wall. Would it be so hard for you to put your dirty drawers in it?"

Tasha ignored Cissy's complaint against her slovenly ways. "Another concert, huh? Do you really like lemanthev music that much?"

Cissy put an armload of outfits into the chute and gathered more. She was determined to see Tasha's floor. "I love lemanthev. It's so raw and energetic. Rimnastin is better, but those bands are few and far between still. Not enough of them know how to play decent guitar. So, lemanthev it is."

"I'm surprised you still can hear after going to all those shows. Your eardrums should have bled out by now."

"It makes me feel alive. You should try a live show. I bet Dramok Diltan would be tickled to death if you suggested he take you to the concert."

Tasha chuckled. "Rolat might be into lemanthev. Maybe Wal, too. He strikes me as the type who'd try anything at least once. Somehow, I doubt Diltan would be the type to cut loose at such an event. He might do rimnastin, though. I'll have to ask."

She stood up and twirled around for Cissy's inspection. Her pink skirt was a cute, flouncy thing for a garment that ended just below the knees. Tasha's white blouse was buttoned all the way up to the collar. Her shoes were dressy but flat. "Do I look okay?"

Cissy sighed. "Impeccable. You're just right for Clan Uptight."

"Gee, thanks." Tasha stuck her tongue out. With the pink ruffles, she seemed more like a pouty pre-teen than a woman just sneaking into her thirties.

The only signal Dear Sister is sending out is one that yells 'stop,' Cissy thought. *Has she had any sex since we got here? She was humping like a rabbit the whole trip from Earth. Why this ladylike shit now?*

Before Cissy could interrogate her twin, the door announce went off, signalling Clan Diltan's arrival. Cissy's mouth went dry and her heart sped up.

Tasha checked the chronometer on the wall and smiled. "I'm ready just in time. Damn, I'm good. Be a sweet girl and say hello to my dates."

With a wink, Tasha left the sleeping room. Cissy followed her to the greeting room, making sure doors to messier areas were all closed. If Mr. Perfect Diltan saw what a slob Tasha was, he'd probably run away and not look back.

She glanced at the door that connected her quarters to her twin's. Despite the order to greet Clan Diltan, she should leave Tasha alone with her dates. Yet her feet wouldn't move in that direction. Instead, they carried her to the middle of the greeting room. Tasha smoothed her outfit over one last time before calling to her door to open. Cissy quelled the urge to fuss with her hair.

I don't care what they think of me. I don't. I don't.

The trio of Clan Diltan entered at Tasha's invitation. Right away Cissy realised Tasha had overdressed for her date.

Diltan was as classy as ever despite wearing a casual, well-fitted tunic and slacks. It was the most dressed-down Cissy had seen him and she swallowed a thick wad in her throat at how his clothes clung to a powerful body. Stupid, handsome thing.

Wal and Rolat were similarly dressed, their clothing casual but hiding none of the very nice attributes of their bodies. With his mass of curls tied back in a ponytail and his shirt untucked, Wal looked like a professor on vacation. Apparently, his face never shed that thoughtful, worried expression except when he smiled that devastating smile of his.

Rolat had on shorts, which revealed a lot of corded leg muscle. There were scars, too, thick, jagged ones on one tree-trunk thigh. Those marks upped the Nobek's savagely masculine quotient. Cissy wondered if she should find it as sexy as she did. Heaven have mercy.

The clan bowed to Tasha, though they gazed at her outfit with uncertainty. Then they noticed Cissy standing there. Three pairs of eyes widened.

Cissy couldn't imagine why the men drew up so suddenly at the sight of her. Her clothing was sedate compared to how they'd seen her last time. It was just jeans and a blouse. Okay, so the blouse was a little low-cut and she had a generous amount of cleavage showing. Still, it wasn't like her nipples were waving in the air or anything. Hadn't Clan Diltan ever seen boobs before?

After a pause, the Kalquorians bowed to her, too. That was more like it.

Diltan spoke first. "Good evening, Matara Cecilia. You seem…well." He swallowed and managed a forced smile.

"Right as rain, Dramok Diltan." Her heart thundered in her chest, as if it would jump out just to defy her nonchalance.

Of them all, Rolat seemed the most comfortable with her presence. His gaze was warm on her, making her feel good all over. "Tell me you're not staying in this evening? The weather is perfect for a beach stroll and dinner outdoors. That's what we planned for tonight." He looked over Tasha's outfit again, as if trying to hint at her to change. She only smiled in return.

"Scintillating," Cissy said, though a beach stroll in the warm spring weather did sound pretty good. "I'm hitting a lemanthev concert at one of the clubs tonight. It should be fun."

She watched for Diltan's reaction. He didn't surprise her, his tone matching his pained expression. "Those lemanthev concerts can get out of control, given the number of younglings that attend. Young Kalquorian men do not always handle their urges with great maturity."

Cissy hated the paternal tone, though Diltan had a point. There had been a couple of altercations between the dates she'd gone to concerts with and other attendees. Lemanthev tended to wind the young men up. They always wanted to show off to the few Earther girls in the crowd.

Still, who did this clown think he was telling her what she should do? Cissy planted her hands on her hips and looked Diltan in the eye. "They can't handle themselves, huh? Then I guess I'll have to handle their urges for them."

Rolat made a sound that had a suspicious resemblance to a snicker. Wal ducked his head, but not before Cissy saw the transforming smile taking over his face. Tasha rolled her eyes while Diltan glared.

Cissy switched to her Big Fake Smile that she used when her patience had run out. "Don't worry, Pops. I'll be okay."

Confusion darted over Diltan's face. He didn't know what 'pops' meant. A prime insult gone to waste.

Tasha didn't wait for him to ask for clarification. With another glare for Cissy, she flapped her hands towards the door. "Shall we go? See you later, Cissy."

She fairly shoved the men out ahead of her. They seemed reluctant to leave, but Tasha managed the job. She pulled a face at Cissy just before the door shut behind her and her dates.

Cissy shook her head. Well, what had she expected from Diltan? That he might suddenly find his inner cool? Just once she'd like him to look at her with something besides disapproval.

"Yup," she told herself as she headed for the connecting door that would take her into her own apartment. "Rolat and Wal don't seem so bad. I think I'd like them if I had the chance to get better acquainted. That Diltan, though—that Diltan sure does have one huge stick lodged way up his proper, pretty ass."

It didn't make him any less tantalising. Damn it, of all the men to be infatuated with, why him?

* * * *

"So it turns out Cissy had hidden the liquor in the shuttle. By the time the liaison figured out where we'd gone to, we'd drunk his private reserve of leshella."

Rolat and Wal roared with laughter, their humour mixing with Tasha's tinkling giggles. Even Diltan had to chuckle over the exploits of their date's sister. It was no surprise to hear how rowdy Cissy had been on the transport from Earth to Kalquor. What was surprising was how much he enjoyed hearing about it.

Diltan's mind was not on his date, however. Even her funny stories couldn't hold his attention for long. His thoughts had wandered during the dinner they'd enjoyed and he couldn't make himself appreciate the beach that they now walked upon. His mind wasn't even on how inappropriately Tasha had dressed for their outing. The long-sleeved blouse she wore had to be too warm even with the breeze blowing off the sea. She had to gather her skirt in her fists to keep it from fluttering up to her waist. Wal carried Tasha's shoes, since they were a far cry from beachwear. Diltan had told her to dress casually, yet she'd done the opposite, appearing as buttoned up as her sister was showy.

These things barely touched on Diltan's consciousness. Instead, he worried over what he'd discovered in Zarl's records.

If only he'd glossed over that letter as yet another unimportant bit of the former emperor's meticulous attention to detail! That Diltan had stumbled across such a document had his mind twisting in one direction then another.

How could he expose the evidence of Zarl's complicity in the Earther women's abductions with the powder keg of rebellion the Empire now sat upon? How could he hide such a thing when he believed in utter transparency of Kalquor's government to its people?

I'm in over my head. This task is too big for me.

The burst of laughter from his companions brought Diltan out of his confused thoughts. Damn it, this was not the time or place for him to worry over political concerns. He needed to pay better attention to Tasha. After all, this might be his last chance to attract her to his clan.

He returned to the conversation in time to hear Rolat say, "Your sister is a wild one for an Earther."

Tasha chuckled. "I suppose it sounds that way, but she's got a good head on her shoulders. It's only since we've gotten free of Earth that she's gone a little crazy. We've never known this level of liberty before."

Diltan eyed her prim outfit. Tasha could take a lesson about loosening up, he thought. She didn't need to be as crazy as Cissy, not by any means…but it would be nice if his potential mate showed a little more enjoyment of her newfound freedom.

Tasha laughed harder than ever. "You should see the soaksuit Cissy got. It's utterly scandalous!"

Wal's gaze went distant. "Oh yes." The Imdiko's tone was breathy and Diltan knew his clanmate was remembering how Cissy had looked in her scanty sunbathing wear.

That brought on a lustful turn to Diltan's thoughts as well. What the hell—it was better than dwelling on his troubles at work.

Yet he was supposed to be attending to Tasha. He plastered a smile on his face. "You've managed to hang on to your dignity despite being free to express your, ah, freedom."

Tasha shrugged. "I had my own little wild period on the transport. I figured I'd never see those people again anyway, so why not?"

"Too bad," Rolat muttered in an undertone. "I would have liked to have seen that."

Diltan kept his mouth shut while Wal bit his lips together.

Unaware of their reactions, Tasha continued, "I don't like passion to rule my actions. Bad things happen." For a moment, her face went dark. It cleared so quickly that Diltan thought he must have imagined the strange expression.

Tasha smiled, seriousness done. "Still, I like to cut loose from time to time."

"But not as much as your sister?" Diltan had more and more difficulty imagining Tasha cutting loose at all.

Tasha wrinkled her nose. "These days, she's wild enough for both of us."

Rolat sighed. "She is something."

Wal sounded even more wistful. "Yes, she is."

The expressions on his clanmates' faces told Diltan what he'd suspected since their first date with Tasha—they were far more interested in Cissy than her sister.

Mother of All, that's just what I need on top of everything else that's going on.

Yet in his present state of mind, Diltan could no longer deny that it was Cissy who filled his thoughts when he wasn't focused on work. Tasha's assertion that her twin's outrageous behaviour was a reaction to leaving a repressive society behind made sense.

Maybe Cissy will calm down a little, while maintaining some of that lively spark. Maybe she'll stop goading me every time I set eyes on her. And maybe I can stop judging her just because she's a bit rough around the edges. Rolat and Wal are right – I'm still something of a snobbish bastard.

Whether or not Diltan would ever be able to tolerate Cissy and vice versa was beside the point. It was Tasha he'd set out to woo, with the knowledge that he'd have to find common ground with her sister if things worked out. Now he knew there was no reason to worry over how to cope with Cissy. It was painfully clear to the Dramok that Tasha was not the Matara for his clan.

If only they'd been triplets, with one girl a happy medium between the other two!

This was the wrong time to contemplate any woman. All his attention was needed to figure out how to deal with Zarl's records. The worst part of it was that Diltan would have to do that on his own.

There was nothing he wanted more than to confide in his clan about the issue. Unfortunately, Wal's position as a high judge discounted any hope of that. If Imperial Fathers Yuder and Tidro had been aware of Zarl's order to abduct Earther women – if they had been part of that decision – they could be indicted. To speak of the matter with Wal would mean his judge clanmate would have to make the issue public. It would be wrong to expect the Imdiko to keep such a matter quiet. Rolat's work within the justice system made talking to his Nobek hazardous as well.

Diltan needed to speak to someone, though. He needed to confide in someone who would know what to do, someone who was all for honour and Empire. Someone with a record of putting what was best for Kalquor above everything else. Oiteil would be his first choice, but his mentor was busy assembling a task force on investigating the Bi'isil issue. Spearheading the allegations of Bi'is' involvement with the Basma and Earth's former Holy Leader was fast becoming Oiteil's obsession. He'd already expressed relief that Diltan had made overtures to Maf—

Diltan could have slammed his skull against a wall. The answer had been there all along. How could he have forgotten? He'd already made the agreement to ask for help from the very man who should have been given the assignment of reviewing Zarl's records in the first place.

Diltan thought the matter over. Maf was amongst the government leaders dedicated to tracking down those ultimately responsible for the order to abduct Earther women. He was no fan of Earthers and Kalquorians breeding together, calling for more scientific enquiry into figuring out how to make Kalquorian women fertile again. Maf was one of the few who thought they had given up on their own females too soon despite overwhelming evidence that it was a lost cause. He often spoke of the superiority of Kalquorian women. Some said he even preferred that their culture die out over continuing it with Earther blood, a position in line with the Basma's madness.

Yet Maf was also known as fair, even when it went against his preferences. After all, he'd issued a glowing, if slightly grudging report of Haven Colony that many claimed was an open invitation to mix the species. It was proof that the man could be objective when it was called for. He did not let his prejudices stand in the way of doing what was correct.

A weight lifted from Diltan's shoulders. He found himself giddy from relief. Maf would know how to handle this. Despite all his calls to have an investigation launched into who had ordered the abductions of nearly two thousand women, precipitating a war with horrific casualties, Maf would not want to expose Zarl's orders if such exposure could harm Kalquor.

Diltan smiled with feeling for the first time that evening. Even looking at proper Tasha and seeing Cissy's taunting smile instead couldn't erase the sense that tragedy had been averted. It didn't even matter that the conversation had flagged yet again into uncomfortable silence.

Everything was going to be all right.

* * * *

Rolat felt more than a little relief when their date with Tasha was over. He could stop pretending interest in stories that didn't include her twin, Cissy.

Tasha was nice. Too nice. Too sedate. Not enough spark. He could tell Wal felt the same way. Even Diltan seemed hard-pressed to exhibit any enthusiasm. More than once, Rolat had noted his Dramok's distant gaze and the line between his eyes deepening with some internal worry.

Even my prestige-loving clan leader is second-guessing this particular link to the royals. Thank the ancestors, because I can't see myself clanned to Tasha, no matter how lovely and sweet she is.

Along with his clanmates, Rolat bowed to Tasha in front of her quarters as she murmured her good nights. Then the door closed and the date was over. A few of the knots in Rolat's shoulders untied.

He opened his mouth to suggest to his clanmates they all go out for a few drinks. The Nobek had been planning on doing so for the last two hours. It might sweeten Diltan's mood a touch and Rolat would tell him they needed to give up on the lovely but boring Ms. Salter. If Wal was on board with that—and Rolat was quite sure his Imdiko was—Diltan would concede the issue.

Before the invitation for a few rounds of bohut could leave the Nobek's mouth, the thudding of uncertain footsteps came from the corridor around the corner. Someone was approaching. Judging from the lightness of the steps, it was a female. To Rolat's sensitive hearing, that someone walked as if she'd had a few drinks herself.

His chest squeezed tight when Cissy stomped into view. She caught sight of the men and stopped in the middle of the hall.

Mother of All was the most rational thing that Rolat's mind spit out. He was vaguely aware that his clanmates were staring as open-mouthed as he.

Cissy was a vision in black leather. Her halter top covered everything salacious and yet still managed to tease what with the exposed midriff and shoulders. Her skin had turned a deep gold from the sunbathing she indulged in. A few freckles had appeared on her shoulders. Rolat had the insane urge to lick those freckles.

Her skirt wasn't too tight and it wasn't too short, brushing just above her knees. Yet its cut accentuated the wondrous curves of her delectable body. She looked soft enough to wallow on all night. Rolat's cocks jerked at the idea.

The silver stiletto heels of her ankle boots were at least four inches high. Rolat had the searing image of her wearing nothing but those boots…with her feet up in the air. His cocks jerked again, with stronger demand.

The one bit of colour Cissy wore was the polish on her fingernails. The bright red tip of her index finger tapped the huge bottle of bohut she held in her hand. Rolat's brow rose to see it was half-empty. Few Earthers could handle more than a glass or two of the potent drink. Between the high heels and alcohol, it was not surprising her walking sounded off-balance.

Then she smiled her cocky smile at them. That particular expression always made Rolat want to put her naughty ass in the air for a sound spanking. His cocks did more than jerk—they filled with warmth. Damn, damn, double damn. When Cissy lurch-swaggered towards them, it was all he could do to not hurry over to meet her.

She purred throatily. "Well, well. Clan Diltan is back from romancing my sister. May I assume you got her home safe and sound?"

Diltan bowed stiffly, though Rolat could see the heat in the Dramok's eyes. "Of course, Matara Cecilia. Tasha's well-being is of the highest priority."

Rolat noted that, as always seemed to happen when Cissy was around, Wal appeared as if someone had hit him over the head with something particularly hard and heavy. Tasha never made his Imdiko look like that.

Cissy drew to within a couple of feet of them and paused. She stared at Diltan with an expression that was a mix of several emotions—irritation, bemusement and…desire?

Rolat's eyes narrowed. Diltan wore a nearly identical expression. Up until now, the pair had rubbed each other wrong every time they met. It would be humorous indeed if attraction mixed in with their otherwise combative acquaintanceship. Maybe a mutually unwanted attraction was why they couldn't get along? It was an interesting thought.

Cissy shook her head at the Dramok councilman. "Damn, man. I can't believe you'd wear such a casual outfit."

He frowned. "Why?"

"Because you are the stuffiest thing I've ever met."

Rolat bit his lips together to keep from laughing as Diltan stiffened. His Dramok managed to keep his tone polite as he answered, "Somehow, I doubt that."

"No, I'm pretty certain of it. I've met Earther priests that aren't half as uptight as you."

Diltan skewered her with a look that might have hurt her feelings had she not been tipsy. "There is a difference between being uptight and having dignity, Matara. If you weren't so determined to shock everyone around you, you might recognise that."

Rolat winced. Ouch. But Diltan did have a point.

Cissy's glare was hot enough to set a fire. She poked Diltan in the chest with one red-polished nail. "I'm not out to shock everyone. I'm having fun, long-overdue fun. What would you know about it? You weren't there on Earth, Mr. Tight-Ass."

Diltan looked at the finger poking him. "I see."

"No, you don't. You weren't a woman on Earth watching her every move in terror of doing the wrong thing. Hell, we didn't have to do the wrong thing! Every woman, no matter how careful she was or how proper she was, could be sent to prison or executed just on some man's say-so. We were as prudish as dusty old maids, but one wrong word or look could destroy our lives in an instant."

Cissy stepped back and scowled. "Here I can drink. I can wear tiny bikinis. I can swear. I can have sex. For the first time in my life, no one has the right to judge me for it. Especially not a guy who probably never feared for his life or the lives of his loved ones for one single second, at least not over stupid shit like cutting loose and having some fun."

Something in Diltan's eyes softened at her diatribe. He blinked a few times and exchanged glances with Rolat and Wal. The Nobek saw his own pain for what Cissy had been through reflected in his Dramok's and Imdiko's eyes.

In a quiet tone, Diltan said, "You're right, Matara. I have not been through what you have. I suppose if I hadn't been allowed to be young and a little crazy, I, too, would not worry so much about appearances."

Cissy stared, as if startled that he had agreed with her. After a moment, a little smile tugged at one corner of her mouth. "You are the last person who should be worrying about appearances, Dramok Diltan."

"Do you think so?"

She offered that amazing throaty laugh. "Damn right. You are an incredibly delicious man. You could probably wander around naked all day and get away with it. Why don't you give it a try?"

With an unsteady gait, she walked past the men as Diltan stared at her, open-mouthed with shock yet again. Cissy went to her quarters' door and triggered it open. Instead of disappearing into the dimly lit room beyond, she leaned against the open doorway. Her smirk was back as she looked from Wal to Rolat.

"Tell me, boys. How do you put up with your clan leader being so damned upright and uptight?"

Rolat couldn't help himself. "We get him drunk as much as possible."

Diltan turned his glare on the Nobek as Cissy shrieked with laughter. Rolat thought he'd probably pay for the remark later, but for now he didn't care. Cissy gave him her full attention. That was worth Diltan being pissed off.

When Cissy recovered, she said, "You—Nobek Rolat. I knew I'd like you. You've got a sense of humour and can obviously let loose."

Her gaze slid over to take in the still-silent Wal. The Earther's eyes narrowed. "Then there's the silent one of the bunch. You know what they say about the quiet ones, don't you, Rolat?"

Rolat couldn't help but chuckle. "They're the ones you need to watch. You'd be right about Wal, Matara. He's a despicable one, this Imdiko. An outright fiend."

Wal reddened, but he grinned from ear to ear. He knew better than to dispute Rolat's confirmation of his naughtier tendencies.

Cissy laughed again. "Despicable, you say? Then he's worth knowing." She glanced at the big bottle in her hand. Her eyes widened as if surprised to see it. Then she directed her gaze at Rolat again. "You know, boys, I do hate drinking alone. What do you say we have some fun?" She pulled a face at Diltan. "You can come, too, if you promise to loosen up a little. Show this poor, repressed Earther girl how to kick back Kalquorian-style."

Diltan stood there, nonplussed by the abrupt invitation. However, Rolat was not about to miss his chance to spend time with the too-reckless but absolutely entrancing Cissy. He slung his arm around his Dramok's neck and tugged him towards the woman. After the barest of pauses, Wal followed them.

Rolat gave Cissy a nod as he reached her door, Diltan still in tow. "Thank you, Matara Cecilia. I was just about to suggest to my clanmates we have a few drinks."

He half-dragged Diltan into the woman's quarters. The night was looking up.

Chapter Nine

The men moved aside as Cissy joined them in the apartment. She walked past them and into the small kitchen area next to her greeting room. She opened a cabinet and pulled out some glasses.

As she poured them all healthy draughts, she arched a brow at them. "By the way, I go by the nickname Cissy. Cecilia is too formal. Can you handle that, Diltan?"

Diltan had recovered his usual demeanour. In the haughty-amused tone he usually reserved for when Wal was being difficult, the Dramok said, "Are you going to antagonise me the whole night?"

"Oh, you were planning to stay the whole night? Rather lowbrow of you to make such an assumption, sir."

Diltan's mouth dropped open yet again. Rolat couldn't help but burst out laughing.

"My Dramok, you can argue a councilman or emperor into speechlessness, but look at what this woman does to you!"

Wal also chuckled. He nudged Diltan. "I think you have met your match."

Cissy brought the drinks to them on a tray. She gave Wal a smile that was warm instead of saucy. "Oh, so you can talk."

Wal took a glass, still snickering. "You are an overwhelming creature, Matara Cissy. You steal every word from my head."

She cocked her head to one side, setting down the now-empty tray on a nearby table. "Is that a good or a bad thing?"

"I haven't reached a verdict yet."

She laughed at his wry grimace. He grinned back. Rolat had the idea that once Wal relaxed, Cissy might be in for a few surprises of her own. The Imdiko was no wallflower.

Cissy sat on one of the floor cushions arranged in a semicircle. When she indicated they should as well, the men joined her in relaxing with their drinks.

She gave Diltan another one of her challenging looks. "Okay, so I'm overbearingly loud and brash and you're a stuffy snob."

Diltan scowled into his drink. "I am not stuffy."

It was time Cissy cut Rolat's Dramok a break. "Diltan is much better than he used to be. At one time, he worried too much about his rank and status. Nowadays, it's more about what is right for those around him."

"Are you telling me there's hope for him?" She sounded disbelieving.

When Diltan shook his head, Cissy unexpectedly softened. "Okay, I admit to being a jerk. Something about you gets my back up, but that's my problem. I'll call a truce if you'll stop looking down your nose at me."

Diltan reacted with surprise. "Is that what you think? That I feel I'm better than you?"

"You don't?"

"I am sorry I gave you that impression. I didn't understand how difficult things had been for you back on Earth. I heard the bluster and saw the rowdiness and never attributed the behaviour with relief at being free."

Cissy appeared moved by his attitude. She gazed at Diltan with tremulous hope, a vulnerable expression for such a rambunctious creature. "Good. I don't want us at each other's throats. After all, your clan is dating my sister. It could be we're stuck with seeing each other on a regular basis."

Rolat blew out a breath. "I wouldn't bet on that."

When Cissy and Diltan both started, the Nobek shrugged apologetically. "I mean no offence to Matara Natasha, but I don't feel a real connection to her, my Dramok. She is sweet and no doubt one of the nicest women I have ever met—"

"Damned straight," Cissy muttered.

"But there just isn't that spark I'd hoped for," Rolat finished.

Diltan protested with little strength. "We only get so many chances, my Nobek. It could be you will find that elusive quality given time." He didn't sound like he believed his own words.

Wal spoke up. "I don't know, Diltan. I like Tasha, too, but I've got my concerns as well." He offered Cissy a placatory smile. "Your sister is a wonderful girl. I would be honoured to be her Imdiko, but I don't think she feels any attachment. We're not a good fit."

Diltan's shoulders sagged. He huffed and stared into his glass again. "Fine. If we're being honest, I don't feel it, either. I want to. I've tried my damnedest to. You're right, though. It's not there." He glanced at Cissy, his expression suspicious. "So we're not going to pursue your twin any longer. Are you going to throw us out?"

She'd watched them all with surprise and what looked like chagrin. However, Cissy recovered enough to smart off to Diltan. "Are you kidding? You think I'll make you leave just when you're beginning to act human?"

No sooner had the words left her mouth when she winced. "Damn, I said I was calling a truce. Behave, Cissy." With that self-discipline, she gave Diltan a pleasant smile. "I'm glad you aren't going to string Tasha along. She hasn't found any clan yet that gets her excited, so don't feel too bad."

Diltan returned the smile. "I hope she finds good men. She more than deserves them."

Cissy nodded and raised her half-emptied glass. "To my sister, Tasha. May she find a clan that breaks her out of that prim and proper shell."

Diltan chuckled. "But not too much. I can't imagine how Kalquor would survive if there were two Mataras like you."

"Diltan, why don't you tell me how you really feel?"

That made them all laugh, Diltan and Cissy included. Rolat sensed the tension between the Dramok and the Earther dissolving. It amazed him to note how similar they seemed in their stubbornness and quick release of angst.

Wal helped himself to a second pour. "What of your prospects, Cissy? You seem to be enthusiastically pursuing your options."

She shrugged and surprised Rolat by turning pink with embarrassment. "I don't know that I'm into the game yet. I'm goofing off with guys too immature for me. I suppose I should be a good girl like your Dramok wants and take this lottery thing seriously. I know I'm acting foolish with the clothes I wear and the men I see."

"And the things you say." Diltan snickered when she blew a raspberry at him.

"Yeah, yeah. I act like a soldier on a weekend pass on Dantovon. The trouble is, we women were all straitjacketed by Earth's insane morality for so long. I've always felt like I was suffocating. When it was safe, when it was just me and Tasha and our cousins, I would unload a little craziness. I had to let off steam somehow. That usually meant saying outrageous things."

"I can imagine how hard that must have been," Rolat said. Taken in context, Cissy's antics made sense.

"Then there were all those months we had to go into hiding when Jessica became empress. Earth Gov wanted to scapegoat us for her 'sins'. Armageddon was a tragedy, but it set me free for good. I guess I'm enjoying my liberty with a vengeance."

Diltan nodded, his expression sympathetic. "So we've noticed. It is understandable now that I think about it."

"Completely," Rolat agreed. "It's a surprise you aren't going to greater extremes considering."

Cissy said, "Believe it or not, I am trying to rein some of my exuberance in. I haven't let anyone lure me into a pleasure club yet."

Before he could censor himself, Rolat blurted, "If you decide to do so, please allow me to accompany you."

Diltan choked on his bohut. Wal laughed hard enough that he nearly fell off his seating cushion.

Cissy blinked at the Nobek. "So if one sister won't do, you want to try the other?"

Rolat flushed with embarrassment. He hadn't meant to be so bald about his attraction to Cissy. It had just popped out. "It's not that, though I won't pretend I don't find you tempting. Safety is a concern. Pleasure clubs can get extreme. You should have someone who can take care of you when you walk into such a place."

"Take care of me how?"

Cissy let the innuendo creep into her tone, but Rolat didn't miss the tremor that was there, too. She was interested but a little afraid of him. Well, well. The bold girl had a trace of self-preservation after all. The idea of making her even more nervous threatened to arouse him.

Rolat was not a man who cared for games, however. Teasing over a long period of time was not his style. When he wanted to fuck, he made it loud and clear…just as he was going to do now.

He leaned closer, capturing her gaze with his. In his most no-nonsense tone, he told Cissy, "I will take care of you in every way you need—including making you come so hard you scream."

For once, it was Cissy's jaw that went slack with surprise.

Diltan guffawed. "The rebel is shocked into silence. Perhaps that reckless behaviour was an act all along."

Cissy stared at Rolat for another long beat before dragging her gaze free of his. She made a face at Diltan, but there was no rancour behind it. Her voice sounded a touch breathless as she defended herself. "He startled me. Everyone has been tiptoeing around getting intimate since I got here. Even the young men are cautious, as if afraid they'll scare me away. To hear a man just come out with it is jarring."

Rolat put a finger under her chin and made her face him once more. He sensed Cissy's reluctance to look him in the eye, but he gave her no choice in the matter.

When her gaze locked with his, the Nobek said, "I am quite blunt, little wild one. In fact, I prefer to be up front with what I want. What I want is you."

With that, he leaned in closer…close enough to kiss. He did so, pressing his lips firmly against her so-soft ones. When she melted against him, he pulled her into his lap.

By the ancestors, Cissy Salter felt like heaven in Rolat's arms. Her delicious, curvy frame fit wondrously in the circle of his embrace. She seemed to have been made for him to hold. He gathered her closer still, holding her against the wall of his chest.

Cissy moaned. It parted her lips and Rolat was quick to take advantage. He slid his tongue into her mouth, tasting this little Earther like a man dying of starvation. Her tongue was velvet against his coarser one. He sucked on it, drawing on it, devouring her.

The sensation of holding a soft, compliant woman in his arms overwhelmed Rolat. His cocks filled with heat, demanding. He broke the kiss, gasping for breath.

There was no relief in that. Now he looked into Cissy's face, seeing how her eyes had glazed over, the way her lips were reddened and puffy from his attentions and the soft glow of want in her expression. His cocks jerked. The thought of feeling her pliant around them, yielding to their hunger…

No. No, I've been without a woman for too long to let things happen that quickly. I may not get another chance with this particular beauty again. I want more than a quick fuck and release. Much, much more.

Rolat knew what act he wanted to start with.

"You've been naughty, little Cissy," he rumbled, his voice soft and purring. "Starting with the first time I saw you. Dripping wet in a soaksuit that barely covered your luscious body, flaunting yourself in front of me and mine."

Cissy licked her lips. Her eyes were still dazed, as if Rolat had cast a spell over her. "What are you going to do with me?" she asked in a whisper-thin voice.

Good. She still exhibited that potent mixture of excitement and anxiety that Rolat liked. How far would she let him take her?

He moved one hand down her spine, smoothing his palm over the black leather until he cupped her bountiful ass. He squeezed one cheek, the one that had haunted his fantasies since the moment he'd first laid eyes on Cecilia Salter.

"I'm going to finish what you started," Rolat said. "The handprint you left on this delectable flesh was not nearly enough. Your whole ass needs to be red, covered in *my* handprints. You are in dire need of correction, young lady."

Even as he spoke, Rolat worried he was taking this too far and too soon. Kalquorians as a rule enjoyed pushing limits when it came to sex. Domination, bondage and rough play were as natural to men like Rolat as the instinctual act of fucking. However, Earther limits on such were legendary. That race wasn't viewed as repressed for no reason.

Even someone as outrageous as Cissy might not appreciate all the activities Rolat delighted in. Just because an Earther opted to live on Kalquor and join a clan didn't mean that Earther was the right fit for every clan's preferences. She might be extra sensitive to pain play. She might despise being bound. Some women were as commanding in personality as the men, necessitating an agreement to switch dominance.

Besides, they had established that Cissy was going through a phase in which she was testing her limits. It could be that a spanking would be beyond hers, especially dealt by a man she knew little about.

Rolat hoped she would give his brand of sexual play a chance. That ripe, round ass did need a spanking. He was just the man to deliver it.

Cissy stared into the dark purple eyes of the man holding her. Had Rolat really said he wanted to put his handprints all over her ass? Was he talking about spanking her?

Cissy had been more than willing to experiment with the Kalquorians on the transport that had brought her to the Empire. She knew how dominating the men were and some of the wilder sexual activities they preferred. Spanking had always been high on the list.

She'd allowed half a dozen men to bend her over benches or their laps. Getting her bottom warmed had resulted in varying states of pleasure and pain, depending on her partner's expertise in the matter. Her butt had met hands and straps and overall found the experience to be agreeable.

Cissy tried to think responsibly about the immediate situation. She'd had too much to drink tonight. She wasn't outright drunk, but her head buzzed pleasantly.

Her thoughts felt muddy, too gooey to come through clear. Plus she had little personal experience with Rolat. Tasha had told her enough that Cissy was sure he was a safe person to be with, but who really knew?

Yet there was a security safeguard here in the complex. Sensors would have picked up that three men had entered Cissy's room with her. Fifteen minutes after their entrance, if they weren't gone, the computer would automatically send a message to check on Cissy. If she didn't respond to it with her code, it would signal security to come to her room and forcibly enter.

It seemed to Cissy there was more to be worried about…some important detail she was missing. With the bohut making her loose-limbed and Rolat's stare and threatened spanking warming her below the waist, she had trouble thinking. Good heavens, she could drown in the deep blue-purple of this man's eyes. And then there was that huge hand squeezing her ass. Such a big hand, a hand that would deliver the kind of spanking that would make her thrash…and wet.

"Naughty girl," his deep voice said, rumbling from his chest to shiver through her. "Are you ready to make up for your bad behaviour?"

Cissy wasn't sure what she would say. She wasn't even sure she could speak. Yet her mouth opened and formed the word, "Yes."

"Have you bothered to learn any Kalquorian yet?"

"Lina. Kenich guer." A little. Not terribly well. Her numb tongue stumbled over the guttural pronunciation.

Rolat understood it anyway. He nodded and smiled. "Do you know the word for 'stop'?"

"Sholt." It had been one of Cissy's first Kalquorian words. Her lovers always cautioned her to use it if the sex play got too rough.

A spanking often led to sex with the aliens. A spark lit in her gut, eclipsing that warning feeling that she was forgetting something important.

I'm being stupid and tipsy, but I don't care. I want this man to spank me with his big, heavy hand. I want him to make my ass hot then I want him to fuck me. I want, I want, I want.

Rolat's thrilling stare filled her vision. "I will be careful to not cause any damage. If the pain becomes too much or you are upset with the chastisement, you will say *sholt*. If you understand my instructions, say, 'Yes, Nobek'."

"Yes, Nobek." *A million times yes and a million times more.*

He picked her up off his lap. More hands grabbed her and Cissy remembered it wasn't just the two of them. For heaven's sake, how had she forgotten Diltan and Wal were there, too?

As her head swam with arousal and confusion, they turned her over so that she lay over Rolat's muscled thighs. Scarred flesh of a dangerous man. Damn if his legs weren't each nearly the circumference of her waist and she was no dainty girl. Was she really giving herself over to this beast for a spanking?

The familiar mix of concern and anticipation filled her being. The anxiety was more intense than usual. First of all, Rolat was bigger and badder than the men she'd played with on the transport that had carried Cissy from Earth to Kalquor. Second of all, he had help. There was more than one pair of hands hiking her skirt up, pulling her panties off and rubbing her bared derrière.

Cissy had never played with more than one man at a time before. Most of the men serving in the Empire's fleet were unclanned Nobeks. The majority of the Kalquorians she'd entertained were young with as little experience with females as Cissy had with males.

Diltan's clan was not made up of wet-behind-the-ears boys, nervous with immaturity. The sense of assuredness transmitted through their touches, the way they massaged her rump and thighs. That they knew what they were doing offered a strange mix of security and terror.

"By the ancestors, I've been thinking about this ass for weeks," Diltan groaned. "Serve her well, my Nobek."

"Of course. Will you keep an eye on her for me, Wal? I'm not sure such a stubborn creature knows when to say when."

One pair of hands left off its eager kneading. A moment later, warm palms cupped Cissy's face, tilting her head up. She looked into the Imdiko's face.

His pupils had nearly swallowed the purple of his irises. Wal's parted lips showed his fangs had descended from his palate, peeking out from behind his flat teeth. Yet he smiled as Cissy's gaze met his and his attractive features transformed to become almost as dazzling as Diltan's.

"Hello, my lovely. I'm going to watch to make sure you're all right while Rolat gives you discipline."

"Okay." Cissy's brain refused to come up with a better response. She stared at Wal, amazed that he could appear so forgettable in one moment, so gorgeous the next.

One of the two pairs of hands still rubbing her flesh drifted down her legs, stopping halfway down her thighs. They gripped her firmly. The other set of hands stilled. One held a fleshy buttock while the other traced its way up her spine. It stopped at the nape of her neck. Rolat's fingers curled around, holding her.

"Now, my wayward Earther. You will hold still until I've turned this delectable ass red enough to satisfy me that you've learned your lesson. Next time you feel mischievous, remember the spanking I've given you."

That he invited Cissy to misbehave again went unsaid. She sucked on her lower lip, anticipating future spankings as well as this one. Plus there was the bonus of irritating Diltan for real…

Rolat's hand lifted from her ass.

"Relax," Wal whispered. "It will be more enjoyable if you don't tense up."

Cissy drew in a deep breath. Blew it out while concentrating on making all stiffness release from her body. Her pussy was warm and wet with anticipation.

Bring it on, big guy.

The heavy palm crashed down on her right buttock. Pain flared white-hot and agonising. Cissy shrieked.

"Fuck!"

"I do hope we get to that." Rolat chuckled. "But first, this. Oh, what a lovely handprint on that sweet ass. Time for another."

Cissy moaned, unsure if she wanted another one. The first blow was fiery hell. Maybe she didn't want this after all. Maybe she should call a halt.

Her gaze was still on Wal's face. He'd glanced away to see the effects of his clanmate's discipline and his expression filled with bald want. It made her sex pulse to see such naked desire.

It distracted her enough that she didn't finish considering whether or not she wanted the spanking to continue. Rolat's hand slammed her left ass cheek this time. Cissy howled.

Tears leaked from her eyes. She jerked in an effort to get free, to escape the flaming agony of the Nobek's correction. However, he and Diltan held her down, keeping her from getting away.

Caught. Can't move. No escape…

Another slap, this time to a part of her right buttock he hadn't struck before. Cissy had plenty of backside to paddle, something that had delighted previous playmates. If Rolat was going to turn the entirety of her ass red, he still had a ways to go.

"Look at her dance." The Nobek chuckled. "I do enjoy a good lap dancer."

"You told her to keep still," Diltan said. His cultured voice was breathy.

"I did. I'm glad she's so disobedient. I like the show and it gives me an excuse to keep spanking her for not minding me."

Another slap. More flames. Cissy sobbed and writhed. No matter how she bucked, she couldn't get loose.

They had her helpless. It was that sensation of utter vulnerability that enticed her every time.

Even as pain rained down on her flesh, a part of Cissy revelled in her lack of power. Immobilised, defenceless, she had no hope of physically overcoming the men. For whatever reason, it made her insides melt. Even as she sobbed and struggled against them, her body woke as it never did for sex alone. She felt more alive, more vital right that moment as Rolat spanked her.

Through it all, she gazed through tear-blurred eyes at Wal. He watched what his Nobek did to her but only for quick moments. Most of the time his stare riveted on her face. Despite her throbbing butt and the fact that she was held down with no hope of defending herself, Cissy felt safe under the Imdiko's regard. It made no sense to feel protected when a man held her legs prisoner and another walloped her ass, but a sense of security enveloped her just the same.

Her rear was on fire. Her sex heated, excitement percolating with every strike. Moans interrupted Cissy's cries as lust went to full boil. Pain was an aphrodisiac, feeding her arousal so that it bit hungrily throughout her gut. Her struggles were no longer about escaping Rolat's discipline. She rubbed her mound against his thigh, reaching towards fulfilment.

When the Nobek stopped spanking, she shrieked with dismay. "No! Keep going!"

There was an instant of startled silence. Wal's eyes went wide and he looked up at his clanmates. Then they all burst into laughter.

Cissy couldn't see the other two men from her position, especially since Rolat still gripped her neck and Wal her face. However, she saw the Imdiko had as many tears streaming from his eyes as she did. Their hilarity made her mad.

"It's not funny, you bastards! Damn it, I was close!"

"Ma-Ma-Matara," Rolat guffawed. "Oh, you wonderful, wonderful creature!"

With the help of the others, he turned her over, careful to keep her smarting butt off his thighs. He rocked her cradled in his arms, laughing still.

Diltan collapsed back against the lounger. "Now this is a woman. Were you really near orgasm?"

Cissy didn't see what was so hilarious. "Yes, you jerks! Why did you quit?"

Rolat shook his head, disbelief mingling with the humour. "I quit because your ass is so red. I told you I would not cause damage, so I had to stop. By the ancestors, I've never been with a female who responded so well to a spanking."

With his frank expression of delight, Cissy's frustrated anger calmed. They were impressed with her. No one was making fun. They were glad she'd been aroused by the Nobek's discipline.

Her face warmed with embarrassment. She'd never become turned on enough by a spanking that she'd come close to climax. Cissy thought that maybe something was weird about that.

Diltan leaned close again, his gaze searching her face. "Now, no withdrawing, you lovely rascal. Let's see if you are in need of our continued services."

His hand slid beneath her rumpled skirt, which had moved when Rolat shifted her so that it just concealed her sex. Knowing fingers slid along her slit.

Cissy's first impulse to slap him away short-circuited as desire leapt, full and demanding. Instead, she moaned with longing, her legs falling apart to give Diltan better access.

"Soaking wet," he murmured. "She did enjoy herself."

With no warning, Diltan pressed two fingers inside Cissy. His thumb brushed her clit. Her body resounded, like a gong that had been struck. She arched with a cry as he filled her. At the same time, she slammed her splayed hands against his chest, trying to fend him off. It was too much sensation, bringing her right up to the edge of destruction.

"Hold her," the Dramok commanded.

Wal's arms circled Cissy from behind, pinning her to his chest. Rolat grabbed her wrists and held them, stopping her desperate shoves against Diltan.

The clan's leader pushed Cissy's skirt up, exposing her mound. "There you are," he breathed, his mouth curling in a happy smile. "What a lovely pussy, Matara. And a greedy one, too. I do believe she's trying to yank my fingers off my hand."

"Careful, my Dramok," Rolat said.

Diltan arched a brow at the gasping Cissy. "Now, my rebellious beauty, if you take my fingers away, I won't be able to do this to you."

The two digits buried inside her curled. Diltan pulled them outward, dragging his fingertips hard along the front of her sheath. The friction was an electrical jolt to Cissy's system. Her hair stood on end as a shockwave rumbled through her body.

She uttered a strangled cry, her insides heaving with near-cataclysm. Just like that, Diltan had her on the verge of orgasm again.

Wal's voice teased her ear. "She's a wild one, all right."

"Indeed," Diltan agreed. "I think there is only one way to tame a woman like this. Positive reinforcement."

With that, he pumped her pussy with those wicked fingers. His thumb stroked her clit.

With the second thrust, Cissy detonated. Her head jerked back against Wal's shoulder as a mighty force broke loose inside her guts. She screamed as that force heaved. It felt as if a physical entity fought to escape her body.

"Good girl. Do you have another for me?"

The brute teasing the monster inside her continued to fuck her, his fingers pounding hard against her, just the way she liked to be taken. The ravening desire drew in on itself for a moment before tearing through her once more. Cissy bucked against the men holding her, wild with release. They held her immobile, forcing her to accept climax so intense that it was almost painful.

When at last the storm subsided, the first thing Cissy noted was her sobbing breath. She hauled in air like she'd just run a marathon. What the hell, she felt that worn out.

"Easy, little rebel. Drink this."

A cup pressed to Cissy's lips. She gulped cold water until the glass was empty.

The cup was taken away and she met Diltan's gaze right in front of her. On either side, Rolat and Wal also stared. Their expressions were identical—awed and amused.

"That was something else," Rolat said.

Before Cissy could decide whether to be humiliated or proud, an insistent beeping sounded in the room. It was followed by an electronic voice that stated, "Matara Cecilia Salter, it has been noted you are not alone in your quarters. Please submit the code for your safety status."

She started to speak but issued only a weak croak. She cleared her throat and tried again.

"Code H-L-I-A-A-L-L-W-R-T-F."

"Received and acknowledged. You confirm you are safe with your companions. Would you like another check-in in fifteen minutes?"

Cissy eyed the three men watching her. Was she safe? Not from gut-wrenching orgasms, but who wanted to be guarded against that?

"Negative on the check-in. Clear current guests for duration of visit."

"Acknowledged. Please remember to input new security code at your earliest convenience."

It clicked off. Rolat cocked his head to one side inquisitively.

"I know your code was made up of Earther letters, yet I could discern no pattern. Are you a cipher expert?"

Cissy snickered. "No. Those were the first letters for the statements 'Holy Leader Is an Asshole. Long Live Women's Right to Fuck'."

Rolat threw his head back and laughed, as did Wal.

Diltan shook his head. "Am I to assume that we may continue enjoying ourselves…and you?"

The dangerous light in his eyes made things inside Cissy's belly tremble. Dear heavens, they'd brought her screaming just with a heavy hand and busy fingers. What would full-on sex be like with these three?

There was only one way to find out. She pointed a shaking finger towards the bedroom door.

"That way."

Chapter Ten

Diltan wasn't sure he'd ever been so hard in his entire life. So far, Cissy was more amazing than he'd dared to fantasise. Her brash persona translated to an exuberant libido that had his knees knocking together. Damn, she excited him.

However, there was more to be thrilled with than her willingness to be spanked and have sex. He'd detected an almost hidden desire to submit behind all her outspokenness. Was there something softer beneath the rowdy strength she seemed determined to show the world? A secret urge to be overcome and dominated?

Surely he couldn't be so lucky. Yet the possibility was too much to not explore.

Letting the steel that made up the greater part of his personality move forward, Diltan spoke with the command he'd been born to wield. "Maybe we'll take this to your sleeping room later. For now, I will have you here in the manner I wish."

Cissy's hazel eyes went wide. For an instant, she melted back against Wal, her face softening. Then the brassy light filled her gaze once more. She gave Diltan a mocking smile. "Is that how you think it's going to go?"

The Dramok fought off an ear-to-ear smirk. She did want to surrender. He'd seen it for that fraction of a second before her strength of will took control.

I'll have to earn her submission. Maybe this woman isn't so far off the mark for me after all.

Instead of letting his face light up with anticipation, he gave Cissy a no-nonsense look. "That is exactly how it's going to go. Please remove her clothing while I search for something to bind her wrists with."

Not waiting to see if he would be obeyed, Diltan rose from the lounger. He went into Cissy's room, ignoring her startled yelps and squeals as his clanmates got to work.

He noted with appreciation how tidy Cissy kept her sleeping room. Diltan preferred organisation. Moreover, he hoped it meant he'd not have trouble locating what he wanted. Opening Cissy's closet confirmed his hopes—the more outrageous clothing items were kept separate from what the Earther chose to lounge around in when she wanted to be comfortable. He found a robe with a silky sash. Perfect.

Diltan stalked back into the greeting room to find Rolat and Wal had discerned exactly the position he wanted this naughty Matara in. She sat naked between Rolat's muscled thighs. The Nobek held the backs of her knees level with her shoulders. The position tilted her pelvis up and splayed her legs wide open. Wal stood behind the pair at the back of the lounger, Cissy's wrists gathered in his hands. Her arms were back behind Rolat's head, pointing her bared breasts upwards.

Diltan tossed the robe tie to Wal. Quick as a flash, the Imdiko snatched it out of the air while keeping hold of Cissy's wrists with one hand. He set about tying the Earther's wrists together.

For her part, Cissy's expression wavered between want, anxiety and anger. She glared at Diltan.

"You've got these two trained to a tee, don't you?" she spluttered. "You say 'jump' and they don't even bother to ask how high."

Diltan dropped a quick wink to his snickering clanmates before answering, "I'm the Dramok. I lead this clan. I'm used to being obeyed."

Wal turned his face away for an instant. Again, Diltan was hard-pressed to keep from smiling along with his clanmate. His Imdiko was often the worst behaved of the group. It would have been more accurate for Diltan to say he was used to fighting to be obeyed. He'd had to earn surrender from his clanmates more times than he could count.

That was fine. Diltan preferred not to have things handed to him. It was more fun to wrest control than to be granted it.

He eyed his latest obstacle, looking forward to winning dominance over this particular opponent. At that moment, Diltan decided Cissy would beg him to take care of her needs. No, she would scream for his dominion.

He might even grant it.

His gaze settled on her upturned breasts. Lovely, heavy teardrops of flesh, golden and lush, they begged for attention. Diltan got down on one knee before Cissy and Rolat. He cupped the globes in each of his hands, filling his palms with warm flesh.

Cissy gasped at the bold touch. By the ancestors, had none of the men she'd been with handled her body with confidence before? Everything they'd done to her so far had been greeted with reactions that hinted she found them audacious. Coming from her, it was funny. Then again, maybe her daring nature had intimidated others into being far too careful.

Let's see how you like being on the other side of that, Diltan thought.

He slapped the undersides of Cissy's breasts in turn, bouncing them lightly and making them jiggle.

She cried out. "What the hell do you think you're doing? Stop slapping my tits!" she yelled.

"*Your* tits?" Diltan snorted. "I think not. Tonight, these belong to my clan. Every inch of you does. Your body is ours to do with as we desire. If you behave and do as you're told, we might even allow you another climax. If you don't, we'll go home. It's as simple as that."

Cissy glared in disbelief. Her arms strained against the sash secured around her wrists and Wal's hold, which pinned her arms to the back of the lounger. She kicked, but Rolat held her legs too far apart to allow her to escape or land a blow to Diltan. She yelled as she struggled.

The juices creeping from her open pussy and the rush of soft female scent told Diltan Cissy enjoyed her helplessness. Nevertheless, he reminded her, "Saying 'stop' in Earther means nothing tonight. Only *sholt* tells me you've had enough."

"You big jerk!" she yelled. "Who are you to tell me I belong to you? Where do you get off, pal?"

"Keep mouthing off and I'll gag you," Diltan warned. "Now, where was I before you so rudely interrupted me? Oh yes, these luscious bits."

He leaned in and captured one peachy-pink nipple in his mouth. Moaning with pleasure, Diltan sucked on the delectable flesh, rubbing his tongue over the tip to make it hard.

Cissy's struggles immediately ceased. She panted as the Dramok mouthed one peaked nipple then the other.

Her flesh is so sweet. I'd swear she could melt on my tongue.

It took real effort to release the delicious orb. Diltan managed to do so but only because he knew he could reclaim it at any time.

He went back to bouncing Cissy's breasts in his palms, striking the undersides enough to deliver stinging punishment. She yipped, her hazel eyes going wide again. Between the tiny cries of pain, she gasped harder than ever. Diltan's quick glance at her pussy confirmed she continued to cream. Either pain or being controlled or both were her weaknesses. He would capitalise on that knowledge.

"Magnificent breasts, aren't they?" he asked his clanmates.

"I can't wait to maul them myself," Rolat agreed. Quiet as ever, Wal simply grinned around his fangs.

"Why—why are you smacking them?" Cissy panted. She looked as if she were trying to be angry. If that was the case, she failed miserably. Her expression tended more towards softness. Her eyes had glazed over.

"Because I can," Diltan replied. To underscore that assertion, he gave the side of the left breast a loud slap, cupping his palm to deliver more sound than pain…but further pain than his earlier swats had offered.

Cissy's reaction was instantaneous. She moaned, her gaze growing hazier. She arched away from Rolat at her back, as if to beg for more of Diltan's harsh attention.

"Just as I thought," Diltan whispered, more to himself than anyone else. "A little pain and much restraint in intimate affairs to balance out the fierce independence on your public face."

"Perfection," Wal murmured.

Diltan glanced up at his Imdiko to indicate his agreement before focusing on Cissy once more. "All right, young woman. Now that I know where your head is, let's see how well I can capitalise on it."

Awareness had begun to seep into her expression, realisation of the situation she had put herself in. Diltan had the idea Cissy wasn't used to being where her instincts preferred her to be…under a man. He suspected that the crew aboard the transport that had brought her to Kalquor had been too grateful to fuck a woman to push for real dominance.

They did themselves and her a disservice, Diltan thought. *It's time to correct that.*

Before Cissy could come all the way back to herself and perhaps speak the one word he had promised would end their tryst, Diltan gave those delicious breasts an authoritative smack apiece. As Cissy jerked and yelped, he darted forward to seize one pretty pink nipple in his mouth. As he sucked it in deep, he carefully pressed his teeth against her flesh.

At the same time, he rubbed his fingers over her slit. He found her wetter than ever. Cissy cried out into his mouth, her ass thumping against the lounger. Held by

Rolat and Wal, and bracketed between the Nobek's thighs, it was as much motion as she could manage. She was well and truly at Diltan's mercy.

I have you, my reckless rebel. Now that I do, let's see just how submissive you are.

Cissy's body was a maelstrom of sensation. Diltan's mouth and hands delivered equal measures of torment and delight. Zings of pain from his careful biting mixed in a hectic, mind-stealing brew with the pleasure of his mouth sucking her breast. He rubbed the outsides of her nether lips, creating amazing friction on the sensitive flesh. A calloused thumb brushed her clit, sending jolts through the erect nubbin.

All that excitement was made more poignant by the fact that she could not deny the Dramok's attentions. Bound, brought under the Kalquorians' control, Cissy had no defence against the luscious assault. It made her head swim. She couldn't think coherently, not with such exacting delights pouring through her body.

No one had made her feel so vulnerable…so intensely excited. The realisation was a dim whisper in the back of her mind, barely noticed in the cacophony of sensual chaos.

A weight settled on the top of her head, pulling it back to lean against Rolat's shoulder. Cissy looked into the deep blue-purple of Imdiko Wal's eyes. His gaze was sharp, unsettling against his tranquil face. He smiled, transforming those unremarkable features into something breath-taking yet again.

"Lost in the thrill of my Dramok's touch, are you? I know the feeling well. I'd like to make you drown in those sensations."

With that, his face drifted close. Wal filled Cissy's gaze, that handsome visage blurring as his breath wafted over her lips. His mouth settled against hers. Instinct parted her lips. Coarse velvet warmth invaded. The Imdiko tasted her, his tongue sliding sweet and sure against Cissy's. She moaned a welcome.

A rough voice murmured in her ear. "You are so lovely, giving yourself this way. Not that you have a choice, though, right?" The chuckle vibrated in her ear and rippled down her spine. "No, we claim this wondrous body. You will give us all we desire."

Rolat's confident words etched themselves on Cissy's mind. Hearing him assert entitlement to her left her weak and shaking in their grip.

Wal drew back at the same time Diltan released her breast. She opened her eyes. The three men watched her, looking at her face.

Through the fog of arousal, Cissy realised how exposed she was to them. She was naked. Wal had placed her bound wrists behind Rolat's neck. The Nobek held her legs wide, displaying her sex for them all to see. Even her clit was blatant, having come out red and swollen from behind its hood at Diltan's prodding.

Being bared to them made Cissy's will dissolve even further. Captive to their desires, vulnerable to their whims… Her snared limbs trembled with weakness.

"So, the woman with the spirit of a wild zibger becomes a trembling girl when faced with real men," Diltan breathed. "I am surprised. And gratified. How lovely that I can be strong for you instead of forcing you to allow me to be so."

His words were so much noise to Cissy. All she understood was that she was helpless against these men, that she found the vulnerability exciting and that they were drawing out the anticipation of what they would do to her next.

"Deny us nothing, precious," the Dramok said. "Bend yourself to us for this night. It will be the best decision you've ever made."

Two of his fingers, which had teased her pussy lips and clit all this time, dived inside Cissy. Diltan shoved them all the way into her core. Brutal need rose hard and fierce. She shouted and jerked at the sudden impaling.

"Hungry little pussy," the Kalquorian crooned, shoving in and out with amazing friction. "Pretty pussy wants to come again."

His thumb drew circles around Cissy's clit. She sobbed and shoved towards his hand. Ravening need eclipsed the little bit of awareness she'd held. There was only the stunning man before her and his touch.

Her skin flushed with heat. Bright excitement filled her gut. Climax was on its way. He would give it to her now that she was his to control. He would make her come whether she wanted it or not. She wanted it, though. She wanted it with all her being.

Diltan's fingers escaped her eager flesh, leaving her empty. Her wail of loss was interrupted as the Kalquorian gave her ass cheek, still smarting from Rolat's spanking, a couple of light slaps. The blows were gentle, but she was sensitive from the earlier punishment. Pain lanced through her hindquarters, making Cissy yell.

Diltan's fingers pushed inside her again. His thumb went back to work on her clit. The shard of agony from his strikes washed into something much more exciting as arousal consumed her once more.

"That's it," he encouraged as she voiced throaty groans. "I like that you enjoy both pain and pleasure and being made to take both. Good girl."

Cissy's insides clenched, readying once again for orgasm. She made moaning pleas to Diltan to let it happen this time. She'd forgotten how to form words, so her begging was made up of nonsense sounds. He understood her anyway.

"So soon? I'm not sure I should let you. I'm not a sadist, but I like how you suffer for me right now. Allowing me this power is too sweet a gift to squander."

Fingers gone again. More pats on the ass. However, the feeling was of intensity this time rather than pain. Cissy whooped in air. Her body still inched towards climax, though slowly.

Diltan's rolling voice wove through the roaring in her ears. "Oh, is that how it is? You're more fun to play with by the moment, Matara. Wal, I believe you have a free hand?"

"Thank you, my Dramok."

Diltan lightly paddled the sides of Cissy's buttocks, where Rolat had done the least spanking. Wal reached down to pinch her breasts. He alternated that with spanking them from side to side. Searing heat came from their touches. It streaked fiery trails to her pussy. Cissy shrieked as pressure built. She needed to come.

"That's it, Cissy. Nowhere to go. Nowhere to hide. All you can do is sit there and take the torment." Diltan's smile filled her gaze. "You have to come for us. You have to surrender everything. The only way out is through."

He and Wal took her higher. Cissy's cries rebounded through the room as they swatted flesh. Just as exciting was how Rolat held her helpless for their attentions.

It started with a tiny spark, a concentrated mote of white heat in the depths of her sex. The combustion swept out from that point, devouring everything in its path in a great wave of rapture. Cissy disintegrated in an instant. Engulfed, lost, consumed. She could not survive such force and did not care.

The climax wrecked her. It shredded her from the inside out, leaving nothing intact. She didn't know how long it lasted or if it would ever end. It was as if she'd fallen into a shaking abyss with no bottom.

At long last, a voice called her back to life. "Drink, Matara. This will help you get your strength back."

Something pressed to her lips—the rim of a bottle. Thick, fruity liquid dribbled into her mouth. Cissy thought of berry smoothies and swallowed. It was one of her protein drinks that she liked to have for breakfast.

"Good girl. Keep drinking."

Cissy obeyed. More voices joined the first person's, an unimportant chorus as energy crept back into her body.

"Have you ever known any woman to respond so eagerly?"

"Never. Not that I've ever had an Earther before. Certainly none of the other races have had such a positive reaction to pain and bondage play."

"Not even our own, at least not the two I've had."

"What happened to this species being repressed?"

"I think we've already established Cissy is bolder than most of her kind."

Laughter. The bright, happy sound of it made Cissy want to see their faces. It was only then that she realised her eyes were closed.

She blinked them open. She lay on her back, her head and shoulders slightly elevated with the three men of Clan Diltan looking down on her.

"She's returned to us. Hello, young lady." Rolat's rolling thunder of a voice tickled deep in her ears.

She swallowed the last of the drink. Wal removed the bottle from her lips.

They were still in the greeting room. Rolat remained on the lounger and Cissy lay naked across his thighs, her head and shoulders cradled in the crook of his beefy arm. Wal sat next to the Nobek. Cissy's calves rested on the Imdiko's legs.

Diltan knelt at Rolat's feet. He smoothed Cissy's hair back from her face. "Are you with us once more, Matara?"

She swallowed, trying to get her thoughts in line. Her brain felt fogged, with clarity glimpsed here and there. With difficulty, she made her lips form words. "That wasn't half bad."

The three men roared with laughter. Cissy managed a weak grin.

A sharp scent similar to cinnamon filled her nose. She tried to think what food she had in her apartment that would give off such a tasty aroma. It took a few seconds for Cissy to remember that Kalquorian men put off an arousal scent. Their cocks lubricated and that clear, slick substance smelled and tasted like cinnamon.

Cissy groaned. She'd come hard and felt as weak as a newborn kitten. Yet the men had not yet received their pleasure. Judging from the smell and the hard heat poking at her thigh from Rolat's lap, they were eager for sex.

"Stim tab," she croaked. The small dissolving tablets were better than coffee for energy boosts. She would need them if she was to make sure Clan Diltan didn't end up screwing an unconscious Cissy.

Wal produced the clear tab. "I thought you might want one. I hope you don't mind that I looked through your kitchen cabinets for it."

"If I can't trust a judge, then who?" she managed, opening her mouth for the proffered stimulant. Her wrists were still bound and rested at her waist.

It took only a few seconds for it to hit her bloodstream. The clouds lifted from her brain at last. All traces of the alcoholic buzz went with them, too.

"For heaven's sake," Cissy groused, angry with herself. "I'm not usually this easy, okay? Don't get that impression. I always make my dates say good night at the complex's entrance."

"Would you prefer we leave you?" Diltan's tone was light, but there was a forced quality to it. He didn't want to go.

For some reason, that pleased Cissy.

"When I've just gotten my second wind?" Cissy gave him her naughtiest grin. "Or have I intimidated you, Dramok? Can't handle the Earther girl?"

The sudden darkness in his eyes made it hard for her to not squirm. "I think we've handled you quite well thus far. Would you like another demonstration?"

He didn't wait for her answer. Diltan grabbed her wrists and pinned her arms over her head with one hand. The other grasped her thigh. He hugged her leg to his torso.

Still holding Cissy cradled in one arm, Rolat snagged her other leg. Once more Cissy splayed open. Her breath caught.

Want surged anew in her belly as she saw intent in the three men's purple eyes. "Oh hell. Not again. What are you maniacs doing to me?"

"What you like best, apparently." Diltan snickered. "What is it that makes you more excited, Cecilia? The pain or bondage?"

Somehow, the Dramok using her proper name made Cissy want to placate him even more. The authority in his voice made it clear she must bend to his control.

"I don't know," she whispered, strength running out of her yet again. "I-I think being helpless. I've had to protect Tasha since we were little. I've had to be strong. Not being able to be in control I-I don't know why it does this to me."

Wal smiled. "It must be a relief to let go of responsibility. To have your needs taken care of instead of expending all that effort to see to the requirements of others."

Diltan nodded at his Imdiko. "I've had those moments myself, as you well know."

"Indeed. Few can shoulder such weight all the time."

"Perhaps you'd like to be the first of us to demonstrate how well we take care of those in need?"

Wal gave Diltan a delighted look. "Thank you, my Dramok. I am always happy to be of service."

He moved so that he knelt at Rolat's side, between Cissy's splayed legs. She whimpered as he looked her over. That sweet, gentle face held something darker now.

His palms covered her breasts. Wal rubbed the mounds, testing their malleability. He plucked at her nipples, bringing zings of delight stabbing through her. His hands flattened out and swept down her ribcage. Without pause, he kept going, stroking over her wide-open pussy. Cissy's body lit once more. She jerked helplessly. She moaned a complaint when the Imdiko's hands left her.

"I'm going to fuck you." Wal sounded almost as commanding as Diltan in that moment. Cissy wasn't sure if it was his bald statement or the tone that made her insides bubble.

He swept his shirt off. Cissy drank in the sight of muscled male. Wal was beautifully formed. He wasn't simply a fit specimen. His body was long and elegant as well as chiselled. Her mouth watered at the sight of him.

A grin pulled at one side of his mouth as humility battled his enjoyment of Cissy's overt ogling. "Do you like what you see?" Wal asked.

"A blind woman would like what I see," Cissy choked.

"Thank you. There is more, you know. Quite a bit more."

His teasing made her snicker. The quiet one, indeed.

Wal stood up and tugged his shorts down, pulling them over the jutting lengths of excitement at his groin. They slithered off his hips and slid past his thighs. He kicked off his shoes and the shorts and looked at Cissy to gauge her reaction.

"Oh wow," was the smartest thing she could say. Even if Wal without a smile appeared ordinary, his body was anything but.

Cissy had seen plenty of Kalquorian dual appendages during her trip from Earth. She'd seen all widths and lengths. Yet Wal still managed to delight her.

His two cocks were identical, save for the shorter length of the rear one. Smooth and tapered like bullets, they stood out straight from his gorgeous body. Slightly darker than the rest of his brown skin, they showed a delicate tracing of veins on their glistening surfaces. With his cocks lubricating, they gleamed in the room's soft light.

Despite the graceful shapes of his penises, Wal was thick. Cissy knew from experience she enjoyed a thick man, even over length. Greater girth made things rub just right on the inside.

"I'm glad I do not disappoint," the Imdiko murmured. He knelt between her legs once more. "Relax. You need preparation to take me."

He bent over and sucked Cissy's clit into his mouth. She yelled and yelled again when he pressed two fingers deep in her pussy. She hadn't been prepared for the suddenness of the pleasuring. Her body jerked. It was then that she was reminded that Rolat and Diltan held her prisoner.

"Oh," Cissy groaned. That wonderful vulnerability that made her weak swept over her again. She trembled in the Dramok's and Nobek's arms as Wal pumped his fingers in and out and rolled his tongue over her clit.

He released her for a moment, flipping his curly black ponytail over one muscular shoulder. "So wet," the Imdiko said, sounding as if he praised her. "I can't wait to shove my cock in here."

Wal's blunt words about what he planned to do with her made Cissy's insides jolt. These powerful men had her number, all right. She had the nasty suspicion that if they wanted her to beg them for sex, she'd do it in an instant.

The Imdiko bent to her clit once more. Instead of him fingering her pussy this time, he went for her anus. Cissy had tensed with the delicious sensation of that talented mouth on her and it took a moment for her to force relaxation onto the tight ring of muscles guarding her nether entrance. She did so just in time for the first thick digit to slip within.

She'd grown used to anal penetration. Yet she'd not had sex since landing on Kalquor almost three weeks ago. The intrusion might have been uncomfortable had Wal not distracted her with stroking her sensitive nub with his raspy tongue. With heat exploding in her clit, she barely noticed him stretching her, even when he added the second finger.

Over her head, Diltan spoke to Rolat. "I love watching someone take a good fucking."

The Nobek's voice had an animal growl quality. "Especially someone as lovely as this girl."

Cissy could barely attend their words. Her brain uncoupled again. Wal's mouth and fingers were the most important ingredient in this lustful brew, but being held down before an audience turned the blend intoxicating. Her chest heaved as she gulped air. It went still when Wal straightened, taking mouth and hands off her. He grasped his ready lengths with one hand. He used the other to brace himself against Rolat's massive shoulder.

"You will take my cocks now," the Imdiko told Cissy. "It's time for tonight's first fuck."

She panted again as Wal positioned himself at her entrances.

"Nowhere to go," Rolat reminded her. "No escape."

Wal gave a quick, short thrust. The first couple of inches of his primary cock slid easily into Cissy's pussy.

Her ass took the first inch of his smaller a bit more grudgingly. A sudden, marvellous ache drove all the air from her lungs.

"That's right," the Imdiko said, going still once more. "I'm inside you, just a little bit. There is a lot more to go, little Earther. You will take every last inch of me."

Cissy uttered a garbled cry. It was meant to be agreement, but words failed her yet again. The Kalquorians kept robbing her of the ability to speak.

Wal shoved again. As he went, his cocks widened, giving Cissy that wonderful girth she enjoyed so much. Her pussy gloried in the friction that found her interior sensitivity. Her ass complained against the invader.

Somehow, it was the throb in her rear that excited Cissy most. It brought home her lack of power against these men. It thrilled her beyond comprehension.

Wal again stopped before she could experience real pain. A small part of her mind recognised that despite the forceful attitude, the Imdiko gave her body time to adjust to him. He was careful not to cause injury, though he easily could have done with her as he wished.

The realisation gave Cissy permission to move even further into the intoxicating desire that enthralled her. She was helpless but safe. They could hurt her, but they wouldn't.

Diltan enhanced the fantasy by bending to seize a breast in his mouth. He tugged at Cissy's nipple with his teeth, delivering exquisite shards of pain without causing real harm.

With vision made hazy, Cissy gazed up at Rolat. The Nobek watched as Wal pressed hard into flesh both welcoming and reluctant. Rolat's eyes were dark, the cat pupils spreading wide. His lips parted in a soundless snarl. Fangs peeked out. His erections jabbed Cissy's hip. When Wal finished with her, when he'd sated his lust with her body, Rolat and Diltan would take their turns. They would have her and there was nothing she could do to stop them.

Wal thrust in ever deeper, making her yield to him. Discomfort was pleasure and pleasure was ecstasy. Every nip from Diltan's teeth, every push Wal made into her ass and pussy, made her more pliant to the men.

She didn't know how long the glorious torment lasted before Wal's groin met hers, the Imdiko fully embedded within her. He paused. His hand trailed over the softness of her belly, caressing with gentle ownership. His fingertips sent heat deep into her gut.

"Now I fuck you until I fill you with cum," the Imdiko said.

That was all the warning Cissy got before Wal's hips swung back, pulling him nearly free of her. The sweet chafe of his flesh dragging against her interior walls made her hair stand on end. She arched against Rolat's thighs, orgasm already threatening.

The Imdiko shoved back in. Cissy legs kicked as violent pleasure crashed within. She howled as Wal took her hard and fast. It was her favourite way to get fucked—powerfully, with no quarter given.

The Kalquorian rode her rough, his body slapping against hers. Cissy's head tossed back and forth. She couldn't deny the whirlwind of sensation galloping through her. When she came, it was as if her body would turn itself inside out. Passion twisted her guts, wringing her out.

She heard a man's throaty yell while she tossed in the maelstrom of climax. Something slammed deep within her core, sending daggers of mingled pain and pleasure throughout. Cissy screamed with renewed elation.

The walloping pleasure gentled, slowed and stilled. She blinked up at the faces hanging over hers. Wal gasped and shuddered, as if he'd just run a race.

This time they gave Cissy water as she recovered. As she drank it, they stroked her lax body. Their bold touches kept her arousal simmering. The eagerness surprised even her.

"Just call me Ms. Libido," she said, shaking her head.

"Excellent," Diltan said. "I have always wondered how difficult it is for the women, both Earther and Kalquorian, to keep up with three men."

"I guess it's easy with the first flush of novelty," Cissy guessed. "Plus, you three seem to know what you're doing. How did you become such masters of sex?"

That made them laugh. "We've had experience with someone not always thrilled with our intentions," Rolat snickered. He winked at Wal.

The Imdiko sighed. "Foolish youth. When my clanship with these two was arranged, I was…shall we say reluctant?"

"More like dead set against it," Diltan snorted. "Wal hated us. Me, especially."

"Oh, so I'm not the first to resist your charms," Cissy teased. She gazed at Wal. "So what did he do to piss you off?"

"It was more a case of who he wasn't," the Imdiko answered. He shrugged. "As I said, I was a foolish youngling."

"As we've all been at some point." Diltan stroked Wal's cheek affectionately, earning a smile from the Imdiko. Whatever issues had existed between them were long gone in a distant past.

"I'm no youngling," Rolat said, "but my libido is pretending I am. Are you sure you're all right to continue, my lovely?" He smiled at Cissy, as easy-going as if his cocks weren't trying to poke a hole in her hip.

"Perhaps another stim tab is due before my Nobek has his way with you?" Diltan suggested.

Cissy looked the big warrior up and down. He still wore a pullover shirt and shorts, but there was no doubt he was a big, strong man. His desires felt pretty strong, too. "No, but keep them close at hand. I have a feeling this bruiser is going to wear me out."

"You'd be surprised at just how gentle I can be," Rolat said. "Now don't look disappointed, lovely Cecilia. I've seen how much you like it hard and fast, but allow me to show you how uncompromising demand can be expressed in another fashion."

Wal chortled as he chugged a protein drink. "Oh, I bet I know what's coming."

Rolat didn't respond. His smile was evil enough to make Cissy's stomach flip-flop. Diltan laughed and stepped away from the lounger.

Cissy tried to figure out a way to ask the Nobek what he had in mind without sounding like a wimp. Before she could order her thoughts, Rolat stood, hefting her in his arms as he did so.

"I think we need your bed, pretty girl. This lounger isn't quite right for how I want to fuck you."

"Um, okay. It's a small apartment, so I guess I don't need to show you the way."

Rolat swept through Cissy's quarters, carrying her into the bedroom within mere seconds. He tossed her onto her bed. She bounced a little when she landed, startled by his strength. She weighed a good deal more than a small child.

"Lie right there where I put you," the Nobek ordered her, peeling his shirt off. "You do not move unless you want that pretty ass to be sorer than it already is."

Cissy swallowed hard. Standing shirtless over her, Rolat looked a hell of a lot bigger than Wal. Even in the dimmer light of her room, she could see the sculpted musculature that made up his arms and torso. Scars confirmed he was a dangerous person to the wrong people. They tracked over his chest and stomach, lines of varying widths and lengths. He was a brute. He had to be to have survived those injuries, some layered over others. The violence they spoke of added to Rolat's aura of strength. It made Cissy wonder what he'd done to those who had dealt them.

The man was all power. Just looking at him left her trembling. She stayed splayed out on the bed as she'd landed, feeling frightened and aroused under the big man's stare.

Her peripheral vision caught Diltan and Wal coming into the room to watch. However, her gaze didn't move from Rolat.

The Nobek slid his shorts off. In Cissy's nervous state, his cocks looked more like battering rams than sexual organs. Veins knotted the surface of the tapered lengths. Rolat grinned at her.

"That's right. I'm going to fuck you with these and there's not a damned thing you can do about it."

With that, he crawled onto the bed, right over Cissy's prone body. She mewled her want and anxiety. Instinct made her try to slide away.

"Oh no," the Nobek whispered. "Absolutely not."

He grabbed her still-tied wrists and stretched them over her head with one hand. Rolat's weight settled on her, pinning her down. He was careful not to crush her, but she couldn't move out from under him. His cocks, pulsing as if they possessed minds of their own, sat hot on her thigh.

"Trapped, little Cecilia," Rolat told her. He smiled when she whimpered. "Be my good girl and submit. Or fight, if you think you can. Either way, I am going to fuck you."

His granite thighs squirmed between hers, spreading her open. Cissy couldn't help but resist. The Nobek was so damned big and intimidating! She panted as panic tried to assert itself.

His hand reached down to position himself for the first thrust. The wet tip of his primary cock burrowed into her pussy, followed by the pressure of his smaller cock at her ass. Cissy kicked, but Rolat's wide legs kept her from landing a blow.

"I feel the heat and wet pouring out of you," he whispered. The low tone was more frightening for the quiet. His eyes stared into hers, pinning Cissy's head to the mat as surely as his body held her down. "You struggle, but there is nothing but want in your gaze. I will give you all you desire and much, much more."

He pushed in. Rolat did not take her quickly or slowly. His was a steady, uncompromising pace. It was neither rough nor gentle. It was matter-of-fact demand, pure and simple. The Nobek moved inside Cissy as if he had every right to do so and expected her compliance.

The attitude of entitlement rocked Cissy's senses even more than being held down. Her body no longer felt like her possession. It belonged to Rolat. He owned her in that moment.

She might have felt like just a warm body for him to fuck and that was an exciting fantasy as well, but it was not the case. Not with the Nobek's eyes staring into hers. Rolat studied her face, as if to memorise every line, every pore, every twitch. Cissy could almost see him cataloguing everything for later analysis. He wanted to know her, not just fuck.

That didn't mean he wasn't doing a good job of the sex. He forged in, pressing deep to possess her. Pleasure swirled as her body yielded to him. The weight of the Nobek pinning her to the bed reminded Cissy that she had no choice but to surrender. No choice but to accept the long, thick intruders deep inside, to let him take all he wanted until he achieved his pleasure. She moaned, her struggles quieting.

"That's it," Rolat murmured.

He gave her all he had, his primary cock bumping something in Cissy's pussy that sent shivery shards of exultation through her core. Sheathed deep within, Rolat continued to stare into her eyes. Cissy was aware of the heavy body on hers. The Kalquorian's large torso covered her. The lower part of his chest mashed her malleable breasts nearly flat. The movement of his diaphragm as he breathed pushed rhythmically against her belly. His hips pressed hers into the soft sleep mat. She couldn't move.

Trapped beneath the delicious prison of the Nobek's body, Cissy's nerve endings exploded as he rubbed his groin in circles against hers. The motion ground her clit against the hard muscle of his flesh. Her body tried to involuntarily bow against him, but there was no room to move. Her heels thudded against the bed as fireworks erupted in her belly.

Rolat arched his back, sliding his cocks out without lifting his weight. He shoved back in, hitting her cervix once more. His hips circled again, making Cissy take insane friction. She squirmed, the pleasure overwhelming her senses. She couldn't budge.

"You see?" Rolat purred in her ear, the rumbling voice vibrating her very being. "A nice, steady fuck without the pounding force you prefer. Yet here you are, moaning and crying out, writhing beneath me because the ecstasy is so great. Are you learning your lesson, girl? Shall I continue with your instruction?"

He didn't wait for an answer. His cocks slipped out once more, their thickness rubbing everything inside hard to curl her toes. Even if she had found her voice, Cissy wasn't sure she could have provided one. The ecstasy was exquisite in its torment. She didn't know that she could stand carrying on with it.

It wasn't as if she had a choice. Rolat showed her how relentless he was in making her suffer gloriously. His thrusts were steady and strong without being violent. He continued to massage her clit with his groin with every in stroke. All the while, he kept her restrained beneath him while his gaze bored into hers, leaving her vulnerable in every way possible.

Her moans grew into sobs. Cissy's body went into full riot. It fought the continuous rapture that tortured rather than delighted. Rolat's pace made every sense excruciatingly alive, yet release kept its distance. Cissy couldn't climax. She couldn't move in order to bring on orgasm. All she could do was lie confined while the Nobek fucked her.

"Please," she choked. She was desperate for him to relieve the pressure that made her guts ache.

"No," Rolat answered. His tempo never varied.

Damn it, didn't he need climax as badly as she? Cissy tried again.

"Please."

"No."

Tears spilled from her eyes. This was torment. Beautiful torment, yes, but still an agony that Cissy thought might drive her insane. She wanted to come.

"Please? It's too much, Rolat. It's too intense."

"Then suffer for me." His slight smile held no mercy.

For the first time, Cissy struggled for real. She tried to yank her arms free of his grip. His only reaction was to arch a brow at her. He kept fucking as if nothing were happening.

She tried to buck him off. Despite her greatest efforts, she didn't budge the Nobek one bit. Cissy tried squirming, hoping to slither out from under him. She remained trapped, not making any headway at all. Rolat's expression didn't waver this time, but she got the sense of him being amused.

And still his cocks moved in and out. His groin continued to abrade her clit.

Cissy wailed. She shook her head from side to side. She begged him in a piteous voice, "Please, please, please," until the words vanished into sobs.

"No." He kept fucking her.

At last, Cissy surrendered to the knowledge that the Nobek might never stop. He could hold her prisoner on her own bed all night, making her body accept his at that never varying pace. She had no power to work her will. No chance of coercing him to give her completion.

Nothing she could do or say would make the agony end.

That moment of helplessness was what something in her psyche had been waiting for. Knowing she was Rolat's with no hope of realising selfish desires caused a surge of pure carnal elation.

The climax was on Cissy before she knew what was happening. All at once her pussy seized, a spike of searing bliss driving deep within. She shot high up on its peak, hurtling towards a blazing light as bright as a sun.

The man on top of her shuddered. A thunderous groan reverberated in her ears. The flesh within hers jerked. She crested again, a fresh spasm barrelling through her at the knowledge of her captor's release.

They lay still for several minutes after that, catching their breath. Rolat boosted himself up and smiled down at her.

"Now you have a small idea of what a good mind fuck feels like coupled with a physical fuck. I do hope we can soon explore more of how that pretty head of yours works."

"You—you…what the hell?" Cissy managed, looking at the Nobek with mingled awe and fear. Had he known all along that she would get off on accepting her helplessness against him? How?

He laughed and got up. Wal came forward to revive her with water and another stim tab.

"Rolat is a little too smart for comfort when it comes to playing with people's heads. I've never met anyone so intuitive when it comes to figuring out weaknesses."

"If he wasn't a Nobek, he'd have been a wonderful psychologist," Diltan said. He still leaned up against the wall.

Cissy paused in slurping water. "Nobeks can't be therapists?" she asked.

Rolat stretched his wondrous body, looking as content as a cat with cream. "We don't have enough patience, as a rule. If I had to listen to some man cry about his life, I'd end up shaking or punching him for behaving like a child. It wouldn't matter how reasonable his trauma was, either. If it's not the pain of a clanmate or close family member, I'll lose my tolerance for such."

"But not women?"

The Nobek considered a moment and then shook his head. "A woman experiencing hurt would be even worse. My overriding instinct is to make the person or people responsible for her suffering pay. I don't think that would go far in solving her issues."

Humour stretched across Wal's face. "Nobeks are heavy-handed when it comes to remedying emotional storms." He glanced at Rolat, as if to communicate something private.

The other man laughed. "You'd know better than many, my Imdiko."

Diltan stepped forward. Judging from the heated look he gave Cissy, he had little interest in the conversation.

"Are you recovered from playing with my exacting clanmate?" he asked her.

Cissy handed her empty water pouch to Wal. The Imdiko got up and left her alone on the bed.

She told Diltan, "I don't know that I'll ever recover fully from that, but I'm as good as I'm going to get. Bring your irritating but gorgeous ass on over."

Diltan grinned. The man was too devastatingly handsome when he did that. It was wrong for any man to look that good. Cissy wished she could continue to despise him for it, but she'd called a truce. Plus she didn't have it in her heart—or other significant body parts—to resume their disputes.

He came closer, stopping just out of reach. His hand went to the collar of his loose-fitting shirt, and he pulled.

The resealable seam down the front purred open. Diltan shrugged the shirt off, letting it first expose his chest and abdomen. Cissy's mouth went dry.

It's so unfair. Even Jessica's Nobek Bevau is barely better made than this obnoxious fiend. Why does Diltan have to be so damned perfect?

Cissy's gaze roamed over the planes of the Dramok's chest, over the sculpted beauty of his abdomen. As he peeled his shirt off his arms, she had to contend with the beauty of those limbs, too. He was an alien god, some holy being made to sit upon a golden throne amid golden-tinged clouds. It was downright ridiculous how good he looked.

Bastard, her head muttered. She didn't want to desire him so much. However, her body was very glad to see what it was about to enjoy.

Unable to keep looking for fear of her tongue falling out of her mouth and giving Diltan the pleasure of knowing his full effect on her, Cissy dragged her gaze to Wal. The Imdiko sat cross-legged on the floor nearby.

"You tried to reject him for another Dramok, huh?" she asked.

Wal laughed. "Young and stupid, remember?"

Diltan's voice cut through the air. "I want your attention on me now, Cecilia."

Cissy's head snapped around at the commanding voice before she could think. Her mouth dropped open.

The Dramok had taken his shorts off in the brief moment she'd given her focus to Wal. The flawless structure of his upper body continued all the way down. The lines of his legs were clearly defined, muscular and graceful all at once. Even the man's cocks appeared like works of art to Cissy. The tapered lengths were without fault, smooth and glistening and ready for her.

Diltan strode to the bed with purpose. He held out his hand. "Give me your wrists."

Cissy didn't know whether to be disgusted or amused at how she responded instantly yet again. Her arms shot out to obey Diltan, letting him cradle them in that hand. How did he command her obedience so easily?

As he untied her wrists, the Dramok smiled down at her. "Holding you down has been fun. However, I want to test your ability to let yourself go just because I wish it of you. I want you to put your entire self, mind and body, under my authority."

Cissy arched a brow at him. "What, you demand and I obey?"

"Exactly."

She scowled and rubbed her freed wrists. "You don't ask for much, do you?"

"Only everything." Diltan smirked. "Nothing excites me more than having someone surrender to me sexually. Not because they have to but because I want them to. If you can't handle it, say so. I'll get dressed and say good night."

The obstinate part of Cissy wanted to do just that—tell Diltan to put his clothes on and get out. That easy way he had of assuming dominance nipped hard at her pride. Yet stinging her pride just as much was the phrase *if you can't handle it*.

The arrogant son of a bitch is playing me. Who am I kidding, though? I'll regret not fucking that amazing body. I think he knows it, too.

Then she thought, *Maybe I can get some of it back by playing his game. Dramok Diltan must have never heard the phrase 'Be careful what you wish for'.*

Cissy had to fight to keep the smirk off her face. She didn't want Diltan to have any idea what he was in store for if she got the chance.

"All right, Dramok," she purred. "Order away."

For an instant, Diltan's eyes narrowed. The man might have had the ability to push Cissy's buttons like no other she'd ever met, but he was no fool. Cissy gave him what he expected—a challenging look that said *do your worst*.

He stepped away from the bed. "On your knees before me."

Cissy did as she was told with no hesitation. She was eager for what she hoped Diltan would tell her to do next. It would put her in more control than him and he would be the one left shaking and weak.

She knelt before him, gazing up with what she hoped was an expression of surrender. What happened next shocked her to her core.

Diltan stood over her, tall and beautiful and strong. The resolve in his face was softened by a hint of gratitude. He might have been used to being in command of his clan, but Cissy had the impression it was something the Dramok did not take for granted. He was in control because Rolat and Wal—and, for the moment, Cissy herself—allowed it.

Only a truly strong man would merit something of that nature from people like his clanmates, Cissy realised. *A man they trust not to abuse such power. I see it as a game, but Diltan has earned his place with them.*

Does he want to earn that same respect from me?

All at once it was no longer about winning against Diltan and getting laid in the meantime. Cissy had the urge to give him pleasure, to make him feel good. Not because he would accept it as his due but because he would appreciate it. Her surrender would mean something profound to him.

Perhaps the realisation showed in her eyes. At any rate, the usual haughty expression Diltan wore around Cissy was nowhere in evidence as he gave her a warm smile. "All right, my lovely. I hope your tongue is not as sharp as the words you sometimes use. I wish to feel it as well as your lips on me."

Looking up at that beautiful face hovering over her, Cissy could only manage, "Yes."

"You may take me in your mouth then."

Cissy started to reach for him, but that gentle consideration in his eyes made her pause. Uncertainly, she asked, "May I also use my hands, Dramok Diltan?"

Diltan's eyes widened just a little before he nodded. "Yes, you may."

Knowing she had just surprised him, maybe as much as he'd surprised her, gave Cissy reassurance. *We're both on shaky footing right now,* she thought. *We're learning things that neither of us expected of each other.*

Cissy gripped a cock in each hand. As she closed her mouth over the tip of the smaller one, she rubbed the thick, rigid sexes from their bases, all the way up on the primary and to her lips on the other. Diltan sighed with pleasure.

Cissy stroked up and down while continuing to kiss and mouth the bottom-most cock. She took her time. Damn if she didn't want to serve this man to the best of her abilities, prolonging his pleasure. Somehow the idea of putting his needs ahead of her own excited Cissy. Her pussy, already well served by the other two men, oozed honey to streak down her inner thighs.

Diltan's cocks had lubricated with the sharp, spicy fluid that exuded from his pores. It sizzled on her tongue before resolving into sweetness. She twirled her tongue all over the flesh, seeking more.

She sucked so hard that her cheeks dimpled.

Diltan groaned. "Very nice," he mumbled. "Very, very nice."

Cissy peered up at him. He watched her with heavily-lidded eyes, his lips wet and parted. His hands were on his hips, very much the master over her, granted by divine right to have his cocks sucked by his slave.

A ticklish heat spiked high in Cissy's belly. *I put that expression there,* she thought. *I make him feel good. I'm on my knees, I'm serving him, but he can't feel powerful without me.*

The thought and the resulting pleasure it gave her made her work even harder to excite Diltan. Cissy poured all her effort into his gratification. She wanted to be the reason he was fulfilled as a man. She didn't quite understand why she had the need to do so, except that it also fulfilled her.

He can't be strong without me. He finds his power in me.

It was an amazing realisation.

Cissy took Diltan's secondary cock as deep as she could, to the verge of gagging. Both cocks jerked at her action and Diltan gasped. Thrilled at her success, Cissy bobbed her head back and forth, drawing in more and more each time. She'd succeeded in taking most of the smaller when Diltan put a hand on her head.

In a thick voice unlike his usual smooth tones, he said, "Now the other one, my lovely girl. Suck the bigger cock. That's my good girl."

Cissy drew back. She was gratified to see the iridescent drop of pleasure waiting for her on the end of the larger one. Without one bit of sarcasm, she said, "Thank you, Dramok," before accepting the offering with a careful flick of her tongue.

Diltan's moan was music to her ears, almost as wondrous as the sweet-spicy-salty flavour that filled her mouth. He was happy with her service.

Cissy tongued the length of his main cock, drawing his precious juices into her mouth and down her throat with passion. Diltan's hand, still on top of her head, closed in a fist. The pull on her hair was slight but exciting. She had put him in control and he accepted that responsibility.

Cissy again worked to claim as much of his flesh as she could. She only got half his cock in her mouth before she felt as if she might choke.

I must take more. I must show him how I am his, all of me. I must prove myself worthy of him.

Part of her knew it was supposed to be a fantasy, nothing more than a part in a play. Yet the need felt real to Cissy. She was driven to pleasure him.

She set to work. She fought to relax her throat, to accept more and more of the Dramok's length, to delight him as he'd never been delighted before. As Cissy crept steadily up towards the wide base of that choking cock, Diltan's strained whispers encouraged her.

"Yes, my beauty. Do it. Swallow me. Oh, it feels so good. That warm, soft tongue on me. Sweet, wet mouth surrounding me. Those lips tight around my cock. Carefully, now. Yes. Yes. Yes, Cecilia. Yes."

At last she had almost all of him. Apparently it was all Diltan could take, because he shifted his hips, sliding his cock out of her mouth. Cissy whimpered at the loss, though she'd no longer been able to draw breath.

"That's enough, Cecilia," Diltan said with a firm tone. "You will hold still for me while I fuck your mouth."

The fist in her hair tightened and Cissy quieted her soft protests. It was not her place to argue but to obey. Obedience made her master happiest of all.

Diltan's hips swung back and forth, pumping his cock between her lips. He didn't go as deep as she'd fought to take him moments ago, leaving her plenty of room to breathe. Cissy concentrated on rubbing her tongue hard on the underside of the flesh that drove against it.

"That's right," Diltan plunged in and out. "My mouth to fuck. My pussy to fuck. My ass to fuck. My Cecilia. Mine in every way I wish to have you."

His, his, his. Diltan felt it with every mote of his being as he watched his throbbing cock move back and forth in Cissy's accepting mouth. By the ancestors, he couldn't stop claiming her in his head.

He'd expected her to fight him tooth and nail for control. They'd been at cross purposes since the moment they'd met. Yet she knelt before him in an attitude of perfect surrender. She'd fought to take him fully in that gorgeous mouth he plumbed now. She was giving him the most precious thing he could ever ask for—herself.

That Cissy had chosen to do so made Diltan's knees wobble. She knelt as if it were her duty to let him fuck her warm, welcoming mouth. By the ancestors, did she have any idea how gorgeous she was like that?

Yet there was still that indomitable spirit in her eyes, that spark that said Cissy was yet very much her own woman. She had not lost her will at all—rather she had turned it so that it matched his as well. She met Diltan's needs because they suited hers.

I see you, you little rascal. I see you in there and I know you could turn on me if I show one moment's weakness. Only a strong, sure man can hold one such as you, even for just one night. Am I up to that task?

He was determined to find out.

Diltan enjoyed using Cissy's mouth for a few more strokes before taking a step back. She made a mewling sound of want as he slid from between her lips. Hearing her desire made his hips jerk involuntarily. Molten heat slid up his secondary cock, eager to spill into the larger one. Diltan drew a deep breath and forced himself to calm down.

I will claim every bit of her that I can. We will both be satisfied before this encounter ends.

After that little cry of hunger, Cissy went quiet again. She remained on her knees, looking up at him with yearning. Diltan's pricks jerked.

He swallowed hard before ordering, "On the bed. Spread your legs for me and hold them open. Offer me your pussy."

Cissy scrambled with a haste that gratified Diltan. Could she be that eager for him? Or was it all an act? Damn, he hoped it was real. If he found out she was playing him—

Yet she lay on the bed, grabbing hold of her knees and parting them wide to offer him access. She looked like an offering of sexual sacrifice and something deep in the Dramok's loins wrenched. He had the fleeting urge to take her hard—violently even.

Cissy made his head spin. Ancestors help Diltan if she had even a glimpse of how crazy with lust she drove him.

He went to her, walking in slow, measured paces. She watched him, her hazel eyes wide, her moist lips parted as she drew quick breaths. The want in her expression was naked. Diltan bit back a groan. To see such lust, shown without inhibition, made his cocks swell tighter.

To think this woman who has driven me crazy with irritation could be the only thing that I want in this whole universe right now…

Diltan stood over Cissy, trying with all his might to order his thoughts. He couldn't, not with his cocks demanding her warmth, not with his whole being centred on making him part of her.

The Dramok gripped his members, leaning in towards her heat. She was wet, her soft, pink sex glistening an invitation. Her rear entry was still open from its liaisons with his clanmates, enticing him to fill it once more. Diltan voiced a groan and leaned over her. He forged deep into Cissy.

She cried out a glad welcome, her body straining to meet his even as she kept her hands on her knees, maintaining the position he'd demanded. Heat pulsed in his dicks, molten goodness that nearly made him cross-eyed.

Just as wondrous was the firm warmth holding him. Diltan was enclosed in soft, tight flesh, trembling flesh that not only yielded but flexed, drawing him deeper still. Cissy's body welcomed him with an embrace that felt like coming home.

Diltan's instinct was to move hard and fast, to meld with that wondrous part by emptying into it. Yet looking into the face beneath his, at the rapturous expression gazing into his, brought him up short. It gave him the same feeling he got when making love to Wal or Rolat—the fervent need to serve the one serving him. An irrefutable responsibility to give every bit as good as he got.

With that, Diltan slid slow and sure out of Cissy until only the tips of his cocks remained within her sweet body. Then he shoved in again to make her gasp and arch. Her mouth opened wide for her high-pitched cry, and her passages tightened hard around him. Diltan hissed between his teeth as lust surged in his groin.

That was it. That was just what she liked.

Diltan kept the rhythm of slowly withdrawing and slamming back in. Cissy rewarded him each time with a little scream. She managed to hold on to the backs of knees, but her feet kicked in the air. Her head tossed back and forth, as if to deny the pleasure she received.

The Dramok would not let her do so. Propped on one hand over her, his hips continuing to whipsaw back and forth with determination, he reached between them to gently grip the lovely's clit between thumb and finger. Cissy squalled as he rubbed the slick nubbin with delicate friction.

"Pretty little rascal," Diltan breathed. "You will come for me. You will come for me now."

He slammed into her, pinched down. Cissy at last lost her hold on her legs, grabbing hold of Diltan's arms as her body bowed back. She shrieked as her pussy spasmed hard around the Dramok's length. Diltan was forced to still, brought to the brink of release by her explosion.

Seconds later, the Earther fell limp to the sleeping mat's surface, her breath sobbing as the last of her convulsions ebbed. Diltan felt the familiar and still-wonderful surge of power from bringing a lover to complete release. It was like a drug, one he could never get enough of.

"You are so beautiful when you climax," he purred to the shaking woman. "You will do it for me again."

Cissy blinked, coming to her senses as Diltan did the slow withdrawal from her as he had before. "I don't think I can—"

"Oh, you most certainly will." He thrust back in, seizing her clit once more and rubbing.

It took two more strokes, but Diltan had his way. Cissy's screams of completion were beautiful to hear.

He could have listened to her cries all night, but Diltan knew from the pounding in his groin that he'd reached his limit. He wasn't going to last much longer.

The Dramok freed his livid cocks from the sweetly clinging sleeves of his still-moaning lover. He picked up her shuddering form and turned her over onto her stomach. He scrubbed at his smaller cock with the antiseptic wipe Wal handed to him with a grin. It took no time for it to grow slick with lubrication once more. Damn, he needed to come soon.

Grasping Cissy's hips in both hands, framing that luscious ass, Diltan lifted her bottom to his groin. Whether from weakness or relief that he granted her a reprieve, Cissy went lax in his grip.

Not for long, my irreverent beauty, he vowed as his primary cock entered her ass.

Cissy thought, *Stick a fork in me. I'm done.*

Diltan had made her come so hard that her insides felt like a washcloth after a bath—wrung out. It was a relief to have him coming at her from behind. Let him have his fun and get his cookie. He more than deserved it after the amazing and heart-stopping climaxes he'd treated her to.

It had almost been too much. Cissy's throat was raw after the yelling she'd done. The Dramok had overwhelmed her with his knowledgeable fucking and fingering. The man definitely had a leg up on the younger men Cissy had a habit of enjoying.

She did her best to ignore the agreeable ache of having his thicker girth pierce her ass and the gorgeous friction of his smaller cock rubbing the front of her womanhood. Yeah, it felt good. With time, it would make her come again. She didn't want to, though. Those last two orgasms had nearly blown her head off her shoulders. She'd had enough.

From the sound of Diltan's panting, he'd get his pretty soon. Cissy was exhausted, but she made herself move beneath him, greeting his thrusts with her own, giving him the pleasure he'd earned. Damn the man. Gorgeous, charming when he wasn't being an ass and talented in the sack to boot. Had anyone ever made her scream like that before? No. Not ever.

"Too quiet, my pretty rebel," Diltan grunted. "I like it better when you make some noise."

His hand shifted, sliding from her hip to her mound to seek. Cissy gasped and grabbed his wrist. He was not stroking her clit again. She was not going to have another of those excruciating orgasms.

She never felt him move. All at once, Cissy found her wrists pinned at the small of her back by one strong hand…and the other was again groping for her nubbin.

"Wait! Wait!" she cried, trying to get away from him. His cocks kept her skewered in place, like a bug on two pins. Diltan's finger and thumb snared its prize.

"Come for me, my rascal," he said, fucking and rubbing her straight to the verge of climax.

"Please! Please! *Please*!" Cissy shrieked as rapture flared bright. Then the tidal wave was on her, eclipsing all but wild sensation.

She screamed long and hard into the linens that covered her bed. She screamed and screamed and still orgasm tore through her, taking her beyond reason. It was as if Diltan reached inside her to rip it out of her loins.

Then it was over, followed by shuddering aftershocks. Diltan's groaning sounded far away. His weight shifted and he fell over onto the mat, landing on his side and carrying Cissy with him. They lay gasping and shaking all over.

Two more large, warm bodies crept onto the bed with them. Cissy found herself nuzzling into Wal's wide chest. She had the impression that Rolat lay behind him. A hand that could only be the Nobek's stroked her hair from her sweaty brow.

She wasn't sure how much time passed before Diltan spoke. "If we may not spend the night with you, Matara, can I at least have enough time to discover where my legs have gone to?"

That was greeted by laughter from the other two men. Cissy managed to smile at the sally.

"Shut up and go to sleep, Dramok. I'll kick your sadistic ass out in the morning."

Maybe. Or maybe she'd let them talk her into letting them stick around for breakfast. Or longer. At this moment, it was hard to think about getting rid of Diltan and his amazing clan.

Chapter Eleven

When Cissy woke, it was with the sense of being warm and safe. She revelled in it, feeling the strength of a male body against hers, her face snuggled in a smooth, muscular chest. Lovely.

For a minute or two, she thought she was back on the Kalquorian transport that had taken her off Earth. Then she remembered she'd made it to Kalquor and the Matara Complex. She was a woman sought after, a woman enjoying all the thrills and pleasures denied before.

Legs tangled in hers. Then she realised there was not just a man in front of her but behind her as well. Oh hell. Where had she ended up last night? She'd gone overboard with the bohut, that was for sure.

Cissy's thoughts were sluggish. What had happened the night before? Dancing at the concert. Drinking. Who were the boys she'd played with? She couldn't recall the faces of her dates last night. Well, this was going to be awkward as hell. After the past few weeks, all the young men looked alike.

Cissy was readying excuses as to why she had to jump up and leave right away when her brain decided it would join her body in wakefulness. She remembered now, all right. But not the men she'd met up with the night before. She'd ended up with entirely different fellows…men with faces she'd not likely ever forget if she lived to be two hundred. She'd sucked down the bohut just to keep them out of her head…and in her drunken state, she'd let them in other places.

I am never going to drink that much again. Oh fuck, I'm in some serious shit now.

She was afraid to open her eyes. She did so anyway. An expanse of brown skin greeted her gaze and she slowly tilted her head back to look into Imdiko Wal's attractive face.

He smiled and became stunning. "I thought you might be waking when the rhythm of your breathing changed. Good morning, Matara."

Before she could respond, a big body reared up behind Wal. Rolat grinned down at her. That meant that behind her, spooned up nice and tight, his hard cocks nestled in the crack of her ass, could only be—

She turned her head, feeling like the heroine in a horror film. There lay the devastatingly handsome monster himself, lit in golden light from the vid playing a morning sunrise. Dramok Diltan. He too was awake and looking at her.

Cissy realised something else she'd forgotten the night before, something eclipsed by booze and lust. Something that made her nauseated and ready to cry all at once.

"Oh, blessed Buddha. What the hell did I do?"

Rolat's voice rumbled like thunder. "Enjoyed yourself, I hope."

Cissy blinked at him, feeling as if the tidal wave of guilt would crush her before she could drown. Flailing, trying to get out from between Diltan and Wal, she snapped, "You've all got to get up. You need to leave right now."

Diltan had his superior, you-exasperating-female expression again. "By the ancestors, now what is your problem?"

Cissy could have slugged him. "What do you think? I fucked you! You're dating my sister!"

Wal cocked his head, confused. "I thought we'd established that we would not continue to pursue that avenue. Besides, we were not exclusive to Tasha at this early juncture. In turn, she was not expected to be faithful to us. That is the nature of the lottery."

Were they dense? Did they think any of that mattered? Cissy spluttered, "Tasha doesn't know that you're giving up your interest in her. She doesn't know! And I'm her sister!"

Rolat seemed as perplexed as the other two. "The lottery contract states that all parties may pursue multiple interests at once. We're allowed to demonstrate our attraction to all of our options, which includes you."

Wal added, "You said Tasha wasn't that interested in us, either, which was already obvious."

Cissy managed to untangle herself from bodies and linens. She lunged off the sleeping mat to stand at its foot. She glared at the three men. "Tasha wasn't interested, but what if she changed her mind? No matter what the lottery contract states, I've got no excuse for this behaviour, not when it comes to my own flesh and blood. Shit. This is screwed up. Please leave."

Diltan slid off the bed and stood. "We need to talk this over. Perhaps we should include Tasha in the conversation if you believe there is a problem."

Cissy tried not to notice how stupendously stunning the man looked. How amazing they all were, truth be told. She was pissed off with herself more than any of them, but Diltan always made an easy target. She wanted to lash out at him, throw some of the blame his way.

Stop it. They're right about the lottery rules. He and the other two haven't done anything wrong. It's me. I fucked up and I only have myself to blame.

One thing was for certain—she didn't want to discuss anything with Diltan, no matter how innocent he was in the matter. What she needed was the time and space to figure out how to admit to her sister what she had done.

"I'm waiting, Cecilia." Diltan crossed his arms over his chest.

His domineering attitude made her fired-up temper flare hotter. She went on the attack.

"Okay, Diltan, let's talk. Why don't you start with why my cousin Lindsey doesn't like you? I'm interested in why she hinted we should avoid getting involved with you."

Cissy didn't know what she'd expected the Dramok's reaction to be. She hadn't expected to see him go deathly pale. The man's jaw snapped shut so hard she thought he might break his teeth.

His clanmates watched him with confusion. Rolat asked, "What's this about, Diltan?"

In a tone tight with fury, Diltan snarled, "It's something we don't need to discuss in front of her." His glare was enough to make Cissy cringe "At least Matara Lindsey can be counted on for discretion. You might learn a thing or two about that."

He turned on his heel and stormed into the bath facility. Cissy heard the water run and loud splashing.

Recovering from her surprise at his reaction, she called out, "Are you saying I have no discretion?"

The water switched off. Diltan came back into the sleeping room. Without pausing, he grabbed up his pile of clothes from the floor and kept going towards the door that led to the greeting room. As he went, he said, "It is not your strong suit, from what I've seen."

Unmindful of her nudity, Cissy hurried out after him. Diltan stood in the middle of the room, yanking his clothes on. He seemed intent on pretending she wasn't there.

Hurt by the rejection, Cissy yelled, "You don't know anything about me, you pompous, self-important jerk!"

He stepped into his shoes, finishing his quick dressing. He brought his eyes up to stare at her. "I know this."

With that, he made two quick strides to stand in front of her. Before she could react, Diltan grabbed the back of her neck and pulled her close. His mouth fell on hers.

Cissy instinctively parted her lips. Diltan's tongue forged in, taking. At the same time, the hand not holding her in place slid over her pussy, stroking and fondling. Cissy's senses lit, arousal filling her gut and making her clutch the man with need. Honey slid from her to cover Diltan's talented fingers. She moaned, grinding hard against his touch.

The Dramok released her and stepped away. Cissy reached for him before she remembered she was mad at him. That she'd already screwed up once with men that courted her sister. Her fingers trembled as she forced her hands down to her sides.

She didn't miss how one corner of Diltan's mouth twisted up in a moment's victory before he called to his clanmates still in the bedroom.

"I'll be waiting for you two at the complex's main entrance."

With that, Diltan turned his back on Cissy and left her quarters. She stood there, confused, angry and crazy-aroused.

Behind her, she heard the disappointment in Wal's voice as he told Rolat, "Damn. This is not how I anticipated starting the day."

* * * *

Diltan's head ached. His thoughts churned in chaos. It was damned hard to smile as if nothing was wrong as he passed aides, sycophants and fellow council members. It felt like it took forever to navigate the corridor that led from his chambers to Councilman Maf's.

First and foremost were his concerns over Cissy. He could have handled that situation better than he had, but her bringing up Matara Lindsey had thrown him off. That was a can of worms he wanted nothing to do with opening. The thought of his behaviour with the empress' sister two years ago was enough to make his face burn in humiliation.

Dumbest thing I've ever done and I've done some stupid things in my life. Damn it! At least the Imperial Sister held to her promise to not tell anyone about it.

Diltan couldn't blame Lindsey for feeling she had to warn her cousins about him. He'd been reprehensible in his dealings with her.

He could even understand Cissy's sense of betrayal to her sister after sleeping with his clan. Though the rules of the lottery were clear, Diltan had learned that Earther ideas of morality tended to be much different from Kalquorian expectations. Women not repressed by the old spectre of their former government still dealt with the memories of its punishments. Had Diltan not been so rattled by the mention of Lindsey McInness, he would have been more accepting of Cissy's concerns this morning.

Okay, he'd messed up. There must be some way he could make it up to Cissy. It pleased him to know that, despite her sometimes rough behaviour, she had that kind of decency.

The very decency I've fallen short of. The memory curdled Diltan's guts. If Cissy learned what he had proposed to Lindsey, her reaction would be withering at best. It shamed him to know he was capable of something so low.

Sometimes my ambition sickens me. I can only imagine how much it would disgust Cissy.

It didn't occur to him to wonder why he attached so much importance to how Cissy would feel if she learned Diltan had once tried to take Lindsey from her clan.

He drew near Maf's chambers and fought to bring his scattered thoughts into focus. Right now he needed to deal with the other source of stress in his life—Emperor

Zarl's records. Diltan paused just outside Maf's door and drew a deep breath. His colleague would know what to do. That would go a long way to relieving the brutal headache that pulsed behind Diltan's eyes.

Bolstering his resolve, Diltan stepped into the offices of Councilman Maf. Maf's assistant, Dramok Sitrel, a man who managed to be handsome despite a long face and thin lips, stood up from behind the desk where he worked. He bowed. Diltan returned the courtesy.

In his usual quiet, cultured tone, Sitrel smiled at him. "Councilman Diltan, always a pleasure. What may I help you with this morning?"

Explain women to me and why I act the way I do around those strange and wonderful creatures was on the tip of Diltan's tongue. Instead, he responded, "I don't suppose Councilman Maf would have a moment to speak to me?"

Sitrel gave him a pleasantly concerned look. "He is always glad to see you, but at the moment, he is meeting with one of his constituents."

Diltan nodded. He knew he should have commed instead. "That's all right. I'll be glad to make an appointment when it is more convenient for him, if you don't mind."

Sitrel sat down and tapped at his computer. "He has time open this afternoon. Will that be soon enough?"

"That will be fine."

More tapping. For some reason, it made Diltan's headache worse.

At least Sitrel was a quiet man. Most of the time, people were unaware of his presence in a room. "May I enquire as to the subject of discussion?" he asked Diltan.

"Emperor Zarl's records. I've come upon a concern that would benefit from his objective opinion."

Sitrel paused in his typing and gave Diltan a look that was sharper than usual. "Will you excuse me for just a moment, Councilman?"

"Of course."

Sitrel stood, bowed and announced himself at the closed door that led into Maf's personal office. After a few moments, it opened for him and he went in.

Diltan watched all this with bemusement. So Maf wanted to know anything to do with the Imperial records, did he? Once he heard the revelations Diltan had come across, he'd no doubt feel vindicated. He was about to get the answers he'd demanded for so long. Now he could join in Diltan's struggle as to what to do with them.

Less than a minute after going into Maf's inner chambers, Sitrel came out again. At his side was a Kalquorian woman of singular beauty. Diltan recognised her right away—Matara Feyom.

The statuesque woman was the lifemate of another councilman and a well-known face around the Government House. Too well-known. The gossip surrounding her was thick and not complimentary. There were those who made remarks discussing how many of Feyom's dozen children were the progeny of her clan. Even Diltan, who felt rumour mongering to be the activity of lower, petty minds, could not help overhearing such tales on occasion.

Had Feyom been leaving another councilman's inner chambers, Diltan had to admit he might have thought the worst himself. He hated that his thoughts turned in that direction, making him no better than other judgmental men. For all Diltan knew, Feyom made it a habit to visit other councilmen to argue for her Dramok's political agenda.

And even if she was the kind of person others alleged her to be, it was not Diltan's place to condemn her. He'd done his share of unethical activities. Matara Lindsey's face flashed in his mind and Diltan felt that squirmy sense of shame in his gut once more. No, it was not his place to judge, not by far.

Besides, it was poor, twisted Maf Feyom had been visiting. The idea of such an amazing example of femaleness having a liaison with the deformed Dramok was laughable. Feyom shone dazzling bright.

She did not appeal to Diltan beyond her surface beauty. As he bowed in respect to the lifebringer, he reflected how hard her otherwise perfect face was. Though Feyom's appearance was flawless, she missed something, something warm and lively. The Kalquorian woman would have benefitted from a touch of the fire that Cissy Salter possessed. Diltan thought his lover of the night before compared well against the woman who gazed at him with cold calculation.

Trying to put his mind back on the here and now, Diltan straightened from his bow. "Good day, Matara," he said before glancing at Sitrel. "I do hope I am not the reason your visit is cut short?"

Feyom looked him over. Her gaze was a bit too evaluating for comfort, making Diltan feel perhaps her reputation was not without merit. Her return smile was appreciative but bored.

With a husky tone, she replied, "Not at all, Councilman. My business with Maf concluded some minutes ago. We were simply chatting as old friends will." She smiled at the Dramok aide. "Sitrel."

Sitrel bowed and she walked out. The aide said to Diltan, "Councilman Maf will see you now, Councilman."

"Thank you."

Diltan walked past Sitrel and entered Maf's chambers. The senior councilman's office was much like those of most councilmen. There was an informal seating area with a table that visitors could gather around. There was the more official desk for business talks, with a hover chair suspended behind it and four chairs ranging in front of it. The desk had two computers, a com unit and a couple of awards from businesses and advocacy groups. More awards graced the walls, along with still vids of Maf in the company of various dignitaries. A bar and news vid, set on mute, completed the room's attributes.

Only one detail varied from the norm. All of the seating, including that around the informal visiting area, was the kind that kept one off the ground. Floor seating cushions were noticeably absent. It was little wonder—Maf's infirmities did not allow him to lounge comfortably on the floor.

The man himself came from the small round. His gait lurched, his twisted legs carrying him without the easy grace of most Kalquorians. Diltan hardly noticed anymore, except to feel the familiar stab of sympathy he always did for Maf.

Maf made the awkward dip that counted as a bow for him. "Diltan, what brings you all the way down to my end of the corridor? Can I get you a drink?"

His bright, cheerful voice brought a responding smile from Diltan. He waved his host back towards the sitting area. "Nothing for me, please. I'm afraid this is more business than pleasure."

Maf wobbled back to the chair that sat at just the right height for him to perch easily on. Diltan sat across from him, glad that the other councilman didn't stand on much ceremony. Procedures were rigidly held to in council and committee meetings, but in the environment of his office, Maf had always been affable with Diltan. Heated confrontations on the council floor had never found a place here.

"Tell me," Maf invited as soon as they were both settled.

Diltan drew a deep breath and plunged in. "I have come across some delicate matters in the records of Zarl when he was the emperor. What I have found is disturbing, perhaps too much so for it to be made public."

Maf crooked a brow at him. "You know the rule of transparency, my friend. We hide nothing from the people of the Empire."

"Not even when it might mean a break within the Empire?"

Maf blinked. "Is the matter that sensitive? It must be for you to question our openness with the people of Kalquor. I've never known you to be secretive when it comes to public policy."

Diltan felt a rush of relief that Maf saw to the heart of his dilemma. "It is to the greater good that we keep no secrets, save those of the military, from our people. This is something you and I have always agreed on as members of the Ethics Committee. When possible, everything must be laid bare."

Maf blew out a heavy breath. "Nothing brings an empire crashing down faster than the weight of its own secrets."

"Which is why I try to live by the creed of honour and Empire." Diltan winced, thinking of Cissy being upset that morning and his shame getting in the way of doing well by her. He'd missed honour in a big way that time. "I do not claim to always get it right, but I try."

Maf chuckled. "As do we all. But, Diltan, let's cut to the chase of why you feel differently about whatever has brought you to me today."

"I'm torn, Maf." Unable to sit still, Diltan got out of his chair and paced back and forth. "There is no room for secrecy in our Empire. Yet the truth could destroy it. Which way does one lean when the two are opposed? Do I toss aside honour to safeguard the Empire? Or do I stick to honour, knowing I may be sacrificing our people? "

Maf's forehead wrinkled as he considered him. "Are you sure it would be a sacrifice? Diltan, change is difficult in any case. Sometimes it is forced upon us, as the acceptance of Earther Mataras has been forced upon all of Kalquor in order to continue our culture."

"Most of us don't feel as if the women have been forced onto us." He thought of Cissy and his chest warmed.

"There are those of us who struggle with this issue more than you might imagine. It has wrought fundamental change on everything we have held dear for centuries. Will we be stronger for it or will we crumble in the end? That has yet to be answered. Meanwhile, terrible things have happened in the fight to find our way through it."

"Like the end of Earth. The Beast of New Bethlehem." Diltan's warm feelings crumbled as horror filled his being.

Maf nodded. "Greater yet is the end of our own species, to be replaced by those we defeated. Still, the Empire has not fallen apart yet. Adapting to such immense circumstances may be the end of life the way we know it, but it is not the end of life in the universe. Civilisations come and go and yet the cosmos continues."

Diltan could see that Maf had devoted a great deal of time to the question. Perhaps his views were opposite of most Kalquorians', but Maf had not reached his conclusions haphazardly. It made him feel he had done right to come to the senior councilman.

He dived in. "I find it interesting that you would bring up the Earther Mataras."

"You do? Tell me."

"That's the matter in Zarl's records. Maf, I have irrefutable proof that Zarl not only knew the abductions were going to happen, but he sanctioned them as well. I have the order that sent our people out to kidnap the Earther women and bring them against their will here to Kalquor."

Maf's mouth dropped open. His eyes widened and a hectic light bloomed within them. "Did you bring the file?"

Diltan took a file drive, no bigger than his thumb, out of the pouch he wore on his belt. "I brought a copy."

He handed it over, putting it in the clawed hand held out to him. It shook, as if Maf had been seized by a great tremor.

As the file passed from Diltan's fingers, it felt as if a terrible burden passed with it. Perhaps it was cowardly of him, but he was more than happy to share it with someone like Maf…someone who could decide best if secrets should remain hidden or brought out into the light of day.

Maf stood and limped to his desk as quick as his twisted limbs would take him. He wasted no time in plugging the file into one of his computers and looking over the damning document.

Diltan sighed in relief, relaxing in the chair. His mind approached a semblance of serenity. He waited as the other councilman perused the contents of the record that had been Kalquor's supposed salvation…and could lead to its collapse.

* * * *

Cissy sat in her sister's greeting room at the low table, alternating between chewing on her lower lip and sipping coffee. Tasha sat across from her. Cissy kept her gaze down. She couldn't bear to meet her sister's eyes.

Despite her resolve, it had taken Cissy two hours to summon the courage to knock on her twin's door after sending Clan Diltan on their way. Tasha was a late sleeper anyway. Putting off the coming confession had been all too easy. However, Cissy finally made herself go to Tasha, determined to clear her conscience and somehow make things right.

She heard the amusement in her sister's voice. "Okay, what did you do this time?"

Cissy's shoulders slumped. "Something tacky and stupid. And totally wrong."

"This should be interesting."

Tasha almost sounded as if she were laughing. A flare of temper blazed for an instant in Cissy's gut and she quickly quashed it. She was in the wrong, not Tasha.

Cissy made herself look up into the face so much like her own. She struggled, but she managed to meet her sister's gaze. "Tasha, I owe you a huge apology. I know you said you weren't into Clan Diltan, but there's no excuse for what I did. I got drunk, but that doesn't justify my actions, either. I would never hurt you in a million years."

To her surprise, Tasha looked delighted. "Oh, so you finally decided to give them a chance? It took you long enough."

Cissy's mouth fell open. "Wait. What?"

Tasha erupted into giggles, rocking back and forth on her seating cushion with glee. "For heaven's sake, Cissy. I wanted you to get with them. That's the only reason I went on the second date! So you could see them and maybe realise how infatuated you were."

"You—me, infatuated—what?"

Tasha nearly fell over with laughter. "Oh my gosh, the way you ranted about how much you didn't like Dramok Diltan. It was a dead giveaway. I knew you had a crush on him."

Shock and anger fought for the upper hand. Cissy fell squarely between them, unable to choose which one felt right. "Hey, now hold on! You played me? Your own sister? And no way I had a crush on Dramok Stuffy Pants. That guy is a jerk!"

No, not so much a jerk. However, Cissy was determined to let Tasha have a piece of her mind, even if that piece wasn't entirely truthful.

"A jerk you like. When you weren't snarling at him, you had those big moon eyes all over him and his clan." Moving into brat mode, Tasha sang, "Cissy and Diltan, sitting in a tree—"

Cissy picked up a smaller pillow lying next to her on the floor and pitched it at her twin. "You are such an ass."

Unperturbed, Tasha dodged the pillow and finished her ditty. "K-I-S-S-I-N-G! Man, I thought last night would never end. I spent our whole date telling stories about you to get them interested. I hoped those three would get the hint to move on to you."

Cissy at last came down on the side of anger. She yelled, "I can't believe you would do such a thing! Here I was, feeling awful I'd slept with them, only to find out you sicced them on me!"

Tasha gave her wide eyes. "You already gave them sex before a trial date? No kidding. Damn, you do have it bad for them. So when is the clanning ceremony?"

Cissy folded her arms over her chest. The nerve of her sister! "The clanning ceremony is scheduled for never. We had a fight this morning and I made them leave. That's what your matchmaking results in, you meddler."

Tasha groaned. "Of course you had to pick a fight. After I wasted an entire night making sure they knew how great you are under all that…that Cecilia-ness. You are too much."

"Not half as much as you," Cissy spat back. "Who asked you to play Cupid anyway?"

"Well, I won't do it again," Tasha snapped. "Go back to dating those silly young boys who will never make you a decent clan."

"I will."

"Good."

"Fine."

With that, they sat silently, sipping their coffee and refusing to look at each other. Cissy thought about stomping back to her apartment. It would irritate Tasha more if she just sat there.

The whole thing would blow over in a matter of minutes. The twins could never stay mad at each other for any length of time. Pretty soon Tasha would remark on the weather or suggest they go down to the spa. Or Cissy might mention something about the art show she heard would be coming to a local gallery, one she knew Tasha would love to see. They'd act like their little disagreement had never happened.

For now, however, Cissy was content to pout. After all, Tasha had connived to put her in that jerk Diltan's arms—that sexy, gorgeous, melt-in-his-arms-when-he-kissed-her Diltan. Right where Cissy had wanted to be all along but couldn't bear to admit to it.

Chapter Twelve

After going through a weapons scan and search, Diltan walked the gauntlet of Royal Guards on the palatial uppermost level of the Government House. He was on the Imperial Level now, heading for Emperor Clajak's chambers. The grandness of the hall with its vaulted ceiling made little impression on the councilman.

Over an hour ago, Diltan had thought he had unloaded a great weight. Yet after replaying his conversation with Maf several times over and recalling the other councilman's reaction, the burden had returned. No, not just returned. Tripled. With each remembrance of Maf's unholy excitement over evidence of the royals' wrongdoing, Diltan realised all the terrible things that could happen. Now his shaking knees tried to buckle under added pressure. His headache had gotten so bad that he felt nauseated.

He had little hope of it lessening any time soon. Only of perhaps adding to it. He felt crushed under responsibility to the Empire. It was due to his well-meaning but colossal mistake.

Diltan had to face up to that error by speaking to Kalquor's highest leaders. All the members of the Imperial Clan were busy people. Clajak was known to be hands-on when it came to his duties. He demanded to know everything going on in the Empire. A man once considered to be an irresponsible playboy, the Dramok Emperor had silenced his adversaries on that count.

Yet Diltan had to see the man immediately. If Clajak would not grant a spontaneous audience, Diltan would beg Empress Jessica for her time. The matter could not wait.

He reached Clajak's reception area. He noted how crowded it was with others who had appointments and who hoped to be squeezed into the emperor's busy schedule. There were no places to sit in the room save for at the desk of the receptionist. The lack of seating was a smart move, meant to discourage too many people from hanging about and begging for Clajak's precious time. It didn't deter everyone, however, as was evidenced by how near to capacity the room was filled.

It didn't matter. Diltan had made a massive error and he had to warn the Imperial Clan of what was about to happen. If anyone wanted to call him out for letting Clajak know ahead of time what was coming, let them. The welfare of the Empire came first…an Empire beneath which the foundations might soon shake and crack.

It's a good thing I no longer want so much to curry the royals' favour because they will not be happy with me now. But how was I to know what Maf's agenda was? He always seemed so fair-minded, even though he opposed us breeding with the Earthers. Surely I wasn't the only one to be fooled into thinking he could be objective about the matter!

The ancestors were smiling on him for a change. Diltan had just pushed his way to the receptionist's desk when Empress Jessica emerged from Clajak's inner chamber. She was a pretty little thing with straight chestnut hair lying like a sheet over the shoulders of her imperial purple robe. However, discounting her for her size was always a huge mistake. Of all the Imperial Clan, it was Jessica who would invite a fight before even her temperamental Dramok.

Her bright blue eyes lit on Diltan and she gave him a look of mock horror. "Uh-oh. What did we do now, Councilman?"

Then Clajak himself leaned out of the doorway to grin at Diltan. His eyes matched his official purple robe. "I don't remember seeing you on my itinerary."

Diltan bowed to them, as did the rest of the people waiting. "I'm not scheduled for an appointment, my emperor. I apologise for my presumption, but something of great importance has come up." He noted equal measures of dark, impatient looks and curiosity. He turned back to the emperor and empress and beseeched, "I am terribly sorry, but the matter I bring to you can't wait. I must speak to at least one of you."

The desperation in his expression and tone were enough to convince Clajak and Jessica. The Dramok emperor said, "You are not a man to seek an immediate audience without just cause, Diltan. Come in." To his receptionist, he added, "Tell Korkla to join us please."

Diltan wove through the others to enter Clajak's inner chambers behind him and Jessica. The empress's light floral perfume was a sweet trail to follow, but it did nothing to calm Diltan's nerves. He barely noticed the luxurious appointments of the room, the well-wrought desk, chairs and cushions making no impression on him at all. His hectic gaze skimmed over the fine art and statues that decorated the room. He paced as Clajak sat on his desk and Jessica perched very un-empress-like on the edge of the finely carved surface. They watched him with concern as he tried to order his thoughts.

How was he going to break the news to Clajak about what his fathers had done? And how could he tell him that the Empire itself might teeter on the brink of disaster?

Dramok Korkla, Clajak's aide of many years, entered the room. The sharp-featured man, as efficient and pleasant as Diltan had ever met, gave him a cursory smile before addressing Clajak. "You called for me, my emperor?"

Clajak waved Korkla to one of the hover chairs floating before the desk. "Councilman Diltan says he has something important to tell us. I assumed I would need you in on this."

"Good to see you, Councilman." Having acknowledged his employer and the empress, Korkla bowed to Diltan before taking his handheld computer from a pouch on his belt. He sat and readied to make notes.

"What's wrong, Diltan?" Jessica prodded.

He took a deep breath. "My empress, my emperor, I was selected to go over Imperial Father Zarl's records."

Clajak's eyes flashed with interest. "Yes, I am aware of that."

"I found something. Something…troublesome. Something the then-emperor kept secret."

Clajak's brows drew down a little. "With our code of transparency? That doesn't sound like my father."

"He had good reason to keep this quiet." Diltan swallowed. "This matter I've uncovered—it made me fear for the Empire's stability should it become known. I consulted with Councilman Maf because I needed guidance."

Korkla nodded approvingly. "Maf is well regarded, smart. It was wise for you to have done so."

At least Diltan could claim he wasn't the only one who had thought that way. Korkla was known as a good judge of character.

It didn't calm his despair. "No, Dramok Korkla. It was a horrific mistake because Maf will now make the matter public no matter how damaging it may be to Kalquor. The man was downright gleeful to have this evidence! His joy over the trouble that it will cause was obscene!" Diltan appealed to the two royals in the room. "I swear to you that I had no idea how much he loathed the secrecy of the Matara abductions. I would have come to you first had I suspected."

Clajak stared at Diltan, his expression thunderstruck. He rose from his seat. In a voice hushed with shock, he said, "My father Zarl made mention of the initial kidnappings of Earther women? He knew who was behind them?"

"He implicated himself as the main instigator. He also implicated the rest of your fathers."

Clajak sat back down heavily, as if his legs had gone out from under him. "How bad is it, Diltan?"

Diltan took a small amount of comfort in the level of Clajak's stunned response. It was obvious that the current Dramok emperor had no connection with the abductions. The face framed by its waves of smoky steel-coloured hair had drained of all colour. The present Imperial Clan could at least claim they had nothing to do with the kidnappings that had led to the war.

Jessica and Korkla looked almost as shocked. Their mouths hung open. Silence reigned in the room.

It took all Diltan's strength to answer his monarch. "The situation is the worst possible, my emperor. Zarl specifically wrote the order to carry out clinical tests on an Earther woman for purposes of breeding. He also ordered that if the results of those tests were positive, the abductions of between fifteen hundred and two thousand Earther women would be carried out. It was an action that led to hostilities between Earth and Kalquor, which culminated in the destruction of Earth."

For several moments, no one spoke. It was Empress Jessica who drew herself up, standing as tall as her petite frame allowed. "Councilman Maf wishes to pursue litigation?"

"I am sure of it, my empress. He will call the Ethics Committee together to discuss the necessity of such action." He raked fingers through his hair, the enormity of the situation pressing ever harder on him. "The only thing that kept the Galactic Council of Planets from indicting Kalquor for the destruction of Earth was that no one knew precisely who was behind those abductions."

Korkla pursed his lips. "Zarl is out of the reach of justice. If he did not name Tidro and Yuder specifically as accomplices, they may still face an enquiry. However, with no proof and no witnesses, there is no reason to believe they are in danger of being held responsible."

Jessica's glare was stormy. "They will still have to face questions…or at least Yuder will. Father Tidro is several weeks away in seclusion." She shook her head. "Zarl gave the order! Most suspected Haven's Governor Ospar, who was our ambassador to the Galactic Council at the time. Councilman Rajhir, too, since it was his clan who claimed the first Earther Matara, Amelia Ryan."

Korkla added, "Since so many councilmen clanned those first Mataras, a huge government cover-up was alleged by those opposed."

Jessica sounded bitter as she said, "I love Ospar like a brother, but I always thought he was devious enough to pull a stunt like that."

Diltan said, "Dramoks Ospar and Rajhir may very well have had a hand in the abductions. Zarl's communications were coded to keep the recipient of his orders concealed, but they traced as going off-planet. As the ambassador to the Galactic Council, Ospar would be the most likely candidate. He is known to have ways of making things happen outside of proper channels. Since Councilman Rajhir's clan had a hand in testing the first Earther Matara for breeding compatibility, it is highly likely he was in on the conspiracy."

Korkla looked at Clajak, horror filling his expression. "Rajhir is your cousin, a direct link to the Imperial bloodline. The ramifications are huge if it comes out he knew Zarl made the order."

"That's not the worst of it," Diltan muttered. "I have no doubt that even if Imperial Fathers Tidro and Yuder are innocent of any wrongdoing, Maf will demand they be interrogated. At the very least, the Galactic Council will demand we surrender your fathers to them for investigation, my emperor."

In a voice that suggested she had plunged into a nightmare, Jessica said, "The rebellion will use this to gain followers. The Basma could get enough traction to challenge us directly. It is a danger to the Empire."

Clajak stood. His face worked, but Diltan couldn't tell if the emperor was terrified or furious.

His fists clenched, Clajak came around the desk and headed for the door. Staring after him, Jessica called, "Where are you going, Clajak?"

Clajak whirled to face his mate. His words slurred because his fangs had descended, he snarled, "To find my father Yuder. He has much to explain."

With that, he left the room in a swirl of purple robes. Jessica chased after him, calling over her shoulder, "Korkla, we'd better get Bevau and Egilka. Send them straight to the Imperial Fathers' suite."

The aide was already clicking for a frequency on Clajak's desk com. Diltan watched him, his soul feeling helpless.

* * * *

Nobek Yuder stood on his home's balcony, facing into the wind. It whipped his long, steel-coloured hair back from his face, streaming like banners behind him. It reminded him of the night his Dramok had died. Storm clouds scudded across the horizon in ominous warning, threatening to eclipse the day. The sea crashed as passionately as it had the night he had talked his Imdiko into leaving Kalquor, sending off his last surviving clanmate.

At least the weather had warmed. Yuder was almost too hot. His solid black formsuit left his muscled arms bare, but he was starting to sweat. Nevertheless, he still missed the weight of his old Global Security uniform with its armoured padding.

It was hard to be retired, though Global Security still consulted him on matters important to the home world's safety. The Imperial Clan also asked for his input, but that happened less and less as they grew comfortable with their roles as rulers. Yuder had his lover Tara and every moment with her felt like being reborn. Still, it was hard for a Nobek to no longer be in the middle of activity.

I am losing my purpose in life, he thought with uncharacteristic sadness. *I am getting old and useless.*

Yuder heard the door to his home open. It wasn't necessary to respond to the instinctive need to find out who had come in and be ready to defend his clan if required. Zarl was dead. Tidro was safe elsewhere. Tara was doing volunteer work at the hospital. Besides, his contingent of Royal Guards only let certain people enter the home without first clearing it with Yuder.

Safe and useless, he thought. Then he heard the thudding footsteps, the kind of purposeful stomping approach that always heralded the arrival of an angry Clajak.

Yuder wondered if the moment he'd dreaded had arrived. He hoped so. Secrecy had never sat well with the warrior. Being emperor had afforded him many opportunities to exercise his need for justice and action, but the trade-offs had barely been worth the challenges. Zarl had been so much better with the intrigues that came with the throne.

He turned as his son burst out upon the balcony, the purple robes of his office billowing in the fierce wind. Without preamble, Clajak yelled, "Zarl gave the order for the Earther abductions. You and Tidro supported this?"

Tension bled out of Yuder's body at the accusation. At last, the worst decision he'd ever made had been discovered. The secret was out, at least to Clajak. His guilt in the matter could at last be made right.

Yuder dipped his head in a slow nod. "We did, my emperor. How far has the information spread?"

Clajak stared at him. Now that he had confirmation, his sometimes violent temper eased. It was yet another sign of his maturity, that Clajak had at last grown into the man Yuder had hoped he would. He could perhaps become known as the Empire's greatest emperor…if his fathers' mistakes didn't derail that. If Clajak didn't try to protect them in misguided familial loyalty.

The younger man's fists clenched. "Councilman Diltan didn't know what to do with the information, so he consulted with Dramok Maf."

Yuder's eyes narrowed. "Then it will become public knowledge that we gave the order. Maf is head of the Ethics Committee and dedicated to absolute truth."

Clajak's voice rose again. "Do you know what this will do to the Empire?"

Yuder nodded. "The Basma's rebellion will gain support. It was our short-sightedness that didn't see the revolt coming. We didn't realise there would be so many who preferred our extinction to mating with the Earthers."

Clajak whirled to pace back and forth. His robes snapped in the wind, expressing the passion he fought to not give vent to. "It's not just that. You went behind the backs of the people! You opened the way to war, which led to Earth's destruction!"

"I cannot refute that. I do not refute it. I accept full responsibility."

Clajak stopped in front of him. He was bigger than Yuder and stronger. Yuder had seen Clajak kill another man when Jessica had been threatened. He was still nowhere near as dangerous as Yuder. However, had his son raised his hand, the elder man would not have defended himself.

Clajak did not make any attempt to attack. "What was found in Zarl's records…is that why Tidro left?"

Now came the hard part, the part where Yuder would ask Clajak to behave almost as unethically as he had. The Nobek had no choice, however. He had to protect what was left of his clan.

Yuder said, "Your Imdiko father has spent these last years caring for Zarl to the detriment of his own well-being. Tidro is old and broken, Clajak. If Zarl did not mention him by name in those records, then I refute he knew anything of the matter. You must let me assume full guilt."

Clajak's expression betrayed only a moment's pain before he asked, "What of our cousin Rajhir? Matara Amelia was the woman tested, the woman he took as his clanmate. What about Dramok Ospar who was our ambassador to the Galactic Council then? If Rajhir was part of this, then so was he. You can't tell me that conniving creature isn't in this as deep as you."

Yuder closed his eyes. "Ospar has always acted in the best interests of the Empire. His methods, like ours, may not have always been the most principled, but you know his heart lies with our well-being."

Clajak continued as if he hadn't spoken. "What of over half the Royal Council which benefitted by gaining Earther mates from the mass kidnappings you ordered? Over half! This will shake the very foundation of our realm!"

Yuder sighed. "Ospar is the only one I know for certain who was aware the order came from the Crown. He was bound to act under our authority and cannot be blamed. As for the rest, I'm not sure if Rajhir and the others knew who was ultimately behind the abductions. They have always sworn they didn't."

Clajak's gaze was dark, his fury regaining strength. "I think it's time we found out."

Yuder wanted to warn Clajak from looking under every single stone for fear of what he might find. How many had been fully aware of who ordered the mass kidnappings? Had Zarl or Tidro confided in anyone beyond their clan and Ospar? Had Ospar spoken to anyone on the matter? There was no telling who would be dragged out into the light now that the matter had been discovered.

Yuder also had no doubt Councilman Maf would chase every lead down, determined to flush the conspirators out. The man presented himself as fair-minded, but he had long been quietly amongst those who voiced objections against interbreeding with Earthers. Maf had been amongst the first to insist those behind the abductions be brought forward.

Yuder thought, *Ancestors help us if it went beyond my clan and Ospar. There will be no end to the outrage. The Empire might well burn before it is over. I must find a way to keep that from happening, even if it means sacrificing myself.*

He bowed his head. “My emperor, I will cooperate in every way possible for the good of the Empire and its continuance.”

Chapter Thirteen

Diltan was only too happy to get home at the end of the day. He knew nothing more of the drama unfolding now that he'd revealed Zarl's secrets to Maf and the Imperial Clan. The Government House was rife with rumours what with Maf shutting his chamber doors for most of the day and the Imperial Clan first dashing throughout the halls then making themselves unavailable as well. When it became known that visits from Diltan to those people had preceded these strange goings-on, he'd been forced to close his doors and ignore coms. He'd even avoided Oiteil. He did not want to discuss the brewing trouble with anyone anymore.

He kept himself busy by continuing to peruse Zarl's documents, hoping to find evidence that would keep the matter contained to the former Imperial Clan and show the Royal Council was untainted by the controversy. He ended his day disappointed even though he'd stayed an hour later than usual to avoid his fellow councilmen.

Entering his home at last, Diltan wasted no time in searching out his clanmates. He needed the friendly faces of those who cared about him.

He found them in the common room, with Wal snuggled against Rolat on the lounger. The pair were having small glasses of bohut and sharing a plate of bite-size wisba-coated ronka. Apparently they'd been content with conversing, since none of the entertainment, music or gaming systems were running. They smiled at him as he entered.

Wal pulled free of Rolat's encircling arm, sitting up. "Welcome home, my Dramok. Would you care for a drink?"

"Please. Thank you, Wal." Diltan let his legs fold beneath him, collapsing rather than settling onto a seat cushion at Rolat's feet. He leaned against his Nobek's legs, closed his eyes and made his mind go blank.

Diltan listened to the sound of the nearby fire crackling in the pit. He let it fill his ears, concentrating on that and not remembered snatches of conversation from earlier that day. He put the troubling events out of his mind, sinking into the safety and security of home. Here, no one could trouble him. He could pretend the Empire was as strong as ever, that no rebellions waited in the wings, that nothing bad could ever happen.

Diltan was aware that Rolat and Wal spoke to each other, but he kept them in the background. He let his worries quiet until he felt a glass press into his hand, which lay curled on one thigh. Only then did the Dramok open his eyes to consider the small glass of bohut Wal had given him.

He stared at it for a few minutes, gazing into the liquor's reddish-brown depths. When he raised it to his lips, he downed the smoky-sweet drink in one gulp.

Fire traced down Diltan's throat and he winced. It brought him back to the here and now. He laid his head back on Rolat's knee and looked up at his clanmates. Wal had curled at the Nobek's side again. Both men watched him with affectionate concern.

"Someone had a rough day," Rolat observed.

"And then some," Diltan said.

Wal stood again, took Diltan's glass and refilled it from the bottle now sitting on the low table before them. "Do you wish to talk about it?"

I can't. If Yuder and Tidro go on trial, you'll likely hear the case.

Even if Diltan could have discussed Zarl's records and how he'd mishandled their information, he didn't have the heart for it. He told Wal, "By the ancestors, no. I fucked up and I can't even begin to comprehend the repercussions of it."

Diltan took another swig of bohut, but he didn't drain the glass this time. The anxieties of the day were back on him. *How bad is it going to be? It's going to shake the Empire but will it be enough to make the very foundations crack?*

In a careful tone, Wal said, "If you can't talk about your work, would you appreciate distraction?"

"Immensely."

Rolat grinned at him. "Good. Let's discuss Tasha and Cissy."

Diltan groaned. "Speaking of fuck-ups I've committed. Damn it, I could have handled this morning better."

"Perhaps. At any rate, Wal and I have agreed we'd like to switch our suit from one to the other."

Diltan's head pounded. His headache was making a return. "You wish to pursue Cecilia? Not chalk last night up to drinking and mere physical attraction?"

Wal shook his head. "She's more to our liking than Natasha. Tasha is sweet, but Cissy is…" He paused then laughed loudly. "Astounding."

Diltan finished his second drink. "She's blunt and rude. She possesses little decorum. In short, the second Ms. Salter is all the things I would not wish in a Matara."

"All the things you thought you didn't wish in a Matara," Rolat countered. "Yet you are drawn to her. Don't deny it, my Dramok. She fascinates you every bit as much as she entrances us."

Diltan scowled at him before glancing at the bottle on the table. He knew better than to drink just to soothe his nerves, but the bohut was damned tempting. Still eyeing it, he said, "The last thing I need right now is a complicated dating situation, especially when it comes to those who are connected to the Imperial Clan."

Wal's light voice held an undercurrent of suspicion. "Speaking of which, don't you think you should share the issue Cissy mentioned you having with Imperial Sister Lindsey?"

Pain stabbed Diltan's temples. Fuck. He did not want to have this conversation. However, today was determined to be chock full of shit.

He griped, knowing it would do him no good. "Damn it. If you knew the day I had, you'd give me a break."

"Let's compromise," Rolat offered. "I will pour you another drink to help loosen your tongue and settle your nerves. Then you will tell us what happened." He took Diltan's glass and reached to pour the last of the bohut into it.

Diltan got to his feet. "Being the Dramok of a clan is nothing like what I expected it to be. Clanmates who refuse to obey orders, who order me around to boot, and insist on enticing the wrong Matara to join us. As Cissy might say, the whole package sucks lemons."

Rolat smirked and offered Diltan his drink. "Your biggest problem is not us. It's your ambition, my Dramok. You reach high, so you will inevitably fall from time to time."

Diltan took his glass from the Nobek and retreated a couple of steps away. If he was going to confess his wrongdoings with Lindsey, he was not going to be within arm's length of Rolat. Just being in the same room was too close for comfort.

Steeling himself for the censure of his Imdiko and Nobek, Diltan told them, "I reach too high, on occasion."

"Can one do that?" Wal mused. "I think a man should go for whatever his dreams are, however impossible they may seem."

"Including another clan's Matara?"

"Well, I can't countenance that."

Diltan sighed. "Then you'll be very disappointed in me."

The Imdiko's eyes widened. "Oh, Diltan. No."

Rolat glared, his anger already on the rise. "Not with Imperial Sister Lindsey. Diltan, I swear I will beat you black and blue if you laid a hand on her."

Diltan held one hand and his glass up in surrender. "I promise I never touched her. I did try to get her to de-clan her mates in our favour, however."

Rolat made a sound of disgust as Wal stared at him in horror. "My Dramok, how could you?"

Diltan slumped. Since it didn't look as if Rolat was going to launch himself at him to administer sound punishment yet, he quaffed his third drink and set the glass down on the table. Once he recovered from the river of liquid fire burning its way down into his guts, he said, "Young Clan Bacoj had no rank, not enough to warrant their clanning the sister of Empress Jessica."

"Says you," snarled Rolat. "That is inexcusable, Diltan. Even you shouldn't be able to sink that low with your ambitions."

Wal shook his head, looking more sad than angry. He didn't speak. He didn't need to. His expression told Diltan how he'd let him down.

Somehow that was worse than Rolat's anger. It made Diltan sick to his stomach.

In a small voice, he said, "It was an awful mistake I made, a cracked-skull move. Maybe my worst."

Or second worst, he privately countered, thinking of the coming trouble over Zarl's records.

"One of many horrific mistakes," he amended. "I lost all honour when I did that."

Rolat's initial fury ebbed. "Is that why you financed the start of their businesses? I'd like to think the guilt made a better man of you."

"I'm glad to say it was only a small part of why I invested in Bacoj's, Vax's and Japohn's futures." Diltan had to smile a little, knowing how he'd given deserving men a chance to realise their dreams, even though the road leading to that had been rough. "Their proposals had real merit, as is evident from the success all three men have enjoyed."

"You recovered your investments within two years, didn't you?" Wal said. "And then you told them to keep the rest of their profits for themselves, if I remember correctly. No interest charged, no residual percentages taken. I thought that was generous of you."

"I didn't feel good about riding on their success after what I'd done," Diltan admitted. "Unlike me, they are good, decent men. They deserve happiness with their Matara."

"The Imperial Sister kept quiet about the matter. How kind of her." Rolat's tone oozed sarcasm. "I wish she would have had her sister announce what you did on the council floor in front of all of Kalquor."

Diltan sighed. He needed to clear his conscience about the matter once and for all. That meant telling them the most humiliating part of the story.

"She wasn't the only one who kept my shameful actions a secret. The mothers of Clan Bacoj found out about my proposal to Matara Lindsey. They shamed me for being such an ass. Giving Clan Bacoj my financial support was the price for their silence on the matter."

"A bargain for you," Rolat snorted.

"They verbally flayed my hide and I still cringe to think of it. One of your beatings cannot come close to the tongue lashing they laid on me. I have never felt so small and worthless as I did that day."

Diltan lowered his gaze, humiliated. Being reproached like a naughty youngling by the Mataras had been the most embarrassing moment of his life. He would have taken a thousand punches from Rolat before enduring the scorn of the three mothers.

Wal huffed. "If I didn't know that under these occasional bursts of arrogance lies a very good man, I'd whip you myself."

"I might still do so," Rolat said. "Damn it, Diltan. What were you thinking?"

"About myself, of course. About my standing, about proving my rank. That's what usually gets me into trouble, isn't it?"

The silence stretched long and heavy. Diltan felt their eyes on him, judging and finding him pathetic. Which he was. Along with vile, repugnant, horrible…

Wal's chuckles broke into Diltan's thoughts. The Dramok looked at his laughing Imdiko with surprise.

Wal's merriment increased as their gazes met. "I would give anything for a vid recording of those men's mothers letting you have it. To see proud Councilman Diltan chastised by a group of angry mommies! Tell me you looked as miserable as you do right now."

Rolat joined him in the hilarity. "That must have been quite the sight. I think we should implement prisoners' mothers' wrath in the penal system. I can think of no worse punishment than having to listen to a mother's rant."

The two men laughed together as Diltan stood there and took it. He didn't like being the butt of the joke, but he deserved it. Nevertheless, his face burned.

After a few minutes of being doubled over at the thought of Diltan being told off by elder Mataras, Rolat gasped, "My Dramok, life with you is never boring."

"I'm glad to keep you entertained," Diltan said in a flat voice. "Just beat my ass and let me off the hook."

"Oh no." Rolat's grin turned evil. "Beating you would be far too easy. I have a better idea, at least a little something to start with."

The Dramok felt a twinge of unease. "I can't wait to hear it."

"Now that we know how thoroughly you fucked things up with the Imperial Sister, let's move on to someone else's sister. Except this time, you're going to do things in an ethical matter."

Diltan saw where he was going and groaned. "Rolat, no."

"Yes. You are going to court the woman Wal and I want to entice back into our bed. I'm not saying we have to clan Cissy, but we will make every effort to see if she is the woman for us."

Diltan thought about opening another bottle of bohut. "She's so bawdy and unreserved." *And she hates me.*

Wal's grin was as devilish as Rolat's. "Which we like. You know, I think courting Cissy would be a valid form of punishment for what Diltan did to Matara Lindsey. My Nobek, you are without a doubt one of the most intelligent men I've ever known."

"Thank you, Wal. Though I think courting Cissy will be only a start for Diltan's punishment. I'll have to think on further repercussions for the serious wrong he's done." Rolat skewered Diltan with his demanding stare. "No just going through the motions on this either, Diltan. I want to see you chase after Cissy with all the fervour of a man in love."

"If she'll even see us," the Dramok pointed out. "If you recall, she didn't seem so keen on us this morning."

Wal's smile faded, replaced by his stern 'judge look', as Diltan thought of it. "You will fix it so she changes her mind," he commanded.

Diltan scowled. Yet he remembered how warm it had made him feel on the inside when he'd woken to Cissy's face first thing this morning. It had been the only moment of happiness he'd felt all day. Sinking into her warmth last night after weeks of thinking about her had been an unparalleled joy.

Who was he kidding? After dealing out hard truths all day, he had to face his own uncomfortable slice of reality. He was every bit as intrigued by Cissy as his clanmates. She irritated him, but she excited him as well.

Perhaps the only reason I find her infuriating is because she's someone I don't think I should want and yet she still stirs me so damned much.

It was an interesting notion. However, Diltan was not willing to own up to the thrill of pursuing the rebellious little Earther to his clanmates. They might decide on some other awful form of punishment for his attempted indiscretions with Matara Lindsey.

Rolat stood. "You look presentable enough. Since you've had three glasses of bohut, I'll pilot the shuttle."

Diltan started. "What, you want to go talk to her now?"

"Absolutely. Move or I'll carry you."

Diltan's heart rate sped up at the thought of seeing Cissy. However, for Rolat's and Wal's benefit, he put on a long-suffering expression and said, "Won't this awful day ever end?"

* * * *

Cissy was poking around in her cooling unit for something to snack on when Tasha burst into her apartment. "Cissy, you have to come over to my place now."

Cissy stared at her flushed twin. "Why? What's going on?"

"No time. Come on!"

With no further explanation, Tasha rushed through the door that led to her quarters. Wondering what all the excitement was about, Cissy hurried after her.

She stopped short to see Clan Diltan assembled in Tasha's greeting room. As one, the men bowed to her. When they straightened, Wal and Rolat looked to Diltan, who stood between them. He scowled at them in turn before giving Cissy his attention.

With a stiff smile on his stupidly handsome face, Diltan said, "Good evening, Matara Cissy. I am glad to see you again."

She narrowed her eyes at him. "Sure you are. We parted on such lovely terms this morning. What is this all about?"

Beaming, Tasha tugged her down to one of the seating cushions surrounding the low table where they'd had coffee this morning. Tasha waved the men to the other cushions. "Please sit down, gentlemen." She said to Cissy, "I told them you confessed to what happened last night and that I'm all right with it."

Cissy snorted. "Did you also tell them you plotted for what happened last night to happen?"

As they settled down to sit cross-legged across from the sisters, Rolat and Wal looked amused. Diltan was obviously startled and banged his knee against the table.

"Careful!" Tasha called.

Cissy silently thanked the table.

Wal's devastating smile made her heart thump, but it was aimed at her sister. "So you wanted us to end up with Cissy. Is that why we were treated to so many stories about your sister, Matara Tasha?"

Tasha blushed. "Sorry. I know I wasn't subtle. However, I could tell we weren't working out so well and she obviously had a thing for you."

Diltan's brow rose. Cissy hated the smirk that tried to turn the corners of his mouth up. "Is that so?"

Cissy gave him her most unimpressed look. "Tasha overstates the issue. I like Rolat and Wal. You, on the other hand—"

Tasha pinched her and told Diltan, "She never shuts up about you, even though much of her incessant ramblings have to do with what an awful person she says you are."

Rolat winked at Cissy. "My Dramok does have his moments."

Diltan rolled his eyes.

Tasha kept talking as if no one else had spoken. "As Shakespeare said, 'The lady doth protest too much, methinks.'"

Cissy rubbed her thigh where Tasha had pinched her. "As some other wiser person said, what I wouldn't give to be an only child."

Tasha ignored her. "I like your clan, Dramok Diltan. I think you are wonderful men with much to offer the right woman. However, I don't think I'm the one you should be offering it to. That particular honour, if you can stand her, belongs to Cissy."

The three men bowed their heads to Tasha. Diltan said, "Matara, it was indeed a privilege to be considered by you and we thank you for the honour. However, my clanmates have agreed that they, too, are not convinced we would make good clanmates for you."

Rolat made a low sound in his throat.

Diltan sighed. “I also agree. We hereby rescind our interest in you for our Matara.”

He turned purple eyes to regard Cissy. That hint of a knowing smirk returned and she bristled.

Oh, so you think I’m a sure thing, do you? Well, you just go ahead and ask if you can date me. If you dare, I’m going to turn you down flat, you pompous ass. You are not the Dramok for me. You piss me off and no number of amazing kisses or great nights in bed are going to make up for that.

Wal nudged Diltan. The Dramok shot him a glare before drawing himself up. “Matara Cecilia, as tempestuous as our meetings have been thus far, they have also been…interesting.”

Cissy made an ugly sound.

Diltan didn’t react. “Will you consider my clan’s offer to explore compatibility for possible clanship?”

Cissy opened her mouth. *Hell no, not in a million years, not if you were the last man on Kalquor.* “Thank you, Dramok Diltan. I accept.” Her teeth snapped shut, making a loud clicking sound. She moaned, “Oh crap, what did I just do?”

Wal snickered. “Funny. I once said that myself when I gave in to joining his clan.”

“Not quite.” Rolat corrected him. “You used more colourful language.” He turned and bowed his head to Cissy. “Don’t worry, Matara. Wal and I will do all we can to make up for our Dramok.”

Tasha’s smile was blinding. “Yep, these are the men for you, sister of mine.” She giggled.

Cissy clapped her hands to her face and squeezed her eyes shut. “I am an idiot.”

“You are so wonderful for my ego, Matara,” Diltan sighed.

Tasha excused herself to get ready for another date. Wal was amused to hear himself say, "I hope you have a lovely time." He was more amused to realise he meant it. Tasha was not the Matara for him.

When his clan first applied for the lottery, Wal had vowed that he would do whatever it took to claim the first Matara who showed the least bit of interest in their clan. The chance to attract a lifebringer and become a father had felt like the holy grail of his existence.

Yet like so many things the Imdiko had believed he wanted throughout his life, this wish had turned out not to be so important after all…at least not where attracting just any woman was concerned. No, now he knew it had to be the right woman.

You'd think after all these years, after all the mistakes I've made, I'd figure out I don't have half the answers I thought I did. By now, I should realise that I don't know what I want until it hits me over the head.

Wal's gaze settled on Cissy. Maybe it was this woman he wanted, just as it had been Diltan and Rolat he wanted instead of that awful Dramok from his boyhood. He knew one thing for sure. If Cissy rose from her seat right now and excused herself to get ready to meet another clan—other men—jealousy would tear his gut apart.

If we could get her and Diltan to stop fighting long enough to explore the possibilities, this might be a good match. Better than good.

Cissy glared at Wal's Dramok even now. Why was she angry again? She'd agreed to see them as potential mates. Maybe it had something to do with the satisfied look on Diltan's face. Wal thought about kicking him to make the expression go away.

As he contemplated the amusing notion, Cissy sighed and stood up. She motioned to the door that connected her rooms to Tasha's. "I guess we should talk about this. Come on, I'll fix us all some drinks."

Having seen the woman crumble with passion before, Wal believed he had a better idea. It beat giving Diltan and Cissy another opportunity to snipe at each other. Before his clanmates could make a move towards the door, he said, "Talking is so overrated."

Rolat and Diltan turned to him, their gazes questioning. Cissy gave him a surprised look. That delighted Wal. She'd startled him so many times, it was good to return the favour for once.

The delectable Earther recovered and smirked at him. "You should know. You do so little of it."

Wal offered his own challenge. "I listen to lawyers nitpick codes and laws and precedent all day. If we're going to court you, I prefer we dive right into the matter."

Her amazing blue-green eyes narrowed. "In what way?"

"Let us take you home and introduce you to our playroom."

A low growl, perhaps too low for Cissy to hear, issued from Rolat. Diltan's eyes widened.

Meanwhile, Cissy stared at him with confused amusement. "A *playroom*? I'm younger than you by a bit, but I'm not a child. What are three adult men doing with a playroom anyway? Do you have kids you haven't told me about?"

Wal spoke with the deadly quiet voice he used in court. It was the tone that got a lot of attention from troublesome prosecutors and defendants alike because of the threat in its undercurrent. "Oh, it's definitely not a room meant for little ones. This room, with all its toys, is one for grownups only."

Cissy's eyes grew large. Good. She'd heard the intimate menace he'd wanted her to hear. After last night, she had an inkling as to how demanding sex with his clan was. It tickled Wal to see the way she swallowed hard. He didn't want her afraid of him, but the Imdiko enjoyed seeing her nervous. Diltan seemed to relish her hesitation as much as Wal. "Where is the adventurous Matara we've gotten used to? My Imdiko, I do believe you've made her uneasy."

The challenge from the Dramok made Cissy ready to fight back. She folded her arms over her voluptuous chest. Her suspicious gaze met Wal's. "It's just that I'm not sure what you're up to. As we've discussed before, it's the quiet ones a girl should look out for."

Rolat confirmed, "In Wal's case, you would be right. There is a lot of evil behind that sweet face."

Diltan dismissed Cissy with a wave of his hand. "She won't go for it. Last night was her limit. This little Matara is brash up to a point… Then when you call her bluff, she runs."

"I'm not running from anything." Her jaw jutted out.

Cissy played right into their eager hands by getting pissed off enough to become reckless. This time drinking too much was not required and that pleased Wal. He ached to have her beneath him again, with no excuses to hide behind. Her rashness might be ill-advised, but in this case, the Imdiko was all for it.

His hopes were confirmed as she marched to the door that led out to the corridor rather than the one to her rooms. She gave them an impatient look over her shoulder. "Well, what are we waiting for? Let's go."

Wal was at her side in an instant and offered Cissy his arm. She took it with bravado, though he caught a glimpse of uncertainty in her eyes. He made sure his smile offered approval.

"As you wish, Matara. I am glad to see your spirit of adventure."

Wal walked her to the in-house transport, which would take them out of the complex.

How he looked forward to getting her into the playroom at home. There, they would find out just how adventurous little Cissy was.

* * * *

With Rolat and Diltan walking with them, Wal escorted Cissy to the cliff where the clan lived. It was a two-mile jaunt, giving the group time to talk. During their short journey, Cissy learned Diltan had been born into money (no surprise), that he'd felt uneasy about it (surprise) and that he'd gone out of his way to make his own way rather than rely on his parents' generosity (bigger surprise).

She also discovered Rolat had not set out to be a prison administrator but a Global Security officer. He said he'd been devastated when he hadn't been accepted by the organisation as a youth.

"It's not an easy task to be accepted in their programs," he told her. "You not only have to pass a lengthy testing process—"

"Which he did," Wal pointed out.

"But a lot has to do with who you know. People without connections face an uphill battle."

Diltan was quick to add, "They invited Rolat to apply again five years after his initial attempt."

The Nobek shrugged. "By then I was already making substantial gains in the Department of Penal Colonies. I had been awarded commendations, promoted twice and discovered that, while not as glamorous as Global Security, I enjoyed the work. I turned Global Security down."

During the walk, Cissy also found out that Imdikos typically didn't pursue work as lawyers and judges. Wal laughed, "My parents continually asked me if it was really what I wanted to do the entire time I studied law. We even argued about it. When it comes to the court system, my breed usually gravitates to advocacy for victims and defendants, along with support work. However, my Dramok father was a lawyer and it always fascinated me. I used to watch him argue cases. I knew that was what I wanted to do."

Diltan's smile for Wal was filled with pride, far more than when he'd talked about his own successes. "Wal was stunned when the Court General asked him to consider becoming a judge, but he merited the honour. His pursuit for real but compassionate justice has taken him all the way to the highest court on Kalquor."

Wal said, "Sometimes I still wonder if I'm equal to the task, but no one has told me I need to step down yet."

"They'd be fools to do so," Rolat declared with warmth.

"Absolutely." Diltan's tone filled with conviction.

Wal ducked his head and smiled. Cissy could tell their approval meant a lot to him. That they gave it without hesitation made her happy for some reason.

Moments later, they were at the beach-level entrance to the cliff where the three men lived. The sudden stab of anxiety told Cissy how at ease she'd become during their walk along the beach. She hadn't noticed she'd been conversing so comfortably with even Diltan, not until that casualness was gone.

By the time the transport opened to Clan Diltan's door, Cissy was downright nervous. As Wal ushered her into the home, she wondered why she felt so jumpy. She'd already had sex with them after all. Damned good sex in fact, the best in her life. Yet there was something dark and knowing lurking in their smiles that told Cissy they were up to no good.

"Lights up three-quarters," Diltan called as they entered the first room.

Cissy's unease disappeared as her surroundings lit up. Her mouth dropped open and she gasped.

"Wow. Wow!"

Cissy let go of Wal's arm and stepped away, turning in a slow circle to take in the immense space. It made her think of the ballroom in a fairy-tale castle. The stone walls, no doubt the rock of the cliff they were inside of, were polished to a marble finish. The floor beneath her feet was the same, though it was of a slightly deeper gleaming grey, as if it had been stained. Pillars on either side created alcoves where seating arrangements waited in rich gold and deep purple hues. Over those were huge paintings, the real things rather than vid projections.

The ceiling was similar to the lighting panels Cissy typically saw in Kalquorian walls, but it lit in complicated patterns that were as artistic as functional. There was even a raised platform along the far wall where a band might play. It was a grand and gorgeous space suitable for Cinderella's ball.

Cissy couldn't believe her eyes. She felt as if she should be wearing a silk and taffeta gown, hoping that Prince Charming might choose her from other maidens and waltz her about the room. Suddenly self-conscious, she looked down at her the scuffed boots, jeans and flannel shirt she'd thrown on earlier that day.

Talk about underdressed, she thought. *Fairy Godmother, where are you and the mouse-drawn pumpkin?*

She choked out, "You live here?"

To his credit, Diltan sounded a little embarrassed. "This room is much grander than the rest of our home. It's done this way because we throw the occasional get-together in this room.

Cissy gazed at him in wide-eyed disbelief. "Get-together, huh? Just you and your one thousand closest friends? No wonder you can hardly stand the sight of grubby little old me."

Diltan paled. His slight smile soured in an instant. He even looked angry. "You have a habit of dressing beneath yourself, but I would not call you grubby. Not by any means."

Cissy was newly startled when Rolat patted Diltan's crotch. "From the feel of things, my Dramok likes the sight of you just fine."

Wal chortled, the smile doing its usual magic of transforming his face into something beautiful. Diltan, who stood between the two, shoved them both aside and walked up to Cissy.

"Ignore them. Let me show you around and prove we're not as snobby as this room says we are."

He offered Cissy his arm. She took it with a lifted brow and grin. Diltan returned the smile, making something in her chest tight.

She drew a deep breath. *Oh, you merciless bastard. You are so charming when you want to be.* He'd actually looked affronted when she'd put herself down.

Diltan gave her a tour of the home. The dining room was as grand as the greeting/party room. "Well, it is part of the public area of the house," he explained when Cissy rolled her eyes at him. "We have dinner parties from time to time. Our private rooms are a better reflection of the men we are."

The rest of the home was indeed less intimidating to Cissy, but it was still luxurious. What Diltan referred to as the common room was outfitted like a family room on steroids. There was a huge lounging couch, three vid-enabled gaming tables, a massive vid and entertainment system, a bar and even a small kitchenette…and they already had an immense full kitchen near the dining room!

Plus the men had suites of their own, like self-contained apartments of three or four rooms each. There were no beds in the men's private suites, so Cissy was not surprised to see the separate sleeping room. It too was immense, with separate dressing rooms and lavatories for each man…plus an extra for their missing fourth clanmate.

The home boggled the mind with its endless string of rooms and the series of balconies that overlooked the ocean. Cissy had seen inns on Earth with less space.

Her favourite room by far was an atrium located in the centre of the house. It had a glass-like ceiling that could be retracted to open to the sky above. Much like the spa area of the Matara complex, it boasted a pool and carefully tended plots of flowers. Large circles of lavender and blue grasses dotted the tile flooring, inviting lounging. Cissy could imagine lying down in the softly scented bits of lawn to read or just stare at the clouds passing overhead.

The home of Clan Diltan was by far the grandest thing she'd ever seen. Even though she was the cousin to the empress, Cissy was out of her depth with such men.

She gave the three a wry smile. "You were right to court Tasha. She's a much better choice for a life like this."

Diltan fixed her with a stern look that made her stomach do flip-flops. In a no-nonsense tone, he told her, "You can stop that right now."

Cissy shook her head at him. "No, you have no idea. This is a place for someone ladylike, someone who knows what fork to use for salad course at high tea. I'm not that woman. I've always been a tomboy and a loudmouth. I got the most beatings at our school of any kid."

Rolat scowled. "They beat you?"

Cissy nodded. "A couple of times for not behaving as a lady should. I got into some fights. If anyone messed with Tasha, I'd pound on them or—"

She stopped. Cissy had once done something much worse than beat up a classmate for picking on her sister. Something terrible, something she dared not speak of.

She rushed through the rest of it. "I made them pay. Long story short, I don't do classy well. It's not me."

Rolat didn't look put off at all. "A protector for your sister. I see nothing wrong with a strong woman not afraid to speak her mind or defend those who she loves."

Diltan surprised Cissy by agreeing. "Neither do I. Although I have certain ideas on propriety, particularly when it comes to behaviour around the kind of men I work with, I know real class has nothing to do with how you dress or use your manners. It has everything to do with how you take care of those you love."

Wal gave her his devastating smile. "Absolutely," the quiet Imdiko said.

They were being so nice, even Diltan. Okay, especially Diltan. Cissy had to let them off the hook.

She looked around the atrium with appreciation, even though such settings were wasted on a rough-around-the-edges girl like her. "Your home is beautiful, but I'm not made for this. Thank goodness we aren't formally seeing each other as far as the lottery is concerned. You don't have to blow one of your five chances on me."

It was Wal who said, "I think that determination has yet to be made. Shall we move on?" Without waiting for Cissy to answer, he took her hand and tugged her out of the atrium and towards yet another room.

Cissy allowed herself to be led, though she couldn't help but wonder why they insisted on bothering with her.

Chapter Fourteen

Cissy stopped and stared at the room the men ushered her into next.

What the hell is this? Some sort of torture chamber?

Wal cracked up, his laughter echoing in the space. "From the look on your face, I accept your earlier statement that you never entered the pleasure club on your transport."

Cissy blinked. This was the home version of a pleasure club? She tried to see the various tables, benches and devices as a sensual playground, but the items were too foreign…too scary.

She told the men, "I'm almost afraid to ask what all this stuff is."

Rolat stepped beside her and looked about the room. Delight registered on his face, as if remembering many happy times. Then again, he was head of Kalquor's prison system and Kalquorians were known for brutal punishments of felons.

The Nobek's voice was easy as he said, "There is no reason to fear us. Anything you do not wish to try, we will respect."

Wal put his arm around her shoulders, tugging her close to his body. He guided her towards what looked like a low, padded balance beam, except it had tethers on its supports. With his arm holding her so firmly, Cissy felt both safe and vulnerable under his power. A thrill ran through her, sending a ticklish excitement straight to her pussy.

The Imdiko smiled, as if he knew the effect he had on her. "Here, let me explain the toys we have."

"Toys, my ass," she muttered.

Diltan's evil chuckle raised the hair on the back of her neck. "Some of them are for that, yes."

Cissy shot him a dirty look. He seemed amused at her reaction.

Wal directed her attention back to the balance beam, which was about at the level of his waist. "The spanking bench. As you'll note, your ankles would be tied to the supports. The loops on the other side are for your wrists, or you can hang on to them if you feel you can be trusted to submit to discipline."

Cissy swallowed. She liked spankings… She liked them a lot. Being bent over the bench had plenty of appeal, though she wasn't so sure about the implements hanging on the nearby wall. The black leather thing was most definitely a whip. The flogger was nearly as intimidating. There were straps of different widths and thicknesses, paddles of wood and leather and something that resembled a riding crop with a small, flat spatula head. Ouch.

She realised the men watched her, gauging her reactions. Could they tell that she found the bench itself arousing? That the whip flat-out scared her?

Wal moved her along to a pillar with tethers, enough to bind more than one person to it at a time. "This is used for bondage, also to mete out discipline. I think you'd look lovely stretched along it, surrendering to a light flogging."

"Light?" Cissy flushed to hear how breathy her voice sounded.

Wal glanced at Rolat, who nodded. The Nobek said, "Just enough to leave some pretty pink stripes on your back, ass and thighs. Maybe while you wear a clit stimulator with a vibrating dildo shoved inside your pussy."

That sent a stab of pure want through her body. Cissy almost moaned at the idea.

There were more objects to be trussed to, along with devices that would fuck a person in ways Cissy had never imagined. There was a basin which filled with a water-like liquid that Wal told her was safe to have sex in with no worries for bacteria or infection. A massage area. A corner of the room had balloon-like coverings that reminded Cissy of the bouncy-houses that used to be featured at kids' parties on Earth. She giggled to think of bad, bad Rolat or snooty Diltan careening off the black walls and floor while trying to have sex. Did they have that kind of playfulness?

Most of the room was dedicated to pleasures of the darker variety, however. Cissy had to admit it turned her on to think of being strapped to most of the apparatuses, made helpless while the men played with her.

She snorted disbelieving laughter to think of where she'd come from to end up here. "Back on Earth, we were told sex was not for any reason but to produce children. It was a sin that could damn your soul to engage in it for pleasure's sake."

Diltan made a face, showing Cissy what he thought of that line of reasoning. "Sex is more than breeding. It is discovery. Closeness. The opportunity to learn about each other physically and emotionally."

Cissy swatted a manacle hanging from a chain attached to the ceiling to set it swinging. So much of the stuff looked suited for a dungeon. "Yes, screaming in terror is an emotion," she cracked.

Rolat gave her a knowing half-smile. "You're not afraid. Oh, I see some reluctance here and there, but mostly you're excited."

"Says you."

"Says your scent." The Nobek's half-smile became the full item.

Wal chuckled. "You are aroused, little one. It's impossible to miss that aroma, especially since I grew so familiar with it last night."

Cissy squirmed. They could smell the honey seeping from her sex? As if she didn't feel vulnerable enough.

Diltan leaned up against a padded gadget that reminded her of stocks. He folded his arms over his chest and gave her a smug expression. "Aroused or not, I bet she doesn't let us try the first thing in here."

Damn it, she hated it when he acted superior. "Sure, I'll try something. Or is that wishful thinking on your part? Maybe you're the one who is intimidated by the idea of getting me in a compromising position."

He raised an eyebrow at her. His attitude stated she should make a decision.

Cissy snorted and gazed around the room. Now that the time had come to choose something to try, the room was a torture chamber again. Everything she considered was scarier than the last.

Rolat wandered over to something close to the middle of the room. The toe of his boot nudged a huge cushion with handles. "Why not this? You seemed interested in it when we showed it to you."

Happy to turn her back to Diltan, Cissy went over to Rolat. The cushion was a red wedge-shaped device meant to drape one's body over. The handles were perfect to hold on to if one needed to brace herself. It sat upon a mat that her boots sank into. The whole setup seemed soft, comfortable…and without anything that suggested helplessness or pain. It seemed harmless enough.

Rolat gave her ass a light pat. "Not one bit threatening, is it? A good toy to start with. However, there are some rules that go along with its use."

"Like what?" Cissy asked.

"Like you obey our every command. That you do whatever you are told without question."

Her mouth dropped open. "Complete obedience? Without question? Are you serious?"

Diltan's voice slid silkily into her ear. "That's the price of not being tied helpless, which this wedge doesn't allow. You have to give up all control to us."

Cissy frowned, both because the Dramok's too-kissable face was barely an inch from hers and because of what the men wanted. Giving up all control would not be easy for her.

"What if I hate what you're doing or telling me to do? Don't I get any say if it's the most horrible thing ever?"

Wal eyed the wedge with a smile. "Of course. You can end the whole thing at any time. All you have to do is say *sholt*."

"The word for stop," Cissy remembered. "So just to be clear on this. I let you guys order me around and do whatever you like to me, but if it's too much, then I can say *sholt* and you'll quit right away?"

Diltan nodded. "You give us the power we crave, but ultimately it still rests with you. It takes a certain amount of courage to play with Kalquorians, however. Experienced men, not the boys you've been carrying on with up until now. It's nothing to feel bad about if you think you can't handle us."

He was baiting Cissy and she knew it. Even being aware that he was goading her didn't keep her from getting mad at the challenge.

Cissy planted her hands on her hips, tossed her hair back and glared at the Dramok. "I've handled a lot worse than you, Diltan."

He shrugged. "If you say so. Is that a yes, Cecilia?"

She pretended her heart wasn't hammering fit to bust out of her chest. "Sure. We'll give this thing a shot."

Rolat rubbed his hands together. "Lovely. I have quite a few ideas after seeing your reactions to some of our toys."

"Which ones?" Spoken offhandedly, as if she didn't care. However, her gaze flicked worriedly to the whip hanging on the far wall.

Rolat grinned. "Why don't I surprise you? Strip."

The order was so abrupt that Cissy stared at him. The Nobek's smile faded, replaced by grim command.

In a tone that said Rolat expected immediate compliance, he said, "Are you going to cooperate with us or not? If you are, it starts now and you do what you're told. If not, say *sholt* and we'll take you back to your quarters."

Cissy thought she should bristle at his dictatorial attitude. Instead, her entire body flared hot. Every cell prickled with eagerness to know just how forceful the big man could be. Bending to his will felt like the only thing that mattered in that moment.

Hell no, she did not want to go back to her apartment. Not with that huge, strong man demanding her acquiescence.

It was only a lifetime of portraying the tough gal that kept Cissy from dropping to her knees before Rolat. It was also that steel that made her sneer, "Fine, oh lords and masters. I'll do what you want, no questions asked."

Diltan had his hatefully handsome smug face on again. "You know, I like the sound of that. You may call us 'Master' while we're in here."

Cissy's jaw dropped. "Seriously?"

"I insist. There will be no more of your smart mouthing, either. Speak with respect or be punished."

When Cissy stood there blinking in surprise, Rolat prodded her with the same commanding tone he'd used earlier. "How do you answer him, girl?"

A small part of her brain remembered Diltan was a jerk not deserving the title of master. However, the majority of her consciousness looked up at the three delicious beasts of men who were eager to do things to her body she couldn't contemplate…and she wanted to know what those things were. Cissy could not pretend the situation didn't excite her. She thought if she touched her pussy right at this moment, she'd explode with orgasm.

What the hell, she could call a stop to this at any point. If it came to that, she could tell Diltan where to stuff his 'master' bit. In the meantime, she'd see how things would play out.

Mindful of Diltan's warning to not smart off, Cissy gave him her blandest look. "Yes, Master."

There was a quick succession of expressions that flew across the Dramok's face. They went so fast that Cissy would have missed them if she hadn't been staring right at him. First came the startled widening of eyes, as if Diltan hadn't expected her to go through with it. Then the handsome features softened in a look of…gratitude?

Really? Was he that pleased with her going along with this? Ridiculously handsome Diltan appreciated getting laid with rough and loud *her*?

Before Cissy could contemplate that astonishing expression, Diltan's mien smoothed, giving him that cocksure attitude with a hint of smugness again. "Very good. Clothes off."

Cissy stripped, keeping her emotions to herself. She frowned a little at the marks her jeans had left on her waist. Great, just great, she was putting on weight again. Suddenly she could not look at the men's faces anymore. There they were, hot and muscled and perfect…and still clothed…while she stood there naked and chubby. Self-consciousness made an abrupt appearance.

Got to lay off the booze and sweets, she told herself. *A little fluff is fine, but I'm not buying clothes another size up! And I refuse to feel uncomfortable getting naked with these guys.*

No one said anything about her padding. Instead, Rolat rumbled, "Lay over the wedge. Put that gorgeous ass in the air."

Her heart thudded as Cissy moved to obey. She draped over the wedge, her hips fitting over the rounded apex of the triangular cushion. At least it was comfortable. It had just enough give to hold her gently, allowing her to sink a little into it. It would have been wonderful except she felt so damned vulnerable.

Wal's tone was quiet but no less commanding than his clanmates'. "Hold on to the handles. Spread your legs wide. Then do not move from that position."

Cissy again complied. Damn it, had she felt exposed before? With her ass in the air, legs spread, pussy on full display, she had never felt so open or defenceless. Her fists, clutched around the padded handgrips on either side of the wedge, tightened until the knuckles turned white.

Meanwhile, the three men went to the wall where the spanking implements hung. They muttered in their own language. Cissy had learned a little conversational Kalquorian, but the trio spoke too low for her to pick anything up. She strained up to see what they might select from their treasure trove of torment, but the broad backs kept the view hidden. If one of them grabbed that damned whip, she was out of there.

They turned and Cissy put her head down to keep them from seeing that she'd attempted to spy. One set of footsteps approached, heavy and deliberate. Another set, lighter, went somewhere behind Cissy and headed her way. Was the third man hanging back?

"Look at this lovely little girl, waiting patiently for her masters." Diltan's voice was all warmth, warmth that filled Cissy's chest.

"She is behaving quite well. You didn't think she would," Wal teased his Dramok.

"Diltan has been known to be wrong." Rolat chuckled.

That was answered by a snort. Cissy rolled her eyes at herself, feeling the fool. Of course she'd only heard two men approaching her. Nobeks were trained to be silent. As big as he was, Rolat would have made no sound as he walked.

He was silent, all right. When fingertips, raspy with callouses, stroked the inner lips of her pussy without warning, Cissy yelped and nearly flew off the wedge.

A heavy hand clapped down on one ass cheek. "Wound up, are we?" Rolat said in an amused voice. "Stay still, naughty girl."

Her butt throbbed from the strike, but the rest of her body sang from both that and the sensual touches to her female parts. Cissy groaned and made herself settle. "You startled me." At his silence, she belated added, "Master."

"I didn't ask you to speak, girl."

Well, wasn't that rude? Cissy glared at the padded mat beneath her. *So you want me to wait for permission, do you? I'll speak when I damned well want to, you goon. In fact, I'd make your ears burn right off your head if I hadn't agreed to play along. If you weren't making my undercarriage so damned happy right now. Aw, man, that does feel good. Fuck. I wish he'd shove those fingers in me.*

Her temporary pique faded fast under the Nobek's tender strokes. Trembling overcame her body as Rolat caressed. Juices ran hot over his fingers and Cissy's eyes rolled in her head. Dear heavens, it was all she could do to not kick the floor as passion surged through her gut.

"Sensitive little girl. The right man, the right touch, and you fall apart."

He made it sound like praise and Cissy couldn't help the glow of pride she felt. That in turn made her feel ridiculous. *Yeah, it's all me. Your wonderful magic hand has nothing to do with it.*

When Rolat removed his fingers from her eager flesh, the loss was very real. Cissy moaned a note of grief. The Nobek chuckled and patted her rear.

"Don't worry, little one. Your masters have much more in store for you."

She sensed the men moving, getting ready for something. Cissy wanted to raise her head and look over her shoulder to see what they were up to. A sense of preservation and fear that the play would end kept her in the position they'd demanded. Rolat's caresses had primed her for sexual delights.

A low hum sounded and Cissy went still. What was that? An instant later, something moved against her pussy again. More specifically, it moved against her clit. Gentle vibrations travelled through her most sensitive part, sending resounding pleasure through her body. She clutched the handles and groaned.

"Lovely," she heard Wal say through the roaring in her ears. "You like how that feels."

It wasn't a question for her to respond to. Cissy wasn't sure she could have formed words anyway. Profound bliss coursed. She caught herself straining back against the thrumming instrument Wal touched to her clit.

"All right, my Imdiko," Diltan said, his voice sounding a million miles away. "It's our turn now."

The vibrator disappeared. Cissy moaned and waited for whatever the men had in store for her next.

It was not what she expected. Something slapped her left butt cheek. The initial contact felt light, but then a brand of pain erupted there. Cissy cried out and stared over her shoulder.

High above her, Diltan grinned. He showed her the spanking instrument he held, the one that looked like a plastic spatula at the end of a crop. She thought she could feel the square imprint of it on her ass.

"Shit," she swore as sensation pulsed from the blow he'd landed.

"Surprise number two," said Rolat.

A streak of stinging hurt fell across her rear, missing where Diltan had whacked her. Cissy sucked in air and blew it back out. She turned her head to see the Nobek holding a crop—one without that flat square head—over her.

At least it's not the whip, she thought.

She'd no sooner had the notion when Diltan brought his instrument down on her right cheek. The smart made her gasp. Rolat followed that with his crop. Then another smack from Diltan. Another line of pain from Rolat.

The humming vibrator nestled against Cissy's clit and the throbbing grief disappeared. All was heat and excitement in an instant. Now she cried out for an entirely different reason.

As waves of pleasure filled her, something hard and slick pressed against her anus. A moment later, something thick—but not Kalquorian-cock thick—popped inside her. With the heat of spanked flesh and the enthralling pulses of the vibrator, the invasion was pure nirvana.

A small part of Cissy's mind registered Wal had placed an anal plug inside her to stretch the tight ring of muscles. Playing with Kalquorians these last few months had made the sensation almost routine. Routine, that was, until now. With everything else that was happening, the plug felt glorious.

Pleasure arced higher and higher. Cissy ground back against the wide surface of whatever Wal used on her, reaching for realisation. As soon as she did that, the Imdiko took the vibrator away.

Diltan and Rolat peppered her rear with their spanking implements. This time intensity sizzled where there had been pain before. It brought her no closer to orgasm, but overall passion increased, especially when Cissy thought of how she bowed to their punishment, as if she had no choice but to surrender to it. As if they were indeed her masters to be obeyed no matter the cost to her.

Yours. I am yours. I belong to you, to be done with as you please. My will is yours. My body is yours. Yours.

"Look at how she moves under discipline." Rolat's voice seemed to come from another planet. "Have you ever seen anything so perfect?"

"Lifting her ass for every strike." Diltan's delighted tone sang through Cissy's senses. "Even after last night, I never would have guessed she would give herself so well."

A few more strikes and the vibrator returned. Cissy screamed as shattering pleasure poured through her, driving her right up to the edge of orgasm. The vibrator disappeared. The plug was eased out then back into her ass. She sobbed, shifting her hips to fuck the thing, hoping it would somehow finish her off. Wal moved it around and around, stretching her, readying her.

Another quick touch of the vibrator. Cissy thought her head would blow clear off her shoulders then the excruciating pleasure backed off once more. Crop and spatula-crop pattered her ass. Another blast of ecstasy. More plug-fucking. More spanking.

When the vibrator touched her clit momentarily once more, Cissy shrieked, "Please! You're killing me! Please!"

Everything paused. Wal's voice was choked with humour. "She does ask nicely."

Rolat, just as amused: "Even if it is at a deafening volume."

Cissy sobbed. They would never let her come. Never.

Then Diltan's commanding tone silenced the tiny snickers of the other two. "She has served us without complaint. Now my Imdiko may serve her. Cecilia has earned her reward."

"Yes, my Dramok."

Heavy warmth lay over Cissy's shuddering body. Wal was there, his lips touching her ear as he whispered, "Are you comfortable enough on the wedge?"

'Comfort' wasn't exactly a word she would have used, not with her pussy pounding its need like a second heartbeat. But Cissy knew what the Imdiko asked.

"I'm fine in this position if it is what you wish, Master. Thank you."

His soft lips brushed her tear-streaked cheek. "Good girl. I'm going to reward you for your obedience."

She heard the sound of resealable seams parting behind her. A pair of heavy, slick lengths of heat thudded against her spanked rear. Cissy moaned and wiggled against Wal's livid groin. "Please," she whimpered again.

"Yes, sweet girl. Yes, good girl," he murmured into her hair.

Wal lifted a little of his weight, allowing him to hold the back of her neck with one hand. She felt his other fist close on the ends of his sexes, placing them so that they readied to enter her. Cissy tried to spread her legs even wider, begging him to enter and relieve the awful emptiness.

The Imdiko pressed in careful increments, his larger cock spearing into her ass. Cissy was still tight, but the plug, spanking and vibrator had made her eager. She strained to capture more of him.

His smaller back cock nudged into her soaked folds. She made a glad cry to feel him pushing into her, filling her as only a Kalquorian man could. Even better was the pressure of the twin girths pressing against the magic spot in her pussy.

As close as Cissy was to climax, Wal's careful movements kept her from coming. Some small part of her appreciated his caution, but impatience was more demanding. She tried to shove backwards onto the Imdiko. The grip on the back of her neck held her pinned to the cushion, however. She couldn't claim her prize.

She wailed a protest. "Please, faster! I need you, Master, please!"

Wal huffed a breathless laugh. "Your ass is tight, my girl. As much as I'd love to fuck you without care, I am not interested in hurting you. You will have to take what I give you at the pace I feel is best."

Cissy wailed again. She kicked the padding on the floor and strained to meet his groin. No good. She couldn't move. She needed to be fucked hard, but she couldn't make that happen.

Being overpowered by the man skewering her made arousal even worse. Knowing that she had no ability to take what her body demanded, that she was helpless to enact her will, brought excitement spiking in Cissy's gut. Her climax was dependent on the Imdiko and he could grant or withhold it from her on a whim.

Not caring that she'd lost all pride, Cissy sobbed the one word that thus far failed her in a long string of begging. "Pleasepleasepleasepleaseplease..."

And still Wal kept his methodical pace, ensuring her safety even as he drove her insane. She screamed in frustration.

His hand released her neck, wrapping around her hair to pull her head back. His breath warmed her cheek as he said, "What's the matter, naughty Cissy? Is Master making you wait? Is it making you crazy that you can't have what you want until I decide you can have it? If I decide you can have it?"

Cissy rolled her eyes to the side to look into the alien purple of Wal's. The hard light in them showed none of the Imdiko's usual gentleness. He appeared as dangerous as Rolat.

Shaken by the realisation that making demands on Wal could be every bit as perilous as doing so with his Nobek clanmate, Cissy whimpered, "I'll do anything you want, Master. Anything."

His grip in her hair tightened. "Yes, you will. Right now, you will hold still and take this nice, slow fuck I've decided to grant you."

Tears filled her eyes at his words. *Nice, slow fuck*. What he wanted. What she had to want because she had given herself to him. Cissy had no choice but to acquiesce.

A knowing smile quirked the corners of Wal's mouth. "That's it. You are here for my pleasure, beautiful slave. I can tell you like that. I feel your pussy trembling. I feel the wetness pouring from you over me. I feel how your body clutches at my cocks. You want to serve my desires."

A tiny sob drifted from her lips. Yes, she wanted him happy. But it was so hard to remember that when her body clamoured for him.

Those soft lips found hers, as if Wal would sip the torment from her mouth. His kiss was every bit as languorous and careful as the way he melded his body to hers. Cissy concentrated on losing herself in that embrace, filled with a heart-breaking sweetness.

She was so taken by the thorough gentle kiss that she didn't realise Wal had at last joined with her until his mouth drifted away from hers. His groin snugged up tight to Cissy's ass and pussy, buried to the hilt in her warmth. He smiled.

"You see? Now we are one, my lovely little servant. Now I have you and you have me in the most delicious way possible."

For some reason Cissy wasn't entirely sure of, she said, "Thank you."

"You are welcome. Now give me another of those kisses."

As his mouth closed over hers once again, Wal pumped, emptying and refilling her in smooth, easy strokes. His tongue slid over hers, lending greater pleasure to the fire blazing hot in her belly. Cissy moaned into Wal's mouth as sumptuous friction brought all her senses to life. She felt every stripe Rolat and Diltan had placed on her flesh, every rasp of Wal's rough tongue, every glorious inch of the cocks plumbing her depths.

Orgasm laid hold of Cissy, starting at the point where the Imdiko's cock rubbed wondrously against the hottest cluster of passion at the front of her pussy. From there it billowed out, suffusing her entire body. Wal held her head in place, swallowing her cries with his kiss as she combusted.

Even when the first massive surge of pleasure ended, endless ripples continued to make her moan steadily as Wal loved her. The Imdiko's pace quickened, maintaining Cissy's long, delightful orgasm as he sought his end. At last Wal groaned, his body straining as it draped over hers and he spent his passion.

Snuggled under the big alien's warmth, Cissy sighed. With Diltan's clan, she had become ruined for the younger, less experienced Kalquorians she'd been playing with. She could not imagine having sex again with those eager but naive men.

"I suppose I have to get up now," Wal mumbled after a few moments of recovery.

"I could always pick you up and throw you across the room to get you out of my way," Rolat said in a cheerful tone.

"I'll manage," the Imdiko said.

He rose, taking his weight off Cissy. "Thanks for laying on me in such a way as to not keep me from breathing," she smarted off.

Wal tweaked her nose. "Smothering my lovers is not one of my games, pretty girl," he laughed.

Cissy managed to get to her knees, but her legs felt wobbly. "I'm not sure I can stand," she giggled to the men.

"Then you may crawl," Rolat told her with the same grin he'd given Wal when he'd threatened to toss him. "This way."

Cissy blinked at the Nobek as he started to walk to the next play area, where a swing with straps depended from the ceiling.

Chapter Fifteen

Crawl? He couldn't be serious.

Noticing she didn't follow, Rolat stopped after two steps and turned to her. "I believe your master gave you an order, girl."

Cissy looked from the Nobek to his clanmates. Diltan's and Wal's expressions were alike in smiling confusion. The Dramok lifted a brow as she stared at them.

"Was his command not clear enough? What has you so stunned, Cecilia?"

"He told me to crawl."

"Yes, I did." Rolat's slight shrug told them he was as lost as his clanmates.

From her kneeling position, Cissy crossed her arms over her chest. "You don't think that's demeaning? Disrespectful?"

Rolat cocked his head. "In a scenario during which I have assumed power over you, no. I am the master and you are the servant. Having you crawl is a display of the control you have granted to me."

He came back over and knelt on the floor before her. "Have I done anything to make you feel I do not regard you as a beautiful and intelligent woman that excites me in body and mind?"

Cissy thought about it. "Up until now, no."

"Why is telling you to crawl different then? How is that so much worse than telling you to take a spanking, which causes actual pain?"

Cissy scowled. "I'm not a dog. I don't like being treated like one."

"What is a dog?"

The question gave her pause. Kalquorians didn't have dogs. "It's an animal we kept as pets on Earth."

"Like a wild animal in a zoo? Or more an animal put into service like kestarsh on farms and ranches?" Rolat's brow was drawn in the effort to figure the matter out.

It was Diltan who answered. "No, dogs are more like companions for Earthers, often treated like children. There have been petitions put forth in the effort to allow these animals onto Kalquor because they are held in such high regard by the Mataras. Our laws regarding alien species prohibit them because of the impact they might have on the natural order of our planet."

Cissy's eyes widened. "You don't have pets like that?"

Wal shook his head. "Here, it's considered unnatural to take an animal out of the wild to keep like a possession. We do need some work animals such as the kestarsh, and their captivity and breeding are heavily regulated. We know some aliens enjoy keeping animals as companions, but it is not something we Kalquorians do."

"We're getting distracted here," Rolat pointed out. "Cissy, when I tell you to crawl, it is not because I see you as a lower life form. I think I understand now where you might get that idea from, since many animals do crawl. In this instance, however, I am only maintaining our roles as master and servant. I am dominant to you and you crawling where I tell you to is an expression of the play." His eyes twinkled. "Besides, you said you couldn't stand yet. I thought I was doing you a favour."

Cissy felt a sense of relief at his words. Rolat had meant no insult. It was just part of the game. "I guess I took offence where there was none intended."

He shrugged. "A misunderstanding. If it bothers you, I will not insist on you crawling for me."

She felt foolish. "I've made a big deal out of nothing, apparently."

Rolat reached to brush a tendril of hair from where it had fallen over her face. For a man with such big, blocky hands, his touch was tender. Cissy found herself leaning her cheek into his warm palm.

He smiled at her gesture. "If it makes you the least bit uncomfortable, it is a big deal to me. Never feel you cannot tell me what bothers you. I will stop in my tracks any time you need reassurance."

Diltan added, "That goes for all of this clan. If one of us is not enjoying what's happening, then none of us will. Speak up any time you need to." He threw his head back to laugh. "As if I have to tell you to let me know what I'm doing wrong!"

They all chuckled at that.

Rolat gave Cissy a searching look. "Never doubt I have the utmost respect for you, Matara. Any female who threatens to make me a woman is one I'll watch out for."

Cissy snickered. "I need to stop being so obnoxious. But if you could have seen your faces when I told you that—it was worth it."

"Shall we continue then? And how shall we continue?"

She considered. She believed Rolat was not trying to make her feel bad about herself by commanding her to crawl. It was part and parcel of the scenario they had agreed to. She could live with that. And if it turned out she couldn't, she could always say *sholt*. More than ever, Cissy trusted the three men to respect her limits. Besides, seeing Rolat with that crop and feeling his strength was a huge turn-on. She liked being his to control.

She smiled at the Nobek. "I will crawl for my master."

He nodded and rose to his full height, towering over Cissy, making her feel small, making her feel vulnerable…but somehow making her feel safe as well. "Then follow me on your hands and knees. Be quick about it."

He moved over to the swing, Cissy crawling in his wake quickly to keep pace with his long strides. She waited for the sense of degradation to overwhelm her.

For a moment it sat on her heart, a tendril of hurt winding within. Then Rolat looked over his shoulder at her. The approval in his gaze warmed her, shrivelling that mote of discomfort. She saw something else in his expression as well—gratitude.

It really wasn't about him lording power over her. It wasn't about him degrading her. It was about him earning her trust enough for her to hand him control. The knowledge rocked Cissy, slowing her pace for a bare instant before she pushed herself to follow him even faster.

There was a lot of stuff going on behind their so-called play, she realised. They were building the foundations for something much bigger than mere sex games. Something for the future, perhaps.

They arrived at the swing. Rolat bent and lifted her in his arms. Cissy revelled in his strength, strength he would apply to her security should they stay together. Yes, there was plenty going on here beyond kinky play.

With that caring smile that made all concern melt away, Rolat placed her in the straps that served for a seat. She was surprised to find it was comfortable and supported her weight without a single creak.

It hung from two thick straps, which were hooked into the ceiling. There were soft fabric cuffs attached to those straps, which Rolat cinched around Cissy's wrists. The bonds stretched her arms all the way over her head, pulling her upright in such a way that her breasts were lifted high. The Nobek growled at the sight and lightly slapped the mounds. Cissy squirmed at the tiny stings that roused her libido from its sated state.

The wide strap that supported the back of her head had smaller straps that ended in adjustable loops. Rolat unfastened a loop and bent one of her legs up. Cissy gasped when he wrapped fabric around her thigh just above the knee and reconnected it to make it a loop once more. He tightened it around her leg, imprisoning the limb so that it was held high and wide.

"Any pain in the hip? How is your circulation?" the Nobek asked, running a finger between the loop and her leg.

"I'm okay," she said, sounding anything but. Her voice was higher than usual in a blend of nervousness and excitement. Rolat had trussed her like a sexual sacrifice, making her helpless to anything he might do to her.

He must have heard the emotion, because he chuckled deep in his throat. It was an evil sound that gave Cissy chills.

Rolat bound her other leg the same as the first. She was wide open to him now and unable to move.

He wandered away, going to some shelves where small items were scattered. Cissy couldn't see much beyond jars and bottles there. Rolat picked up a jar of golden liquid and something that resembled an artist's paintbrush. She doubted he was going to paint her portrait.

The Nobek's smile was just as evil as before as he approached her with the jar and brush. Cissy was dying to ask what he was up to, but didn't dare. She was afraid of the consequences of questioning her 'master'. Plus she wasn't sure she would like the answer even if he chose to give it.

Rolat opened the flip-top jar and stuck the bristles of the brush in, swirling it around to saturate them. Then he painted the golden-hued fluid all over her pussy. Cissy noted he caught any drips before they could reach her vulnerable asshole. She shivered to feel the soft bristles playing about her softest bits, especially her sensitive clit.

Rolat capped the jar and handed it and the brush to the nearby Wal. Cissy noted how the Imdiko, along with the watching Diltan, grinned from ear to ear. Fuck. Whatever Rolat was up to, it was something they looked forward to seeing her reaction over.

Rolat rubbed her breasts with the expectant air of a man waiting for something. As long seconds spun out, she thought whatever the stuff he'd used on her was supposed to do, it had failed. Not that she cared. She liked having her breasts played with. The big, rough hands massaging them were getting her juices bubbling all over again, sending warm tendrils of pleasure down to her sex…

Her pussy flared bright with heat. Cissy sucked a startled breath in as excitement suffused her sex.

"Ah, I see you are ready. We are going to play a little game now. I am going to try to make you come and you are going to try not to."

Cissy stared at him as her parts below spasmed with desire. The warmth had a little tingle to it now, making the very air currents feel good. Had the Nobek lost his mind? With this kind of enticement, why on Kalquor would she deny herself orgasm?

Her disbelief must have shown, because Rolat gave her that stern look he did so well. "Every climax you have means a swat from Diltan's paddle when he takes his turn with you."

He nodded toward the Dramok, standing a little off to one side. Diltan stood there with a huge smile and an even bigger wooden plank. Cissy's eyes widened to see the paddle. He'd break her ass with that thing.

Rolat tried to remain firm, but Cissy detected the way the corners of his mouth trembled, as if restraining laughter. "You understand the rules then. Let's begin."

He held out his hand. Wal brought him what appeared to be a thick wand with a fat, round cushioned tip. Rolat thumbed a switch and it hummed loudly.

Shit. Cissy knew the trouble she was in right away. Before she could brace herself, Rolat pressed the vibrating tip to her clit.

The soft surface of the thing thrummed hard and fast against her avid flesh. The heat and tingling exploded in her clit. Her whole body galvanised, every mote of her consciousness coalescing on that bright exaltation that erupted within seconds.

Cissy strained and screamed in the swing as climax stampeded through her. She'd barely finished tumbling from the first swell of rapture when Rolat stepped away.

As she sobbed in violent gasps, Rolat turned to the chuckling Diltan. "That's one. You'd better warm up your arm, my Dramok. From how fast she gave in, I think you're going to have quite the workout."

"Fine by me. This little lovely has been a thorn in my side since she got to Kalquor."

Rolat moved close once more. "All right, Cissy. Let's see if you can do better this time."

Cissy tried to assemble her thoughts and her will. She must not allow another orgasm. She was not going to give Diltan the satisfaction of punishing her.

However, her libido had fully awakened. She'd been stopped before her climax had enjoyed its full expression. Plus her pussy was sensitive from the stuff Rolat had smeared all over it and the vibrator neared her trembling flesh once more…

Sensation blasted through her. Cissy didn't feel it just in her pussy but in her entire body. Vicious bliss shot straight up her spine and into her skull. Orgasm ripped through her once more, heralded by her shrieks.

This time Rolat didn't take the vibrator away. He ground it against her pussy, making her take the brutal excitement. Another lurch of ecstasy barrelled through. Cissy writhed in the swing, trying to get away from the vibrator. She was unable to do so and she rent the air with cries of release.

Only then did her tormentor back off. Cissy sobbed in her binds, her whole body shaking in reaction.

When she could see again, Diltan's delighted leer was the first thing to come into view. "Two that time. I would love at least five, my Nobek."

Rolat nodded, looking obscenely happy. "I would be delighted to comply. Here it comes, Cissy."

She kicked and cried out as the humming machine closed in on her swollen pussy. Rolat took his time about touching her, prolonging the anticipation. Cissy steeled herself but the battle was already lost. She could not resist that thing. Diltan could threaten her with the paddle forever and a day and Cissy would not be able to keep from coming. She was too sensitive and the vibrator was too strong.

The vibrator was on her again, shuddering against the tender flesh of her sex. Pleasure swelled, grew big and exploded. Cissy squalled as elation had its way with her once more.

When Rolat relented, she hung limp, sobbing helplessly. The Nobek was a demon. Worse than a demon. Cissy had never known pleasure could be an instrument of torture.

The Nobek sighed, his expression damned near joyful. "Lovely, lovely. I am enjoying our game, little girl. Obviously, you are, too. What a beautiful mess you are with your body perspiring and your makeup running. So exciting."

He got her again, renewing her screams. "Oh yes. Stunning, my pet. You're so wet. Wet and wide open for me. By the ancestors, it's too much."

Rolat tossed the vibrator aside. Cissy felt like screaming again, but this time in relief. Yet her reprieve was all too brief. The Nobek opened his trousers, releasing his cocks. Nearly shaking in excitement, he grabbed her hips, simultaneously pulling her close and stepping forward to thrust inside.

He took her hard and fast, just as she'd wanted Wal to do earlier. This time, however, Cissy was not seeking relief. She'd gotten her thrill and then some. Yet her pussy remained warm and aroused, no doubt from the hateful liquid. Rolat's cocks stretched her with their combined girth, rubbing interior hotspots with ceaseless friction. His groin chafed her exposed and swollen clit.

Climax yawned wide yet again to consume her. Cissy surrendered with a mournful groan, knowing she had no choice but to let it have its way.

Rolat's head fell back and he yelled to the ceiling the moment before he let go. Veins stood out on his bare arms as he strained against her, filling her.

"Fuck. Fuck," he moaned as his cocks continued to jerk. "Fuck."

He was beyond any other words for at least two minutes. Cissy didn't care if he never spoke again. She didn't care if he never moved again. Her guts felt turned inside out.

At last the Nobek revived. He kissed her lips, his body still shuddering in the aftermath. At least it wasn't just her that had been so greatly affected.

Wal pressed water to her lips as Rolat and Diltan freed her from the swing. Cissy was hydrated but nowhere near recovered as Diltan slung her over his shoulder and walked to another area of the playroom.

Oh hell, she was due a paddling from the Dramok. Cissy had no strength to resist. She didn't even have the strength to protest.

She found the energy to whimper when he placed her in the stocks, however. First, the medieval-looking instrument was lowered so that she was forced to kneel to rest her head and wrists in the padded holes. Cissy wondered if Diltan positioned it out of consideration for her shaking legs or because it was such a subservient pose. Either way, the paddle was long enough for him to wear her out without having to bend the least little bit to reach.

Before he went to work on her poor, defenceless ass, Diltan came around to kneel before her. His expression was forceful, his eyes intent with power. With a sense of resignation, Cissy felt her libido perk up yet again. Damn that beautiful man and his dynamic personality.

Diltan's smile was appreciative. "You are a beautiful mess. I've never had a woman who would allow her makeup to smear, to let herself appear so well-used."

Hell, was she that wrecked? Some of her hair hung over her face in tangled clumps. Oh no. It was unfair that she should look anything less than her best around this gorgeous man. She was overwrought from the intense emotions of the last hour. Tears came to her eyes.

Diltan brushed them away when they spilled over. "No, don't cry. Don't you know how sexy a well-loved woman is? How exciting you are right now? Haven't you noticed what you are doing to me?"

He gestured to his crotch. His trousers strained to hold his arousal, the seam slightly unsealed. The fabric was dark, too, telling Cissy that he lubricated freely.

She was captured in the stocks, incapable of doing anything to the Dramok, and yet she felt a jolt of power. Cissy might be imprisoned, but somehow she was the one with a hold on the man before her.

The moment her eyes turned off the waterworks, Diltan gave her his smug smile. "I believe I owe you five swats, my lovely. Plus, my cocks are eager to fill you. You may be ready to call it quits, however. Do you wish to say *sholt*? I understand if you cannot take any more."

Cissy would have preferred to claw her own eyes out over coming yet again. Yet Diltan's superior expression had its usual effect on her—she'd be even quicker to claw her eyes out than to lose to him. It didn't matter that she knew he was being genuinely kind and not arrogant. Even his consideration was a challenge to her. She would meet it if it killed her.

She arched a brow at him. "Absolutely not. Unless you're the one ready to call it quits?"

Diltan chuckled. "That just earned you an extra swat, my headstrong girl. Feel free to keep pushing me."

Oops, she hadn't intended to get into more trouble. As Cissy eyed the paddle Diltan held, her retort died on her lips. She didn't dare mouth off to the Dramok when he was on the brink of whacking her with it.

Diltan looked behind her and jerked his head. Wal and Rolat stepped forward into her field of view.

"Rolat and Wal will be right here to keep an eye on you. I know you're tired and perhaps overwhelmed. The moment you need this to end, tell them."

Her gaze jerked from the monstrous paddle. Diltan's eyes on her were searching, concerned. Caring.

For a moment, Cissy was struck dumb by the Dramok's expression. Where was the pompous jerk who pushed all her buttons? Who was this man, this gorgeous, warm creature watching her with compassion in his eyes?

Somehow, she managed to choke out, "Yes, Master." She told herself that she spoke with her heart in her voice because she didn't want to give him a reason to spank her longer than what she was already in store for. Certainly it wasn't because she'd do anything right this moment to keep that kind look Diltan gave her. The look that said he might feel affection for someone as rough around the edges as Cecilia Salter.

Not possible. But Cissy felt warmth under what appeared to be genuine fond regard.

Diltan gave her a nod. His smile—a real smile, not the superior smirk that drove her nuts—never faltered. His gaze held Cissy's as he moved towards and around her, their eyes staying locked until he disappeared behind the stocks that held her.

Wal and Rolat knelt before her. Their expressions were as tender as Diltan's had been as they both reached to stroke tangles of hair back from her face.

"He will not be vicious," Wal told her in a low voice. "This is, after all, about pleasurable pain. But you must speak up if it gets too much. We have been playing strenuously, after all."

Rolat added, "Do not let pride keep you from calling out. As much as you two lock horns, this is not a competition. Be responsible, Cissy."

Before she could respond, there was a loud and happy sigh behind her. "Gorgeous from all angles. I am going to enjoy wearing this ass out in so many different ways."

Cissy thought of that huge paddle he held and her mouth went dry. When Diltan gently patted her ass with a warm palm a moment later, she squealed. Her face flushed in embarrassment. She'd let herself get keyed up.

His chuckle made her clench her fists. "All right, since you sound so impatient to begin. I won't draw the anticipation out any longer, my dear. Relax. A tensed butt makes it hurt worse."

Fuck, Cissy thought. *I don't think I can relax.*

The first swat from the paddle was anticlimactic. It made a soft thud against her butt. Cissy drew a sharp breath at the contact, but there was only a light tingle of pain and generous heat from the strike. She looked at Wal with surprise.

The Imdiko burst out laughing. "I think she believed you would knock her across the floor, my Dramok! You two need to develop better understanding."

"Hmmph," Diltan grunted. "She deserves a real walloping for assuming I was out to hurt her."

Cissy scowled. She didn't miss that she was a little mad that it hadn't hurt more than it did. She'd psyched herself out for nothing!

"Don't worry," Rolat said. "This is one of those things that builds in pain as it goes on."

He was right. Diltan continued to paddle her ass with light strikes. By the time he reached the fourth strike, Cissy's butt felt blistered and her skin sizzled with hurt. She especially felt it where he and Rolat had already striped her ass. She panted as she readied for the next blow. By that time, she blessed the extra fluff she'd put on her body that cushioned the paddle.

Number five burned like fire. Cissy yelped on that one and her body instinctively tucked in an effort to shield herself from the final spank. However, there was nowhere to go. She was stuck and at Diltan's mercy. As usual, the situation had her excited as well as suffering. She cursed her libido and wished she didn't like discipline so much.

She could hear the laughter in the Dramok's tone. "One more, my precious servant. No hiding now. Stick it out there for me like a good little slave. Take your punishment, bad girl."

Cissy ground her teeth together to keep from telling Diltan where he could shove his paddle. She didn't need to be giving him any ideas that might rebound on her, after all. It was one more swat. Just one more. It meant pain, but it also meant pleasure. She could handle it.

Even with psyching herself up, it still took a lot of fortitude to obey Diltan. Tilting her butt up, inviting that final swat, made her wince with anticipation. It also made another kind of heat roil in her gut. Cissy had no choice but to admit she liked being under the Dramok's control.

Instead of giving her the expected whack, he caressed her ass. She groaned at the contact, which sent thrilling sparks of hurt through her flesh. Cissy pressed back into the painful petting.

"Sweet girl," Diltan said. The approval made Cissy smile. Then two of his fingers shoved deep into her pussy, making her squeal. "Very sweet girl. So wet for your master."

He pumped in and out, flicking his thumb over her clit until Cissy moaned in continuous bliss. Her hips rocked in tandem with the thrusts, welcoming effervescent delight to the fore.

"Pretty little Cecilia," Diltan sighed. "I think you want to come for me, don't you?"

"Uh-huh," she breathed, feeling the first delicious spark that heralded release. "Master."

His thumb ceased flicking and stroked a thought-stealing circle over her straining nub. "That's right. Closer and closer. It feels so good to give yourself to Master."

"Aahhh." Cissy's whimper was a high note, almost like singing. A stronger spasm shot through her pussy, choking the sound off. Her sex seemed to gather itself, readying to explode.

"That's it. Almost there now. Let it go."

Cissy arrived right on the verge, only seconds away. Her pussy tightened around the driving fingers, drawing on them.

"Here you are. Excellent."

Diltan's fingers disappeared. Barely a second later, the paddle cracked against Cissy's ass.

She detonated. The blast of hot, ecstatic pain provided the final push into orgasm. Cissy's pussy seized, carrying her into rapture.

The first swell of passion had barely ebbed when Diltan's thick cock pressed into her. He took her in one smooth thrust, filling her pussy with his primary dick while the second rubbed hard against her clit. Another bolt of elation shot through her body, taking her far from conscious thought.

Cissy was vaguely aware of being fucked hard and fast by the Dramok. Some part of her knew that was why the seizures of desire rampaged over and over, leaving her screaming. It was an eternity of vicious delight before the body behind hers stilled, but for the shudders that accompanied the sensation of the interloper within her twitching.

In the wake of the intense climax, Cissy's mind drifted. Everything turned floaty and dreamlike. Hands drifted down to release her from the stocks, arms gathered her close to a strong chest and she was swept from the playroom. The corridor drifted past. She was borne to another room, an immense washroom where a bathtub the size of a small pool waited filled with water.

In her fuzzy state, Cissy watched Diltan and Wal disrobe, showing off their gorgeous bodies. They descended into the basin and she was handed down to them. The water was heated to the perfect temperature. A cup of cooler water was pressed to her lips. Then Rolat was in the huge tub, too, smiling down at her.

Their voices were distant as they spoke. Cissy was too caught up in the warmth of the bath, of the secure feeling of arms around her to hear what they said. She smiled at the men. Their faces stretched in laughter.

Hands stroked and rubbed all over next, washing her. Every now and again, water and protein drinks were offered for her to sip. She took her time about coming back to the world. She luxuriated in the wonder of being doted on. It was the sweetest sensation she'd ever known, on the heels of being roughly and thoroughly satisfied. She could have spent eternity like this, with these three men.

* * * *

Diltan had never thought of himself as possessing many Imdiko tendencies, but tending to Cissy gave him an incredible rush. Seeing to her needs when she didn't have the ability to take care of herself made him feel stronger than any other time of his life. Nothing compared to it—not proving himself capable of amassing his own fortune and not rising in the political arena.

He'd had hints of it before with Rolat and Wal. There had been times when he'd taken care of his clanmates in some form or another. But they were strong men in their own right. Diltan's experiences in having another lean on him so completely had been nothing compared to this.

All his irritation with Cissy's brash ways, with her impetuous rush into experiencing life after being kept under Earth government's thumb for so long—which he now understood—all of that had vanished. Seeing her soft and vulnerable, feeling her melt trustingly in his arms, knowing what lay beneath that frantic need to be her own woman had him enraptured. Diltan could see what his Imdiko and Nobek saw—a potential lifemate. Cissy was a woman he felt a need to care for and keep secure.

How could he do that when trouble for all of Kalquor peeked over the horizon? The worries he'd had over Zarl's records came back tenfold. If the things he'd uncovered and unwisely divulged to Maf incited real unrest, would it put Cissy in danger? Or, ancestors forbid, what if it fomented outright rebellion? Earther Matara abductions had lessened recently, mostly due to more stringent safeguards. However, the Basma was determined to rid the Empire of its last hope for survival. Cissy and all the other women could find themselves in a great deal of danger in the next few days.

It was not a matter to be discussed now, if ever. Particularly since Wal might be called to judge the matter if Imperial Fathers Yuder and Tidro were brought into his court to answer for Zarl's misdeeds. Yet Cissy's safety hung in the balance. She needed to know how precarious the situation might become. Wal and Rolat needed to know if they were to help protect their potential Matara.

As awareness inched its way into Cissy's gaze, Diltan made his decision. He prayed that this time it was the right one.

He smiled down at the lovely woman nestled against his side. "How are you feeling?"

She blinked at him, her blue-green eyes halfway between dreaming and awareness. "Weird. My brain feels like it's coming out of a fog. That whole thing we just did…it was crazy. Crazy but wonderful."

Wal cuddled close to her. On his opposite side, Rolat smiled. "I'm glad to hear the wonderful part."

"I quite enjoyed myself," Wal said with joy that matched the Nobek's.

Cissy returned the smiles. However, her look sobered when she glanced up at Diltan. "Okay, what did I do wrong this time?"

He started. "Not one damned thing. You were amazing and I thank you for sharing yourself with us. I know it can be a difficult thing making love to such demanding men, especially when you are a demanding woman."

She stretched. To his delight, she cuddled against his side once more. "I am demanding. I worry a lot, especially about Tasha. She's the nice one of the pair, you know."

Wal snorted and raked his fingers through his mass of curls, making the cloud of hair stand out in crazy corkscrews. "I don't know any such thing. I find you nice in many ways."

"Wickedly nice," Rolat added. "The kind of nice a horny Nobek enjoys very much."

The three men chuckled. Cissy shook her head at them, though a smile played at her lips. She rolled her eyes at Diltan. "*You* know what I mean. Tasha is such a good person, so ladylike. I've always needed to stand up for her and make sure she's not hurt, along with being tough for myself. What just happened here…I had to give up control. I had to give myself over to you."

Diltan nodded. "That had to have been scary. You had a moment or two of being uncomfortable."

"A little. A lot of it was a relief. Even getting my rear beaten was—I don't know. How can I explain it? It was all out of my hands. I didn't have to think or worry or do anything but put up with you guys and your freaky urges."

That brought another round of laughter and they nodded their understanding.

Diltan said, "You got to go on a little holiday. No responsibilities except to do as you were told."

"I was free. I let you make the decisions for me and nothing awful came of it." She cocked a warning brow at him. "Don't think I'm going to make it a steady diet, though. I like being away from all those awful laws and rules of Earth telling me how to act and live my life. I'm not about to hand you control over everything I do."

Rolat stroked the back of her head. "Nor would we want you to."

Wal agreed in a firm tone. "I have enough trouble trying to keep these two in line. Corralling three of you would be way too much effort."

Diltan told Cissy, "We do our best to not let our domineering personalities interfere with each other, at least not where career and such are concerned. Believe it or not, I do let my clanmates have a vote in the things that concern us all."

Rolat made a gruff sound in his throat. "Then he tries to do as he wants anyway."

Diltan gave him a wry look. "When was the last time you let me get away with that?"

"Never."

Cissy laughed and the Dramok shrugged. "In the realm of sex, however…we do become assertive."

She gave him a mock look of chagrin. "That's one word for it."

"How did you feel about submitting to us?"

Cissy frowned a little. She didn't answer him right away, debating whether or not she should answer at all.

If they were to have a real go at making her the clan's Matara, Diltan needed to nip Cissy's reticence in the bud right away. In a firm tone that managed to not be too demanding, he said, "Cecilia, we cannot have a relationship without the truth. We must be open to each other when it comes to such matters. Answer me right now—how did you feel about surrendering control to us?"

"Right." Cissy's mouth dropped open in shock, as if he'd surprised the answer out of her before she could stop it. Her stammering attempts verified that. "I mean—I don't want—oh shit."

Wal twirled a strand of her hair around one of his fingers as he strove to calm her with understanding.

"It's not something to be frightened of, you know. It's apparent that you have a natural need to be able to give yourself up to men you feel safe with. You need that space where you know you will be cared for. We have provided that for you and you responded."

Rolat chimed in. "It got scary every now and again. Upsetting even. Keep in mind that though we can be demanding, you have nothing to fear from us. We just like making you a little nervous."

His smirk made Cissy kick out at him. She gave him her patented scowl and Diltan was glad to see it aimed at someone else for a change.

Cissy said, "Fine. It feels good to let everything go with you three. I guess something in me recognises I can trust you."

Her words reminded Diltan of how vulnerable she could be if things went bad in the Empire. Having visited the Matara Complex twice now, he thought of how it was well guarded against intruders who might try to sneak in. But would it withstand an angry mob bent on creating havoc?

Cissy's impatient tone roused him from his thoughts. "There you go again with that worried expression. Maybe it's time you share a little truth, too. What's up with you, Diltan?"

He looked at her. Damn it, she was lovely. More importantly, she was smart. Cissy would keep him on his toes if she was his Matara. The idea that she might join his clan was no longer so farfetched. It scared Diltan.

He said, "There is trouble coming to Kalquor. It could be big and I'm certain the Imperial Family is going to suffer for it. As part of Empress Jessica's life, you could be in danger."

As Cissy's eyes widened and his clanmates stared at him, Diltan addressed his Imdiko. "Wal, what I'm about to say could affect you as a judge and it's unethical for me to share it with you in particular. However, for Cissy's sake, it might be for the best if you know in advance what I should keep secret from you."

His Imdiko stared at him in surprise. Then he glanced at the woman between them and his expression firmed. He raised his gaze to Diltan once more. "If it affects Cissy, I want to know. I can always recuse myself from any proceedings I have no business presiding over."

Diltan took a deep breath. Let it out. And told them all about Zarl's records, Maf's reaction to their contents and his own fears of how the news would rock the entire Empire.

Wal's face became drawn, confirming Diltan's fears of the legalities of what the Imperial Family would face. Rolat also appeared grim.

Cissy's expression hovered between concern and confusion. "Could the public finding out all this really bring on a full rebellion?"

Wal snapped a nod. "It is a possibility. At the very least, there will be protests, especially if a large portion of the Royal Council is called into question. Damn it, Diltan, this could get ugly."

"I know. I wish I had kept it a secret."

Wal shook his head and reached to squeeze the Dramok's shoulder. "That would have ended with your reputation in shambles. Scholars would have gone over the documents and discovered the matter at some point anyway."

It helped Diltan's conscience a little to realise his Imdiko was right. Still, the impending trouble allowed little of the dread to be alleviated.

Wal offered a tight smile that was probably supposed to be comforting. "So much of historical significance happened at the end of Clan Zarl's reign. No, you did the right thing."

Rolat blew out a heavy breath. "There is little doubt the Empire will experience a tremendous upheaval, perhaps within a few days. The leaders of the would-be rebellion will make this their rallying cry."

Cissy looked from one man to the next, worry clouding her pretty face. "Can it be avoided? I mean, you're talking about the potential for civil war, aren't you?"

Rolat considered. "A lot will depend on how the current Imperial Clan handles it. It's going to be natural for Emperor Clajak to protect his surviving fathers. However, if the entirety of Clan Zarl ordered those abductions, then the surviving members have to stand trial both here and at the Galactic Council. It's the only way to keep the peace."

Diltan thought of the furious disbelief on Clajak's face earlier that day. The Dramok Emperor had shown himself to be a man of honour since assuming the throne, devoted to the good of the Empire. Yet there could be little doubt he would want to protect Imperial Fathers Tidro and Yuder…and if he did, all hell would break loose.

The safety of Kalquor and its people depended on whether Clajak's loyalties lay most with his kingdom or his fathers. Diltan wondered which side would win…or if there would be nothing but losers in the end.

Chapter Sixteen

Feeling hungover from fatigue, Cissy walked down the corridor of the Government House's Imperial Level. She'd commed ahead to make sure Jessica had time to see her. Her cousin's Imdiko receptionist had responded with a warm, "The empress always has time for her family."

That might change in the near future if things get as bad as Diltan fears, Cissy thought when she got off the com. She had the feeling Jessica's life, along with that of her clan, would be turned upside down by the coming revelations.

She was tired, though it only bothered her here and there. Mostly she basked in the sleepy feeling and wonderful aches that reminded her of the night before. After giving her a bath, Diltan's clan had taken her to their bed and tucked her in between their magnificent bodies. Cissy had fallen into a deep, dreamless sleep that had ended all too soon with her companions waking early to prepare for their workdays. Wal had made a breakfast that was more like a feast. He'd also seen to it that her clothes had been laundered and pressed so she wasn't forced to put on grubby things. Cissy had teased him that he made for a great wife.

She'd known about the strange Kalquorian tradition of men feeding the women. Cissy protested it, of course, because she was an independent woman who didn't need to be fed like a baby. Rolat laughingly put her in a headlock and Diltan used the opportunity to smear iced pastry over her lips and chin. Then Rolat licked her face clean, making sure he kissed her into arousal in the process. After that, Cissy didn't argue about being given a food facial or what came of it afterward. She'd ended up making the men late for work that morning. She did not apologise and no one complained.

Wal had accompanied her back to the Matara Complex. "I hope to see you again soon," he said in his quiet but intense voice.

Cissy grinned. "I think you can bet on that."

Cissy had been sure Tasha would still be asleep. Guessing that Jessica would have to rise as early as other gainfully employed people on Kalquor, she'd made her appointment to see her cousin. The receptionist told her to come right over.

With the large breakfast in her belly reminding her of how displeased she'd been with her figure the night before, Cissy elected to walk. The morning air was cool, the skies were blue and she set off with memories of Clan Diltan's playroom in her head and a cup of coffee in her hand.

An hour later, she arrived at the Government House. The late night, early morning and walk were telling on Cissy by then. She yawned as the in-house transport deposited her in the palatial corridor of the Royal Chambers.

The interior of the cliff's rock had been polished to a high sheen from the floor to the arcing ceiling. A rich runner of soft carpet ran the length of the long hallway, which was lined with the red-uniformed Royal Guards. Had Cissy not indulged in Clan Diltan the night before, she might have viewed the muscled and armed Nobeks guarding the Imperial Clan like a buffet. As it was, she gave them an appreciative but passing glance once she let them confirm she was Jessica's blood.

Emperor Clajak's love for fine art was in evidence from the gorgeous paintings hanging on the walls to the exquisite statuary that dotted here and there. Cissy was impressed to see a couple of Earther pieces as well, rescued from her destroyed world. It made her smile while her eyes misted to recognize pieces from home.

Despite half a dozen other early birds waiting in Jessica's reception room, the empress's aide waved Cissy through to the inner chamber. Jessica greeted her with hugs and kisses. Cissy was just as happy to see her cousin. After being apart for so many years, the joy of reuniting had not dimmed.

Jessica eyed her with a delighted smile. "Look at you! You seem relaxed and happy."

Cissy shook her head in pretend humiliation. "For the most part. True to my contrary nature, I'm seeing a clan with a Dramok I could kick in the ass on a regular basis."

Jessica pulled her over to a seating area consisting of a low, polished table and billowing seating cushions. "Why am I not surprised? So Diltan drives you crazy, huh? No reflection on you because you're wonderful, but I'm surprised he swapped out Tasha. He's got a thing for appearances. I didn't think he'd go for the jeans and T-shirt type."

Cissy stared at the younger woman as Jessica plopped on a cushion. "How did you know?"

Jessica poured herself a cup of coffee from the carafe sitting on the table. Cissy noted the room, with its elegant pieces of furniture that belonged in a mansion, was still arranged for comfort. The effect was cosy, far warmer and more home-like than the corridor outside.

Jessica motioned for Cissy's cup and refilled it. "You're my cousin. That means your activities are scrutinised and gossiped over relentlessly. People are dying to know if Tasha and the rest of us are ready to disown you for stealing her clan."

Cissy sank down next to Jessica with a groan. She'd never expected to be a subject of rumour, not over dating a clan. "You have got to be kidding me."

Jessica gave her a wry smile. "Welcome to the Imperial Family, babe. So what's up besides your incredible love life? There is an incredible love life, right?"

"Incredible would be one word for it." Cissy thought about the playroom. A big, unselfconscious grin bloomed on her face. Once again, she felt all the aches from the night before, aches she thoroughly enjoyed at that moment.

Jessica laughed outright. "Being with three men who want to rule and serve you at once. It's good stuff."

"Damn right it is."

"So did you come here to fill me in on all the dirty details? They'd better be dirty, cuz."

Cissy shook her head at the roguish look on Jessica's face. "I'm sure you have a few tales of your own, but no, I'm not here to brag on my love life. I wanted to check on you."

Jessica sipped on her coffee, merriment leaking from her face. "I take it your pillow talk wasn't all about future dates then."

"Diltan told me about Imperial Father Zarl's records and the trouble they could cause. Could it really erupt into a full-blown rebellion here on Kalquor?"

Jessica set her cup down and met Cissy's eyes. The worry in her gaze was palpable, answering the question before her words did. "I think it could. We're in a hell of a spot, Cissy."

"Diltan says it could mean putting the Imperial Fathers on trial."

Temper sparked in the younger woman's face. "Clajak's dead set against it, as am I. But how can we not allow it? On one hand, I'm not about to serve up Zarl's legacy and Clajak's other two fathers to those who would demand they pay for Armageddon. On the other, to not do so will invite the anger of those who want to blame them."

Cissy pointed out what she thought was the best point of defence. "It's not Kalquor's fault Earth's cities were rigged by our leaders to blow up in the event of an invasion."

Jessica was just as quick to voice what Diltan and Wal had the night before. "No, no one could have ever predicted that. Still, it would never have happened if the Empire hadn't abducted all those Earther women."

Cissy rolled her eyes at the conundrum. "What was Kalquor to do? Roll over and die? You know if the shoe had been on the other foot, Earth would have felt justified doing the same thing."

Jessica sighed. "It doesn't change the fact that the kidnappings were, at their root, wrong. That can't be denied."

Cissy saw how it weighed on her cousin. "Others had to have been involved, though. The emperors at the time couldn't carry out such a thing on their own."

If anything, Jessica turned paler. "The motives of the others would have been the same as Zarl's—save the Empire. It's what guides many of these men's lives."

Cissy hated to hear the pain in Jessica's voice. "What do you do? Is there anything you can do?"

Jessica stopped pacing to look down at her. "I have an idea. It's flimsy as hell, to be honest. It's a defence tactic that has little to do with the truth of what the Empire did."

"Then how can it miss?"

That made Jessica laugh a little. "I'm not going to get into it yet because I haven't figured everything out. Wish me luck. Maybe your sweetheart Diltan will help me."

"Sweetheart," Cissy snorted even though her being warmed at the thought of the Dramok. "How is Aunt Tara doing with this? Her lover is wearing a bull's-eye on this one."

Jessica wrung her hands. "She's being a good Buddhist, reminding us life is difficult and full of changes that we must accept. I know she's hurting, though."

"No doubt."

Jessica flicked away an escaping tear with impatience. "I wish I had half Mom's strength. Despite everything, the Imperial Fathers are good men, Cissy. I loved Zarl as much as my own father. Yuder makes Mom happy. Tidro is too old to go to prison. Damn it, I can't think badly of them no matter what they did. They felt they had to save Kalquor."

Before Cissy could reply to that, the door to the reception area slid open. Prince Wayne and Princess Noelle dashed into the room with glad cries.

Cissy couldn't help but chuckle as the children threw themselves at their mother. Five-year-old Wayne was a miniature version of Egilka with Asian-looking eyes and sharp features beneath his child-pudgy cheeks. His black hair was a wild tangle, his hugs exuberant enough to worry Cissy for Jessica's well-being. The kid was physical, prompting Jessica to say, "Gently, Wayne!"

Noelle was more sedate but still enthusiastic about greeting her mother. With Clajak's steel-grey hair and an elfin face that seemed a darker version of Jessica's, the three-year-old was a riveting sight.

An Imdiko followed the children in, moving to untangle the enthusiastic Wayne from Jessica. "Too rough, boy," he said in a quiet tone. "Do you wish to hurt your mother?"

"I'm sorry, Ripua. I'm sorry, Mother," Wayne said, going shamefaced. His purple cat's eyes found Cissy sitting at the table. "Cousin!" he bellowed. He would have launched himself at her if not for Imdiko Ripua holding him back.

"Hello, Wayne," she laughed. "If you promise not to tear my head off with those strong arms, I'll have that hug."

"I promise!" he yelled. Even so, Ripua hovered while the boy hugged Cissy, delivering a wet and sticky kiss to her cheek as well. His breath smelled of sweets.

When Noelle came over to shyly embrace Cissy, Wayne raced across the office to jump on the lounger there. He bounced across the upholstered piece, whooping with frantic energy.

Ripua bowed to Cissy before addressing Jessica. "I'm sorry to interrupt your cousin's visit, my empress. Since the children will be gone overnight visiting Emperor Bevau's parent clan, I thought you would want to say goodbye."

"Of course. Noelle, I know you'll be a good girl."

The little girl ran from Cissy back to her mother. "I be good. I like staying with Grandmother."

"Because she spoils you with shopping and getting your hair done," Jessica laughed. She called to her son, who had calmed enough to pace the back of the lounger like a tightrope walker. "Wayne, no tantrums. If you break one door or punch holes in any wall, I'm giving your Nobek grandfather permission to punish you thoroughly."

The boy stopped, wobbling on his precarious perch. "I swear to be good, my mother. No biting, no fighting, no breaking. On my honour." He puffed his chest out. Despite having Egilka's features, his suddenly fierce attitude reminded Cissy of Bevau. "Besides, I can't break any walls or doors tonight. My grandfathers are taking me camping outdoors. We eat for dinner only what we catch!"

"Sounds like fun," Jessica said, but she rolled her eyes at Cissy and pulled a face that said she thought otherwise. Cissy fought not to laugh.

The empress shook her head at the balancing boy. "All right, I believe you. Come down from there before you break your neck and give me a goodbye kiss."

Again the children clambered all over her, though Wayne did manage to hold himself in check better the second time around. After a full minute of hugs, kisses and proclamations of love, Ripua took the children out.

Jessica's smile faded into something sad as the door closed behind them. "Until the last year, it was Noelle's temper that worried me most. Wayne's getting wilder and wilder by the moment, though. If that boy isn't a Nobek, I'll take the blame for the Earther abductions myself."

Cissy inhaled sharply. If Wayne was a Nobek, he was required by Kalquorian law to live in a training facility until he reached adulthood. "Do you really think so?"

Jessica came back to the seating area and settled on her cushion. She sighed. "We're all pretty sure. He's energetic to the point of hyperactivity, quick to anger and destructive. He's impulsive enough to put himself and others in danger. He loves Noelle, but you saw how extreme he was while hugging me. He's no longer allowed to touch his sister for fear of hurting her."

"But to have to give him up—I can't imagine." Cissy could have cried for Jessica.

"At one time I would have agreed with you. However, it is for the best given his behaviour. He needs to be in the care of those who can help him learn control. Bevau is on the board of the training camp he went to and he says Wayne will do well there."

"When?"

"The formal testing for breed categorisation takes place in a couple of months." There was a catch in Jessica's voice.

Cissy reached out to take her hand. "I'm sorry, Jess. He's so young to be sent away!"

Jessica pulled her shoulders back and sat up straight. "He'll only get more violent as he grows older if he's not given the tools to cope with his nature." She gave

Cissy a brave smile. "It's only training camp, not prison. It's not like I won't see him again once he goes in. We'll have a visiting schedule and he'll come home for holidays."

Cissy saw the struggle behind the courageous act. "Is it really necessary? Can't he have tutors, something like that?"

Jessica shook her head. "I've researched this thing back and forth ever since I began to suspect what breed he would fall into. Tutors are not the answer, not for all the support a young Nobek needs. Training camp is highly structured and the one Bevau went to turns out the most successful Nobeks in the Empire. The facility is newly upgraded and some of the best minds teach at that place. Colleges back on Earth would have killed for this staff."

"I guess you know best," Cissy said, but doubt coloured her tone.

"Trust me, it's not easy to hand my son over for others to raise. But whatever it takes to give Wayne every chance for success, I'll give him." She even managed a snicker. "If you saw the state of my home right now, you'd understand. A cyclone would be kinder than my little Wayne."

Cissy squeezed her hand. "I support you then. Whatever you need, I'm here for you."

Jessica squeezed back. "Just having someone to talk to helps a lot. I've done a lot of wailing to Lindsey, Mom and my friend Michaela. Still, I'm always happy to have another person to bitch to."

Cissy laughed. "Bitch away. Threatened rebellions, your son going off to boarding school— what else do you need to unload?"

"I didn't introduce you to Imdiko Ripua, did I? That was rude. I hope I didn't hurt his feelings. I guess I've got too much on my mind to do everything right."

"What is he, like, the Kalquorian version of a nanny?"

Jessica nodded. "He's been with us since Wayne's birth. He's practically one of the family. He won't be with us much longer, though, so I'm whiney about that. Ripua is getting clanned to a Dramok on the other continent. He put in his notice two days ago."

Cissy clucked sympathetically. "As empress, you need all the help you can get. Particularly if Wayne is having all the problems you mentioned."

Jessica looked despondent. "On a planet with damned few children born in the last decades, decent childcare is hard to find. Hardly anyone is qualified."

Cissy moved closer to wrap her arm around her cousin's shoulders. "Is anything going right in your life right now?"

Jessica laughed at that. "I could use a good party. How soon can you join Diltan's clan so I have an excuse to throw one?"

Cissy gave her a shove. "Don't even try that, woman. I think Rolat and Wal are definite winners, but that Dramok still has a lot to prove to me. Don't go renting a hall or ordering the cake yet."

Jessica gave her a knowing look. "You know, I once felt the same way about Clajak and Egilka. Sounds like love to me."

"Lust, you idiot. I want to screw that gorgeous man silly. Nothing more right now."

"Mmm-hmm."

Cissy contemplated punching her cousin in that mouth. Jessica's smirk reminded her way too much of a certain irritating man she knew.

Chapter Seventeen

Diltan went over some pending matters with his aide, postponed a few appointments and made sure nothing of an emergency status looked ready to erupt. With two hours left in the morning, he departed the Government House and walked the half mile to get to the cliff complex that made up the Imperial Justice Centre.

Wal's chambers were as large as Diltan's, but the Imdiko managed to make his office space feel more intimate. It might have been the soft floor covering that Diltan's expensive shoes sank a good two inches into. Or the pleasant landscape paintings on the walls that displayed only simple sky and earth. Perhaps it was the billowing cushions that made up the two seating areas. The low table in one of the areas looked lived in with cups and carafes, upon which Wal's legal aides had casework notes spread over most of the polished surface. At Diltan's arrival, the judge had shooed out the young Dramok assistants he presided over.

It might have been the low lighting of the room that gave the room its cosy vibe, set dimmer than what Diltan saw in most offices. Wal's eyes were sensitive, spurring headaches when his surroundings were too bright. Even on cloudy days, he did not venture from the indoors without prescription eyeshades.

Wal rose from his desk as his legal aides departed. The desk was a crescent moon shape, surrounding the judge as if it would hug him—another item imparting intimacy. Its surface was just as covered with work as the one sitting area, though more organised. Wal sat in the midst of two computers, a multi-frequency com unit and half a dozen library tablets that contained the whole of Kalquor's vast documentation of legal precedents, laws and decisions. It also sported pictures of Diltan and Rolat, along with one shot of the entire clan.

When the last of his aides filed out of the room and the door closed to give Wal and Diltan privacy, the Imdiko's face relaxed into a warm smile. Diltan, despite his concerns, could not help but return the caring gaze of his long-time clanmate. Things were tough and likely to get worse long before they got better, but at least he had his Imdiko and Nobek. It made some of the tightness in his chest ease.

He and Wal went to the seating area with the clean tabletop. They sat across from each other. Wal's smile disappeared as he put on what Diltan thought of as his 'judge' face.

"Record conversation. High Justice Wal discussing matter of Imperial Father Zarl's records and its legal ramifications with Royal Councilman Diltan. Note that the councilman is this judge's clan Dramok and agrees to the recording of this interview."

Diltan nodded. "Dramok Diltan, Royal Councilman of the Kalquorian Empire, hereby confirms my understanding that this record may be made public."

Wal flashed a quick, encouraging expression before going back into judge mode. "I have gone over what we've discussed as clanmates and checked legal precedent for the matter moving into a discovery hearing. A lot depends on the timing of the matter. Upon any indictments made by the Royal Council, the court is required to hear testimony and recommend whether or not the case goes into trial in an expedited timeframe."

Diltan pursed his lips. "Which my esteemed fellow councilmen, particularly those in the Ethics Committee, will insist upon."

"A number of factors are in play that mean I would probably have to sit on the hearing and perhaps even a trial, if it comes to that."

Diltan's eyebrow lifted. "You have inside information through me, even though I've kept the specific details from you. We are courting a woman with blood ties to the Imperial Clan. These won't have a bearing on your being selected?"

Wal shook his head. "We are short on judges at this time. If I am called to oversee anything to do with the Imperial Family, I will try to recuse myself from the proceedings. However, even with you giving me advanced notice and our seeing Cissy, it might not be enough to keep me off the bench. My oaths to perform my duties by the laws of Kalquor assure the public trust that I will put Empire before anything else."

He didn't have to remind Diltan of the penalties that would befall him if he should break his oaths. A long prison term with brutally hard labour and financial ruin that the clan could never hope to recover from would be the mere beginning.

Diltan offered a wan smile. "I guess it doesn't matter one way or the other what I tell you about the case then."

Wal held his hand up, warning Diltan off. "Let's not muddy the waters too much, my Dramok. Diltan, I have to be impartial about this case if it comes before me. I must be impeccable in my pursuit of the truth and justice, no matter how harsh."

"I know. It's just that the Empire could be at stake if the Basma uses this scandal to rally enough Kalquorians to his cause."

"Even if revolt is threatened, I cannot allow that to subvert our laws. Kalquor's government is all about openness. Zarl knew that, which is why he committed his dealings to his records and left them there for you to find. The truth must be known."

"He's right."

Wal and Diltan started. They turned to the door, which they had not heard open to admit Emperor Clajak.

Diltan and Wal shot to their feet and bowed. It was Wal's office, so it was he who spoke first. "Greetings, my emperor. I had no idea you were coming to visit."

Clajak gave him a tight smile and motioned for them to sit back down. "Honourable Wal, excuse my rudeness at showing up without warning. Councilman Diltan, I hope you will pardon the interruption and that I listened to a little of your conversation before announcing myself." He bowed before selecting a cushion at the table and sitting down.

Exchanging concerned looks, Diltan and Wal resumed their seats. The Dramok's thoughts swam at what was surely an unprecedented move on Clajak's part. Had he come to try to sway Wal in the matter of his father Zarl's records? Diltan could not think of any other reason for Clajak's sudden appearance.

Clajak addressed the Imdiko. "Perhaps my being here will keep you off the bench on this case. I do not wish my cousin Cecilia's future happiness thwarted by ongoing events. I worry your clan will be forced to give up your suit for her, albeit temporarily."

Wal recovered from his surprise at last. In typical caring fashion, his first act was to warn the monarch, "I am recording this discussion. Anything said here will be a matter of public record, my emperor."

Clajak never flinched. "Good. Enough secrets have been kept already. I did wish to consult with you on one issue to do with this affair of the abducted Mataras. Imperial Father Tidro is on retreat, dealing with the trauma of Imperial Father Zarl's death. I hesitate to recall him since Imperial Father Yuder swears Tidro had no idea of what transpired as far as the kidnappings were concerned."

Wal's brows beetled together as he considered for a few moments in silence. "Is Imperial Father Tidro's health of great concern?"

There was an instant of profound pain on Clajak's face then all expression smoothed away once more. "There are no life-threatening complaints at this moment. However, he is very old as well as devastated by his Dramok's passing. The trip to retreat was harder on him than expected. Physicians attending him say he should not attempt a return for at least two months. Maybe not ever. They think he may be grieving himself to death."

Wal again took his time considering before nodding to Clajak. "As no hearing has been scheduled yet, I would advise you to let him remain on retreat for now. Should close examination of Zarl's records and questioning of Imperial Father Yuder necessitate Tidro's return, the court can deal with it at that time. We would also take into account Imperial Father Tidro's physicians' reports. It could be a recorded deposition would be ordered before we would subject him to the rigors of space travel."

Clajak rose to his feet gracefully and bowed to the Imdiko. "Thank you for your advice, Honourable Wal. Tidro will remain on retreat unless otherwise ordered."

The emperor bowed to Diltan, who had also risen. "Councilman Diltan, I appreciate the diligence you have shown in the matter of Zarl's records, no matter how this turns out. You did exactly as you were supposed to—you did your job as a trustee to the Empire's welfare."

Diltan couldn't help but ask, "What will you do now, my emperor?"

Clajak's expression was grave. "Kalquor must be able to trust its leadership. I will do whatever is necessary to not betray that trust. The people will be served."

With that, Clajak left.

Diltan met Wal's gaze. His Imdiko looked every bit as morose as Diltan felt.

Wal sighed heavily. "Are we finished discussing the matter?"

"For now."

"Conversation adjourned. End recording."

Diltan rubbed his forehead. Yesterday's headache was returning with a vengeance. With feeling, he said, "Fuck."

"I agree." Wal patted Diltan's shoulder. For once, the Imdiko's touch was not comforting.

His heart heavy and head pounding, Diltan returned to the Government House. In the lobby, he summoned the in-house transport. It opened a second later, telling him it had already been on its way.

He could hardly believe his luck when Cissy stepped out. She jumped a little and gasped to see him waiting there. They stared at each other. The Dramok returned the smile creeping over her pretty face. All at once, Diltan felt a lot better.

He laughed at his reaction. He was actually glad to see the rascal. From the way she gazed at him, Cissy felt the same. Would wonders never cease?

Cissy arched a brow and peered about as if about to impart a secret. In a loud whisper, she said, "We must stop meeting like this, Councilman. People will talk."

Instead of hurrying out as Diltan half-feared she might, Cissy drew closer to him. The Dramok caught himself inhaling deeply of her scent. She smelled clean, but he fancied he detected a hint of his clan's mixed aromas on her. Warmth swelled in his cocks as he thought of her lovely, lush body and all they'd done to it last night and this morning.

Knowing how hopeful he sounded but not caring, Diltan said, "I can't be so lucky as to be the reason you're here."

Cissy flushed. Could it be delight that he would want her to visit him that made her wiggle a little? It lasted only a moment before she put on her exasperated face. "Oh, you think you're so irresistible." She relented at once, grinning again. "No, I did not come to see you, but that is a pretty smooth line, you charming bastard.

I came to see how Jessica was holding up, given what's going on."

That sobered Diltan right away. "I hope she is all right."

Cissy shrugged. "Things are tough, but then so is she."

Much like Cissy herself, Diltan thought. The idea brought him up short. He had always admired Jessica's strength and her spunk…even her temper that masked genuine, heartfelt caring. Why had he been letting that same force of personality deter him from courting Cissy? He should have seen through the brash façade from the beginning.

I see this woman now and I will not be blinded by surface appearance again, he decided. "It's a little early, but not too soon for my midday meal. Will you join me? I know a nice place not far away."

Cissy glanced at her jean shorts and plaid shirt with its rolled-up sleeves. She pulled a face. "Such a jokester. I'm not dressed to be seen in a nice place with such a high-ranking Dramok. Stop being a jerk."

Diltan snorted. Now that he was thinking with his heart and not his ambition, he would not let something like Cissy's preference for comfortable clothing be a cause for embarrassment. It helped remembering the delicious body inside those clothes.

Besides, if other men found her appearance off-putting, Diltan wouldn't have to blacken their eyes for looking too closely.

The heat in his voice was genuine as he said, "You are perfect, my lovely. Whether dressed like a man or naked in my bed, I see nothing I don't like."

Cissy shook her head as if to say she wasn't buying it, but her face lit with pleasure. "You *are* a smooth devil.

You deserve to be seen with the likes of me, if only to punish you for such shameless flattery."

She looped her arm in his. Diltan turned his back on the in-house transport, more than happy to leave behind his concerns in order to spend time with her.

As he led her out onto the sunlit beach at the foot of the cliff, he teased, "Admit your heart pounds to be in my company. I always knew you liked me. I knew it from the moment we met."

Cissy offered her wonderful bellow of a laugh and shoved against him. "Shut up before I take a swing at you."

Feeling her warm at his side, Diltan found it impossible to wipe off the stupid grin he knew he wore.

* * * *

Lunch at A Taste of Home was busy, but Diltan had no trouble getting them a table. Cissy noted that though business was brisk, it wasn't as crowded as at night. Conversation was a steady hum through the eatery and waiters moved at top speed to get the patrons fed.

Cissy had only seen the place at night, with its dim, intimate lighting that made each table feel like its own private island. During the day, it was bright and cheerful, with the walls emitting full-size vids of the seaside, complete with the salty smell and dull roar of the ocean. The table Diltan got them was next to one of these vid-walls and Cissy felt she could have walked out onto the sand. She swore she could even feel a slight breeze.

It might have been the serene feeling that kept her from getting mad at Diltan when he confessed he had tried to woo Lindsey from Clan Bacoj. Instead of giving him hell over it, Cissy rolled her eyes at his temerity, called him a few rude names and let the matter go. Diltan seemed genuinely contrite as well as embarrassed over his admission. In the end, she felt the matter was best left between him and her cousin…and the mothers of Clan Bacoj. Diltan's account of how they had raked him over the coals put Cissy in stitches even as he turned a blistering red.

Cissy privately admitted she was impressed he had the decency to admit to his wrongdoing. Most men in her experience would have kept such a thing hidden for as long as possible. Diltan was an ass but an ass that attempted to rise above that particular shortcoming.

Once he'd come clean about the issue between him and Lindsey, they settled down to lunch. The pair ordered more food than they could possibly eat, tantalised by the menu. They laughed over their many platters and Diltan insisted Cissy try everything. Her protests about her figure had him waving her off.

"If you knew how good your soft, yielding body feels against mine, you wouldn't worry," he scoffed. "I adore your curves. If not for the worry over your long-term good health, I'd beg you to add to them."

Cissy was all too happy to have an excuse to sample the full menu. Vax's recipes were the best she'd ever had.

At one point, she groaned around a mouthful of heaven. Hiding her face behind her hand, she said, "That man does things to chicken that no one on Earth ever imagined possible."

Diltan nodded his happy agreement. "He is a talent. I'm so glad being an asshole didn't keep me from being one of his investors."

Cissy had to shake her head at the Dramok again. "Quite the story. Lindsey is still mad at you and I didn't think she was the type to hold a grudge for so long. You truly are a jerk."

He reddened yet again. He managed a devilish look nonetheless. "I'm the biggest jerk in existence. Yet I have moments of being a good guy and it throws everyone off-guard."

They laughed. Cissy felt no real anger at Diltan, not with him so determined to be honest about the matter. She had to tease him, however. "You should have been born ugly or stupid. Arrogance is not crippling you enough. It would do you some good to be instantly reviled once in a while."

"Are you kidding? You came close. Admit it, you wanted to punch me within a minute."

"That's probably a record, huh? I was the quickest to resist your charms."

"Almost. You've been a real pain in the ass from the start, but it's nothing compared to how much or how fast Wal hated me."

Cissy blinked at him. "Seriously? I know you've mentioned you didn't get along at first, that he had it bad for another Dramok."

Diltan nodded and speared a piece of ronka in peas and gravy. "He could have cheerfully pushed me off one of the cliffs when we first met. I almost felt like I needed to check my food for poison any time I ate or drank in his presence. He despised me before he ever laid eyes on me."

Cissy leaned forward, fascinated with the idea that sweet, quiet Wal could harbour such loathing for anyone. "Oh boy. You really had to lay on the charm, huh?"

Diltan snickered. "No, I only had to prove how awful the other man was. He didn't need much help as it turned out. Then when Wal couldn't pretend the man wasn't an utter asshole—worse than me, even—he hated me for making him face the truth." He shook his head. "It's more Wal's story to tell than mine, so we'll leave it at that."

Cissy was dying to hear more, but she could appreciate that Wal might not like being talked about without his knowledge. She put her curiosity aside.

Her stomach gurgled a warning, feeling tight and overfull. Cissy considered the delicious food still waiting to be eaten with sadness. To distract herself, she invited Diltan, "Tell me more about you then. Where does this horrid sense of propriety come from?"

Diltan grinned and pushed his own plate away. "Ambition, ambition, ambition. I wholeheartedly admit to my need for rank and status."

"Pushy parents?"

"Not really. My parent clan was well-off, they were generous and I never went asking for anything. It bothered me, however. Somehow, being handed everything made wealth seem empty and meaningless. I felt like others looked at me as if I didn't deserve what I was given."

Cissy regarded him. "So even though you could have anything you wanted for the asking, you were compelled to earn it?"

Diltan shrugged. "I have a ridiculous drive to be and possess the best that there is, but it has to be won. I've always been like that. Even before I finished basic schooling, I worked odd jobs to make my own money. I studied business and marketing at an advanced level when I was barely in my teens. I amassed a small fortune of my own before the age of twenty by investing my allowance and earnings. Pretty soon I didn't have to work at all because my investment income was so phenomenal."

"Well, at least you aren't lazy." Cissy laughed. "You are what I believe we from Earth call a Type A personality. Ambitious, status conscience and able to work yourself into an early grave if you're not careful."

Diltan sipped the kloq he'd ordered with his lunch. "Wal is constantly on me about pushing myself too hard. It's true that I love the trappings of success. I want the Empire to remember I was here after I'm gone." He sighed, gloom settling on his handsome face. "The way things are shaping up with this whole Earther abduction affair, it looks like I might get that. It wasn't the way I envisioned making my mark."

"Be careful what you wish for. That's what they say anyway." Cissy didn't like the despondent expression he wore. How could she make him feel better? "Hey, you're just doing your job, Diltan. It's not like you arranged those kidnappings or anything."

He raked his fingers through his hair. Damn the slug, he looked sexy with it mussed. "If I'd just known Maf had an agenda where those records were concerned! He's going to make a big deal out of them and set Kalquorians against one another. He might do a better job of it than the Basma has."

Cissy was determined to make Diltan relax. He took too much responsibility for others' shortcomings. "Come on, you big snob. We're here to relax and get our minds off the end of the Empire. Let's talk about good things. What are you most proud of that you've accomplished?"

Diltan drew a deep breath, settling himself. He took another sip of kloq and made the attempt to smile for her. "Since we've had so many children born on Kalquor in the last four years, seeing that they have the best possible education has become my primary focus. I've put in to form a council committee on it."

"You don't already have an educational system?"

"We hardly have any Kalquorians under the age of thirty left. Before Earther women came and began having our babies, we had fewer than a hundred births total the prior decade. The only real systematic approach to learning has been directed at the Nobeks, who go into training camps around the age of five."

That reminded Cissy of her nephew, Wayne. Jessica was positive her son was going to end up in a training camp within the year. *Well, at least his education won't fall through the cracks,* she thought.

She asked Diltan, "What about the Dramoks, Imdikos and Mataras? What have you done about their schooling?"

"Because there are fewer of those breeds, small classes or individual tutors have become the rule. The Temple of Life often fills in the academic gaps in smaller communities. Priests are always ready to serve others."

"Our schools on Earth were heavy into religious study," Cissy said. "Not to mention pro-government propaganda."

"The Temple of Life has an edict against teaching specific spiritual philosophy to small children unless the parents ask for that," Diltan said. "The first classes are always comparative in nature, allowing younglings who are curious to learn different ways of thinking. The Temple of Life tries hard not to tell people what to believe and to be open to those who have different faiths."

"Interesting."

"As for language, arts, mathematics and the sciences, the need for formal academics will soon grow far beyond what we have in place," Diltan continued. "In the last five years, since the first hybrids were born, we've had something of a population explosion. It's at just over ten thousand births right now, but there are more babies on the way all the time. Plus we have more Earther women coming to Kalquor to join clans, which means more children… We've got to take a serious look at the issue before it has the chance to become a problem. We are talking about Kalquor's future, after all."

His tone grew more passionate as he spoke. Cissy could tell Diltan was heavily invested in getting proper education for the children of Kalquor. It impressed her. "You are devoted to your Empire."

"Our society has been hailed as one of the greatest by the known worlds. I don't want to see it end. What is the point of saving ourselves from extinction if we aren't going to be the best versions of ourselves?"

They were quiet for a moment, digesting food and thought. Diltan roused himself and looked at Cissy with surprise. "I just realised I know nothing of what your vocation is. What is it you did on Earth and what would you like to do for a career? If you wish to have a career, that is."

Cissy grinned brightly. "You're going to love this."

"Uh-oh. Now I'm wishing I hadn't asked." Diltan chuckled.

"I was a teacher on Earth. I'd like to return to that. So if you're looking for staff for your first school—"

He regarded her with open-mouthed surprise. Then Diltan's head fell back and he roared with laughter. "Ancestors! You're a teacher? Are you teasing me, Cecilia?"

She shook her head, laughing with him over the coincidence. "Not one bit. I taught kindergarten, the very age group Kalquor's oldest hybrids have arrived at."

The Dramok's eyes lit with excitement and he leaned forward. "We have so much to discuss, you and I. To think that I have access to an expert in education—this is phenomenal! Oh, I know there are a few other Mataras on Kalquor who were once teachers, but very few. Now here you are right where I can confer at any time." He shook his head, delight playing freely over his face. "This is so lucky."

"I wonder why there aren't more teachers here?" Cissy mused.

"The first wave of Earther women brought here were off-planet workers. Not a teacher in the lot. The Galactic Council pleaded with those found after Armageddon to go to an orphanage colony set up for the surviving children of Earth."

Diltan's mention of the first Mataras begged a new question, one that would put them back in the territory of what made him feel miserable. However, Cissy now had a vested interest in what being a part of this man and his clan's lives meant. There was a major truth yet to be uncovered.

With some trepidation, she broached the subject. "Would you have supported the Earther abductions if you'd been in on it?"

Diltan didn't rush to answer. His brows furrowed and he stared at the platters of food they had not been able to finish eating. Cissy knew he wasn't seeing their leftovers, however. He was considering the subject from every angle. Cissy had the insight that he had never thought about what he would have done in Emperor Zarl's place until this moment.

It gave her the opportunity to study the Dramok in detail. That was not an unpleasant exercise. He was a stunning man with that well-formed jaw, that perfectly straight nose, those high cheekbones. He was smart. Funny. Dedicated to his causes. Despite having some personality flaws, Cissy sensed that Diltan was a decent man, ready to help those he could. And damn, he was good in bed.

As for the way they grated on each other's nerves…well, a little bit of friction kept things interesting. Cissy could help Diltan not be so stuffy. He could help her be a little more refined. If they managed to not strangle each other first, the whole lifemate thing might work out.

As long as the Empire doesn't blow up around us, we have time to figure this out. I'm not ready to tell the gorgeous bastard I like him that much…but it's worth a shot.

At last his gaze met hers. "I'm not sure I could have been a part of the kidnappings. Maybe it depends on the individual circumstances. I know that some of the women were in a bad way when they were taken. I've seen Earthers who hid from their own shadows who later blossomed into strong, steady women with the support of their clans. But a few, when given the option of de-clanning and leaving the Empire, did so. It wasn't good for everyone."

"I guess it depends on the woman and what she went through on Earth," Cissy mused.

"You would not have been one to let men whisk you away like that." He sobered again. "The thought of coming upon you and forcing you to come to Kalquor is a hard one. I don't think I could have done it."

"Even knowing you were taking me from a society that thought of women as second-class citizens?"

"And bringing you to a culture that, with a few loud exceptions, cherishes females with near idolisation?" Diltan snorted. "I don't know, Cissy. I really don't. I wish I could say with all certainty that I'm a better man than to have taken your choices from you. It would have been a hell of a tug-of-war with my conscience."

"It sounds like you wouldn't have gone through with it," Cissy said.

Diltan took a few seconds to think about it more. He shook his head. "It's impossible to say for sure unless I was in that position. I have the disturbing feeling I would have initially gone along with it, though."

Cissy gave him a surprised look. "Do you think so?"

"Remember how stupidly I behaved with your cousin Lindsey? That tells me something about myself. My only saving grace is that when I learned how badly she took my proposal, I was aghast. I thought I was doing her a favour, taking her away from a clan with so little status. I couldn't have been more wrong."

"You and status. Someone needs to cure you of that." Cissy went back to teasing because she sensed Diltan was ready to beat up on himself some more.

He responded with his smug grin. "That won't happen any time soon. I must say, I've developed a taste for more distantly related but still royal blood."

Cissy motioned at her less than fancy clothing. "To the casual observer, you're slumming it. By allowing yourself to be seen with me, you can pretend you're not so obnoxious."

"I'll admit that I'm not crazy about the clothes. Yet it has less to do with their cheap construction, terrible fit and that they are more suited to a man than the fact that I know what's underneath them. Even if you were wearing a jewelled gown right now, I'd hate it. The best look for you is naked."

Knowing he found her attractive made Cissy feel warm and happy inside. Not wanting to appear the simpering female basking in compliments, she elected to return his leer. With her gaze raking over that too-fine body, Cissy said, "It's too bad you're working today. I'd let you take my offensive outfit off if you were available."

Diltan appeared gloomy for all of a second before his smile returned. "Who says I can't take the day off? I've already cancelled several appointments this morning. What are a few more?"

Cissy's heart sped up at the thought of Diltan's playroom or his bed. "Really?"

Diltan stood up and offered her his hand. "Why not? As far as I know, we only live once. Tomorrow is going to be a bitch what with me reporting to the Ethics Committee, so I should make up for it with a good time today."

Cissy let him help her to her feet. "Naughty boy. Playing hooky, are we? Whatever will your constituents say?"

His eyes gleamed. "If they had what I did last night and this morning, they'd congratulate me for my good sense. Besides, I can claim that I knew from the start you were a terrible influence. Let's go prove it."

Cissy laughed, moving easily into the circle of his arm. "Far be it for me to challenge your notions of my irresistibleness."

Chapter Eighteen

The instant Diltan ushered Cissy into that grand greeting/ballroom, he stopped her. "Clothes off."

She raised an eyebrow and planted her hands on her hips. "Oh, are we playing at that again?"

"I take play very seriously, my dear." He stared down at her, thinking how delightful she looked despite the stubbornness on her face. Or perhaps he responded to that spark of contrariness. Cissy struck him more and more like a challenge to be won instead of an obstacle to avoid.

The obstinate expression faded from her pretty face, replaced by soft wanting. Her hands slid from her hips, the fingertips skating down those soft, delicious thighs. Her head bowed and her gaze slid from his face. Diltan's chest filled with warmth to see her obey the natural instinct that begged her to surrender. He delighted to see her shoulders remain back and not hunching. She might want to please, but none of Cissy's strength was compromised. If he made one wrong move, a single insulting demand, she would make him pay. Her submission to his desires would be earned, not given.

That suited Diltan fine. It was the way he liked things.

Despite the warm, happy feelings coursing through him, the Dramok used his most commanding tone. "I dislike it when I have to repeat myself, Cecilia. You will be disciplined for not obeying my orders. I suggest you strip now to avoid greater punishment."

Cissy's gaze flashed up at his face. Her expression told him she already debated defiance even as she started unbuttoning her mannish blouse. "You damned Kalquorians. Always so pushy."

He smirked. "You've only gotten a hint of that. Get naked and then crawl to me."

Crawling had been a major issue the night before, one Diltan could appreciate the difficulty of performing. He wanted to see if Cissy trusted his respect for her following their discussion of the matter. Without looking to see how she responded to the command, he walked over to the nearest lounger that sat against the wall.

When Diltan sank down on the plush, red-cushioned couch, he checked on his guest's progress. Cissy glared at him, but she continued to get naked. She'd shed the awful shirt. It puddled at one foot while she wrenched off the shoe covering the other. Diltan didn't miss the blatant hard buttons of her nipples straining the smooth cups of her bra. Her brain might rebel against being dominated, but her body responded with trust. He had to fight off the smile that accompanied the realisation.

The rough denim shorts slipped down her thighs. Cissy kicked them towards Diltan, but they ended up far short of his perch on the lounger. How had he missed how adorable she was when she scowled? Like a little pouting girl who wasn't getting her way with a firm parent. Diltan wanted to laugh out loud at her antics.

The bra came off, revealing those heavy, beautiful mounds with their peachy-pink tips. A growl of appreciation welling in his chest, but he choked it off. He wanted to appear in control, like Cissy didn't affect him so strongly. His cocks, swelling hard against his trousers, gave enough of that indication.

Yet he did groan a little when her plain white panties slid off, revealing Cissy's soft thatch of reddish-brown pubic hair. Diltan had imagined how lovely her pussy would look bared of those curls, but he thought he would miss their softness.

Now naked, Cissy hesitated for an instant. Diltan said nothing. He raised one brow at her. She swallowed and sank to her knees.

The gesture made something in his throat fill. Seeing the gorgeous Earther crawl towards him made it hard to breathe. Her breasts swayed with the motion, as if to hypnotise the Dramok. His cocks hardened at the sight. By the ancestors, Cissy owned him at that moment. Nothing would save him if she figured out she was the one with the real power here. Diltan was hers for the taking.

As she crawled around the table in front of the lounger, he opened his pants' resealable crotch, allowing his avid dicks to spill out. They jutted with eagerness at Cissy's approach. Trying not to sound too strained, he told her, "You may use your mouth on me while I decide on your punishment."

He already knew what he wanted to do to her, but it was best to heighten her anticipation and nervousness. He'd seen how well she responded to that. Cissy's increasing respiration and the darkening of her eyes told him excitement overcame her. She enjoyed this every bit as much as he.

Pushing the issue, he demanded, "I gave you an order. What do you say?"

She crouched now between his legs, her face level with his flushed cocks. She licked her lips as she looked them over. "Yes, Master."

Without further ado, Cissy took his smaller length in her pretty pink mouth. Warmth filled Diltan's cock to match the heat of her touch. He was wet with readiness. The sweet moisture of the mouth sucking him was better still.

Diltan sighed and let his head fall back to rest on the lounger. He closed his eyes, allowing the wonderful sucking sensation to absorb his senses. Her velvety tongue twirled over the tip of his cock, making it feel as if the juices within simmered. He jerked with reaction when her hand surrounded the base of his larger dick, nudging it out of the way so she could go down on its twin.

The Dramok's hands tightened into fists. Cissy took almost the entirety of his shaft into her mouth, letting it enter the top of her throat before slowly, sensuously releasing it. Need came to a boil, lighting a molten fire inside the secondary organ. She took him in again, warming him, wetting him, sucking him. Her hand moved over the larger cock, sliding over its slick skin to deliver wondrous pressure.

She grasped the smaller prick in her other hand as her mouth released it. Then her breath heated the tip of the primary. Her tongue delivered a light, delicate touch on the end and she moaned enjoyment. Diltan guessed she had claimed whatever pre-cum had collected there. Hearing her appreciation of his flavour made heat trickle from his smaller cock to the other.

She took his larger cock in that magical mouth of hers, her tongue twining all about the shaft as she enclosed about half of its length. Her hands moved in tandem with the bobbing of her head, delivering all the sensation he could wish. His cocks grew heavy with aching need, an agreeable torment.

Diltan thought of spilling in her mouth, of feeling her work to swallow his seed. The fantasy was sumptuous, bringing more of the pleasurable agony to his groin. If he weren't careful, it would happen soon.

His voice rough, he ordered, "Stop now. I've decided what I need to do with you."

Cissy released him, drawing back so that she sat on her heels. Diltan saw the flash of concern in her eyes, along with excitement. His cocks jerked at the alluring expression.

He said, "Sit on the table behind you and lie back."

Eyeing him with suspicion, Cissy did as she was told. Diltan looked her over, naked and awaiting his pleasure. The curls covering her slit were soaked. Damn, she was delicious. He thought another position would make her even more tempting.

"Grab your ankles and hold yourself open for me."

Trembling with what Diltan was sure was eagerness, Cissy obeyed. Her legs flung wide, opening her sweetness for his delight. The Dramok was not surprised that he shook almost as much as the Earther.

He licked his lips. With relish he told her, "I am going to spank your pussy. You will hold yourself open for my discipline the entire time. If you close your legs or try to escape, you will receive extra punishment."

Cissy's eyes went wide. Uncertainty fought a battle with lust for control over her features. Her knees closed an inch, as if instinctively to protect her most vulnerable flesh.

Diltan asked in a quiet, undemanding tone, "Do you wish to say *sholt*, Cissy? If you don't think you can handle it, now is the time to say so."

She swallowed hard. He thought she would tell him to go fuck himself, grab her clothes and storm out. Diltan was not a little shocked when instead, her legs spread wider than before.

In a strangled voice, Cissy said, "No, Master. I do not wish to stop."

The Dramok was exultant to hear her acquiesce. However, he felt a little worried now that he had permission to discipline her. Was it desire for his control that pushed her to accept this play, or did Cissy's stubborn streak lead her to go places she wasn't ready for?

Diltan leaned down to look into her hazel eyes. His voice still soft, he asked, "Do we need to discuss any concerns you have?"

Cissy didn't answer right away. She concentrated for a moment, thinking the matter over. Diltan was relieved to see she put caution ahead of pride. It was one less worry for him to deal with.

She shook her head. "My Master will stop if I decide it's too much. I trust that."

Joy that had nothing to do with lust flamed bright in Diltan's heart. Trust. Nothing but love itself could compare with such a gift. It thrilled him to his core.

He caressed her face, letting touch speak the tenderness absent from his words. "Very well then, my sweet slave. Ten spanks for your pretty pussy, naughty girl. You will thank me for each one or I add on more. Do you understand?"

Her eyes shone. "Yes, Master."

Diltan leaned away so that he had easy access to her pussy. He looked at the beautiful flesh spayed open before him, awaiting its correction. Juices slid from between those tender petals. Wet. For him. Eager to please.

It was a good thing his dicks were already out of his pants, bobbing before him with the veins knotting the skin. They were painful enough with being confined.

Diltan took a deep breath. He cupped his hand and raised it. Cissy's eye widened, her mouth dropped open as if in preparation to scream and her body tensed. However, she kept herself open for him.

He clapped his hand against Cissy's pussy. Cupping the palm meant he struck less surface area. He also made sure to avoid her clit, which would be more sensitive than the rest of her flesh. Diltan struck sharp enough to sting…hopefully the kind of sting she enjoyed.

Her sudden inhalation was punctuated by a little cry of hurt. Cissy jerked, her ass thudding against the table top. Yet she kept her legs open for him.

A single tear crept from the corner of one eye. Diltan waited to hear if she would show gratitude or cry for him to stop.

In a breathless voice, higher pitched than he'd heard from her before, Cissy said, "Thank you, Master."

He smiled with delight. "You are welcome, Cecilia. Nine more to go."

Cissy's body was a maelstrom of differing sensations. Her pussy throbbed from the first strike, heat rampaging through the flesh. It hurt even though she knew Diltan had held back. Yet the warmth of it enticed her, pulsing through her core in exciting waves.

Even more enthralling was offering herself for punishment. Cissy could speak one word and Diltan would stop. She could let go of her ankles, get up off the table and walk away. Yet here she lay, on her back beneath a much stronger man, allowing his control to force her to submit to his discipline. She was there because he wanted her there.

Did Diltan have any idea of the power he owned over her? Did he realise that with one severe look, she wanted to crumble to his every whim? That with the imposing tone he adopted when they played in this manner, he robbed her of all strength?

If he had the least idea, he didn't abuse it. Instead, he invited her to return to her rational mind, to weigh the consequences of what they did. Before the first strike, he had insisted she be sure she wanted this. After the first smack of his hand to her tender parts, he waited to be sure she wanted to continue.

Dramok Diltan was a snob, a jerk and a schemer. He also cared. About her.

It made it so easy to sink into the role of his slave, his property with no choice but to do as she was told. Even giving herself over for chastisement, holding herself helpless for correction as he spanked her throbbing pussy.

His hand clapped down again, sending dull agony to reverberate through her. Cissy cried out, tears springing to her eyes and rolling free. In the wake of that pain came the glow of sublime heat once more. Cissy's yelp resolved into a groan as need tumbled through her belly.

I am his. I must please my Master. I must give everything of myself for his pleasure.

"Thank you, Master," she whispered, adoring everything about him—his strength, his power, even his brutality in punishing her for such a minor transgression. He became her world.

Another smack descended on her waiting flesh. This time the pain was not unpleasant. It was still intense but more enthralling than tormenting. She opened her legs wider as she said, "Thank you, Master."

Another one. Cissy's hips rose to greet it and her crotch suffused with brightness at the harsh contact. She moaned her thanks throatily, grateful for every sweet throb.

Diltan's next strike hit much lighter than the ones that had come before, but this time his fingertips landed on her clit. Pain returned in a rush, poignant and immediate. Cissy writhed and screamed with the excruciating blast. Tears poured from her eyes. Her pussy flexed, trying to orgasm. When no further stimulation happened, the near climax backed away, leaving Cissy jerking on the tabletop.

"Thank you, Master! Thank you!" she screamed when she was able to form words again.

Diltan chuckled. "You beautiful creature," she thought he said before he swatted her crotch again, this time not touching her clit.

Cissy spread her thighs as far as she could, wordlessly inviting him to slap her still-spasming clit. She did not dare ask him for it, though. She was being punished. She was Diltan's slave. It was not her place to ask him for anything.

She sobbed when he spanked beneath her clit again, denying her the awful glory of real hurt. The next one was the same. And the next. Her sex was on fire, feeling swollen and pulsing, but it was not the torment she wanted.

"Last one," Diltan said.

At last, he swatted her sensitive nub again. Anguish filled Cissy's gut as pain bolted through her. Heat seared and her body reached, straining for the dissolution that wanted to come with it. She shrieked as climax brushed up against her…and retreated once more. Cissy was left sobbing her final 'thank you' as her legs tumbled limp from her fading grasp.

Diltan stripped off his shirt and lowered his pants to his ankles, displaying that heart-stopping body that matched his face. His cocks were livid, straining towards her as if they would tear themselves right off the Dramok's groin in order to get at Cissy.

He grinned at her, the look both mocking and sinister. "I'm going to fuck this naughty slave now. I am going to fuck my Cecilia hard."

Cissy felt a stab of terror as the man loomed over her like a sexual demon. Her body clamoured for what he promised. "Thank you, Master," tumbled from her lips.

Diltan grabbed her legs, draping them over his muscled forearms. He dragged her close, aiming those twin rams at her pussy and ass. It was only then that Cissy remembered she hadn't been prepared anally. Was she still stretched enough from this morning?

The question was moot. Diltan let go of one leg to gather his cocks in his hand. He positioned them both to enter her sex.

Cissy gasped. She'd never been taken that way before. She wasn't sure she could handle it, especially if Diltan was going to take her hard.

Yet for all his threats, Diltan eased in with care, teasing her open in small increments. Cissy groaned as she was stuffed full, the doubled girth rubbing against her interior walls. About halfway in, she felt a little strained to accept the two cocks. Fortunately, she and Diltan were both sopping wet, easing things. It didn't ache until he was almost all the way in.

"Take it," Diltan said, his gaze intent on her face. "Relax and take me. You want this. Your body will adjust."

He was right. He paused every few seconds, giving Cissy a chance to absorb him. The ache remained mild enough that it fed into the excitement of the moment, enhancing rather than detracting from her desire. Pain was its own pleasure, she discovered. Pain delivered by a commanding and yet conscientious man, at any rate.

Diltan's groin met Cissy's. He smiled approval, making her warm all over. "Very good, slave. Very, very good."

Then he pulled outward, dragging that thick heaviness through her, finding all the sensitive places within. Electrified, Cissy's whole body seized.

"That's it," Diltan said, his voice breathless. He stopped just before his smaller cock could lose its place inside her and shoved back in.

His strength grew with every stroke, thrusting harder and faster each time. The steady friction rubbing inside made it feel as if every hair on Cissy's body stood straight up. Next to Diltan's bunched shoulders, her toes curled tight. She shouted an accompaniment to every smack their meeting bodies made.

"Play with your clit," Diltan snarled, fangs appearing behind his flatter teeth. "Make yourself come for me, girl."

Cissy was on the brink already. Her hands flew to her crotch, fingers reaching. It only took a light, feathery brush.

She strained to deliver the orgasm, a huge billow of sensation that fought to escape her. It felt as if it would tear her apart in its violent attempt to rip loose. Cissy screamed as convulsions rumbled through her, each one stronger than the last.

Diltan pounded into her over and over, feeding the frenzy. Then his cocks jerked inside her, as if possessing their own separate lives. He came inside her, filling her with his seed, releasing into her, his temporary possession.

They yelled and shuddered against each other for what felt like an eternity, forcing pleasure from each other's bodies until Cissy's body went limp and Diltan sagged over her. They lay groaning for a while after that, their chests moving in tandem as they heaved for air.

Little by little, Cissy's thoughts reassembled themselves. She blinked up at the far-off ceiling with its intricately lit patterns.

One thing was for certain. Whatever differences she and Diltan had, sexual compatibility would not be one of them.

The Dramok's big body covered her like the world's best blanket, pressing her into the hard surface of the table beneath her. Cissy couldn't believe the table hadn't collapsed from their combined weight.

"It's a good thing you've got such sturdy furniture," she muttered.

Diltan chuckled lazily in her ear. "It has to be to hold men the size of my clanmates."

Cissy thought about that, of the three muscular men wallowing on this very table, their bodies entwined with one another. Her pussy gave a little twitch. Despite its sated state, it responded to the yummy vision.

"I wouldn't mind seeing that."

Diltan rose on his elbows so he could look down at her. With a laugh, he delivered a sweet, soft kiss to her lips. "I'll see what I can do."

Chapter Nineteen

Diltan's heart pounded as he prepared to wrap up his report to the Ethics Committee. He'd saved the damning part of Zarl's records for last. Once he revealed them, nothing else would receive due attention.

Not that he claimed much attention from the eight-man committee right now anyway. All the councilmen who served on it sat at a raised table, settled in hover chairs. Small vids of history's most important and heroic councilmen lined the walls. A vid floated over the long table, the documents Diltan had gone over from Zarl's reign as Dramok Emperor. In the dimmed light, the report shimmered, allowing the members to peruse the enlarged document.

So far Diltan's report had been boring and mundane. All but Maf and Councilman Terbal appeared on the verge of falling asleep. Terbal made notes on his handheld, the conscientious man he tended to be. Handsome, though rather unremarkable in appearance, the younger man was often quick to challenge the Imperial Clan. However, he did so in a polite way. With his average height, build and unassuming demeanour, Terbal often escaped notice from the others. Much like his mentor Maf, Terbal preferred to let his votes speak for his beliefs.

Maf, however, looked nowhere near inoffensive. His bent body leaned over his end of the table in a pose of rapt attention as he waited for Diltan to get to the admission of abduction. Maf reminded Diltan of the mountain hereso, an arachnid that could reach the size of a man's thigh. Diltan could almost imagine Maf pouncing on a luckless reptilian dril, the hereso's favoured prey.

With evidence of Imperial wrongdoing in his grasp, Maf showed his true colours. While Diltan had known Maf didn't approve of Earther Mataras, he would have never thought the man capable of wanting an actual witch-hunt to protest their presence. It made him wonder what other secrets Maf had kept about himself.

Maf's bigotry, however repugnant, didn't matter. The time had come to reveal the secret that could divide the Empire. Diltan took a deep breath.

"Next item, computer."

The letter from Zarl to its unknown recipient appeared on the free-floating vid. Maf straightened as much as his twisted body would allow. He licked his lips. Terbal also straightened, his eyes moving as he perused the contents of the letter.

Diltan kept his voice as matter-of-fact as possible. "Five years ago, Dramok Emperor Zarl sent this communication to an unknown recipient ordering breeding compatibility testing of an Earther Matara. As we are all aware, that Matara turned out to be Amelia

Ryan, then residing on Plasius. This is the same Amelia Ryan who became Matara to Clan Rajhir. Dramok Rajhir at this time is a councilman of good standing.

"The letter goes on to say that in the event of a positive outcome of such compatibility testing, Zarl commands that all Earther females available to us be brought to Kalquor for the purposes of continuing Kalquorian bloodlines and our culture. Even if it means abducting them against their will."

That brought gasps and exclamations. The committee was awake now, their eyes wide as they stared at the vid.

Maf stood. "There it is. At long last, we know now who is ultimately responsible for the destruction of Earth and the polluting of our two species' genes." He ignored the shouts of anger that came from Dramoks Gamas and Efo. The councilmen had each clanned two of the first Earther women brought to Kalquor.

When he could be heard again without raising his voice, Maf continued. "Not only did the emperors themselves order this, but Councilman Rajhir, a cousin to the Imperial Family, is implicated. He must have had his Imdiko Dr Flencik test Amelia Ryan. After her breeding ability with our kind was confirmed, he clanned her, perhaps against her will."

There were more cries from all the committee members. Diltan rose to his feet and signalled for silence. He was amazed that he got it.

Diltan gave Maf a level look. "If Dramok Rajhir is indeed a part of this, I must point out it would have been by the order of his emperor, Dramok Zarl. There is no way of knowing for certain if Rajhir realised where that order originated from. He has always maintained he was not aware of its author, only that it came with the official governmental seal."

Maf waved him off. "Even if that is so, Rajhir was a councilman at the time, as he is now. Such an anonymous decree should have been brought to our attention. And what of the recipient of this letter? Who would that have been? After all, this person is just as guilty, as he would have known it came from Zarl." He looked at the two councilmen with the angriest expressions. "Gamas and Efo? Your Mataras came from the abducted group of women."

It was the powerfully built Gamas who stood to glower at Maf. "My Matara was not kidnapped, Councilman, and I take offence at your suggestion that I would do such a thing. She joined my clan of her own accord and will tell you so herself. Beyond that, I do not care for your characterisation that she pollutes our race, Maf. Were you capable of defending yourself, I would demand a physical contest. If you had a Nobek, mine would challenge yours in your stead for your insult."

Efo rose to stand next to Gamas. Usually a man with elegant features, he looked as savage as any Nobek in full rage. "The same stands for me. Though you cannot fight, you will hold your tongue or it will find itself cut out of your head."

The situation was getting out of hand. Diltan slammed his fist to the tabletop. "Enough! This is an ethics meeting, not a fighting circle. Committee Chairman, do you wish to say something about the evidence rather than provoking other committee members?"

Maf wasn't smiling, but he was damned close to it as he stared at Gamas and Efo. "I wish to ask these two who told them to fetch their females. Who told you to go out and capture your mates? Where did your orders come from? The summons didn't just magically appear in your hands."

The two men exchanged a look. Their lips pressed together, as if to refuse any words to escape. It had been so with all the affected councilmen these past few years. Without knowing who the power behind the abductions was, the majority of the Royal Council had voted time and again to block investigation into any middle men who had passed the orders along.

Diltan kept all emotion out of his tone. "The Committee Chairman has posed a fair and just question, my fellow councilmen. It is time all the answers be given. We now know Emperor Zarl originated the first wave of Earther Mataras to come to Kalquor. If you know who his go-between was, you must answer now."

"Not doing so in the face of this evidence is grounds to dismiss you from this committee," Maf added with relish.

As the two bristled, Diltan offered the only concession he could. "Telling us who it was only means further enquiry into the matter. It could be this person was simply following his emperor's ruling. Perhaps he felt he had no choice. If that is found to be the case, he may yet avoid indictment and trial."

"He will be indicted. The people will demand it," Maf promised. His eyes were hectic with light.

Diltan managed to keep from scowling. He kept his attention on Gamas and Efo. "That remains to be seen. Still, we must have everything out in the open now that Zarl's part in the affair is known. Once again, who issued you the order to claim your Mataras? Who contacted you with the official governmental command?"

Efo scowled, more savage than ever. Yet he nodded his acquiescence to Gamas, who outranked him.

Gamas gave Maf a dark glare of hatred and turned to Diltan. "My contact was the then ambassador to the Galactic Council, Dramok Ospar. He sent out the orders, which bore the official seal."

Maf's smile was as savage as Efo's glower. "The same Ospar who is now governor of the mixed colony of Haven?"

Gamas snapped a nod. "Yes. However, he never claimed to know the contents of those closed orders."

Before Maf could do any further damage, Diltan grasped at the one straw of hope he could find. "Gamas, Efo. You say your Mataras were willing to join your clans and I prefer to believe you. However, that is not the issue here. Were you instructed to kidnap them or only to seduce in the hopes they would agree to be clanned?"

Again the two men exchanged glances. Gamas closed his eyes and shook his head. Efo's shoulders sagged and most of the fight left his demeanour.

He said, "We were told timing was imperative. The orders said that if we didn't move quickly, the women would be taken away by Earth."

Gamas added, "Their lives were in danger, Diltan. We all know what Earth did to their women, how they were tortured and killed for the slightest offence to their religion. It wasn't just a matter of saving our culture. We went along with it to save our beloveds."

Terbal's mild voice was as inoffensive as ever. "I'm sorry, councilmen, but that was not Diltan's question. He asked you if you were told to kidnap or simply lure the women to the Empire? This is an emotional matter, but stick to the facts, please."

Efo's gaze lowered to the table before him. "The order stated that if the women would not consent to come with us, we were to abduct them."

Maf sat down in his chair. His gloating smile made Diltan feel sick. "I move we call for a council vote at the next open session to file indictments against surviving Imperial Fathers Yuder and Tidro, along with Dramoks Rajhir and Ospar. Councilmen involved in spiriting away Earther women to Kalquor against their will are to be determined and indicted as well."

Gamas' face lit with fresh fury. Efo's shoulders drooped. Diltan's heart was heavy, but protocol had to be followed. "A motion has been made by the committee chairman. All in favour?"

Terbal and Councilman Osem, who was known to oppose Earthers breeding with Kalquorians, called out their agreements. Two other members more hesitantly added their voices.

Diltan shook his head at himself but also said, "I must also vote affirmative as to Imperial Fathers Yuder and Tidro. I dissent as to voting to indict Dramoks Rajhir, Ospar and others who gained Mataras due to those first Earther clannings until more information is forthcoming. Computer, note my dissent."

"Noted," the computer confirmed.

"Those opposed to the motion to order a vote for indictment?" Diltan asked.

Not surprisingly, Gamas and Efo opposed.

Diltan sighed. "Motion carried. At the next open council meeting three days from now, Imperial Father Nobek Yuder, Imperial Father Imdiko Tidro, Dramok Rajhir and Dramok Ospar will be named as conspirators to abduct Earther women, leading to the destruction of planet Earth. An investigation will be launched against those councilmen who participated in the abductions of said Earther women to determine if they too are to be indicted."

Maf's hateful smile had dimmed to something a little more dignified. "Heard and affirmed by Committee Chairman Dramok Maf."

Diltan stared at the damning letter floating in front of him. Wrong or not, he wished he had erased the awful thing the instant he had laid eyes on it. Unfortunately, it was too late.

If Maf had his way, it could very well be too late for the whole Empire.

* * * *

Three days later

With her sister at her side, Cissy stepped into the private viewing gallery overlooking the Royal Council's chambers. The glassed-in enclosure already had two nervous women pacing within its small space—Lindsey and Aunt Tara.

The twins exchanged hugs with their kin. "Nice digs," Cissy kidded in a weak voice. A couple of Royal Guards stood at the door—big, silent Nobeks in red-armoured uniforms. Several hover chairs took up most of the space, along with a table that offered coffee, water, mela, fruit and vegetables.

Outside the glass walls, Cissy could see another larger gallery across the space that hovered over the council chambers. It filled with Kalquorian citizens—

mostly men, but a few Earthers and even fewer Kalquorian women crowded inside.

After greeting her cousin and aunt, Cissy stepped up to the glass wall and gazed down on the chamber itself. The floor below was a great round circle made of the cliff's polished stone. Surrounding half of it in a divided semicircle were carved tiers like steps that seemed to serve as seating. Many blue-robed councilmen were huddled in groups in that area, talking intently.

On the other side of the floor were two daises, one above the other. Chairs that could only be described as thrones, four on each tier, sat over the floor. Men that Cissy supposed were aides busied themselves setting up computers and vids before the uppermost thrones. More Royal Guards were stationed behind the chairs and on either side of the dais.

A large vid flashed to life over the chamber, displaying a view of the currently empty floor at about eye-level. Then smaller vids came online, covering the top third of the gallery's glass wall. Cissy goggled at the different views of the council tiers, the upper dais where the Imperial Clan would sit and multiple angles of the floor.

"Wow. This is better than most sports venues back home. Do you think a boxing match will break out in the middle of the meeting?"

Lindsey managed a small smile at her jest. "Considering what's about to happen, I wouldn't be surprised. Are you all right, Mom?"

Tara McInness looked as serene as ever, though her mouth was slightly drawn. "I think so. Yuder has prepared me for this as best he can. I don't pretend it will be easy to hear him accused of treachery, especially not in front of this crowd. Kalquorians are passionate about their politics."

Tasha sighed. "I hope our being here will give you the support you need to get through this."

Tara hugged her niece, looking tiny and vulnerable next to the taller, curvier Tasha. "There is a season for everything. The past couple of years with Yuder have been wonderful, but change is the only constant of life. We enjoy the good times and accept the challenges that must come."

"Do you think Jessica is ready for what is to come?" Cissy asked.

Lindsey shrugged. "As ready as she'll ever be. Usually, she likes a good fight. I don't think she's looking forward to this one, not with those she loves in the mix."

The door behind them opened and they and the guards turned to see a dark-haired woman with a cherubic face walk in.

Tara opened her arms to the new arrival. "Michaela, how good to see you."

Jessica's best friend wasted no time in accepting the embrace. Orphaned in her teens, Michaela had been accepted as a part of the family. "Hello, Mom. Jessica said I might join you in here rather than jostling in the public gallery."

"Of course. You don't ever have to ask."

Lindsey gave Michaela a peck on the cheek. "Serena's uncles, particularly Japohn, want to know when she's coming to visit us again. Between your daughter and Noelle, I think my clanmates are finally coming around to having children of their own."

Michaela laughed, the sound throaty and deeper than one might imagine coming from a woman. "My little girl has your Nobek wrapped around her finger, doesn't she? Japohn will be impossible if you give him a daughter. He'll never let her clan."

That got them all laughing. Lindsey's Nobek was a fierce creature, but he was quick to play silly games to make Jessica's and Michaela's daughters laugh. The brute melted into goo around the girls.

Michaela turned her grin to Cissy and Tasha. "Okay, which is which? Neither one of you is in sweats or jeans, so I can't tell you apart."

"We're going to make you guess," Tasha teased.

Cissy had decided today's proceedings deserved a nicer than usual outfit, so she had raided Tasha's closet for a simple white blouse and a green skirt. She'd put on makeup and had laughingly called herself Tasha Two.

Michaela's dark eyes sparkled. "Cissy, whichever one of you is you, you look great in a skirt. I'm mad at you, though. You've got nerve missing the last two dance lessons. Explain yourself."

Faced with Michaela's gentle censure, Cissy held her hands up in mock surrender. "I've been…busy. Distracted."

"Good for you. What are the names of these distractions?" Michaela's eyebrows waggled.

Tasha was the one who supplied the answer. "Clan Diltan. Rich men with rank, including a Royal Councilman. Can you imagine?"

Cissy didn't miss the face Lindsey made. She would have to discuss the matter of her relationship with her cousin. Things these last few days with Clan Diltan had gone well. Cissy hadn't been back to the Matara Complex in the last two days until this morning to get ready for the council session.

Sorry, Linds. As much as it shocks me, too, you may have to deal with a lot of contact with Diltan in the coming years. Hopefully you'll see he's not the same idiot who made that awful proposal to you a few years ago.

Michaela took Tara to one side, speaking to her in low tones. Lindsey and Tasha had their heads together, too, allowing Cissy to ruminate over the past few days.

There had been sex. Lots of sex. Tons and tons of sex. Cissy thought about all the ways she'd had sex with Clan Diltan and her body warmed. She had it bad all right, when just the thought of Diltan, Rolat and Wal made her wet.

In between the sex, Cissy was getting to know the men on a deeper level, good and bad characteristics alike. Quiet Wal was sensitive, empathetic to the extreme. He took an interest in the people who had been brought into his court, whether they were victims or perpetrators. Cissy had found out that many years ago, a young man who had a drug problem accidentally killed another man in a shuttle accident. The victim, an unclanned Nobek, had been raising his younger Dramok brother who had not quite reached his teens. Wal had kept tabs on the boy, making sure he was placed with good foster parents. When the Dramok finished his basic schooling, Wal had paid for the young man's continued education. The Dramok had gone on to become a legal representative in the military.

Wal had not focused merely on the victim of the case. In the case of the drug-addicted Nobek whose actions had cost the life of another, Wal had made it a point to get to know the young man after sentencing him to a work camp term. Discovering that the perpetrator had been abandoned to training camp by his parent clan and left to fend for himself once his training was done had upset the Imdiko judge. Wal had kept in contact with the Nobek throughout his prison stay, encouraging him to enter rehabilitation and psychiatric counselling. Determined to save the Nobek's future, Wal had pushed Rolat to mentor the young man.

Rolat had smiled and shaken his head as he told Cissy the story. *'I see addicts in prison all the time. We put them through programmes to get them off the drugs, but it only sticks when they want it to. Many times, they get out and return to their old ways within a few weeks. I had little faith we could make a difference in this particular man's life. He was stubborn, worse than most. But Wal refused to give up on him and he wouldn't let me give up, either.'*

'Did it work?' Cissy had asked.

'Damned if it didn't. That young Nobek ended up being one of the best trustees I'd ever seen. When his term was up, we put him to work as a counsellor and later trained him to be a guard. Now he's an assistant warden for the Empire's fifth biggest work camp. Because of him and the programmes he's put in place, those who go through his camp have the smallest number of repeat offences.'

Wal had been conspicuously absent during Rolat's telling of the story. He was too modest to discuss the matter, other than to say, *'If someone sees the good they can do if given the chance and if someone is willing to give them that chance, they will rise to the occasion.'*

Tara's gasp jerked Cissy out of her reverie. She noted her aunt was still speaking to Michaela. "Oh dear. Of all times for this to happen—"

Michaela nodded, her black curls bouncing about her shoulders. "I know. I don't think she's aware that Rajhir might be facing trouble."

Noticing that the rest of them were looking at her, Michaela explained, "Councilman Rajhir's Matara is pregnant. They just found out this morning."

Cissy felt ill. The past couple of days, when Diltan wasn't concentrating on her, he worried over today's council meeting and the accusations he would set against the Imperial Fathers. He had mentioned that Dramoks Rajhir and Ospar also faced indictments. Rajhir had twins already and Ospar's adored stepson was a special needs child.

A lot of people were going to suffer, including innocent kids. Cissy said, "This situation is going to hell in a handbasket fast."

Michaela made a face in agreement. "No shit. I don't know that this can get any worse, but I'm not going to tempt fate by saying it can't."

Cissy went to the glass wall. Two tiers up, she spied Diltan talking to a couple of other councilmen. She wondered if he'd heard Rajhir was about to become a father again. Then she realised it didn't matter. Diltan had a job to do, no matter how distasteful it might be.

Poor man. He looks like he's got the weight of the world on his shoulders. Well, he does, doesn't he? The weight of the Kalquorian Empire.

His handsome face, so serious with his brows drawn towards each other, gave Cissy a jolt of warmth. Affection filled Cissy's being. Thank goodness that Diltan was as self-assured as he was. It took a strong man to do the right thing when so much bad could come of it. Knowing he couldn't avoid what was coming, Diltan would face trouble with power and dignity.

You wonderful, pompous jerk. If you knew how much you mean to me, your head would explode in disbelief.

Cissy couldn't help but smile a little. She should tell him that, just to see his reaction. Shocking Diltan would never get old.

Everyone came to attention as four people entered through a door and climbed the stairs to the upper dais. Except for the slight shuffling of councilmen taking their seats, the place went silent as the Imperial Clan of Kalquor sat upon the four thrones—Bevau, Jessica, Clajak and Egilka.

The three emperors and the empress gazed across the circular floor at the tiers crowded with councilmen. Their faces, all so different in structure, were identical with grave intent. Beautiful Bevau, elfin-faced Jessica, strong-jawed Clajak and sharp-featured Egilka had the dignified resolve of those bravely facing a firing squad.

Clajak's honey-smooth voice rolled through the hush like the tide coming in. "This meeting of the Royal Council will come to order."

Cissy's heart sped up.

The beginning of the meeting was the usual business—debates over pending legislation, the latest committee reports from Infrastructure, Nobek Youth Affairs and Border Control. Nothing suggested that real ugliness was in the offing unless one noted the tension on the Imperial Clan's faces. Diltan stole a glance at Councilman Rajhir's drawn countenance. Oiteil appeared worried, not because Diltan had told him anything but because Diltan had been so silent. It was enough to tell Diltan's mentor that bad news was coming. To his credit, Oiteil had not pressed for inside information.

As for Maf, he at least had the good breeding to not appear excited. The bent Dramok's manner was quiet but expectant. Diltan didn't know if he preferred the councilman's usual dignified mien or the truth behind that mask. If others saw how enthralled Maf was with tearing Kalquor's peace apart, perhaps they would not be so quick to rally to his side.

But then again, there were plenty of men who wore their prejudices on their sleeves. How many more were like Maf, pretending to be willing to hear all arguments but actually waiting for the slightest note of trouble to scream wrongdoing? It worried Diltan.

The knowledge that Cissy was there, high overhead in the Imperial Family's gallery, was the only thing that gave Diltan a good feeling right now. Her presence bolstered his resolve to get this right. Even that pleasure was tempered, however. Her extended family faced public upheaval. He'd done everything he could think of to prepare her as she tried to be strong for her aunt and the empress. Diltan hoped it had been enough. Thank the ancestors Cissy possessed the strength and the grit that she did. Her propensity to fly in the face of good manners was a boon in a situation such as this. The coming revelations demanded courage to stand up to others, not politeness.

The meeting dragged on, but Diltan dreaded what was to come at the end. Too soon, Clajak's gaze flicked to meet his and the emperor said the dreaded words. "Next on the agenda, the report from Councilman Diltan as to the disposition of former Emperor Dramok Zarl's records."

Diltan rose from his seat on the tier. He had already agreed with both Maf and the Imperial Clan that he would cut right to the chase and reveal the damaging information.

In a carrying voice that impressed with its firmness, Diltan bowed to the emperors and empress. "My emperor, my review of the records of our former ruler and your Imperial father Zarl has been completed."

With equal steadiness, Clajak asked, “What did you find of note, Councilman?”

“I have the unhappiness to report a grave injustice set down by the hand of Zarl. An injustice he visited upon the Empire and the people of Earth.”

That brought a low tide of mutters from the public gallery. Around Diltan, other councilmen shifted, silent as they watched Diltan with wide eyes. All but Maf, whose narrowed gaze kept trained on Clajak.

Clajak nodded. “Proceed, Councilman.”

Diltan stepped down the tiers until he reached the chamber floor. His gaze swept from the emperors, to the public gallery, to his fellow councilmen. He refrained from looking up at the gallery where Cissy stood with her family. It was best not to give any indication of favouritism, however slight.

He told the council, “The nature of the crime Zarl admits to is so heinous that I have already brought the matter before the Ethics Committee. This has led us to move for a vote to indict several people, including Imperial Fathers Yuder and Tidro, along with Councilman Rajhir and governor of Haven Colony, Dramok Ospar.”

He looked Rajhir in the eye. It was not a challenge, only an invitation for the other man to show he had nothing to hide. Rajhir’s face remained tense but controlled and he met Diltan’s gaze without flinching. Good. People would remember that.

The rest of the room hung in quiet shock. It seemed that no one even dared to breathe.

Behind Diltan, Clajak asked, “And the crime the Ethics Committee would have these men indicted for?”

Diltan spoke the dreaded words. “The wilful abduction of one thousand eight hundred and seventy-three Earther women from various colonies, planets and space stations throughout the member territories of the Galactic Council of Planets. Said abductions resulted in war between Earth and Kalquor and the subsequent destruction of Earth, killing several billion innocent men, women and children."

For a moment, the silence spun out, leaving space for Diltan's charge to hang loud and clear. Then the public gallery and tiers of councilmen erupted in cries and shouts of denial, accusation and outrage. Fists beat on the glass walls overhead and councilmen sprang to their feet, shaking fists at Diltan, at the Imperial Clan, at one another. The din was deafening.

The steady *thud-thud-thud* of Emperor Bevau pounding on his podium rose over the bedlam. His powerful voice, aided by amplification, rose over the yelling. "This session will return to order or the gallery will be cleared!"

Between that angry voice and the Royal Guard assuming attack stances, the chamber quieted. A few stray growls drifted from the gallery and council, but everyone seemed to have regained control over his passions…for the moment. Diltan could only hope good sense would prevail. Riots had occurred in the council chamber before. People had been hurt. He could well imagine his report inciting such disquiet.

When he could be heard without amplification, Clajak's smooth but powerful voice rose once more. "The records in question must be presented to the members of the Royal Council and reviewed. Are you prepared to submit these records, Councilman Diltan?"

Diltan faced him and bowed. "I am, my emperor."

"Are the men accused present?"

There was a rustle of robes behind Diltan. He looked over his shoulder to see Rajhir stand tall and proud. "Councilman Rajhir, my emperor."

Diltan added, "Imperial Father Yuder is also present, my emperor. Imperial Father Tidro is in seclusion following his Dramok's death and Governor Ospar is currently at his post on Haven Colony."

Clajak's gaze darted up at the Imperial gallery for a brief moment before calling out, "Let those accused and present come before the Imperial Clan."

Rajhir descended the tiers to stand on the council floor with Diltan. Yuder was ushered in from a waiting room off the council floor. He looked as fierce as ever, his jaw set with determination. Both Rajhir and Diltan bowed to the Imperial Father as he approached to stand with them.

The three men stood before the dais, gazing up at the three emperors and empress. Diltan didn't miss Jessica's pallor, though her expression was as composed as her clanmates'. He knew how close she was to Yuder, however. And she worshipped her mother, Yuder's lover. How this must be tearing her apart!

If Clajak hurt similarly by seeing his father called before him in shame, he showed no sign of it. "Dramok Rajhir and Imperial Father Nobek Yuder, once this council has had the opportunity to review the records of former Emperor Zarl, it will vote on the matter of indicting you for criminal abductions. As representatives of the government, one that prides itself on transparency to its people, this is just and fair treatment. Do you wish to say anything on your behalf before the matter goes any further?"

Yuder gave Rajhir a slight nod, indicating he should speak first. Rajhir said, "I have no statement to make without legal counsel, my emperor."

"Noted, Councilman Rajhir. You recognise this will result in your suspension from the Royal Council until the matter is settled?"

"I do, my emperor."

"So be it." Clajak's steady gaze went to his father. "Imperial Father Nobek Yuder, do you have a statement?"

Yuder lifted his chin. In a tone that had made the Royal Council shake for well over a century, the Nobek stated, "Only that the matter of the Earther Matara abductions rests entirely with myself and my Dramok, Imperial Father Zarl. None of the other men accused, not Dramoks Rajhir and Ospar nor even Imperial Father Tidro, had any criminal involvement in the matter. Neither did anyone else. As the only living conspirator, I take full responsibility for the crime."

Diltan drew a sharp, surprised breath. Rajhir muttered an oath. Around them, the shouting began again. The thudding of fists against the gallery's reinforced glass was louder than before. Royal Guards had their blasters out, letting Diltan know that violence was beginning to break out.

Bevau shot to his feet, his beautiful face transforming in an instant into something bestial as he snarled with fangs exposed. His thunderous shout, deadly with promise, brought tense quiet descending upon their surroundings once more.

The Nobek emperor growled, "One more outburst like that and the gallery will be emptied, Captain of the Royal Guard. You will bring me any man who raises his hand to another so that I may relieve its owner of it permanently."

Diltan's breath froze to see the fury on Bevau's almost purple face. He could well imagine the Nobek ripping away body parts from anyone who pissed him off.

Clajak at last looked upset, his control slipping. Some of the shouts had been for Yuder's life. Still, he managed to keep his tone from wavering. "I have heard your confession, Nobek." Drawing a deep breath, Clajak continued. "Imperial Father Yuder has admitted to culpability in the matter of the Earther Matara abductions. He is to be placed under house arrest until the council has reviewed the records of the late Emperor Zarl and held a vote on whether or not to indict. Councilman Rajhir remains relieved of his duties until this matter is settled. Meanwhile, Governor Ospar and Imperial Father Imdiko Tidro will be informed that they are to be recalled if necessary. The vote as to who should be indicted will take place here on the council floor one week from today. This meeting of the Royal Council is adjourned."

Diltan, Rajhir and Yuder bowed to the grim-faced Imperial Clan. The Royal Guard, no doubt worried fighting might still break out, hurriedly ushered the emperors and empress out.

Yuder was just as quickly escorted out by six more guards. There were a few shouts of 'Execution!' and 'Genocide!' but order remained. Rajhir also had a small contingent of guards, along with a couple of Global Security officers, one of whom Diltan recognised as Rajhir's own Nobek. Between that man's feral snarl and the big, muscled hulk of the other dreadlocked officer, no one challenged the trio as they left.

Diltan went to the council tiers and sat down heavily. When other excited members of the council came towards them, Oiteil warned them off. "Not now, he won't tell you anything further. You will have to review the records yourselves and come to your own conclusions."

Diltan wanted to feel gratitude to his mentor, but instead dread filled him. Yuder had decided to take the fall for the whole affair, most likely in an attempt to protect his Imdiko and anyone else he could. The man courted a possible death penalty or life imprisonment rather than let others get hurt.

Diltan could understand that. If half the council was indicted as Maf wanted, it would rip the Kalquorian Empire apart. Yuder taking the entirety of the blame might be the only thing that would keep revolt from becoming revolution. Still, it made his heart heavy to think of one man burdened with the blame of billions of deaths…deaths he was sure Yuder never could have imagined happening.

The other councilmen dispersed, leaving Diltan alone. Oiteil left, too, heeding his own words, though he no doubt burned to ask questions. Diltan felt thankfulness towards his mentor and vowed to stop by Oiteil's chambers as soon as he felt capable of facing others.

For his part, Diltan pretended absorption in his handheld, tapping keys to build a document of nonsense words and phrases. He knew he hid behind the device like a frightened child, not wanting to address those who tarried. He didn't care if it was cowardice. He couldn't stand to discuss the matter with those who now found themselves in the line of fire or those who wished to be part of the firing squad.

Little by little, the angry muttering of those in the gallery faded as the public onlookers left. Diltan heard hushed voices from the dais at the front of the chamber but still kept his gaze down. He didn't want to talk to the Imperial Clan, either. He felt responsible for Yuder being placed under house arrest, though it was the Imperial Father's fault for speaking out as he had. Still, Diltan had presented the evidence and it had led to the shocking scenario.

A flash of green fabric and a very nice set of feminine ankles and calves appeared in his peripheral vision. At last Diltan's head came up to the surprising and delightful sight of Cissy standing in front of him. If not for that special fire in her eyes, he would have mistaken her for Tasha. He thought her breathtaking in the skirt and blouse ensemble.

"Hi," she said softly, not like Cissy at all. Again, Diltan thought he might be looking at Tasha. Then the woman tugged at the lace collar of her white blouse as if it made her ill at ease. Yes, this was his comfort-loving Cecilia, no doubt wishing she wore something not so prim.

"Hello," Diltan greeted her. "Don't you look lovely. Downright presentable, in fact." He gave her a wink.

"I have my moments. Don't tell anyone or I'll pull your tongue out," Cissy agreed with her more familiar challenging grin. Then her face softened again, giving him a look of concern. "Tough day at the office, huh?"

Behind her, Diltan saw the other women of the Imperial Family huddled with the Imperial Clan. Clajak had his arm around Imperial Mother Tara while Jessica held her hand. Tara's face looked strained, but she seemed to be holding together pretty well considering her lover had been taken out under guard.

Diltan drew a heavy breath and returned his attention to Cissy. "A very trying day. I did not expect Imperial Father Yuder to be led out under arrest."

"No one did, from what I understood was to happen. He was supposed to invoke counsel like Dramok Rajhir did. We had no idea he would announce his guilt."

Diltan wondered if the Imperial Clan would take offence if he pulled Cissy into his arms to offer comfort…and perhaps receive a little comfort in return. Then he decided he didn't care. He put his handheld in his lap and reached for her hands. She came to him willingly, smiling a little. He tugged her down to sit next to him. She felt right with her body next to his, a perfect fit with his arm around her soft, warm frame.

Diltan said, "It seems Yuder is determined to keep everyone else out of trouble at the expense of his own freedom. Typical protective Nobek. I guess if you think about the kind of emperor he was, it shouldn't surprise any of us that he'd do such a thing."

He glanced again at Tara. Jessica's mother was a tiny thing, not substantial in the least. Yet she stood straight with her shoulders back, as unassailable as a Nobek.

"How does she do that? How can she be so calm when her mate's future is in jeopardy?"

Cissy looked at her family. "Auntie Tara? We could all learn a thing or two from her. She's quiet and sweet, but she's the strongest person you can imagine. Jessica says she makes the Temple of Life priests seem like nervous wrecks."

Diltan chuckled. "If only we all possessed such grace."

Cissy snuggled, peering up at him with those amazing blue-green eyes. Cool-coloured eyes that still evoked fire. "Are you going to be all right?"

Diltan's heart warmed. His rebellious little rascal, this scallywag who he would have turned his back on only days ago, was so much more than he'd credited her for. It made him feel good to be the focus of her concerns. He caressed her cheek, hoping she could see how she touched him.

He murmured, "I'll be fine now that I know it matters to you."

They stared into each other's eyes, the moment perfect as unspoken emotion passed between them. It was an instant in which talking of what they felt would have detracted from it. It was beyond mere words.

This is the one. It's not a matter of how she will appear to others when she is at my side. It's not a matter of being the perfect mate for official appearances. Cissy fits me. I think she fits Rolat and Wal, too. Even when we rub wrong against each other, it's still right. Our moments of friction will only mould us more firmly together.

The realisation was sudden. It should have been shocking. Yet it was not.

Diltan had just decided he was ready to call it a day, to play 'hooky' as Cissy called it so he could spend more time with her, when Maf's aide Dramok Sitrel appeared before them.

The sharp-featured man looked from Diltan to Cissy and back before speaking. "Please excuse the interruption, Councilman Diltan. Councilman Maf requests your presence for an immediate personal meeting. He is most eager to get to work on readying for the indictment vote."

A wave of disgust boiled in Diltan's gut. Maf had kept himself restrained during the council meeting. Now that the report was public, it appeared he would proceed with unseemly haste. Damn it, he could have waited at least a day to hear from the rest of the council before rushing headlong into stirring up more anger.

Yet Maf was the head of the Ethics Committee and he was well within his rights to begin proceedings. Diltan had no choice but to do his job. Again.

Without bothering to address the waiting Sitrel, Diltan stood. He felt incomplete without Cissy pressed to his side, almost bereft. He wondered if she felt the same.

He bowed to her. "My apologies for having to leave you much too soon, Matara."

She sighed, making him think that perhaps she did miss him a little. "Some days just don't seem to end, do they?"

Diltan smiled at her. "I hope to see you later."

"I think I can squeeze you into my packed schedule tonight." She winked at him and looked him up and down, not caring that Sitrel hovered close enough to see her bold appraisal.

Her obvious lechery made Diltan want to laugh. Instead he reciprocated, bending down to brush his lips against hers. "Until then, my lovely."

Diltan straightened, not missing the mischievous twinkle in Cissy's eyes before he turned away. He passed by Sitrel without a glance. He felt mean satisfaction that Sitrel was surprised enough to have to hurry to catch up.

Chapter Twenty

Diltan allowed Sitrel to precede him into Maf's office. Despite what was coming, the Dramok was assured. Damned near joyful. With Cissy's support, he could take on just about anything, including Maf's newfound fanaticism.

Don't get too cocky, he warned himself as he crossed through the doorway into Maf's private chambers. *Being high on affection will not do anything to fix this situation.*

Maf sat behind his desk, muttering instructions to his computer. He turned from whatever task he performed as soon as Diltan stepped in.

He beamed at his visitor. "Good, wonderful, I am glad you were available right away, Diltan. There is no time to waste on this matter. As chairman of the Ethics Committee, it falls to me to lead the investigation."

Diltan dipped a little bow and some of his euphoria drained away. "Of course."

Maf waved his withered arm. "Oh, my apologies. I forget myself. Please sit down."

"I need to stretch my legs after the council meeting but thank you." Diltan remained standing before Maf's desk.

The other man caught the coolness in his tone. He exchanged a wary glance with the silent Sitrel, who stood unobtrusively to one side.

Maf smiled again, though with far less wattage than before. His tone remained friendly. "As you prefer. I must have the entirety of Zarl's records at my disposal. Will you give them to me?"

"Of course. Now that I have made the official report, the records are a matter of public record. As of ten minutes ago, my computer loaded them onto the mainframe. *Everyone* has access."

Maf gave him a conciliatory look. "I detect grave concern in your voice, my friend. I realise we are treading on very shaky ground – "

Diltan interrupted him. "Do you, Maf? Do you understand just how shaky the ground is right now?"

Maf settled back in his hover chair, wincing a little. "The former emperors lied. Over half the council benefitted from that lie. Most of our governing body was party to it. They aided and abetted the abductions of nearly two thousand women, which resulted in war, which resulted in an entire planet's destruction. The Earther species is almost as endangered as ours because of this injustice."

A twinge of desperation returned. "I have no argument with you there. It is plain that at least Imperial Father Yuder has many questions to answer. However, I'm not so certain as to the culpability of our fellow councilmen in the affair. I think it is a mistake to try to indict every one of them. Beyond that, I'm asking you to also note the bigger picture."

Maf looked at him as if he'd gone mad. "The bigger picture? What could be more important than genocide?"

Diltan planted his palms on Maf's desk and leaned closer to his colleague. "What about a second genocide? There are extremists out there who have been waiting for something like this to happen so they can tear the Empire apart. You have to know this will divide Kalquor. It may mean those who have opposed the Basma's revolt will now flock to his banner and challenge our way of life."

Maf sighed, his thin face settling into lines of regret. "Of course I realise how polarising the issue could be. That's why it is so important to get to the full truth of it. The Empire is built on a policy of no secrets from its people. Without it, we set ourselves up as despots, playing the common people like puppets."

"If not fed to the public in a cautious manner, this scandal has the potential to blow up in all of our faces. We could have civil war if it is not handled right. Those who are adamantly opposed to the Earther Mataras will use this to further their agenda," Diltan pointed out.

"I oppose the Earther Mataras," Maf said.

"To the point of desiring bloodshed? Of shattering Kalquor?"

Maf shifted in his seat, trying to find a comfortable posture. He grimaced and Diltan wondered if the man wasn't above using his infirmities to elicit sympathy.

Maf said, "Grave crimes have been committed against the Empire and Earth. Those who carried out those crimes must answer for it."

"Even at the expense of the Empire?" Diltan paced before the desk. "I do not support whitewashing this crime of abduction. I can accept the Imperial Fathers must answer for what happened. But to drag every single clan that claimed one of those first Earthers into court? Three men to each clan—that's over five thousand men. As you pointed out, over half the current council is involved. The council itself would crumble, putting our government at risk."

"They have knowingly blocked our investigations into the matter before. Gamas and Efo admitted they knew Ospar was part of it. They are guilty of obstruction at the very least. They must pay the price."

Diltan wheeled to face him. "And what of the innocents who will pay alongside them? What happens to the Mataras and children of those clans, Maf?"

"They receive long-awaited justice for being brought here against their will. At least that's how I see it." Maf gazed at him with kindness, though the light in his eyes was too bright to carry it off. "Diltan, you make good points. Don't think I haven't heard and considered every single word you've spoken. The truth is, it's out of our hands. Demands from the public for trials of everyone involved are already flooding the offices. The people of the Empire insist this be settled. They scream for it. Have you looked outside?"

Diltan blinked at him. Had trouble started already? "No, I haven't checked to see how the people are reacting."

Maf cocked an eyebrow at him. "You should. Minutes after you revealed the contents of Zarl's records, Global Security officers were called in to surround the Government and Royal Houses to keep the crowds at bay. They are talking about bringing in stun devices if the numbers don't disperse."

Diltan stared at him in horror. The situation was devolving faster than even he had anticipated.

Maf nodded. "It has already begun, my friend. Now it is up to us who uphold honour and Empire to do our jobs, no matter how unpleasant they may be."

Diltan choked, "You are one of our more respected leaders. Your voice is as revered as the Head Councilman's. Will you do nothing to try to calm the situation?"

Maf shrugged. "That is not my problem. Only the truth is."

His face was serene. Serene except for the hard-bright glaze of the crusader in the man's eyes.

* * * *

After his meeting with Maf, Diltan made his way to the Imperial level of the Government House. Most of the councilmen had gotten wind of the crowds outside and had left the cliff building. Diltan was grateful no one was around to see him board the in-house transport that took him to the highest level. If it got out that he was visiting the Imperial Clan so soon after revealing Zarl's records, rumours of conspiracy would fly.

I do plan to conspire with the Imperial Clan, up to a point, he admitted to himself as the transport moved beneath his feet. *What else can I do? Maf will let Kalquor suffer in his mania. He does not see that the Empire itself might fall…or he does not care.*

Diltan was beginning to believe the latter possibility was the true one. Maf would let Kalquor rip itself apart in order to get rid of the Earther Mataras and those who had clanned them.

The transport's door opened, bringing him face-to-face with half a dozen Royal Guards, their percussion blasters drawn. One snarled, "Halt. The Imperial Clan will see no one."

Another guard wearing a captain's insignia holstered his weapon and motioned for his squad to follow suit. "This man is authorised for limited access. You're on the list of approved visitors, Councilman Diltan. You may check in with Emperor Clajak's secretary. Do not go anywhere else."

Diltan offered him a bow. "Thank you, Captain."

He hurried down the corridor, his heart thumping fast. "Nothing like having half a dozen Nobeks pointing blasters at a man to raise the pulse," he muttered. He should have known security would be on high alert given the situation. It amazed him that he'd been given access at all.

He stepped into Clajak's outer chambers. The room was empty but for the harassed secretary sitting in the midst of continuously beeping com signals.

The secretary nodded to him. "They hoped you'd come, Councilman, but didn't dare send for you for fear it would look improper. Let me tell them you're here."

Diltan digested that the Imperial Clan wanted to see him as the other man disappeared into the private office. He wondered why. Before he could puzzle it out, the secretary came back and waved him towards the inner chamber. "Please go in, Councilman."

Diltan did so, discovering that not only was the entire Imperial Clan waiting for him, but Clajak's aide Korkla and Bevau's aide Dramok Erybet also crowded into the room. It looked like a war council.

Diltan bowed to the six people. "My emperors, my empress."

Looking calmer than when he'd last seen him, Clajak gave him a slight smile. "Hello again, Diltan. I take it you have some news?"

"Councilman Maf called me into his chambers after the meeting. He demands all of Zarl's records for purposes of building a case of indictment against Imperial Fathers Yuder and Tidro and most of the Royal Council."

Emperor Egilka's sharp face showed no surprise. "As is proper, given his position. Those are now available to him anyway. We saw the documents have been loaded into the mainframe."

"Yes, my emperor. However, I am concerned about his haste in the matter. He is not willing to let this initial trouble pass and the dust to settle. In fact, I believe calm is the last thing Maf desires. I detected an anticipation that borders on enthusiasm to find and convict all involved in the first abductions. He would accuse most of the council itself."

Korkla gave Clajak a worried glance. "That's an overreaching way to behave."

Clajak blew out a gust of air. "I knew Maf was against the mixing of Earthers and Kalquorians for the purpose of re-populating Kalquor, as at least a quarter of the Royal Council is."

Bevau said, "That number has probably grown since the meeting."

"I agree. My father admitting his guilt has only worsened the situation." Clajak asked, "Diltan, I know your concern is for the Empire more than for us. I still wish to know how much we can trust you personally."

Diltan debated that for a few moments, but he'd already been over the matter in his head for some time. He said, "You must not ask me to lie in order to spare Imperial Father Yuder, my emperor. Nor Imperial Father Tidro, Councilman Rajhir and Governor Ospar, if it comes to it. My creed is for honour. Yet before that, I would do what I must to preserve the Empire and its people, whether Kalquorian or Earther."

"What do you think that means, exactly?"

"In this particular situation? I am certain that bringing up on charges those councilmen who are clanned to the first Earther Mataras will harm the Empire. I think it may even feed the Basma's revolt, threatening a real split."

"What are your specific worries on that account?"

Diltan didn't mince words. "Maf is proposing a witch-hunt. It will begin with the Royal Council. Once such a thing gets started, it can be damned hard to rein it in. What of the Earthers that came to us after the first Mataras? Will their clans be suspected of kidnapping? Will they be dragged into court to defend their families?"

Jessica frowned. "Earth's history was full of such things. It starts with one small group being accused or discriminated against and then it grows until entire communities are under siege. Neighbour turns on neighbour, family against family in such cases."

Bevau's aide spoke up. His delicate features made him almost as pretty as a female, but Dramok Erybet was known as a fierce fighter. He'd once been a commander in the almost exclusively Nobek-populated ground army. "We are on a precipice that I have seen before. The first rocks have tumbled down the hill. It will not take much to become an avalanche.

Anyone disaffected will flock to the Basma's banner now."

Clajak's gaze on Diltan was steady. "I will not ask you to lie and destroy your honour, Diltan. However, you are already compromised in a fashion, what with your suit for our cousin, Matara Cecilia."

Diltan's mouth went dry. Surely no one would ask him to give up pursuing his potential Matara? Or would Maf, with his dislike of Earthers and desire to make someone pay, insist on it?

Clajak continued. "All I ask is whatever help you can offer that does not interfere with your ethics."

"Such as?" Diltan's mind was still reeling over the idea that he might be told to have nothing more to do with Cissy.

"The Honourable Wal is your clanmate. You could give us some insight into how a judge might handle the matter." Clajak's face darkened. "I cannot protect my father Yuder, but he swears Tidro knew nothing of the plan to kidnap Earther women. If my Imdiko father can be spared this horror, I wish it."

Korkla added, "You also sit on the Ethics Committee with Maf."

Diltan jerked at that. "I will not spy on him on your behalf."

"Of course not. However, if he is as determined to let his own agenda get in the way of doing his job properly, someone must keep an eye on that. That's all we would ask you to watch out for."

Clajak noted, "As you are doing by coming here today."

The point was well taken. "I am willing to share my concerns on that point. Is there anything else?"

Clajak managed a tight smile. "As bad as things look, we may yet have a chance to quiet the people's anger. If you are willing, I'd like for you to consult with the councilmen who claimed those first Earther mates. My empress has an idea that might help us salvage some of this, if you will hear it."

Diltan looked to Jessica. He had always adored the brave Earther who had proven herself more than worthy to sit on Kalquor's throne. He bowed to her. "I would be glad to listen, my empress."

She smiled at him, a sight that at one time would have made his heart double-beat. Now it only reminded him of another's smile, one that was just as mischievous as hers. "Sit down, please," Jessica invited, motioning towards the nearby seating area.

The group gathered around the table, settling on floor cushions. Jessica offered her proposal and Diltan agreed that it was as slim a hope as she claimed. However, it had possibilities. After an hour of discussion, Diltan agreed to help with the plan.

* * * *

Evening had fallen when Cissy's door announce summoned her from her bedroom. Hope flared bright as a deep voice called out, "It is Clan Diltan, Matara. May we enter?"

It was ridiculous to feel so delighted to hear the Dramok's voice when she spent most of her time wanting to throttle him. It was just as silly for her to finger-comb her hair and smooth down the skirt she hadn't yet returned to Tasha. It wasn't as if Cissy hadn't checked her appearance a hundred times in the last couple of hours, hoping the clan would at least vid-com. She hadn't expected them to show up in person.

She licked and sucked on her teeth, trying to make sure her light dinner wasn't stuck between them before answering, "Come in."

The door opened, admitting the three men with Diltan in the lead. Their faces lit in smiles the instant they looked at her and Cissy couldn't help but beam back. Her whole body felt as if it wanted to grin. Damn, they looked good to her.

Diltan offered a little bow. As Rolat and Wal followed suit, the Dramok asked with a trace of worry, "I hope our unannounced visit isn't a problem?"

"Not at all. At least, not for me." The urge to wiggle like an excited puppy left Cissy and she blurted out the concern that had overcome her following the council meeting. "Should you be here, Diltan? I want you here, but I mean, with me being related to the royal bunch and all, won't you get into trouble or—"

Diltan came to her, taking her in his arms and cutting her off with a kiss. And what a kiss. It started off soft and lovely before turning passionate with desire. Cissy's legs gave out from under her. Her body melted into what was more a lovemaking of mouths than anything so innocent as a kiss.

Diltan held her up as she sagged like a weak little damsel against him. Wal and Rolat chuckled from a million miles away, but it was hard to be sure with the roaring in her ears. Her entire being centred on that kiss, on the feeling of Diltan plundering her mouth in what could only be a claiming. It stole her breath and her mind.

When the Dramok ended the kiss, Cissy's vision blurred. She thought she might faint. Her lips tingled.

She must look like an idiot, gazing up at Diltan with star-struck eyes and clinging to his magnificent body. She fought to get herself under control.

She couldn't come up with anything more intelligent to say except, "Oh. Okay. I guess you don't give a red-hot damn about getting into trouble."

He gave her that patented pompous Diltan smirk, though it seemed a little more tense than usual. "I have reached the conclusion that the issue of Zarl's records is not going to be pretty no matter what I do. So, yes, I've decided not to give a red-hot damn. I want you. Unless I am forced to for the good of the Empire, I will not give up one second with you. Even then, I will come running back as soon as I can."

Wal came over to greet Cissy with a far more respectful kiss on her cheek. "You are more impressive than even you know, lovely. It's not often anyone can get Diltan to go against what would look good."

"You are worthy of worship for that alone." Rolat was on the other side of Diltan. He too gave her a kiss that was almost chaste. Like Wal, the look in his eyes said his thoughts were of a far more lustful nature.

Cissy giggled at their teasing as Diltan rolled his eyes. "Why don't you both shut up? I am not such a fool as to halt this most delightful relationship." He kissed Cissy's still tingling mouth with a loud smack and kept kissing as he spoke. "In fact" —*kiss*— "I want it" —*kiss*— "to continue on" —*kiss*— "and on" —*kiss*— "and on." Kiss.

Cissy pushed against the ridiculous man, laughing and not really trying to get away. "Wait, I thought I was the rebellious one here!"

Diltan's grin filled with dark promise, making her insides tremble. He said, "Oh, please rebel, lovely girl. Feel free to resist all you like."

His ardour, on display without the slightest hint of holding back, enthralled Cissy. Her voice came out husky. "What if I don't want to resist? What if it's the last thing in the entire universe that I want to do?"

This time Diltan's smile showed no hint of the day's tension at all. "That's perfectly fine as well, my beauty. Since you are in such a giving mood, you may kneel at my feet."

Chapter Twenty-One

Cissy's heart skipped a few beats as she looked up at the men gathered around her. What was it about these three Kalquorians that made her so eager to please? She'd always been tough as nails, ready to put others in their place if they dared to encroach on her or her sister's liberties. Yet with Diltan, Rolat and Wal, she became soft. Yielding.

Giving Diltan what he wanted was natural. Too natural. It should have scared her, but it had the opposite result. Cissy lowered to a kneeling position, her body lighting in anticipation.

The men were just as excited, their crotches swelling. The cinnamon scent of Kalquorian male arousal filled her nostrils. They lubricated, their bodies readying to fuck her. Cissy whimpered with avid expectation.

Diltan grasped the crotch seam of his pants and pulled it open. His cocks fell free, glistening and hard.

His honeyed voice sounding a bit breathy, Diltan ordered, "Warm me with your mouth."

Cissy obeyed without hesitation, sucking first the smaller cock in and quickly changing to the larger. Back and forth she moved, her hands curled around the bases. The sharp spiciness of his flavour delighted her.

She wasn't aware that Rolat and Wal had knelt on either side of her until their hands tugged on her clothing. She started for an instant but recovered and continued the sensual assault on Diltan's twin maleness.

Fingers pulled at the front of her blouse. Made on Kalquor, it had the resealable seams her hosts preferred rather than buttons. Cissy thought it was Rolat who made quick work of opening the seam. He tugged first at one wrist then the next as he pulled the sleeves free of her arms. Cissy relinquished her grip on Diltan just long enough to be divested of first the shirt then her bra.

At the same time, Rolat stripped her top off, Wal's gentle hands eased the skirt down her hips. Her panties went to her knees next. Since she knelt, it was too much trouble to pull the articles off entirely. It didn't matter. Thick fingers accessed her pussy without any problem.

Big, hot hands covered her breasts and squeezed. Calloused fingers and thumbs seized her nipples and rubbed. Sparkles of pleasure erupted to swirl down to her pussy, which was stroked with a firm touch. Her hips rocked in tandem. Her body awakened, unfolded, opened wide to the men.

Cissy wanted to be distracted by their knowing touches. It was hard to not be overwhelmed from exciting tugs to her nipples and clit, by the careful insertion of first one, then a second finger in her pussy. Another finger slid along her folds, wetting itself before prodding her anus to stretch the tight muscle ring there.

As good as all that felt, Cissy held on to the urge to serve. Every time her thoughts scattered, she rolled her eyes up to look at Diltan. Seeing him watch her suck his lengths, his eyes dark and demanding, helped her maintain her focus. She was here to pleasure the Dramok. His satisfaction was her responsibility, one she hated the thought of failing to uphold. His disappointment would devastate her.

He grew plumper and harder under her care. His pulse thudded against her tongue. He rewarded her effort with drops of extra sweet saltiness. His cocks gave occasional jerks. Every indication of fulfilment that he gave Cissy encouraged her to work harder.

At last Diltan curled his fingers on top of her head, capturing a handful of hair to hold her still. He took a slow step back, disengaging from her mouth with a look of regret. His gaze flickered to Wal.

"Have you made her wet for my pleasure?"

Wal withdrew his fingers from Cissy's pussy to hold the slick digits up for Diltan's inspection. "Dripping, my Dramok. She is soaked."

"Good. Pick her up for my use."

Rolat and Wal lifted Cissy between them. Arms supported her back while they each took a leg, holding them up and open.

Diltan peeled his shirt off and shoved his pants down to his ankles before drawing close. "You may put me in place for your fucking," he told Cissy.

She grasped his cocks again, aiming them at their intended berths. Diltan tilted his hips, nudging his tapered lengths into her. She sighed. It was strange to note how empty she felt as she readied for him to fill her.

He did so, thrusting in one great movement. Cissy's body yielded to the driving shafts, hurting in the most wonderful way. It tore the breath from her. Her loins seized, close to orgasm all at once. She arched against the arms supporting her as she cried out her elation.

Soft tightness enfolded Diltan, squeezing him with perfect tension. She took him, having no choice in the matter. The Dramok thought perhaps Cissy didn't want a choice. Her glad shout and the flexing muscles clutching his dicks verified that notion.

Fully embedded in her heat, Diltan paused so that she didn't succumb to orgasm too soon. He stood still, buried deep in the luscious little Earther, revelling in the power he held.

The three of them served him right now, giving over all control to Diltan. Wal and Rolat, their cocks straining their pants, had put their own needs on hold for him. They cradled Cissy's lush body so that Diltan might enjoy her. They would wait until he had sated himself on this woman before having her themselves…if he allowed it.

Wal and Rolat were their own men, strong and sure. They had forged careers and success on their own merits. They did not give themselves to be ruled because breed dictated Diltan was a natural leader. Yet there were moments like these, moments during which they handed over all control of the unit to Diltan, when they recognised the force of his personality and conceded he had earned the right to direct them.

Wal and Rolat watched Diltan fuck the woman they also wanted, keeping her in place for however long he required them to. The power added to his excitement, feeding his ardour.

Cissy's spasms calmed while the Dramok contemplated the wonder of being granted the gift of his clanmates' regard. She looked up at him with wide, glazed eyes. Waiting to fulfil his needs. Another amazing gift, one he felt he should earn with all speed.

Having noted her crumbling so quickly from his first thrust, Diltan wanted to see her completely overcome. He grabbed her sumptuous ass, delighting in how it moulded to his grip. He drew almost all the way out.

Diltan plunged back in and kept plunging, over and over, taking Cissy with strength. She squalled by the second thrust, writhing in the arms of the other two men as her sheaths clenched hard around Diltan's driving lengths. Her hands slammed against his chest and hooked into claws. The feeling of her nails biting into his skin, dragging fiery lines down to his belly, sent liquid fire rushing into his secondary cock. Diltan's mouth opened wide, displaying fangs as they descended from the roof of his mouth.

Cissy screamed and twisted in Wal's and Rolat's grip. They held on to her, their fangs also unhinging as they held her prisoner for Diltan.

She would go over in a matter of seconds. Diltan wanted to be responsible for that release. As Cissy scratched fresh furrows down his chest, he pinched her clit.

She detonated, her body straining as he slapped their groins together. Her wails filled Diltan's ears. The wild sound, along with the feeling of her womanhood drawing desperately on his larger cock, brought a thick ribbon of heat surging from his secondary prick into the primary. He was coming.

The fiery trail raced between his cocks, squeezing down, forcing more rapture. Diltan's breath froze in his throat, his world coming to a standstill for the briefest of instances. At that moment, his seed arrived at the end, poised at the border between man and woman. The Dramok's whole body galvanised, frozen at the precipice.

The violent river broke free, pouring from him in heady bursts. Diltan's head filled with blinding brightness. His ears buzzed. Every hair on his body stood on end. His staccato groans announced each surge of release that emptied his straining loins.

At last his body quieted, climax leaving small shudders in its wake. Diltan opened his eyes, his breath still ragged in the aftermath.

At first glance, Cissy looked as if she'd lost consciousness. She lay limp in Wal and Rolat's arms. The two men still held her in place. Their strained expressions told Diltan of their excitement and agony.

"Cecilia," Diltan said. He cupped her perspiration-shiny face in his palm.

Her eyelids fluttered. She blinked as she tried to focus. "Huh?"

He quelled a chuckle at her confusion. Despite his shaky legs and thundering heart, Diltan was not quite ready to relinquish the command they had all given him. There were still two men to be taken care of. He had to hope Cissy possessed the strength to do so.

Making his tone firm, Diltan said, "Now you will suck Wal's cocks. Mind you do a good job of it, little girl. My Imdiko is precious to me and I will not tolerate him being disappointed."

Cissy's eyes snapped wide open at that. Temper flashed like lightning. Diltan thought she might tell him to go suck Wal himself.

Instead, she gave him a look that spoke of hurt pride. "Of course I will do a good job of it, Master. I serve him as I do you."

Again, Diltan had to fight off a grin. Even playing the subservient, Cissy had a rebellious streak a mile wide. She wasn't going to let him get away with questioning her abilities.

Then she noticed the scratches running down his torso. Her breath caught. "Oh. Oh, I-I didn't mean to—"

"To show how much you enjoy me? I'm glad you did. Feel free to demonstrate your appreciation anytime, Cecilia." He gave his clanmates a smug look that challenged, *See if you can do half so well.*

Two pairs of purple eyes narrowed at him. Message received.

Rolat and Wal set Cissy down on the floor, helping her sink safely to her knees. Though her balance wavered a little, an after-effect of the strong climax Diltan had given her, Cissy pulled the Imdiko's trousers open and took his cocks out. Within moments her mouth surrounded him, making Wal groan.

Diltan almost groaned along with him, though his own passions were sated for the moment. The Earther had quite the talented mouth and she used it with spectacular results.

Wal had a weakness for being watched, which no doubt enhanced his pleasure as Cissy sucked him. The Imdiko's gaze went from the woman at his feet to Diltan and Rolat and back to Cissy. His chest rose and fell. Feeling his clanmates eyes on him as he was fellated got to him in a hurry. Diltan thought he detected a minute tremble in Wal's legs.

It was a lovely sight. Pleasant-faced Wal turned arresting when he smiled…and when he was aroused. The lines of his usually tense expression eased. His sometimes too-hectic gaze turned unfocused. Everything about his face softened. Diltan fell in love as if for the first time every time Wal looked like that.

He felt a similar surge of adoration for the woman kneeling at Wal's feet, making his Imdiko look so stunning. Cissy was just as beautiful as Wal right now. Her hair was mussed as befitted a woman being loved. She strained to take as much of Wal's lengths as she could, her mouth stretching wide. She shouldn't have looked gorgeous like that, but she did. Her attitude of giving everything for their pleasure elevated her, just as Wal's smile did for him. Plus she had all those soft curves that made Diltan's depleted dicks twitch anew.

Wal's hands tightened into fists. His eyelashes fluttered. The trembling moved from his legs up his body. Knowing the signs, Diltan called a halt. "That's enough, Cecilia. Strip and lie on the lounger, my Imdiko. Cecilia, you will fuck him until he comes."

His face lost in a dreamy smile, Wal answered, "Yes, my Dramok." He pulled his clothes off.

"Yes, Master." Cissy crawled over to the couch to await the Imdiko.

Wal joined her, his trim and toned body draping prettily over the cushions of the seating. Cissy clambered on top of him. Within moments, she rode the man beneath her. Wal pulled her down so that he could mouth her breasts while she fucked him. Their moans mingled in the air.

Diltan caught Rolat's eye and nodded to a basket of long, blue-plumed reeds that decorated the table. The

Nobek grinned at him. "For pleasure or pain?" he said in a low voice so as not to disturb the lovers.

"Pleasure for him, pain for her," Diltan said.

Rolat fetched them each a reed. They approached the lounger.

Cissy's hair covered the top half of her back. Diltan moved it so it lay over one shoulder. She didn't seem to notice as she slid up and down Wal's cocks. She would notice soon enough, Diltan knew.

Cissy enjoyed the slow build of returning arousal. Wal sucked her breast deep into his mouth and gently bit into the soft flesh. Meanwhile, she bobbed up and down on him, enjoying the friction of his twin girths inside her and the heady jolt of her clit against his groin. She controlled the pace, the depth and the motions. Being in command of the big man beneath her was heady stuff, particularly since she knew Diltan actually called the shots. Plus Wal could decide to overcome her at any moment. With the tiny ache from his bite and that thought, her excitement flared bright for an instant.

Even when I'm in charge, I like the thought that I'm not. Who would have thunk?

Cissy paused to grind her clit against Wal's hard body in slow circles. Nice. So incredibly nice, especially with Wal groaning around his mouthful of her—

Two stinging stripes splashed across her back. Cissy gasped and shot up straight, yanking her breast out of the Imdiko's mouth. She stared at Diltan and Rolat standing on either side of the lounger. They each held switches.

No, not switches. They held those decorative reeds from the basket on the table, the ones with the feathery soft plumes.

Diltan, who stood behind the lounger on her left, frowned at her. “Did I tell you to quit fucking my Imdiko?”

Cissy looked at those reeds, feeling the sting they had left. She swallowed, excitement building. “No, Master. I’m sorry.”

She raised herself over Wal once more, more sensitive than before to how he slid through her channels. Diltan waved his reed before her, letting the soft part circle one of Wal’s nipples. The Imdiko’s breath caught.

Another streak of biting pain erupted across Cissy’s back. She arched with a little cry. The movement made her breasts thrust forward. Diltan tapped the reed stem across the top of them, sending sparks through the mounds. The warm tendrils of pain communicated directly to her clit.

All at once, Cissy was not climbing to arousal. She was there.

Between switching her, Diltan and Rolat traced Wal’s straining body with the velvety fronds. They used the blue plumes to caress his breathtaking face, his throat where the pulse drummed, his dark and pointed nipples and his trembling abdomen. Cissy received a feather-like touch at the crevice of her ass. She knew they teased his rear cock when she rose over him, exposing the base of it. Wal’s pleasure was Cissy’s, too. She experienced every sigh that escaped his lips, every breathless moan that his clanmates’ play elicited.

For her, they served up delightful bites of pain. They painted thin pink stripes on her upper chest with the reeds and she felt every one they laid upon her back and buttocks. That was her pleasure as well. The heat of the switching filled her body. The stings were an exquisite counterpoint to the growing spasms that made her pussy and ass clutch Wal's cocks.

Cissy rose and fell on the man beneath her faster. Her hands planted on his chest, giving her better leverage to slam her sex down on his. She took him hard, riding the building excitement to its crescendo.

Wal howled. He gripped Cissy's hips in a punishing grasp as he strained up. His cocks jerked within her, jetting hot seed deep inside. Then her own orgasm swept in, carrying her up to the blinding heavens.

It seemed they would come together forever, the pair of them grinding hard into each other, extending the heady release for as long as possible. They clung to every ebbing surge, unwilling for it to end.

At last it did and Cissy leaned sideways against the back of the lounger. She sat that way so she could watch Wal's still-gorgeous face, relaxing with the afterglow of completion. She basked in the knowledge that she had help transform that worried visage into this beautiful angel's serenity, if only for a little while.

Rolat's strained voice cut into her contemplation. "Damn, I almost wish I wasn't so aroused. I could look at the two of them that way forever."

Diltan chuckled softly. "It is a sweet vision, isn't it? Have you ever seen a lovelier pair? However, if they have the strength to move, you have waited long enough, my Nobek. Wal, can you get up?"

The Imdiko judge blinked, as if reluctant to wake from a wonderful dream. "I suppose so."

"I'll help get the nicest obstacle out of your way."

Strong arms lifted Cissy. It made her sad to feel Wal slip out of her. He rolled off the lounger and onto the floor, in no hurry to gain his feet. That made the other two men laugh.

Diltan set her back onto the lounger. "Lie face down in his place, little girl. Ass up in the air."

Since he'd put her on her hands and knees, it was a simple matter for Cissy to get in the position he ordered. She knew what the pose invited and smiled. This was going to be good.

Diltan continued to play the role of absolute leader. "Use your hands to spread your cheeks wide. Beautiful, just beautiful. I'm going to enjoy watching this. My Nobek, that sweet ass is yours."

Rolat's gruff voice shook Cissy's bones as he took his place behind her. "Thank you, my Dramok."

The side of Cissy's face was mashed into the cushions. She felt rather than saw Rolat's anticipation of what was about to happen. Rough fingertips skated over her spine. Thick muscled legs pressed the insides of her thighs farther apart. Hard, wet heat poked with brazen insistence at her ass and pussy.

As eager as the Nobek was for her, he didn't rush to claim pleasure. Instead, he rubbed up and down her back. The strong hands would have been relaxing except Cissy was slack from the last orgasm. Rolat's touch felt good nonetheless, making her feel almost sleepy with contentment.

Rolat sighed, a happy sound. "She's pretty with those stripes that haven't faded yet. That round ass open from you two, waiting for me to fill it. Nice, wet pussy that smells like woman and my clanmates all combined in one amazing scent. This is paradise."

His hands left off stroking Cissy's back. A moment later, a row of hard knuckles stroked up and down over her pussy and clit. All at once, Cissy was no longer loose-limbed with relaxation. Her breath caught and a jolt of pleasure rocketed through her core.

"That's it, pretty girl. I hoped you had something left for me."

Rolat ran his knuckles up and down her slit. Cissy moaned and her fingers, holding her ass cheeks wide as Diltan hand commanded, bit deep into the soft flesh. It was all she could do to not pump her hips up and down in time with his caresses.

He swapped knuckles for fingertips, scooping some of the wetness coming from her. He rubbed it against her asshole, lubing her with her own juices.

"She's still pretty wet back here from you two, but it's always good to make sure she's ready."

"Especially with you," Wal said, his voice sleepy. "Your primary cock would make a kestarsh proud."

Cissy thought of how large and thick Rolat's main cock was, the one he was about to put in her bottom. She shivered.

She felt the tapered tip of him settle there. Feverish, she fancied it was burning the smaller of her openings, branding her as his. She shivered again and made herself relax.

Rolat sank into her ass. Having taken Diltan's and Wal's secondary penises, Cissy experienced only a slight ache as the Nobek's girth widened. She sighed to feel how her body accommodated the big man.

His smaller cock parted the folds of her pussy. Rolat gripped it to angle it precisely, sliding into her with ease. Then he reached to pet her clit.

Delight washed through her, a physical rush that made Cissy feel the most alive she ever had. Her senses sparkled with acute awareness, every mote of sensation a glittering gem. She no longer desired to move against Rolat, to claim anything from this third of her lovers. She froze in place, wanting this sweetness to last for as long as possible, to be able to experience it in its entirety.

Wal spoke, telling her he had risen from the floor to stand close and watch his clanmate take her. "Look at you disappearing into her. If I hadn't come so damned hard a few minutes ago, I'd be coming right now just watching this."

"I bet it feels as good as it looks," Diltan chimed in. He sounded awed.

"Better," Rolat murmured. "Fucking exquisite."

Being watched with Rolat enhanced the passion for Cissy. Inside, she felt liquid, as if she melted over high heat, set to boil. The twin thicknesses filling her massaged her interior, as Rolat had rubbed her back…except the effect this time invigorated rather than relaxed. His fingers still played over her clit, rubbing and stroking and tugging her to greater diamond-bright rapture.

Other hands joined in the pleasuring, cupping Cissy's breasts, combing through her hair, smoothing over her belly. As the three men concentrated on her, she felt something beyond mere sexual pleasuring. She felt like the centre of the universe, as if she had been made the most important thing in creation. She was the focus of the clan.

*This—*this *is what the Kalquorians have been talking about. All those times they assured us Earthers that we would be the heart of their clans – this is what they meant. They weren't just pretty words. This is real.*

Cissy would have liked to wallow in that singular sensation, but Rolat was ready to fuck. The hand not engaged in teasing her clit closed around the back of her neck. She was almost disappointed when he started to thrust steadily.

Yet the feeling of being central to the men surrounding her didn't leave. As Rolat's pace grew faster, as their bodies met with louder and louder reports, as pleasure crystallised into exquisite points of bliss that tried to take Cissy's consciousness away, she never lost that feeling that she was all that mattered to Clan Diltan.

She wept as she climaxed hard, feeling a sense of belonging that had only ever been approached by ties to her family. She wanted to be a part of this forever. She wanted to grasp this nirvana tight in her fists and never let it go.

Pleasure ebbed. The wonderful, soul-enhancing sensation did not. Diltan, Rolat and Wal gathered around her afterwards. They fetched her water and food to rebuild her strength. They cuddled with her, keeping her warm and safe. When she was capable of standing again, they somehow squeezed their hulking bodies in her tiny shower to bathe her.

Wal used sheets, pillows and cushions to make up a bed on the greeting room floor that could accommodate all four of them. She snuggled between him and Diltan, with Rolat spooning against the Imdiko.

This is where I need to be, Cissy thought for what must have been the hundredth time. *This is what I was meant for, even if my Dramok is an ambitious jerk sometimes.*

Unaware of her great revelation, Diltan smiled his nice smile, the one he didn't use when he felt pompous. "My day ended a lot better than it started."

"So happy to have been of service, sir." Cissy winked at him, though teasing was the last thing on her mind. Still, she didn't want to scare the men off by moving too quickly. She knew she had her clan, the one that was perfect for headstrong, uncivilised Cecilia Salter. She just had to be patient and wait for them to realise it, too.

Chapter Twenty-Two

Two days later, Maf summoned the Ethics Committee to the conference room. Within minutes, Diltan's temper reached a full boil.

Maf, the object of his ire, spouted the vitriol that had the population of Kalquor screaming for indictments. 'Gangs of thugs', 'a syndicate of sexual slave owners' and 'traitors to the Empire' were among the vile accusations he made. The council baulked at blanket indictments as so many of its members had been the first to clan Earther Mataras. They were open to charging Yuder and Ospar, less so Tidro and Rajhir. Tidro was too old for most to want to drag him through a trial and he had been out of the public eye for the last few years as he tended to the ill Zarl. As for Rajhir, he was one of them, a Royal Councilman. To charge him would open the rest of them to indictment. The conflict in yesterday's open chamber had got ugly.

Leading those shouting for legal proceedings was Maf, along with his ally in the council and on the committee, Terbal. Maf was determined to accuse as many men as possible and drag them into the courts. He seemed to care not at all for the tension in the streets as he pursued his idea of 'justice'.

At the committee meeting, the man's attention focused on one of the easiest targets, trying to get the committee to come to a consensus. Diltan watched him with growing dislike as he spoke and gestured to the documents hanging over the table on the floating vid.

"Further investigation has revealed that three days after arriving at Plasius and allegedly testing Amelia Ryan for breeding compatibility, Dramok Rajhir's clan sent a message to then-Ambassador Ospar at the Galactic Council. That message read, 'Your old friend Councilman Rajhir sends his greetings. Unfortunately, we cannot attend your party because we are viewing the rare flower that blooms bright on Plasius.'"

Diltan scowled and debated him as he had almost every point. "So what? The man likes flowers. I see no conspiracy there."

Maf gave him a withering look. "There are no records of Ospar throwing a party within weeks of that communication. No indication that a gathering of any kind was planned. I believe this message was a code. Rajhir was telling the ambassador that Amelia Ryan was viable for bearing hybrid Kalquorian-Earther children."

Efo rolled his eyes. "That's reaching. You see conspiracies everywhere."

"Do I? The very next day after Rajhir sent Ospar this communiqué, Kalquorian ships in the vicinity of planets and stations where Earther women were employed sent emissaries to meet with them. Many of those emissaries were our fellow councilmen like you and Gamas here. Which begs the question, did Ospar speak to you directly about the matter?"

Gamas snarled, "As I've testified in earlier proceedings, the orders from Ambassador Ospar's office bore the official seal of the Kalquorian Empire. I spoke to no one personally on the matter."

Efo nodded with emphasis. "The same for me. For all I knew, it was decreed by the rest of the Royal Council while I was away at the time."

Maf slapped his palm on the conference table. "We were in recess! Even if the council had been gathered for such a vote, a matter of such magnitude would not have been decided without the Imperial Clan's unanimous decree! This smacks of impropriety."

Diltan pointed out, "Impropriety is not grounds for indictment. There is no real case against Rajhir."

Maf's face creased in a snarl. "Imperial Father Yuder has already implicated himself and Zarl. That indictment is a done deal. Ospar and Rajhir were at the very least in collusion with them and most certainly without the Royal Council's sanction! They must be held responsible as well!"

Diltan couldn't help but take pleasure in reporting, "Imperial Father Yuder retracted his confession yesterday under the advice of his attorney."

Maf blinked and Terbal muttered under his breath as he tapped urgently on his handheld. The papers withdrawing Yuder's confession had been filed late the night before. Only a handful of people, Diltan included, were aware of it.

Maf sputtered, "He can't do that. He spoke before a full council and the live feed that went out to all of the Empire."

Diltan shrugged and settled back in his chair. "He can deny his confession if he has a valid claim of undue emotional duress."

"Being accused of a crime cannot be cited as mental distress."

"But his Dramok's death can be. Yuder is grieving his clan leader of nearly two hundred years. That is no small matter in the eyes of psychology. It is a defence as far as making a false confession."

Maf stared at Diltan for a long beat, his eyes narrow. When he spoke again, it was in a low, insinuating tone. "I see."

Diltan was sure Maf didn't refer to Yuder's legal strategy. "What do you see?"

"That we have the Imperial Clan's mouthpiece in our chambers."

Diltan had known that sooner or later he would be accused of this very matter. However, that didn't keep his temper from sparking heat in his voice. "I am no such thing."

Maf snorted in disbelief. "You have been seen slipping into Emperor Clajak's chambers for private consultations since all this came to light. You are also trying to woo a member of Empress Jessica's family into becoming your Matara. You have an agenda, Councilman Diltan, one that puts you in danger of not doing your job as a member of this committee and council."

Diltan sneered, "I have no more of an agenda than you, Councilman Maf. You've played your hand close to your chest for some time. Yet your dislike of the Kalquorian and Earther races mixing in order to continue the Empire is clear now. With this scandal, you believe you have the chance to pursue nothing short of madness. You hope that others might entertain the ludicrous idea that Kalquorians should die out 'pure' rather than look forward to a grand future with the Earthers. You more than welcome the opportunity to cause dissension—you're jumping on it. Now we see the true fanatic in you. We see the man who would fight for destroying what our society has built…and all because you don't like Earthers."

Disgust pulled at Maf's face. "They are inferior to us. They were monsters who didn't appreciate their lifebringers, who starved the poor in their lust for power. Pathetic weaklings who would not rise against their oppressors though they outnumbered them. Superstitious witch doctors who cried out to a god to save them rather than taking control of their own destinies. This is Kalquor's grand future?"

Diltan's gut tightened. "You have met our empress and think such about them? She is as fierce as any Nobek, as caring as any Imdiko and as dedicated to honour as any Dramok. She is equal to any Matara born of Kalquor."

"She is the exception."

"No, she is the face of the typical Earther. It was their leaders who were the monsters, not the everyday people living their lives. But how could you know that? You have not bothered to talk to many of those people or to hear their stories. Instead, you made up your mind and turned a blind eye to who these Earthers really are. You are the one who is inferior, pathetic and superstitious. You are afraid, Maf."

Maf's expression was set, telling Diltan he had not reached the man at all. "Yes, I am afraid. I'm afraid of men such as you who are ready to give our legacy to these undeserving creatures. We should walk proudly into our destiny, leaving behind our names to legend. The great Kalquorian Empire, which surpassed them all! Instead, we will be lost as a mere footnote. We will disappear into the obscenity of Earther blood and that race's madness."

"Accept extinction? *That* is the madness, Maf. I, for one, refuse to concede to such an ignoble fate."

He got a grim smile for that response. "If the masses rise, you will have no choice."

"The masses will not rise. This temporary hysteria will die down and sense shall restore itself." Diltan tried to make it sound as if he believed it.

"Sense is being restored. If exposing the lies of emperors and councilmen fractures the Empire, so be it! I will not live with anything less than the truth from my leaders and their lackeys." Maf's eyes glittered.

Diltan played his last card, though the game was lost when it came to changing Maf's mind. "Anyone who foments revolution against the Empire is a traitor, Councilman."

The other man's face twisted with fury. "Anyone who seeks to hide the truth from the people is a traitor. I am uncovering the lies now. I have enough evidence of those lies to bring at least Yuder, Ospar and Rajhir to trial."

"The Royal Council will determine that, not you."

"The people call out for it and even this reluctant council cannot ignore the will of the people. Tidro and all the rest of these abductors will follow. If the Empire crumbles, it will be because of the falsehoods propping it up and we are better off."

Diltan had heard enough. He was done with politeness and decorum where Maf was concerned. "If the Empire crumbles, maybe the Basma will give you a nice job as his right-hand man. In his gratitude for doing his dirty work, it's the least he owes you."

The two men glared at each other. The rest held their silence, looking from one to the other. Lines had been drawn and enemies made. Now it was down to the battle.

* * * *

Cissy snickered as Rolat fed her a bite of ytor. It was a delicate mussel from the nearby marshlands. It held just the slightest hint of salty brine that complemented the savoury sauce it had been baked in. Yet she had visions of being fed grapes as she lounged across the Nobek's lap in the sumptuous dining room, lit in the glowing golden light of the dying day. It was impossible not to feel like a queen in the midst of fine drink, food and doting men.

She laughed all during the meal, her giggles punctuated by the clinking of dishes and glasses of leshella. Being fed by three men was too hilarious for words. "I'm going to change my name to Cleopatra," she announced.

"Was she as beautiful as you?" Wal asked with overbearing sweetness, designed to make her laugh harder.

"Reports as to what she looked like are conflicting, but she managed to bring two great men and an entire empire to their knees," Cissy said in a mock-warning tone.

She didn't miss the way Diltan's and Wal's expressions sobered at that comment. After that, the two men were quieter than before. A sense of foreboding lay behind their continued teasing.

As the meal drew to its close, Cissy decided to draw out Gloom and Doom, as she'd begun calling the Dramok and Imdiko in her head. She was pretty sure she knew what lay behind the pinched furrows between their brows. They needed to talk it out.

She sat up on Rolat's crossed legs and looked at Wal on her right then Diltan on her left. "You know, it's hard to have fun when half the room consists of sourpusses."

As the two blinked, Rolat mused, "Sour pussies?"

Unfortunately, he pressed another ytor into her mouth when he said it. Cissy bellowed half a laugh before she started choking on the bite. There were shouts of alarm. Diltan's fingers invaded her mouth to pull the ytor out as Rolat pressed hard on her diaphragm. They cleared her airway so fast that Cissy didn't have time to panic. In fact, she went right back to laughing the moment she could.

"Sour pussies! Oh jeez, that's funny as hell. Sour*pusses*, you big lug. Earther slang for worried faces. Diltan and Wal are pretending to have a good night but they're not."

Everyone relaxed as they realised she was in no danger of dying in their arms. Rolat offered her some leshella to drink. "Yes, I noticed they were not having as much fun as you and I." He looked at his clanmates. "Is it anything either of you can speak of?"

When Diltan and Wal both hesitated, Cissy said, "I bet I know what Diltan's problem is. Jessica said indictments were handed down today."

Concern flooded his expression. "Maf is going after Yuder, Rajhir and Ospar. He's got a list of more to accuse, if he can convince the judiciary."

"Mostly members of the Royal Council," Wal added, even grimmer than Diltan. "Enough to bring the Empire to its knees."

Diltan stared at Wal with growing angst. "They are assigning you to judge the case?"

Wal reached for his half-empty glass of leshella and downed it. When he looked at the bottle on the table, Rolat moved it out of his reach. The Imdiko sighed but said nothing of his disappointment. Instead he told them, "My name is among the first five of a very small list. Some of those on the list I know for a fact will be unable to sit on the panel for various reasons. I will still try to bow out, of course."

Cissy also eyed the leshella with longing. Rolat had told her in private that Wal had been known to drink heavily when he was upset. He was not an alcoholic, but liquor attracted him as a crutch. Diltan and the Nobek had agreed years ago to make sure their sensitive clanmate would not rely on alcohol to numb his feelings.

If Wal couldn't have a drink, Cissy would not imbibe, either. Instead, she faced the issue as her sweet-faced companion must—head on and sober.

She asked him, "Will they let you opt out?"

Wal shrugged. "Possibly. Hopefully. A lot depends on how far removed they believe you are from the case."

"Me?"

He smiled and the concern-ridden face turned beautiful again. "I am courting you and you are a member of the Imperial Family. Can I see you as a lover and remain impartial?"

Diltan frowned at the bottle of leshella, as if it were the focus of all these erupting issues. "My objectivity has been called into question because of that. Maf made a motion to have me ejected from the Ethics Committee if I don't withdraw my suit for Cissy."

Everyone gasped. Cissy's stomach rolled over in a sick wave. She swallowed hard.

She did not want to give up Diltan's clan. Her throat filled with an aching lump more constricting than the ytor she'd choked on. The idea of even a temporary absence left her empty and lost.

Well, fuck me raw. I'm attached to them. Really attached. Cecilia Kaye Salter, did you fall in love with these guys? Is that what you did?

It was a question to be examined later. First things first. She asked them, "Does that mean we have to stop seeing each other?"

It made her heart beat faster to see the furious intent on Diltan's face. "Absolutely not. I refuse to bow to that. Maf can have my seat on the Ethics Committee and I'll tell him where to shove it, too."

Wal glanced at the leshella again. "I agree and I wish I had the luxury to follow your lead, my Dramok. Unfortunately, I don't. If I am bound to sit this case's panel, my fellow judges could command the issue for as long as the trial lasts." He managed a tight smile for Cissy. "However, I will not volunteer who it is I am seeing to the judiciary. We could keep it quiet and hope no one challenges the involvement."

Diltan shook his head. "Maf will not let you get away with it, Wal. He will scream collusion to the entire Empire."

Cissy scowled at the air before her. "I couldn't bear to keep quiet about our relationship anyway. Secrets. Nothing good ever comes from them."

With Rolat's chest against her back, his voice rumbled through her entire body. "And what dark mysteries are you keeping to yourself, little one?"

Only one thing could have distracted Cissy from the current problem facing them. The old horror reared up its dark head to smirk at her.

Yes, Cecilia. Why don't you share the one real secret you've kept from everyone? The one that has weighed on you for so many years? Tell these men who might be the ones you could spend your life with. See what they think of you after that.

She almost forgot to breathe. Her voice barely more than a whisper, she said, "I have no secrets that concern my life now."

Wal took her shaking hand in his and pressed it to his cheek. Gazing into her eyes, he asked, "Then why so upset? Why are you trembling? Cissy, don't you know you can trust us?"

His look was that of a father soothing a frightened child. The care in the Imdiko's eyes enfolded Cissy. It made her feel safe despite the looming danger. Rolat's arms tightened around her, providing shelter from all harm. And Diltan… Diltan leaned close to comfort her. The arrogance he wore like a shield dropped away. Its loss exposed naked concern, along with the resolve of a man who would do everything in his power to help the woman he cared for.

I think I could tell them someday. Now is too soon, though. It must be too soon.

Tears pricked her eyes. When had she ever felt so safe? Cissy had always been the one to watch out for others. She had been strong for her parents and her sister ever since she could remember. Now at last, she thought perhaps she might have found those who would look out for her just as much as she would for them.

If we can get through this mess that's going on right now, I'll be able to find out. I think that it's here, but it must wait a little longer.

Staring into purple eyes that had become too familiar to be alien any longer, Cissy grasped the warmth in her chest and clung to it fiercely. Feeling the men's strength flowing through her, she said, "It happened a long time ago. There's no point in talking about it."

In a gentle version of his 'I am Dramok and lord' tone, Diltan said, "But you just said you hate secrets, my lovely. Cissy, you see the trouble lies and cover-ups have done to this Empire. It could become so much worse. It's enough that I have to live with it outside my private life. Don't bring secrets in here, too."

She reached up to caress his jaw. Its tight set relaxed under her touch. "It's not a secret that concerns what we have…what we're building. I swear it, Diltan. It can wait."

He shook his head. "It can't, not when it puts that pained and frightened look on your face. I can't bear it, my beauty. Show me the trust I need from you. Let me show you I deserve it, that I can be the Dramok you can count on."

Tears threatened again, making Cissy's eyes blur over. "What if what I've done makes you hate me?"

Rolat shifted her so he could look her in the face. "You are incapable of such a thing."

Diltan laughed in disbelief. "Hate you? Cecilia, if you threatening to pull my dicks off and make me a woman didn't do that, nothing would. I told you of the awful mistake I made with your cousin. Whatever you've done in the past, it can't be that bad. I mean, it's not like you murdered someone."

"Actually, I did."

Chapter Twenty-Three

The three men jerked in surprise. They stared at her with identical thunderstruck expressions.

Wal was the first to recover. "Murder? Not you. Never."

Cissy closed her eyes, unable to look at them. She hadn't meant to blurt out her guilt like that. How crazy was it that she, a woman with blood on her hands, had ended up emotionally invested in three men sworn to uphold law and justice?

Karma, how you do love your irony. I knew I would have to pay for my crime eventually, but I never expected it to mean having my heart ripped apart. Going to prison for life would have been easier than losing the chance I had with these men.

Keeping her eyes closed to hide from them, she said, "I didn't mean to, but yes, I did set out to do harm. It ended with me killing a man."

"An accident then." Wal sounded relieved.

"Not really. No, it was murder. I can't pretty it up and call it anything else."

Diltan's tone had more of its commanding edge. "I think you should tell us the story, Cissy."

She drew a deep breath and opened her eyes. She would not hide her guilt or shame from them.

How sweet that Wal looked concerned rather than judgmental. Rolat's expression was one of interest, as if he'd met with a talking dog, got over his surprise and wanted to see what would happen next. Diltan's face was schooled to display nothing of his feelings. His eyes riveted on her face, as if he would learn all her secrets.

There is just this one, you gorgeous bastard. It's big enough to cover a gazillion little secrets that you probably expected.

The cat was out of the bag. It was down to the details now. She might as well get this over with.

"It happened back on Earth, when I was still a child. One of our neighbours was this man who was nice to all the kids in our neighbourhood, about a dozen of us. He would let us use his swimming pool when it was hot. He handed out candy and bought us toys at Christmas. Nothing too expensive, just fun little games and things. We all liked him. We trusted him. He was like everyone's favourite uncle."

Rolat's face darkened like a thundercloud. Cissy could tell he thought he knew what was coming. "Tell me he didn't gain your trust and then hurt you."

"Not me. Tasha."

The men exchanged glares. Rolat's muscled shoulders swelled against the short sleeves of his shirt. Wal's features tightened. He appeared ready to weep and scream all at once. Diltan maintained his stern façade, but Cissy spied the way his eyes widened and mouth tightened. The intensity of his gaze tripled. There was tension playing about him and she thought that if he lost control, he might be more destructive than Rolat.

Cissy wasn't surprised. Sweet, inoffensive Tasha was the last person anyone would want to see victimised. It had nearly driven Cissy out of her skull when she'd found out.

She hurried on with her story, wanting to push it all out before anyone could erupt. "One day while a bunch of us were using this man's pool, Tasha went inside his house to use the toilet. He cornered her in there."

Diltan gave vent to some of his feelings. His voice thick, he said, "By the ancestors. How old was she?"

"Twelve. He didn't go as far as raping her, but he made her take her swimsuit off. He touched her. That's all I know about it because she wouldn't tell me any more. She said the only reason she told me that much was so I wouldn't let him get me alone."

Sickened, Wal asked, "She didn't trust your parents to tell them? To have them confront the monster?"

Cissy swiped at the tears creeping from her eyes. "Even if she had, what could they do? Our laws said a victim of sexual misconduct was as much to blame as the man who attacked her. If my parents had gone after him legally, Tasha might have been convicted of tempting him. She would have been sent to the work camps for her crime…and most who went into the work camps did not come out alive."

She watched as the men fought to absorb this. Wal's head sank towards his chest to rest his face in his hands. Rolat stared into space, his fangs showing as he glared at nothing. Diltan kept his gaze on Cissy, however. He gripped her hands in his, as if to pour strength into her.

Wal raised his head and took her other hand. His expression was filled with pain but compassion as well. "I have heard of how your courts treated victims of such perversions. I had heard, but to know your sister went through the fear of it… There are no words. No words at all."

"Finish the story, Cissy," Diltan urged. "Get it all out. What happened next?"

She licked her dry lips. "I promised Tasha I wouldn't tell our parents. We were scared that since they couldn't do anything legally, they might take justice into their own hands. It was a no-win situation."

"But you decided to do something about this monster."

"I was afraid he would go after Tasha again. I thought he might threaten her into making her do more things. He could have accused her of exposing herself to him, of trying to get him to lie with her. She has a small but distinctive scar under one breast, one that can only be seen if she's naked. He saw that. He could have told authorities about it, proving his case to them."

Rolat growled something. Cissy thought it was *bastard,* but the rumbling quality made it hard to tell.

She continued. "Two nights after he touched her, I snuck out of our house with some matches and lighter fluid. I set the front and back doors of his home on fire, but not the windows. I was sure he could get out. I just wanted to scare him. Maybe make him move away from us. That's all. Okay, if he happened to get hurt, too, that was fine. But I didn't intend for him to die."

Wal's expression eased. "He didn't escape, I take it."

Cissy sighed. "It turned out his fire safety system's wiring had been gnawed on by mice or moles or something. There was a hole in the outer wall where something had gotten in and chewed right through the wire. When the smoke alarms went off, his windows should have automatically opened at a touch, allowing him to get out. They didn't."

Diltan's eyes glittered. "He got trapped."

She nodded. "The newspaper said he did break one of the windows. He tried to climb out, but a sliver of glass cut right across his throat. He bled to death before rescue got there, hanging halfway out the window."

There. It was out. Cissy's fire, meant to frighten the neighbour away, had instead resulted in his death. If that wasn't murder, she didn't know what was.

The men were quiet for a few seconds, absorbing the tale with sober expressions on their faces. They sat there, forming verdicts in their minds. Cissy waited for them to rule on her guilt.

If they hadn't been part of the legislative and justice system of Kalquor, she thought they might pardon her actions. Cissy knew that Kalquorian men were protective enough of women to kill. Tasha, in particular, would incite the most defensive actions of any man.

However, these were men charged with upholding laws and punishing wrongdoers. Diltan had proven through his actions that even emperors were not above the law. They must see her for what she was—an accidental murderer but a murderer nonetheless.

When Wal spoke, he shocked her. "I would say justice was determined to be served, even if you didn't want to be a killer. You did not commit homicide, Cissy."

She shook her head at him, though her heart filled to know he was willing to find her innocent. "You wouldn't say that if you were judging the case."

One side of his mouth twisted up in a weak smile. "Actually, I would. If the crime had been committed on Kalquor, you'd be tried for arson and possibly manslaughter. However, the mitigating circumstances would lead me to sentence you to psychological testing and counselling for the trauma you had suffered. Perhaps some community service, depending on your level of understanding of the crime you'd committed. Probably not, considering you were only a child at the time of the incident. No, intensive recovery therapy would have been my decision."

"But, Wal…a man died."

Rolat snorted. "He went too easily considering his crime against Tasha. Under our laws, a sexual predator of minors would have been executed if found guilty anyway. He would have died a slow, agonising death."

Diltan nodded. "With executioners lined up for the privilege of doing so."

Cissy looked from one man to the next. It dawned on her that nothing had changed between them—save for the pride for her actions that shone in their eyes.

"You mean all that? You don't think it's awful that I killed someone? That I'm a horrible bitch for ending a man's life?"

Diltan held out his arms to her. "Little girl…come to me."

Reassured by the tender expression on the Dramok's face, Cissy crawled to Diltan.

He gathered her in his arms. The other two men crowded close, surrounding her once more. Cissy sank into the sensation of being the one protected instead of the protector. Part of her chided herself for the weakness, but didn't even the strong deserve a moment or two of being cared for? She'd have to ask Rolat.

For now, her gaze centred on Diltan. There was no trace of his trademark smugness on his stunning features. All was tender regard mixed with affection. Cissy basked in it.

His smile was far from the arrogant cast she'd grown used to. It was a smile that made her heart flutter, like some fairy-tale princess meeting her prince. Cissy wanted to groan at the mushy turn of her feelings, but right now the sensation was too right to summon disgust.

Even Diltan's voice felt like a gentle caress. "What a wonderful sister you are, taking care of Tasha like that. You went to your sister's rescue. No one with an ounce of sense would ever fault you for it. Besides, who knows how many other victims that monster attacked?"

Rolat took her hand to press kisses to each of her fingertips in turn. "Not to mention how many potential victims you saved from him. Your actions were those of a loyal, brave person."

Wal cradled the back of her head in his hands. "Even if you had intended his death, there were too many variables to call you a murderer. You were a child, a frightened child taking on a responsibility too great. You have earned no criticism."

Cissy could have argued that. She didn't believe in execution, even for the most heinous of crimes. Her faith taught her that as long as someone lived, they could be redeemed. Her act had not been for vengeance, but the result had taken away a man's chance to redress his wrongs.

Yet as Diltan's mouth pressed against hers, all self-recrimination fled. His kiss was slow, his tongue sliding in to twine with hers. As he kissed her, the other two men stroked her body with feathery touches. She trembled at the care they gave her. It was somehow more profound than the raucous play they had indulged in up until now.

They slipped her clothes from her body. The men continued to kiss and fondle her with devoted attention. Cissy's senses were astounded by how such tender touches could send her every cell alight. At once she felt melting soft and hyperaware. Mouths and fingers stroked soft tendrils of sensation that flared bright until she whimpered and shook in Diltan's lap.

They left no inch of her untouched. Mouths sucked on her earlobes, lips, nipples, fingers, toes and clit. Warm, raspy tongues tasted all the trembling flesh they could find. Fingers explored every hill and fold, discovering the warm places, the sensitive parts, the secrets of her body. When their discoveries made Cissy cry out and strain with overwhelmed pleasure, they held her still as they coaxed storms of ecstasy free. When each squall ended, they started over again.

Cissy was only dimly aware when they carried her to their sleeping room. The billowy cloud of the mattress beneath her back and the warmth of Diltan and Rolat on either side roused her just a bit from her blissful dream. Wal's solid heat covered her and the welcome joining of his body to hers brought renewed desire. He moved over her, his flesh sliding within hers with easy, hair-raising friction.

As he loved her, the other two men continued to kiss and stroke, now dividing their attention between Cissy and Wal. The Imdiko moaned into her mouth and she answered him as they strove for mutual bliss, aided by the urgings of Diltan and Rolat. Their cries rose to crescendo as pleasure swept their twined bodies.

Then Rolat's bulk pinned her. He was careful as Wal had been. The Nobek's restraint made Cissy feel his power as never before. Once more she and the man she made love to were encouraged by the other two. Knowing caresses goaded them towards shared rapture, adoring encouragements spoken in whispers. Cissy had a few wondrous moments of feeling Rolat filling her with his pleasure before her cries joined his.

Then Diltan blanketed her. Her most beautiful lover. Her often irritating opponent. Cissy realised that beneath the arrogance was a strong, loyal man, someone the equal to her strength. Someone who would call her on her rebelliousness just as she would call him on his overreaching ambition.

We were made for each other, she thought. Then his cocks slid inside her and she thought no more.

Long, careful but eager strokes kindled into shared fire as they stared into each other's eyes. They moved together as Wal and Rolat added to the heat, blazing hotter with each passing second. When combustion came, Cissy gave herself fully to the flames, screaming Diltan's name. Her ears rang with his shouts of her name. They burned and burned, feeding themselves to the inferno until there was nothing left but glowing.

Cissy drifted in the arms of the men surrounding her. She thought she must have fallen asleep, because Diltan's voice pulled her into reality from a long way off.

"There now. Will that do as a reward for being such a good sister?"

Cissy sighed, snuggling between her lovers. "Killing is wrong. I believe in that with all of my being, but what you said about keeping that awful man from harming others also makes sense. I feel much better."

She smiled at the three faces surrounding her, her heart filled with warmth. No, filled with more than just that. Filled with…love.

Love. She loved these men. Even the one still lying on top of her, the one who drove her crazy most of the time. Perhaps especially him.

Cissy mentally shook her head, trying to order her thoughts. It couldn't be. It was the afterglow of wonderful sex making her silly, making her think things that couldn't be. Falling in love wasn't possible yet, was it? It felt wrong to be head over heels all at once like this. Yet it also felt perfectly right.

With all the problems they faced right now, heaven help her.

Chapter Twenty-Four

Clajak kept his face impassive as Councilman Maf presented his evidence to the rest of the Royal Council and all of the Empire. The Dramok Emperor had no doubt every man and woman of Kalquor watched the vids. They probably exclaimed as angrily as the onlookers in the filled-to-capacity public gallery.

Every word out of Maf's mouth damned the Empire's leadership. Clajak could not take comfort in the fact that Tidro had thus far escaped extradition, nor that Jessica's family was not in the private gallery watching the proceedings. Not when he could feel the very foundations of his world shaking beneath his feet. Not when, despite all of Yuder's protestations, he knew Tidro was as guilty as the rest of his clan.

The threat of violence was all too real for anyone connected however remotely to the scandal. The cries for revolution grew every day. Public leaders and their followers made accusations of genocide. Many of the people called for the resignation of the entire council, for new elections to take place. There were calls for Yuder's, Ospar's and Rajhir's executions.

More troubling was the dissension coming from the military's ranks. Bevau received reports by the hour from the ground forces and space fleet of a spike in insubordinations. The fighting part of the Empire, the majority of its numbers made up of unclanned Nobeks, was in turmoil. Some even openly sided with the Basma's call for the government's overthrow and expulsion of all Earthers.

Jessica sat to the right of Clajak, the expression on her elfin face impassive as Maf continued to argue for indictments. That alone was a sign to the public that things were not well. Clajak's beloved mate had no problem letting councilmen know when she was displeased with them. People watched council meetings with the Imperial Clan much as a sport because of her. They loved to see their feisty little Earther empress rip apart the arguments of her opposition. That she kept herself under iron control while Maf sneered over the 'evil intent' of his targets, men she cared for, showed she knew her opinions would not be welcome in the present atmosphere.

Clajak did not try to fool himself about what they were on the brink of. Civil unrest waited to spring to life, urged on by untraceable transmissions from the Basma. Demonstrations were already planned. Clajak had no doubt riots could soon follow. With the angry mood of the Empire's populace, injuries were all too expected. Maybe even deaths.

From there, civil war was not so difficult to imagine. The Empire would be broken, torn apart in a horrid cataclysm of fury. And the Earthers who had come to Kalquor, fleeing first a government that allowed no personal freedoms then the atrocity of Armageddon—what would happen to them?

They came here looking for happiness and security, all the wonderful things we promised. Will this snatch it away? Are we all doomed after everything we and they have done to survive?

Equal measures of cheers and heckling came from the public gallery as councilmen rose from their seats to challenge Maf's accusations. Clajak glanced up at those he led, those it was the Imperial Clan's job to guide, protect and care for. Were the two sides as evenly balanced throughout the Empire? Was this small sampling representative of the division of Kalquor?

More and more councilmen jumped to their feet to argue with one another. Clajak noted one man who kept quiet, however—Councilman Diltan. The man watched the proceedings, his handsome face despondent. No doubt he brooded over how it was he who had brought all this ugliness to light.

Clajak didn't blame Diltan for the mess. That responsibility lay with others. The proof of wrongdoing, particularly by Zarl and Yuder, could not be denied. Diltan had done what he was supposed to. He had acted with unfailing honour, as well as circumspection on the matter.

Clajak had little to console himself with, so he clung to the nuggets of brightness that he could find. Diltan was one of these small bits. The usually ambitious councilman had been working with Jessica on the one mote of hope they had of keeping the Empire from ripping itself apart. Once something of an irritating sycophant, Diltan had emerged as the staunchest ally to the Empire's survival.

Dramok Maf, on the other hand… Clajak's gaze narrowed as he took in the bent form of the man shouting down all the rest. Maf had seemingly made it his life's mission to destroy their home's peace. It was Maf who trotted out the evidence with disgusting glee. It was Maf who shouted for justice no matter the price. On and on he went, ramping up the rhetoric. He cried for truth, but his arguments were for nothing less than revolt. Despite his devastated body, twisted from birth, Clajak had never seen Maf as ugly. However, the man's revealed fanaticism was pure vileness.

It took all of Clajak's determined self-control to not let his lips curl at Maf's continued diatribe.

"…and now the Galactic Council of Planets has renewed its call on us to reveal the truth of these horrid crimes against Earth. Our reputation as a realm of justice has been called into question by the other worlds. We no longer have a choice. We must bow our proud heads. We must accept that our leaders have defamed our glorious legacy. We must give them the satisfaction of seeing us fall to our knees in shame. Even though our name be tarnished, we cannot fail to do what is right. We must avenge the deaths of billions of Earthers, killed by our own monarchy! We must have justice for the loss of our birth right by the forced interbreeding with a lesser species!"

His eyes were hectic with victory, his face flushed as he looked around. Shouts for and against his words erupted anew. The widening rift of his people seemed a cause for joy to judge from his smile, a thought that sickened Clajak.

The man had held the floor long enough, Clajak decided. The Dramok Emperor stood up tall, as if his soul didn't feel beaten down by all that must come. His clan stood with him, just as straight, just as silent.

It took a few moments for everyone to notice. The screaming lessened bit by bit, blowing itself out until there was silence. All eyes were on the Imperial Clan. Clajak sensed the Empire waiting with held breath, frightened but eager to know what came next.

Clajak let that silence spin out for a few moments before he spoke. He drew a deep breath to keep his voice steady. Like Jessica, he could not give in to an emotional response, not when so much weighed on his every motion, his every word.

His voice echoed in the vast chamber. "That we would bring the three accused men before the Galactic Council is beside the point for the purposes of this vote. We will concentrate for now on our own laws and justice. Nothing else at this time matters.

"The Royal Council has heard and reviewed the evidence against Imperial Father Nobek Yuder of Clan Zarl, as well as Dramoks Ospar and Rajhir. You will now vote on whether these men, and these three men alone, will stand trial. You will do so based on the evidence before you." His intent gaze swept over the blue-robed men of the council. "I remind you all that this is no matter for sentimentality. Make no mistake—the Empire is watching and will judge you for your actions this day. Our people will voice their opinion on your conduct and hold you accountable. Let it be done."

The Imperial Clan remained on their feet as the councilmen hunched over the handhelds that would record their votes. Clajak was not surprised to see the numbers for yes and no on the overhead vids count up slowly and evenly balanced.

Little by little, the results tallied. The gallery muttered and calls rose as first one side gained advantage then the other. It was going to be close, Clajak realised.

His feelings on the matter were mixed. Rajhir was a decent man. Ospar had a history of being somewhat underhanded in his dealings, but his goal was always for the good of the Empire. And the thought of his own father Yuder standing before a panel of judges… Dread dropped like a stone in Clajak's stomach. He did not want to see any of them harmed. It was unthinkable.

Yet if they did not stand trial, all hell would break loose. Clajak knew it for a fact. Men he cared about and their clans must face potential disaster in order for Kalquor to survive. There was no other way. That meant if the council did not vote to indict, Clajak and his clanmates must overrule. He would be forced to call for trial himself.

The knot in his stomach eased only a little as the vote for indictment gained ground. He would not have to call for his father's prosecution. It wasn't much to be spared from, but he grasped it as he did all the other little pieces of light in the growing darkness.

At last the final vote was counted. Clajak bowed to the cluster of blue-robed men before him.

"The Royal Council has made the difficult decision. You have affirmed that there is no honour without truth. There is no Empire without truth. We must have the truth, no matter how ugly its face may be. Nobek Yuder, Dramok Rajhir and Dramok Ospar will stand trial. The Legal Committee will take charge of the case from this moment. This council is adjourned."

Shouts and arguments renewed both on the council floor and in the gallery. A small contingent of Global

Security officers entered the chamber to assist the Royal Guards should violence break out.

Clajak didn't wait to find out if fists would start flying. With Egilka leading and Bevau watching over their clan with fangs and a knife ready, Clajak gathered Jessica to his side. They left the mayhem under heavy guard.

* * * *

Wal was in the middle of researching case precedent over ongoing litigation when the sound he'd dreaded went off—his door announce. He straightened in his hover chair and bookmarked the document before closing it. He licked his suddenly dry lips.

"Yes?"

The voice that spoke was the one he'd feared hearing. "It's Onziv, Wal."

The Imdiko drew a breath to steady his pounding heart. He rose and called, "Come in."

The door opened to admit the highest-ranking judge on Kalquor. Wal exchanged bows with Dramok Onziv.

Once that respectful pleasantry was out of the way, his visitor did not mince words. "An indictment has been handed down for Imperial Father Yuder, as well as the other two men."

His heart sinking, Wal motioned for Onziv to take the seat on the other side of his curved desk. "As we suspected it would be."

He eyed the senior judge as the man took the seat. Onziv looked his part. Intelligent, resourceful, of unimpeachable honour...all these qualities seemed to be spelled out on his strong and pleasant features. No one had ever questioned the Dramok's right to preside over the Empire's highest court.

He was also a friend that Wal had found he could express any concerns to. He did so immediately. "Onziv, I cannot sit on this case. My clan vies for the Earther lifebringer Cecilia Salter, Empress Jessica's cousin."

Onziv's gaze was steady and kind, though full of regret. "I am aware of your situation, Wal. I am aware…and I am sorry. Daha fell ill last night and was hospitalised."

He referred to the eldest of the high court's judges. Dramok Daha had been in poor health for the past year. It was no surprise to hear he was yet again recovering from some ailment. That it had happened now of all times told Wal he could not avoid the call of his duty.

Onziv continued, his strong voice softened with consideration. "With Nalp and Yij dealing with cases off-planet, you must sit on this trial. I cannot spare you."

A flare of desperation went off in Wal's breast. "Surely the case can wait until one of them returns?"

Patient as always, his friend said, "The Imperial Clan has called for an immediate trial. There is too much unrest following the accusations levelled by Councilman Maf and the Ethics Committee. The matter must be dealt with as quickly as is feasible. Even if you haven't been paying attention to the growing anger—and I know you have—your Dramok would have apprised you of the situation."

Wal could only sit in his misery. He knew what must happen now. For him to preside over the case, his clan would have to give up their suit for Cissy.

Onziv's face scrunched up, as if he had felt a sudden pain. "By the ancestors, this cousin of Empress Jessica is the one for your clan, isn't she?"

It was hard to think when Wal's gut hurt so much. Yes, Cissy was the one for him and his clan. He was in love with her. Right now, that love tore him apart as it became apparent he might lose her.

Onziv appeared almost as miserable as Wal felt. "Perhaps when this trial is over—"

"Who knows how long that will take?" Wal burst out. The pain was no longer in just his gut. His whole body ached. "One minute is too long to not be a part of her life."

He stared at his desktop, unable to look at the man who was taking away the last vital piece of the puzzle that made up Wal's happiness. Cissy's truce with Diltan had grown into affection. She seemed as happy with their clan as they were with her. Yet there had been no words of love spoken, no way to know if her feelings approached the intensity of Wal's. She might wait for them until this mess was over and they were able to take up their suit once more. Then again, she might not. The trial could last months. While Wal sat on the panel listening to evidence and arguments, other clans would pursue his Matara.

More pain thundered through him as his pulse thudded in his head and his jaw clenched tight. The thought of Cissy—his Cissy—with another clan put him in agony as physical as it was emotional.

Onziv's tone was pure sympathy. "I am sorry I can't spare you this, Wal. We must put our duty first, however."

"What of my duty to the woman I love?" Anger made him glare at his friend like an avowed enemy. "I should have Diltan clan her right away so the case will be forced to wait until someone else is available."

Onziv's expression hardened, becoming much like that of a strict father. "Wal, an entire platoon turned on their company commander yesterday. The reason they gave was because his clan's Matara is an Earther. She came to them through the lottery, but his men were screaming 'abductor' and 'traitor' as they beat him. He barely escaped with his life."

Wal blinked, his momentary rage quelled.

Onziv slammed a fist on the desk surface. "This matter has the Empire going crazy. More and more people are calling for Kalquorians to follow the Basma. Violence is breaking out all over the planet. This issue cannot wait. You must do what is right for the Empire before yourself or we may very well lose it."

He was right. Wal knew it, though it sickened him to give Cissy up. Yet there was only one thing he could do.

"I will sit on the panel with no further argument. Forgive my lack of integrity."

Onziv snorted something that sounded like a cross between a sob and a growl. "Don't be ridiculous, my friend. There is nothing to forgive. When you have been blessed with a lifebringer, everything else seems insignificant."

Onziv had clanned an Earther Matara last year. Of course he knew the agony Wal felt. Being denied the woman who made one's heart beat was a nightmare no one would want to live through.

Yet Wal had to do so. Somehow he managed to choke, "Thank you for understanding."

Onziv's usually strong voice had gone feeble. "Good luck, Wal. I hope she waits for you."

So do I. Wal had never wanted a drink as badly as he did at this moment.

* * * *

An hour later, Wal's clanmates clustered around the empty table in the visitor's conversation area of his office. Rolat sat straight up, his legs crossed before him, looking as strong as ever. However, his expression was despondent.

Diltan slumped next to him, elbows on the table, his drawn face propped in his hands. "Damn it. Damn it," he muttered.

Wal gazed miserably at the two men who until now had been enough to keep his life happy. "I'm sorry, my Dramok. I tried my best to get out of it, but there is no way that I can avoid sitting on the panel for this case…unless I resign."

Diltan's head snapped up at that. His gaze riveted on Wal as he reached over and grasped the Imdiko's hand. "You can't do that. You've worked too hard to get where you are."

"But for Cissy—"

"She'd never forgive you or herself for being the reason for leaving your post." Diltan sighed and shook his head. "It's not your fault, Wal. None of this is and I will not have you beat yourself up for it." He scowled. "I never should have revealed what was in those damned records. Both our world and our private lives have suffered for it. What good are honour and duty when the future can be so easily swept away?"

Rolat gave them each a piercing stare. "You did and will do what you have to, both of you. All that has happened is the result of others' actions." He went back to looking dejected. "I keep telling myself that if Cissy cannot wait for us, then we have no business clanning her anyway. Unfortunately, my heart is as stubborn as the rest of me. It does not wish to hear such wisdom."

"Nor mine." Diltan chuffed tired laughter and shook his head. "How did that loud, opinionated rebel get to me? Not that it matters. She did. And now my stomach is churning because we must walk away."

Wal swallowed. At least he wasn't alone with his broken heart. Not that it made things hurt any less.

Diltan asked, "Can we at least have tonight before I retract our suit for her? One last time that will perhaps convince her we are worth waiting for?"

Wal somehow found a wan smile. "I can give us that. Onziv will not register the final judging panel until tomorrow."

"We will make it a night to remember then. One that will hopefully sustain us all until this madness is behind us and we can claim our Matara." In a choked voice, Diltan said, "How did this happen? How is it that no woman other than our uncouth, bratty little hellion will do?"

Wal didn't answer. His throat had constricted, making speech impossible.

Chapter Twenty-Five

Cissy was already naked when she walked into Clan Diltan's playroom. The men had stripped her back in that ridiculously grand ballroom, leaving her clothes in a puddle. They'd done that after the expected news that the courtship was over. Expected, but it was still as painful as Rolat delivering a punch to her gut.

They told her everything that was at stake, why Wal must concede to the high court's dictates. She understood. The matter was bigger than one Earther woman's happiness. She must put her desires aside, along with her happily-ever-after. For the good of Kalquorian and Earther alike, she had to let Clan Diltan walk away.

Cissy managed to not break down. She'd known this could happen if Wal was pulled in on the case. The Imdiko looked as devastated as she felt, which was of some small comfort. At least she wasn't alone in her agony. Rolat and Diltan were resigned and angry in turns. They would miss her and not just because she was a potential mother to their children. Even if they hadn't fallen in love as she had, they still wanted her. There was feeling there, feeling that might have grown had this calamity not befallen them.

Cissy used that knowledge to buttress her strength. She told them she regretted that she would not be able to see them for a while. She thanked Diltan for putting up with her shenanigans. Just to make him roll his eyes at her, she also thanked him for not being as big an asshole as she was sure he was capable of. Instead of making his irritated expression, Diltan uttered a choked sound and pulled her in for a kiss.

"Let's do this night," he whispered. "Something that will hold us during the weeks that we must be separated."

Of course she agreed, but Cissy knew damned good and well that the second she parted from the clan would be the loneliest second of her life. It would be followed by an infinite amount of even longer seconds, seconds that would tick away, one per lifetime.

Cissy stepped into the playroom with her back rigidly straight, shoulders thrown back, jaw clenched closed. One might have thought she marched to her execution rather than a night of pleasure. She needed to be strong to face that these might be the last hours she would spend with this clan. She needed to keep them from seeing her heart ripping apart.

Cissy turned to face the clan. She looked into Wal's sweet, tormented face, into Rolat's stern visage that more than hinted at turmoil and at Diltan's perfection marred by pain. All at once her resolve crumbled and Cissy dissolved into sobs.

Big arms folded around her shaking body, enclosing her in the most temporary of warmth. Wal's anguished voice rang in her ears. "It doesn't have to be this way. Diltan, ask her to clan!"

Rolat's growl answered. "You will be censured if he does so, my Imdiko. You might even be sent to preside over a lower court. Your career would never recover."

"I don't care. It is a small price to pay."

Through her tears, Cissy saw Diltan waver. His mouth was open, the offer on the tip of his tongue. For a brief moment, she almost let selfishness win. She almost let him ask. If he did, she would say yes. Then no force on Kalquor could pull them apart. The matter might be very different the other way around, however.

One question. One answer. One clan to shatter an entire empire.

Cissy put her trembling fingers over Diltan's lips, stilling the words ready to tumble out. "Remember what you told me. Wal would not be the only one to suffer if we do this. Don't say it, Diltan. If you value your people, don't do it. I'm not strong enough to tell you no."

His warm breath shuddered over her fingers. His throat worked. His body tensed. He fought to keep the words from escaping.

The Dramok groaned. His teeth clenched together and his eyes squeezed shut. Cissy sensed the monumental effort he made to contain himself. Her aching heart warmed as she watched him battle to do what was right.

He wants me this much? Does he love me then? Will he wait for me?

Diltan drew himself up, pulling in a deep breath as he took control. His eyes opened and he looked at her. With every bit of Cissy's being begging for it, the love in that gaze came as no surprise. Perhaps it was only wishful thinking, but she could grab and hold on to it with all her might. With everything else in shambles, she had to believe.

Diltan grabbed her wrist and held it steady, keeping her fingers to his lips. He kissed them and smiled at her. Then he looked at his tortured Imdiko with the same steady care.

"Wal, we must not clan her. If we do, you will be taken off the case. Kalquor will lose your objective but compassionate voice in the matter, the very thing this nightmare needs most. Not only that, but the high court will be forced to postpone the trial until a full panel can be assembled. The Empire cannot wait. It is already strained to the breaking point." Diltan faltered for a moment, pain crossing his features. Then it was gone and he was their strong leader once more.

"I will not ask her to clan at this time."

Wal's head dipped, allowing his mass of hair to hide his face from them. Rolat put a hand on his clanmate's jerking shoulder and squeezed.

Cissy couldn't help the sob that broke from her at Diltan's words. He caressed her cheek and bent to kiss her lips. "It's only for a little while, my sweet. I swear when this is done, nothing will keep me from being at your door the very next second."

Wal's breath hitched, but when he raised his face again, it was filled with resolve. "I will permit no delays in the proceedings, Cissy. No one will stall the case for ridiculous reasons. I will fight any and all attempts to do so."

"That's good," she managed in a weak version of her mocking tone. "I hate the thought of Diltan backsliding into being such an ass again without me around to put him right."

That made the three men chuckle. Diltan grabbed her to pull her close against his strong, gorgeous body. "My little brat, if you will have us when this is all over, we will re-apply for your consideration."

If she would have them? Cissy knew there was no other clan for her.

Love isn't all sunshine and flowers. It's not even close. It's more like a version of Hell. But hey, for me it would be par for the course. Everything to do with me has to be contrary.

She gave Diltan a light punch on the chest. "You'd better re-apply for me. I can't keep you from pursuing other candidates, but be warned. If I catch you with any other Earther girl, I will kick her ass all over the Empire."

Rolat made one of his animal sounds. He stared at her in disbelief. "Pursue others? *Fah.*" He made the last sound as if he was spitting out something disgusting. "There are no other Earther girls as far as I am concerned. There is only my Cissy."

Hearing him say that made fresh tears spring to her eyes. *Damn it, when did I become such a weak bawl-baby?* she wondered. But it gave that tiny beam of hope in her heart more to shine about.

Diltan kissed the moisture trailing down her cheeks. In a firm tone, he said, "Enough of this. I don't want tonight spent in regretting what must happen. We will enjoy our time together."

He scooped her up in muscled arms, arms that felt strong enough to shield the entire Empire. It was a shame it was only an illusion. Still, Cissy tried to let the fantasy steal her away from despair.

Diltan carried her to a padded table on one side of the room. It had soft restraints, but the Dramok did not bind her.

"You will allow whatever we wish," he said. His usual commanding tone was soft and his gaze on her filled with pained warmth. "You will obey because you want to, not because you are made to."

"Yes, Dramok." A now-familiar curl of arousal wove within her belly. The idea of surrender made anticipation spike despite her glum mood.

This could be our last time together. It will be if I don't show them how much they mean to me.

She bit her trembling lip and blinked hard against the tears that wanted to come.

Rolat looked to his clan leader. "I think she needs to be taken out of her thoughts, my Dramok."

Diltan nodded, his gaze never leaving Cissy's face. "No one can accomplish that better than your *dysf*, my Nobek."

"An excellent choice."

Rolat turned and left them to stride to the wall where tools of discipline hung. He selected what looked to Cissy like a cross between a fishing rod and a crop. The handle was thick to fit his ham-sized hand, but the length of it was slender, tapering to a tip that looked no thicker around than a guitar string.

Cissy's latest surge of sorrow abated in an instant. She licked her lips as Rolat returned to the table.

His smile was a strange twist of adoration and danger. "This delivers only a slight sting, but the effects can be profound. What do you say if it becomes too much?"

Her voice gone husky with anticipation, Cissy answered, "*Sholt*, Nobek."

"Very good. Raise your arms over your head. Spread your legs. Excellent. Now remain that way until you are told otherwise."

Rolat's arm raised and the slender length of the *dysf* trembled over Cissy's body. She tensed, gripping the edge of the table in her hands, readying for the first blow.

The Nobek's arm flashed in a blur, whipping up and down at fantastic speed. Cissy couldn't even see the *dysf* anymore, so quickly did it move. She didn't feel it, either, not for a couple of seconds.

When the sensation came, it started at her chest, on the upper part of her breasts. Tiny, peppering stings crawled over her flesh. It felt like a slightly sharper version of pins and needles, similar to when her foot's circulation was restored after having fallen asleep. Each swat on its own was not much, certainly nothing to even make Cissy wince. The cumulative effect was another matter.

Cissy writhed beneath the discipline, her body's awareness of sensation coming into sharp focus. She couldn't keep from reacting, but she managed to stay in the pose Rolat had demanded of her. Though it was impossible to follow the *dysf* with her eyes, she felt its effects from her chest to just above her knees. Even her mound felt the tiny bite of the tool, warming under its passage over her flesh.

The sting and heat built until the intensity of feeling had her reeling. Cissy gave herself to it, letting the growing and exciting hurt steal her from the far more painful emotional storms. She lay beneath Rolat's punishment, thrilling at his power over her.

Even as her smarting flesh moved towards real torment, Cissy exulted in it. When Rolat stopped, she cried out in disappointment.

She didn't get to wallow in regret for long. Wal and Diltan stepped forward, one on either side of her.

Hands and mouths descended on her body, bringing renewed sensation to where it throbbed the best. Diltan's fingers and teeth plucked at her nipples. Wal wet his fingers in her font as he sucked hard on her clit. Then the Imdiko plunged those fingers into her pussy and ass, working in and out of her softness.

It was even harder now to stay in position as she'd been told. Cissy's head tossed from side to side as they dealt pleasure as unmercifully as Rolat had applied punishment. Her cries filled the room. Her sex pumped juices over Wal's hand as he fucked her hard with talented fingers.

Diltan rose to slap first one breast then the other. Cissy gasped as the heat from Rolat's switching burst into a conflagration. Then she shouted when Diltan bent and drew a tit deep into his hungry maw.

Her clit engorged, ready to explode as Wal sucked hard. His tongue rubbed over the electrified nubbin, making Cissy feel as if her mind would burst right out of its skull in elation. It wasn't just her pussy and breasts reacting to their attentions. Her entire body turned into one pulsing mote of arousal. It felt as if even her hands and feet could climax.

The first warning jab of oncoming orgasm prodded her pussy. It was that moment that Diltan and Wal released her and stepped back. Rolat came forward once more and his arm moved in a blur.

Cissy screamed and arched against the table, offering herself to the *dysf*. It nipped her as before, but this time it felt more like delight than pain. Her body begged for climax and it tried to make the *dysf* deliver by inviting it to strike the softest bits. Need only roiled higher with every tiny blow. Cissy burned with tension, but release came no closer than to watch with a teasing smile.

It was a relief when Rolat stopped again and the other two men stepped in once more. Handling her as they had before, Cissy would achieve completion in no time. She panted, thrusting her breasts up and spreading her legs wider, ready for the end.

Diltan and Wal had other ideas, however. They had traded spots this time, with Wal lapping at her nipples. Diltan slid his fingers against her pussy lips, wetting them so that he could fill her ass again and work it open with care. His tongue traced slow, lazy circles around her clit instead of touching it directly.

Cissy trembled under them, her body straining for enough contact to detonate. The two men would do no more than taunt her with gentle touches and soft mouthings this time. It kept her burning but would advance no more.

"Please," she strangle-screamed after what felt like an eternity of their sweet torture. "I can't. No more. I can't."

"You can," Wal whispered. The mere tip of his tongue grazed her jutting nipple.

"You will," Diltan confirmed. A third finger teased her anus into letting it enter.

Put in her place, Cissy had no choice but to lie there, shaking under their demands. They were meticulous in their assault, giving her just enough to suffer but not enough for release. Cissy blazed with agonised bliss.

They moved away at last, leaving her quaking and groaning. Rolat returned. He was naked, his cocks flushed purple and livid as the *dysf* moved over Cissy once more. She stared at them through a veil of tears, wishing he could continue the discipline while fucking her with those thick members.

At some point while Rolat whipped her writhing body, Cissy's consciousness decided it couldn't take any more. It floated in a dreamlike state, somehow becoming serene even as she gasped with the feeling of scattered stings. Her flesh raged with the blaze of the *dysf* and desperate arousal. Yet, all at once, it didn't matter. Cissy's thoughts shut off and she drifted in a sea of ecstasy and wondrous agony.

"Good. She's there." Diltan's resonant voice came from far away, like a god speaking from the mountaintop.

"Look at her face. Have you ever seen anything so beautiful?" Wal smiled down at her, appearing out of nowhere like an angel sent from heaven.

Cissy descended. Or the men grew taller, becoming giants standing over her. She now lay level with their crotches. They were all naked, their bodies as eager as hers for salvation.

They turned her on her side. Cissy sighed to feel their warm hands on her, settling her overwrought body. Diltan and Rolat climbed onto the table to sandwich her between themselves, Diltan in front and the Nobek behind.

Someone gripped her leg, raising it so that it draped over Diltan's hip. Cissy smiled to feel hard, hot prods at her pussy and ass. Slick and ready, the primary cocks of the two men filled her. A cascade of delight tumbled through, making Cissy sigh with relief.

Diltan glanced over his shoulder. "Wal, can you manage it?"

A masculine chuckle warmed Cissy's ears. "I'm sure as hell going to try."

A dark object drifted over them. The Imdiko awkwardly crouched over their heads, one foot on the floor as he brought his groin near Cissy's face. Rolat put up a hand to steady him while Diltan gripped Wal's cock and guided it towards Cissy's mouth. She turned her head for a better angle, her lips parting for the gift.

She closed her eyes as the delicious taste and smell of aroused Kalquorian filled her senses. The men all started to move, their sexes slipping in and out of her. New excitement bubbled to life. Fresh sparks caught from the earlier conflagration.

Masculine flesh surrounded her, permeated her. Cissy moved between and beneath hard, muscular bodies, bodies she'd come to know as well as her own. She stroked over Diltan's sensitive nipples, making them pebble as his breath caught. Her other hand reached behind to find Rolat's secondary prick, gripping it so that it slid within her fist as he pumped his primary into her ass. She was rewarded with a drawn-out groan. Her tongue twined about Wal's cock, flicking the tapered tip when he drew it almost all the way out to elicit a shudder.

They knew what to do with her as well. Rolat filled his big paw with her breast, squeezing it to just shy of pain. Wal traced over the nape of her neck, a sensitive area that made every hair stand straight up. Diltan stroked the shaft of her clit, making things below tighten as climax gathered.

She went first. Though Cissy's mind remained serene, her body was too primed to delay gratification for long. She rode the storm of passion, letting it consume her in its glorious violence. When she returned, it was to Rolat's thick groan. Heat poured into her ass. Then Diltan's body stiffened and he added his cries to the Nobek's.

Wal's climax hit just as Diltan stopped shuddering. Salty-spicy-sweetness flooded Cissy's mouth. She had let go of Rolat and used her still-wet hand to milk the Imdiko of every precious drop from his straining cocks. She sensed the other two men touching him, too, but she couldn't tell what they were doing with her face buried against his groin.

A minute or so after he had emptied, Wal stepped to the floor. He staggered a little as he grinned at the others. They grinned back. For the moment, all angst had disappeared from their lives.

He said, "I don't know about the rest of you, but I can barely stand up after that. We can sleep or I have stim tabs."

Cissy was quick to answer. "Stim tabs, if everyone is in agreement. I don't want to miss a single second of this night."

Diltan turned his too-beautiful face to hers and kissed her. "My thoughts exactly. I will waste not one precious moment on sleep."

Chapter Twenty-Six

By the time the eagerly awaited trial of Imperial Father Yuder, Councilman Rajhir and Governor Ospar of Haven was ready to commence, two months had passed since Clan Diltan's goodbye to Cissy. Full spring had arrived, bringing mild nights, balmy mornings and tropical afternoons.

Wal enjoyed little of the fair weather. For one thing, he had been bogged down in fighting off attempts by the defence and prosecution to file delay after delay. Most of the time he had the senior high judge's support in those matters. Onziv himself would preside over the panel for the trial and Wal had little doubt his friend understood the haste he pushed for to get the trial underway. Still, there had been a few snags, postponing the start of the case.

Then there was the matter of missing Cissy. Wal ached with actual physical pain over not seeing the woman his clan coveted. Though the sun shone brightly on most days, the Imdiko felt as if a darkness had fallen over him. It didn't help that Diltan's and Rolat's tempers were testy. Every report that the trial date had been postponed left his clanmates surly. They didn't take it out on him, knowing he did his damnedest to move things at a faster pace. However, the atmosphere of their fine home was tense most of the time.

At last, the day to begin the proceedings arrived. Wal met it with a mixture of relief and worry. After all, the rumblings throughout the Empire were growing louder. Protests against the governing body took place nearly every week. High officials with Earther Mataras had taken to hiring security for their clans. There were reports that entire squads within the military planned to walk out. Men who had failed to clan Earther Mataras thus far had thrown in with the protestors out of jealousy. Unclanned men with little hope of winning female mates, the vast majority of them Nobeks, aligned themselves more and more with the Basma's call for a species-pure Empire.

The courtroom that Wal walked into was a testament to the emotional storm gripping Kalquor. The domed facility, housed at the top of the Imperial Justice Centre, was packed with onlookers. Wal, Onziv and the rest of the judging panel had made it a point to advise the news vids that the first day would be taken up with the prosecution reading documents already available to the citizenry to study. Yet the people had come anyway. The public gallery on the floor could hold no more. The near silence of those gathered seemed ominous to Wal.

The five-man judging panel made their way to their separate podiums on the raised semicircle platform at the front of the court. Wal's gaze immediately went to the prosecutor's dais, since it was located in front of his side of the judging stage. He did not like what he saw.

Sitting in the chairs directly behind the podium along with the prosecutor Dramok Chamar were Councilman Maf and his aide Dramok Sitrel. Diltan's assertion that Maf had gone fanatical over the allegations of Imperial treason appeared to be borne out by his presence there and not in the Royal Council's gallery. While it was common for councilmen to voice their opinions about legal matters that affected the Empire at large, it was unusual for an elected official to be taking such a partisan approach. Maf attending the High Court in obvious favour of one side of the matter was a bold and inflammatory statement.

Wal reminded himself not to read too much into Maf's presence. The man had a legal background, having performed as a territorial attorney general before being elected to the Royal Council. He was adept at litigation.

Wal saw movement at the corner of his eye and looked up to the Imperial gallery balcony on his left. The Imperial Clan filed in along with their red-formsuited Royal Guards. Nobek Emperor Bevau came in first, his handsome face composed though he scanned his surroundings as if to look for enemies. Next came Empress Jessica, lovely as always, her elfin features at odds with the grimly determined look on her face. Emperors Egilka and Clajak entered together, their heads close together as they conversed. On Clajak's heels came his ever-present aide Korkla. Then the Imperial Mother Tara came in. Her face was serene despite the fact that her lover Yuder would be fighting for his freedom and perhaps his life in the next few days.

Then the sight Wal had been starving for came into view—Cissy walked into the gallery with her sister Tasha. Though their features were identical, there was no mistaking which woman was which. Tasha bit her lip with obvious concern. Not a hair was out of place. Her lace white blouse was buttoned to the throat.

Cissy swaggered in, her expression pleasant with an undercurrent of challenge. It said, 'I'll be nice to you as long as you don't give me a reason to tear your dicks off.' Otherwise, she appeared conventional if a touch casual. Her hair was brushed and tucked behind her ears. Her pants and blouse were nicely tailored, the fabric clinging to her body in enticing ways.

A surge of quiet joy as well as trepidation filled the Imdiko. The joyful part gained strength when Cissy's gaze sought him out behind his podium. A smirk quirked the corners of her mouth and one eye slid closed in slow, sexy wink. Wal bit his lips together to keep from smiling. The little rascal. She knew he couldn't appear to be intimate with her in any way right now. However, it delighted him to get that moment of acknowledgement. If she wasn't still interested in him and his clan, she'd avoid his gaze instead of teasing him.

Wal widened his eyes and looked pointedly at the Royal Council's gallery balcony, across from the one where she was now sitting down. Diltan sat at the front with the rest of the councilmen attending this first day of the trial. The Dramok's gaze was on Cissy, waiting for her to see him. They exchanged more frank smiles than Wal had been able to offer. Yes, she was still interested in their suit after two months of no communication. The Imdiko relaxed.

The court official mounting the steps of the judges' platform warned Wal that he needed to attend to his duties. The official conferred for a moment with Onziv then turned to the courtroom.

"This court is hereby convened. Honourable Dramok Onziv presiding as senior high judge of the panel. Let these judges, the accused, the accusers and the citizens attending today conduct themselves with honour in the name of the Kalquorian Empire."

The official left the stage. Onziv raised his hands for quiet, though the room was already silent. A low tone reverberated throughout the room.

The high judge addressed the courtroom. "The trial of the Empire of Kalquor against the accused Imperial Father Nobek Yuder, Dramok Rajhir and Dramok Ospar will now come to order. The prosecution will present its documented evidence at this time."

Prosecutor Chamar rose from his chair and mounted the dais to stand behind his podium. A floating vid appeared in the air over his head, showing documents as he listed the evidence.

For the next two hours, Chamar droned out the case against the defendants. It began with the complaints and condemnations registered by Earth against Kalquor after the Empire had requested breeding compatibility testing. From there were the communications between Emperor Zarl and an unknown person, during which the monarch had ordered clandestine tests on off-world Earther females and their abductions. Councilman Rajhir's strange com to then-Ambassador Ospar about a rare bloom on Plasius was entered into evidence, along with the fact that within twenty-four hours, Kalquorian clans, most of high rank, had claimed Earther women. Sworn affidavits from various planets and space stations documented those clans stalking the women in the days prior.

Wal fought to keep from glancing at Cissy every few seconds as time wore on. He knew every detail about Earth demanding that their women be returned. He'd also been privy to the details of how many Earther women had been allowed to end their regretted clanships due to a new law. That law had been backed by no less than Councilman Rajhir and Governor Ospar, now accused of being behind those clanships in the first place. Those two had also supported the law that stated coerced clanships would no longer be allowed in the Empire. Wal found it hard to attend as he should.

Sparking a little more interest, though still not enough to keep Wal from wanting to stare at Cissy, was an announcement from Earth's Holy Leader Browning Copeland. He'd recorded a message for Earth, which had been broadcast near the end of the war. In that recording, Copeland stated that Earth would destroy itself before it would be taken. He'd also exhorted his people to kill their wives and daughters before allowing Kalquor to take them prisoners.

Last came the final result and the sickening numbers that accompanied it. Earth's destruction when Kalquor invaded, triggered by nuclear devices set to go off if enemy ships entered the planet's atmosphere. Billions of innocent civilian lives ended in an instant. More dead in the aftermath as the poisoned planet lost its ability to support lives. Huge amounts of funds and resources spent in the desperate attempt to salvage as many of Earth's inhabitants as possible. Survivors flung far and wide to try to rebuild their lives, complicating saving a race threatened by extinction.

Though most of the prosecution's report was already known, Wal noted how all those in attendance hung on Chamar's every word. When he was finished, Onziv spoke into the silence.

"We will recess for midday meal. The session resumes in two hours. This court will retire until then."

Cissy filed out with her family. She grinned at Wal before disappearing through the door then puckered her lips in a kissing face. The little minx. She needed a spanking.

He retired to a private room with the rest of the panel where a catered meal awaited them. Realising he was hungry, Wal filled a tray and sat down at the table with the other four men. For several minutes, they were all quiet as they ate.

The Imdiko's thoughts were filled with Cissy and a long way from the case when Dramok Lar interrupted his thoughts. "It has been a long time since this court has had to hear a case against a member of the Imperial Family. I do not like that it has come to this."

Nobek Dorl, the second oldest and longest-serving judge in the high court, scowled at his food. "At least they haven't hauled Imperial Father Tidro before us yet. He is much too old to be sentenced to a penal colony."

Lar pushed a ronka strip around on his plate. "It could be something will come out that will implicate him, however. Tidro was much too savvy and involved in the Empire's dealings to not have known something of it."

Onziv's tone warned them. "I remind my honourable colleagues to not allow yourselves to debate what we have not heard evidence for. We must be careful in this case. Only the facts that are uncovered can be allowed to be shown."

Lar stopped playing with his food and sat back in his chair. "Yes, and the facts could put Kalquorians at each other's throats. It's happening already. This case could well decide the fate of the Empire."

Dorl nodded, his expression grim. "You can't tell me the Basma is not laughing with glee as we hear the case. Mark my words—this will feed his damned revolt."

Gnawing disquiet killed Wal's appetite as it had the others. The five men sat in silence, their food growing cold. Nothing more was said. A heavy pall lay over them, as if they already attended the funeral of their civilisation.

It was a relief to return to the courtroom. It had filled once more, if it had emptied at all during the recess. Wal tried to find solace again in Cissy's face, but now she appeared as sombre as he felt. Whatever the Imperial Family had discussed at their meal had obviously been no more optimistic than the brief conversation in the judges' chambers.

Despite the serious turn, she still looked from Wal to Diltan over and over, as if she couldn't get enough of seeing them. It was much needed-consolation for the Imdiko judge. Kalquor might be on the brink of going to hell, but he had hopes of paradise with the woman he loved.

The court official's voice rang out. "Court is resumed."

Onziv bowed to the woman sitting with two male legal aides behind the defence's platform. Sitting behind her were her clients Rajhir and Ospar. Off to one side, surrounded by grim-faced Royal Guards, sat

Imperial Father Yuder. None of the men showed any trace of emotion.

Onziv asked, "Does the defence have any remarks or business to bring before this bench before questioning begins?"

Matara Nivere of Clan Gegra rose and mounted the steps to the podium. Wal bowed to her, as did the rest of the panel. A Kalquorian lifebringer was a rare and wonderful creature and this particular woman was an accomplished lawyer. She'd won more cases than many attorneys had tried. She was also Rajhir's mother. Wal wondered if that would have any effect on her ability to defend her clients.

She smiled at the panel, though the aura of determination never wavered from her expression. "We do have business to present to you, Honourable Onziv and honourable judges."

"Speak then, defence counsel."

She did so, her voice strong and carrying through the courtroom chamber. "Two of the accused, Dramok Rajhir and Dramok Ospar, will not submit for examination. As their counsel, I concur with their decision."

Finally the onlookers in the courtroom made some noise. Cries of support and outrage echoed through the room.

Maf lurched from his seat, as if he were in charge of the prosecution and not Chamar. "Honourable judges, I most adamantly protest this silence from two of the accused! We are discussing the murder of billions of people, for whom justice must be done. They have no right to refuse examination."

Nivere's only concession to the oddity of Maf speaking was a raised eyebrow. In the anticipatory silence that followed his cry, she addressed the judges. "The evidence against Rajhir and Ospar is circumstantial at best. They were never named in any of Zarl's records as being party to his direct orders to abduct Earther females. Nor has anyone else named them in any traceable documentation during that timeframe. In short, there is no hard proof that Rajhir and Ospar were responsible for the mass Earther Matara clannings which are *alleged* to have been directly responsible for Earth's destruction—an allegation this defence refutes, honourable judges of this panel."

That set off intense mutterings this time, which Wal hoped were better than the previous yelling. Chamar rose to whisper in Maf's ear. The deformed councilman glared for an instant before sitting back down.

Onziv raised his hands, arms held out wide, for silence. He got it, which also boded well for the overall mood, Wal thought. The high judge said, "The session will hold as this panel discusses the matter put forth by the defence counsel."

Wal moved from his podium with the rest of the panel, converging in the soundproof area at the centre of the dais. He already knew the vote he would cast in this first salvo of the battle.

* * * *

From her bird's-eye perch in the Imperial gallery, Cissy watched Wal. It was impossible to hear what the judges discussed, but she saw his intensity as he appeared to argue with his fellows. For an Imdiko, he put on a fierce face.

Since she couldn't guess which way the wind blew over Matara Nivere's motion, Cissy looked across far too much space to meet Diltan's gaze. At least she could see him again. She'd almost been afraid to attend the trial, worried that neither he nor Wal would spare her a glance.

It made the weight she'd carried in her stomach for the last two months lessen to see the opposite was true. Diltan stared at her with so much bald want that her heart threatened to burst from her chest.

If only Rolat had also found a way to be present at the trial. Cissy felt like she starved, her insides yawning wide for any taste of Clan Diltan. Now her eyes feasted on two-thirds of that marvellous entity and begged for more.

Yet it hurt to be so close to Diltan and Wal with no way of being able to touch or even speak to them. Seeing them was just two drops in an arid desert of need. Cissy wasn't sure if not setting eyes on them at all would be worse.

Tasha's voice in her ear was a hushed whisper. "It's tearing you apart, isn't it? I'm so sorry, Cissy, but you'll be with them again."

Cissy glanced at her family, at the men who made up her in-laws. They had been silent for the most part throughout the proceedings, with only a few muttered asides here and there.

She whispered back to Tasha, "Will I? If things go badly for Yuder, it could hurt Diltan's career as a councilman to be seen with me. Those loyal to the Imperial Clan will not forgive his part in this."

Tasha pulled a face. "Diltan doesn't care about that. Look at how he's staring at you. If a man looked at me like that, I'd never let him get away."

Cissy didn't remark at the envy in her twin's voice. Instead she said, "Even at the expense of the man you love? I can't do that." Her words made pain stab her chest. She swallowed the ball of hurt that formed in her throat. "Damn it, I feel like I'm going to die without them. When did I get to be so needy?"

Tasha squeezed her hand. "You're in love. It's wonderful."

"You'd think so. To be honest, it feels like shit."

Their whispered conversations ended as the judges made their way back to their podiums. Cissy saw Wal glance at her as he assumed his place on the high judge's right. The ache came back to her throat and wouldn't move no matter how hard she swallowed.

Judge Onziv addressed the prosecutor and Nivere. "We have reached a decision regarding the defendants Dramok Ospar and Dramok Rajhir refusing to conform to examination by the prosecution. There is indeed no discernible physical evidence that they colluded with Emperor Zarl to effect the abduction of one thousand eight hundred and seventy-three Earther Mataras. By a vote of three to two, these two defendants will be excused from examination at this time."

That set off a new wave of muttering from the people gathered in the public gallery below. It swelled louder. The emperors glanced at one another, their expressions tense.

The court official came forward on the judges' platform, accompanied by two members of the Global Security guards that were stationed all around the courtroom.

The official announced in a firm voice, "There will be silence while the Honourable Onziv speaks. If you do not comply, the court will be cleared immediately."

The temporary furore died down. Cissy and everyone else, with the exception of Bevau, relaxed. The Royal Guards remained on high alert, but then they always were. Cissy suppressed a shiver at the brutal faces of the Nobeks who wore the red-armoured formsuits. She had no doubt the fierce warriors would kill in an instant.

Onziv resumed speaking, claiming her attention once more. “There is enough circumstantial evidence to warrant a penalty for Dramok Ospar’s and Dramok Rajhir’s refusal to speak. Witnesses have admitted verbally that they were given their sealed orders by Dramok Ospar. There is also the matter of Dramok Rajhir’s clanning of the first of these alleged abductees, taken during a time when the Empire’s relations with Earth were precarious at best. For this reason, both men will be taken into custody for refusing to speak. They will remain in custody until the trial ends or they submit to prosecution’s questions. Furthermore, if testimony and evidence are presented that convince this panel the two defendants be required to submit to examination, they will do so.”

He turned to the court official who stood at his station at the foot of the stage. “Have these two men taken into custody.”

The official bent to his handheld. The mutterings of the onlookers were back but much quieter. As Rajhir was led away with Ospar, Nivere put a hand on his arm. He smiled at her and nodded. Cissy looked at the prosecutor’s area to see how Councilman Maf took this ruling. The twisted frame was bent close to Chamar, conferring with counsel.

As soon as the Dramoks left the chamber, Onziv bowed to Nivere. “Does the defence have any further comments or concerns?”

Nivere shook her head, appearing calm despite the fact that her son had just been taken out of the room under armed guard. “We do not, Honourable Onziv.”

Prosecutor Chamar rose and approached his podium. “If I may speak, Honourable Onziv and panel?”

Onziv nodded. “You may.”

“The prosecution begs this panel for a delay of trial until tomorrow, as we were prepared to examine defendant Dramok Rajhir today. This unforeseen challenge, which we will lodge a formal protest against, has placed us at an unfair disadvantage.”

Perhaps Nivere had expected his motion, because she had not taken her seat. From her own podium, she said, “I protest this delay tactic, Honourable Onziv and panel. Prosecution should have its entire case prepared and be ready with all its witnesses before presenting itself in court. The defence is ready to move ahead.”

Onziv considered for a few seconds. Cissy saw how he exchanged glances with Wal before answering. “Having two out of three defendants abruptly move to refuse examination is an unfair burden on the prosecution’s timetable. I will allow the delay. This court will reconvene tomorrow morning at the scheduled time.”

Chamar bowed. “Thank you, Honourable Onziv.”

People shuffled towards the exits as the tone sounded and the official called, “Clear the court. Session has ended for the day.”

Wal shot Cissy a last lingering glance before leaving with the rest of the judges’ panel. Then she directed her attention to Diltan. He backed out of the Royal Council gallery, taking his time leaving despite the Global Security officers ushering everyone out. Finally he had no choice but to walk out but not before blowing Cissy a kiss.

Just like that, she was without even the sight of the men who haunted her dreams. Cissy thought she might choke on her sudden grief.

Jessica's disgusted voice broke through her agony. "Just like court on Earth. A whole lot of nothing got accomplished."

Bevau sighed, the guarded demeanour giving way to his friendlier nature. "Yuder will be examined tomorrow."

"I hope he's ready." Tara McInness let some of her worry peek through. Cissy realised that, as hard as it had been to see Diltan and Wal without getting close to them, her aunt must have suffered greater. After all, her future with Yuder was very much in question right now.

Clajak put his arm around his mother-in-law. "I hope the Empire is ready."

Huddling close together, the Imperial Clan and Tara left the gallery. Tasha slid her arm around Cissy's waist, giving her a sympathetic and knowing smile. "Come on, twin. You need a few drinks."

Cissy nodded, laying her head on her sister's shoulder. Clinging tight to Tasha, she allowed her to lead her out of the gallery in the company of a couple of Royal Guards.

Chapter Twenty-Seven

Wal could tell Rolat's grumpy mood increased with the news that the Imdiko and Diltan had seen Cissy. The Nobek had been stuck in administrative meetings all day, no place for a warrior. Being the only one of them to have not seen the Matara they missed deepened the frown lines etching his face.

He somehow kept any temper he felt from his tone. "How did she look?"

Diltan sighed. "Beautiful." He picked at his meal as they all did. Even though the first day of the trial had been fine, none of them had much appetite. The soothing breeze coming in from the open archway and serene golden light of sunset spilling into the dining room couldn't soothe away the tension of the clan. Even Wal, who had barely touched his lunch, had to force himself to eat.

Rolat gave the Dramok a humourless smile. "I didn't think she would appear otherwise. She is well?"

Wal swirled the bohut in his glass. "Gorgeous." At Rolat's impatient growl, he added, "I think she misses us. Every time I checked, she was watching me or Diltan."

Diltan pushed his plate away. "Which is both good and bad. I hate to be the cause of her unhappiness. It was damned hard to not run up to the Imperial Clan's gallery and steal her away."

Their words seemed to lighten Rolat's mood a little. He managed a weak chuckle. "I can just see you fighting your way past the Royal Guard, my Dramok."

Wal scowled at his drink. "Don't tease him, Rolat. Being so close to her, but not able to touch or speak… Damn it." He quaffed his bohut in one gulp. When he reached for the bottle to refill his glass, Rolat moved it away.

The Nobek said, "I thought about going to the trial. Now I am glad I didn't. You both act miserable."

Diltan shook his head. "It's not all bad. For me, breathing the same air gives some comfort." He covered his face with his hands as if in pain. "Those fucking stupid records. Why couldn't Zarl have erased it all?"

Wal sighed. "He would have released the contents while still alive had the war and rebellion not happened."

"But he didn't. Now we have to clean up the mess he and his clan left us."

Rolat's frown deepened again. "That may take some doing. Even though the trial started rather quietly, there are those who are using it to further their agendas."

Wal caught the tension in the Nobek's voice. He hadn't checked the news vids today, trying to stay as untouched by public opinion as possible. "What's happened?"

Rolat and Diltan exchanged looks before the Dramok said, "A quarter of the fleet and nearly a third of the ground troops have left their positions in protest. Rumour has it many will join the Basma if he comes out of the shadows to lead them."

Wal gasped. "Is this verified?"

Rolat said, "That they left their posts? Yes. That they wish to revolt? Still only rumour but behind every gossip is a touch of truth. I think few will actively go against the current Imperial Clan if they concede to the court's judgment, whatever it turns out to be."

Diltan gave them both an encouraging look. "Emperor Clajak is determined to do that. He will put the Empire's welfare first, even over that of his own family."

Wal wasn't so sure. Seeing one's father on trial for his liberty and life would be a harsh challenge to any son. "Tomorrow's examination of Yuder will be a huge test for our young emperor. I hope he has the will for it."

Diltan refused to let forced optimism fade. "Meanwhile, we will see Cissy again."

Rolat uttered his weak chuckle again. "Now I'm thinking of rearranging my schedule so I can go. I'd face a panel of high judges myself just to look at her." He sobered and reached to touch Diltan's arm. "My Dramok, this forced separation has revealed the depths of my feelings for Cissy."

Diltan nodded, smiling. "And mine. Do you think it presumptuous of me to ask the Imperial Clan for permission to clan her the moment verdict is pronounced? That is, assuming our Imdiko is in agreement?"

Wal found the strength to laugh. "In agreement…absolutely. Presumptuous…perhaps. However, I never want there to be occasion to be separated from her like this again." Feeling the weight of his calling even out of the courtroom, he couldn't help but advise caution. "We will have to see how the trial goes before taking that step. I fear if Yuder is convicted, it may drive a wedge between us and her."

Diltan swallowed. "That has occurred to me as well."

"There is another cause for concern in the opposite direction. The Empire is on the precipice of real trouble if Yuder is not convicted. It could result in violence against those who the public sees as working against them. With our being part of the case, clanning Cissy could put her in danger."

That sparked anger in Rolat's eyes, but Diltan didn't react. Wal was relieved his Dramok had thought of that eventuality.

Instead, Diltan said, "We will keep her safe if she will have us. We'll go off-planet until things settle, if warranted. So tell me, Honourable Wal, what say you to that?"

The Imdiko shook his head at Diltan's pretence of arrogant assurance, knowing it was an act meant to calm him. "Discounting the effects of this trial and its outcome? I say, as much as I want Cissy as my lifemate, tread carefully. Though we are ready for her, she may not be ready for us. Know her heart before you ask, Diltan. We may get only one chance to convince her."

* * * *

The courtroom was packed again the next morning. Wal noted the heightened sense of anticipation the moment he stepped out onto the panel's platform. After hearing of the defections from their armed forces, he couldn't help but eye the ranks of the Global Security officers that secured the court during high-profile cases. There were more than the usual, along with the Royal Guards next to Imperial Father Yuder and up in the Imperial Family's box.

Wal wondered if they would stand should things go an unpopular route during the trial. He checked on Cissy, seemingly safe and secure with the rest of her family. She smiled and gave a little wave. He offered back the slightest of nods and hoped no one noticed. Then he glanced at the Royal Council gallery and saw that Diltan sat next to his friend Oiteil. Rolat was nowhere in sight, so he'd not been able or had decided not to come. Wal tried not to worry.

The court official today was a different one from yesterday. Wal knew this man, a Nobek named Emro. He announced the beginning of the session and the quiet hum of conversation died out. The case got underway in quick order.

At Onziv's nod, Emro said, "The prosecutor calls Imperial Father Nobek Yuder to stand for investigation."

Matara Nivere gave Yuder an encouraging smile. Flanked by his Royal Guards, the wiry Nobek rose to his feet and stalked to the blindingly lit testimony stand between the defence and prosecution podiums. He climbed the two steps to the circular platform. He blinked up at the panel in the strong beam of light that washed his sleek steel-coloured hair silver.

Prosecutor Chamar rose from his seat next to Maf's. He walked forward to the foot of the testimony stand where Yuder waited to be questioned, facing the sharp-featured Nobek. Wal didn't miss the quick glance Chamar exchanged with Maf. It made Wal wonder who was in control of the prosecution.

Before Chamar could ask his first question, Nivere stood and mounted the defence platform. In a polite but strong tone, she said, "Honourable panel of judges, the defence has a request before examination begins."

Chamar jerked at the unexpected delay. His surprise was further demonstrated when he addressed Nivere rather than the panel. "Defence will get its chance to clarify after examination."

Nivere gave him a respectful nod before continuing. "The defendant is willing to submit to examination should our motion be refused. Honourable judges, I would like to change my client's plea. Imperial Father Nobek Yuder submits an admission of guilt for the crimes he is charged with."

The gallery erupted in shocked exclamations. Wal noted no one in the Imperial Gallery seemed startled.

Chamar yelled, "He admitted guilt before and withdrew that plea! Now he's guilty again? What are you playing at, Counsellor?"

Nivere stayed quiet, her face patient as she waited for Onziv's ruling. Meanwhile, Nobek Emro shouted for order and threatened to clear the courtroom. The onlookers quieted and Onziv resumed the session.

His brow furrowed with concern, the high judge asked Nivere, "Are you sure of this motion for your client, Counsellor? Admitting his guilt removes the burden of proving his complicity from the prosecution. It will mean his conviction and we would proceed straight to the sentencing hearings."

Nivere bowed. "We are aware of that, Honourable Onziv. With your approval of this change of plea, we wish to proceed."

"What says the prosecution?"

Chamar glanced at Maf. The councilman scowled, twisting his features to match his body. Chamar shook his head at him, his gaze warning.

Wal watched the exchange with confusion. Why was Maf angry? Holding someone accountable for the abductions and war had been his focus for years. With Yuder's admission of guilt, he should be pleased. Especially since it would probably save Kalquor from any further division and short-circuit the threat of civil unrest.

Chamar addressed the panel. "The prosecution, speaking for the people of the Kalquorian Empire, accepts Imperial Father Yuder's guilty plea in the matter of wilfully arranging the abduction of one thousand eight hundred and seventy-three Earther Mataras and triggering the war that led to Earth's demise."

Subdued whispers eddied through the air and silenced again before Emro could call for quiet. Onziv nodded to Yuder. "Noted and accepted by this court. Proceed with your confession, Imperial Father Yuder."

Yuder bowed. "Thank you, Honourable Onziv. I wish to state that, as emperors of Kalquor, Dramok Zarl and I did order the abductions of the Earther Mataras that were on planets and stations we had access to. I affirm it was done without the knowledge of our Imdiko, then-Emperor Tidro. We acted without his knowledge in the hope of protecting him from future consequences.

"Zarl and I orchestrated the kidnappings, knowing our actions could offend Earth and lead to trouble—perhaps even war—between the two planets. In the wake of Imperial Father Dramok Zarl's death, I assume full responsibility for that act...an act which ultimately led to the destruction of Earth. However, I plead the court's mercy in light of the extraordinary reasons involved. Zarl and I felt we had compelling cause to commit the horrific crime of which I am accused."

Wal frowned along with the rest of the panel. Onziv prodded Yuder. "Compelling cause, Imperial Father?"

"Yes, Honourable Onziv. We acted for two reasons. First, the desperate need to salvage the Kalquorian Empire's culture. As everyone is well aware, we were but a generation away from extinction."

Wal knew Yuder would not be spared a severe penalty for that. Saving one world at the expense of another would never mitigate his crime.

Perhaps that was why Onziv's tone was so forbidding when he said, "And the second reason?"

"The humanitarian mission to save nearly two thousand innocent Earther women from torture and execution."

The public and Royal Council galleries filled with shouts once more. Wal again witnessed the lack of any surprise from the Imperial Family. A look at the Royal Council told him Diltan was not shocked either. In fact, the Dramok had a hint of his familiar smug look.

So that's what you and Empress Jessica have been up to. By the ancestors, Diltan, don't you know you're playing with fire here? How is this going to keep the Empire peaceful?

As Emro shouted for order, Maf rose unsteadily to his feet. His face was purple with fury. "What farce is this?" he raged.

Chamar marched right up to the panel's stage. "I object, Honourable Onziv. There has never been any mention of a humanitarian mission to do with the kidnappings!"

As the furore quieted, Onziv reminded him, "Prosecution relinquished all rights to objections when it accepted the guilty plea from Nobek Yuder. The details and reasons he has stated are a matter for the sentencing hearings, however, which defence counsel needs to remind her client of."

Nivere nodded. "Noted, Honourable Onziv." She wore the twin of Diltan's almost-hidden smirk.

Ignoring the emotions of everyone in the courtroom, Onziv kept the proceedings on track with a doggedness that Wal admired. "Imperial Father Yuder, have you anything further to add that has direct bearing on the case itself?"

"I do, honourable panel. With my support, Zarl ordered my co-defendant Dramok Ospar to send clans to take the Mataras in question. You have seen that communication, which deals exclusively with the issue of our extinction concerns. Ospar expressed hesitation, not wanting to be a party to kidnappings just to save our culture. Then I sent a separate order myself, advising him that these were, in fact, rescue parties. I convinced him the women's lives were in danger, which they were."

"Rescue parties, Imperial Father?"

"This is absurd!" Maf shouted, overcome. Chamar shushed him.

Yuder continued, as if he hadn't heard the interruption. "That is how I presented the order to our then-ambassador. I told him the Mataras were in imminent danger from their own government. I also told him that they were probably not fully aware of their peril—that if they were, they may be in denial of it. There was little time to convince them to flee. Ospar was to see to it that as many of those women as possible were brought to Kalquor for their safety, even over their protests. This was the assumption he operated under. Since time was of the essence, he executed those orders without hesitation and without consulting anyone else.

"As for my other co-defendant, Councilman Rajhir just happened to be in the vicinity of such a woman. He was on Plasius at the time, negotiating trade agreements."

Nivere cut in. "You can check the records on that. The Plasian leader Saucin Israla has agreed to share her documentation of those negotiations with this honourable panel."

Yuder nodded and took up his story again. "Dramok Rajhir happened to be the first to carry out the emergency orders. I believe this is the reason he was unjustly singled out among all the councilmen who aided the rescue effort. In the course of following his duty, Rajhir and his clanmates discovered Matara Amelia was compatible to breed with our species."

Onziv was silent for a moment while mulling Yuder's confession. His expression tense, he asked, "It is your testimony that Dramok Ospar and Dramok Rajhir acted without consulting the Royal Council on the matter because they believed these women were in immediate danger?"

"It is."

Onziv considered again. Wal could imagine he was examining the assertions from every angle of Kalquorian law, just as he himself was. The grim concentration of everyone on the panel told him they were giving the matter their utmost attention.

There was only one decision in the end and Onziv delivered it to the hushed courtroom. "Let the record show a plea of guilty by Imperial Father Nobek Yuder in the matter of the Earther Matara abductions that ultimately led to the war with Earth and that planet's destruction. Let it also be recorded that he assumes sole responsibility for the crime. This panel will deliberate if Dramok Ospar and Dramok Rajhir need to testify further to the matter before proceeding with their cases. In the meantime, we will adjourn until this afternoon, at which time the sentencing hearing for Nobek Yuder will commence. Nobek Yuder is hereby confined under Empire custody until court reconvenes."

In the quiet following the incomplete verdict, a Nobek in the public gallery shouted out, "Let them all be taken away! The whole Imperial Family and Royal Council should be on trial for their lies! Follow the Basma! Free Kalquor from the tyranny of the entitled!"

More shouting rose in the wake of the cry. Within seconds, fists were swinging in the public gallery.

As the fighting heated up and members of Global Security waded in to restore order and empty the room, Wal found a small sense of relief. The only women in the courtroom were those in the enclosed and guarded Imperial gallery and Nivere, who stood next to Yuder. Under the Imperial Father's watchful group of Royal Guards, other members of Global Security led him and Nivere away. More guards took up positions between the panel of judges and the public gallery.

Secure from the violence, Wal checked on Cissy. She peeked at him through a wall of Royal Guards, her worried face appearing between armoured bodies as she checked on him. The Imdiko mustered a smile for her to let her know he was okay. For his part, he was glad she was in the midst of armoured sentries.

Only after he was assured of Cissy's safety did Wal look to see how Diltan fared. All the councilmen appeared to be behaving themselves for a change as they filed out of the gallery. Diltan lagged behind his grave-expressioned colleagues, giving both Wal and Cissy winks and waves to let them know things were all right on his end.

Real trouble had been averted for the moment. Yet Wal was all too aware how much depended on proceeding carefully, even with Yuder's sacrifice.

* * * *

During lunch, the panel couldn't help but talk about what ramifications would result from Yuder's confession. Now that a guilty verdict was in, they were free to discuss the matter as it related to the Imperial Father.

"He's protecting those he can," Dramok Nai said. "Along with his own ass. His assertion of rescue is without merit. He's hoping to exonerate the other two and stay out of prison."

"I know Yuder from back when we both served Global Security," Dorl answered. "He ignores the rules when they don't serve him but always in line with what he feels is best for Kalquor. I think he's giving himself up to preserve the Empire. The intent is noble, though I'm not sold on the method."

"He's going beyond that," Wal said. He had a flash of insight as to what his Dramok and the empress had been about these last few weeks. "If Yuder pled innocent, was tried, declared guilty and sentenced, then we would still have a problem on our hands. It would cast doubt on the legitimacy of the Earther Mataras' clanships. By casting them in a sympathetic light, by insisting on their victimhood, the current wave of anti-interbreeding might lose traction."

"You have a point, Wal," Onziv said. "However, those who were convinced before will still be opposed to integration. Perhaps even more violently so since they'll fight to preserve the stance."

"All the easier to identify those people," Wal said. He felt a sense of pride for his Dramok in that moment. It was a brilliant manoeuvre…if it worked. "If Yuder can present real evidence that the kidnappings did save lives and it turns the mood of the people, even the Basma might be compelled to come out of the shadows in protest."

"If not him, his most ardent followers at the least," Dorl added, his eyes lighting at the prospect. "By the ancestors, I've wanted to get my hands on those who made some of the women disappear when this 'let Kalquor die pure' insanity started."

Wal thought of those few dozen Earther Mataras who had been abducted by the Basma, never to be heard from again. Even the empress had once been targeted by the revolt's followers. She had been rescued from vanishing in barely the nick of time.

He swallowed, thinking about how awful it would be if the Basma targeted Cissy. If she was to disappear, never to be heard from again—

It would kill me. Two months not seeing her while knowing she was perfectly fine was hardship enough. To lose her for good with no idea if she was still alive… I couldn't bear it.

With such daunting thoughts, he headed out with his colleagues for the afternoon session of court. Wal was so worried about the threat hanging over their heads that he almost shouted in relief to see Cissy sitting in the Imperial gallery.

The hearing they hadn't anticipated began. Onziv said, "We will now move on to the sentencing hearings for Imperial Father Yuder. Does his attorney have any witnesses to call?"

Nivere already stood at her podium. She exchanged bows with the judges and said, "I do, your honour. I call for the testimony of Amelia Ryan, Matara to Clan Rajhir."

Prosecutor Chamar stood as Maf glowered. "If you hear such testimony, then this court has reduced itself to a joke, honourable panel."

Onziv crooked an eyebrow at him. "The prosecution has won its case against one of the defendants, who we are now in the process of determining the disposition of. You are excused from any further proceedings except to observe."

Chamar continued a dogged argument. "I will be lodging a formal protest against this. Bringing in one of these Earther women to testify on Nobek Yuder's behalf, one who in fact is clanned to his co-defendant, is not a valid witness. What's more, her Dramok is blood related to Yuder! Her testimony is tainted."

Nivere never lost her composure. "Matara Amelia was the first of the women to be rescued"—Maf's growl tried to interrupt her at the use of that word, but she ignored him—"by our people. Her circumstances are representative of the threat Earth had on her and the other women. However, if it will make the prosecution feel better, I have one thousand three hundred and forty-one more Earther Mataras brought here before the war. I assure Counsellor Chamar that all of those women are also ready—excuse me—eager to testify as to their being rescued, not abducted. I would be happy to bring every last one of them in to satisfy my concerned opponent."

Silence hung over the chamber. Wal and the rest of the panel waited for the prosecutor's response. Chamar exchanged a look with the obviously furious Maf and sat down again.

Onziv turned back to Nivere. "I am sure bringing so many witnesses will not be necessary, Counsellor. Please bring forth the first witness called."

Court officer Emro escorted Matara Amelia into the room and hovered uncertainly as she mounted the testimony platform. The light beaming down on her had been dimmed. She was not on trial and not a hostile witness as far as the court was concerned, so concessions were made for her comfort.

Wal had to admit that the sight of the redheaded Matara was a lovely one. Tall for an Earther female, Amelia possessed a beautifully curved form. The small bump of her abdomen that demonstrated her pregnancy only made her more inspiring to the Imdiko's eyes. He thought of how Cissy might look when she someday carried a child…his clan's child. A lump formed in his throat at the idea. He couldn't help but glance up at her, his heart beating too fast.

Onziv's voice brought him back to the task at hand. "Matara Amelia, in deference to your condition of pregnancy, we will endeavour to keep this examination short."

Amelia bowed her head. Her flaming waves of red hair tumbled forward to brush golden-skinned shoulders, left bare by her long white gown. "Thank you for the kindness, Honourable Onziv."

"Please start the examination, Counsellor Nivere."

Nivere stood at the foot of the testimony platform and smiled up at her son's clanmate. "Tell us how it was that you met Clan Rajhir."

In a strong, carrying voice, Amelia said, "Nearly six years ago, I left Earth to take an exchange artist opening on Plasius. The official reason was for a cultural sharing between my planet and theirs. However, I had far more personal reasons for leaving Earth. I had been raped repeatedly by two men on my home planet and I feared for my life should it be discovered."

Nivere interjected, "Because women who had been raped were, by your government's definition, guilty of tempting men into doing so."

Amelia nodded, her expression turning grim. "Yes."

"Did you ever tempt your rapists, as your government would have alleged?"

"Absolutely not! The first of these men attacked me when I was only fourteen years old, a virgin and unaware of what constituted sexuality."

Wal winced at her account. What Amelia spoke of horrified him. Again he glanced at Cissy, thinking about her story of what had happened to Tasha and how it had moved her to accidentally kill a man. She watched Amelia with a sad but unsurprised expression. It made his heart ache all the more to know Cissy had lived under such a threat.

Shaking her head as if to deny the dreadfulness of Amelia's story, Nivere nonetheless urged her on. "Please continue, Matara Amelia. What of the second man who violated you?"

"He was my work supervisor, in charge of the law enforcement in my hometown. There was no one I could go to, to plead my case in such a situation."

"Awful. So this is what you feared about Earth? That you would continue to be victimised with no legal recourse?"

Amelia's gaze was distant, as if looking across some great divide to a far different world from the one she now inhabited. "That was the least of my worries. I feared being accused of acts of lust. I knew I could never become a wife and mother on my home world. If I was to be so foolish as to marry, any man I took as my husband might report my non-virginal status to the authorities."

"What would have happened in that case?"

"Arrest, torture and execution."

That brought a wave of muttering from the gallery. Even members of the notoriously impassive Royal Guard looked incensed. Diltan and Empress Jessica's plan was working, Wal thought. The tide of anger moved now in the opposite direction of where Maf had sent it.

"So you went to Plasius to escape?"

Amelia shrugged. "The trip to Plasius was a reprieve from potential discovery, but only a temporary one. I knew I would have to return to Earth and live in fear once more."

"But you did not return to Earth."

"No. Clan Rajhir came to Plasius. I met them and they assured me that they would keep me safe from Earth if I would join their clan. After a couple of weeks of getting to know them, I felt sure that they told me the truth. I agreed to come to Kalquor and be their Matara."

"A couple of weeks?" Nivere's brow furrowed. "It does not sound as if you were in immediate danger then, Matara."

Amelia's eyes widened. "But I was, Counsellor. I heard that other expatriate Earther women had accepted the invitations of Kalquorians to come to your planet and live without fear. Earth contacted me and ordered me to go home. I made the mistake of telling them that not only was I also going to Kalquor, but I carried my clan's child—which turned out to be children, as I had twins."

"What was Earth's reaction to that?"

"They sent the military after me. Their plan was to bring me back to my planet for execution after I'd given birth to my children. My babies, Earther-Kalquorian hybrids, would be subjected to testing and experimentation. It most likely would have killed them. The Earther soldiers sent to Plasius caught me. I was beaten. Their commander almost choked me to death."

Another swell of angry muttering broke out. This time Emro had to threaten the gallery with expulsion to make them quiet. While everyone was distracted by that, Wal sneaked a glance at Diltan. His Dramok looked strangely sickened and pleased all at once. Amelia's story had an effect on him, but things were swinging in the right direction.

When silence had been restored, Nivere prodded Amelia to finish her tale. "What happened next?"

The Earther smiled, signalling a happy end to such a terrible story. "At great risk to their own lives, my clanmates—Clan Rajhir—managed to rescue me and our unborn children. They saw to it that we were spared horrible deaths at the hands of Earth's government. For the last six years, I have lived a life I didn't think possible. A life of peace with no fear, safe and secure with my clan."

Despite having heard much of this story before, Wal was newly amazed at the grim horror Amelia had endured. The thought of her children being subjected to medical experimentation was enough to nauseate him. From the repulsed expressions filling the room, he had little doubt his feelings were shared by the majority of listeners.

Nivere turned to the panel. "That completes my examination, honourable panel."

Onziv nodded. "Thank you for your testimony, Matara Amelia."

She bowed her head. "Thank you, honourable judges. If I may, I'd like to offer my sincere gratitude to all of the Kalquorian Empire, which tried its best to see to it that we women of Earth no longer had to live in terror."

With that, she descended the steps. Emro watched her, seeming ready to spring to her rescue should she stumble. He escorted Amelia out of the courtroom and returned.

Nivere addressed the panel. "As I said before, I have many more of these first Earther Mataras who can't wait to tell you their stories. I can bring you as many as you wish to have examined, but I have also recorded their testimonies if you prefer." She held up a tiny file drive. "They are all here, honourable judges."

Onziv gestured to Emro, who claimed the drive. "You may submit the files, Counsellor. We will review them and determine if the women themselves should be brought forth or if these testimonies will suffice for the public record." He checked the chronometer and glanced at the other judges. Wal and the rest murmured their agreement to his unspoken question.

Onziv announced, "We will adjourn for the rest of the day to confer over these latest developments. Objections, Defence Counsel?"

"No objections, Honourable Onziv."

"Very well. We will re-convene in the morning at the regular time. Court adjourned."

Wal looked up to fill his gaze with Cissy for the last time that day. After Amelia's testimony, he found it harder than ever to turn and leave. He wanted to be with her, if only to hold her and promise she would never have to endure the kinds of horrors Amelia had divulged to the court.

She blew him a kiss as she was ushered out of the gallery with the rest of the Imperial Family. Wal lowered his gaze, empty and lost at her latest absence.

At least he could feel good about the direction things were headed in now. The Imdiko did until he saw Maf's livid face. The councilman stared at the floor as his aide Sitrel and Chamar conferred, looking as if he wanted to throttle someone.

Disquiet filled Wal. Maf was not going to be happy with the conviction everyone thought he wanted. He wanted more. Had he fallen on the side of the Basma? Did he wish for revolution?

Matara Amelia's testimony had done the Empire a lot of good, but it hadn't fixed all the problems of the Empire. There was still so much that could go wrong.

* * * *

Two days of testimony on Yuder's behalf followed. Five more women were brought forward to tell of how Kalquorian clans had rescued them from horrendous. The head of the Matara Psychological Council, Dr Govi, also delivered evidence on the Earther trauma he'd seen and treated at the capital city's hospital.

The testimony of two men was not forthcoming. Dramoks Rajhir and Ospar continued to refuse to submit to examination, both for Yuder and themselves. Because the matter of their culpability in the matter was inextricably intertwined, the panel of judges decided it was best to deal with their case before announcing Yuder's sentence.

Another two days was spent examining the allegations against the councilman and governor. The Empire's peace held during that time, but it was obvious from the many protests and demands for action that the public was restless.

It was with great trepidation that Wal mounted the courtroom's platform for what he hoped would be the last time for this case. Cissy's wave and wink were the only things that could lift his heart, along with Diltan's encouraging nod. So much was at stake today. He imagined he could feel Kalquor holding its collective breath, waiting for the final act of the drama that might turn into a prelude to tragedy. Then he saw Rolat in the public gallery. His Nobek was near the front of the spectators, just behind the prosecution's seating. Rolat's steady gaze settled Wal's nerves a little bit more. As always, his Nobek was there, ready to protect him from whatever may come.

I hope your presence is unnecessary, my clanmate. I truly do.

Onziv wasted no time in delivering the first portion of the judgment. "In the matter of the Empire versus Dramoks Rajhir and Ospar, we find the defendants not guilty of wilful abduction of the Earther Mataras."

There was a rise of voices at that. As Wal looked out over the faces, he thought the reaction was about equal on either side of the matter. Half seemed to approve, while the other half appeared angry. The relief coming from the Royal Council's gallery was palpable. With Ospar and Rajhir not guilty, the rest of their number would escape indictment and prosecution.

Some of the public gallery's muttered discontent seemed aimed at that group. However, tempers held and no violence broke out. So far so good.

As soon as the courtroom quieted, Onziv continued. "The prosecution failed to deliver anything more than purely circumstantial evidence. No witnesses could verify these two men did anything but follow their emperors' orders. In that matter, Rajhir's and Ospar's names are cleared."

The two Dramoks in question bowed to the panel, but their expressions remained wary. They knew this was far from over. They were right.

"Furthermore, in the matter of recalling Imperial Father Imdiko Tidro to Kalquor to face trial, there has been no evidence submitted that would encourage this panel to seek charges against him. Nor do we find substantial evidence that would lead us to bring charges against other members of the council or any clan sent to abduct Mataras for their alleged safety, unless any of the Earther women involved wish to bring charges themselves."

That elicited more muttering from the galleries. Those gathered in the Imperial box were relieved, particularly Clajak. No doubt he had lost much sleep over what would happen to his elderly Imdiko father.

One voice rose in dissent. Maf's scowl was an ugly thing as he declared, "This is an outrage."

Onziv ignored him. "As to other matters that have demanded the attention of this panel. Dramoks Rajhir and Ospar, you have defied this court's order to deliver testimony as to what you knew about Emperor Zarl and Emperor Yuder's plans. You refused to divulge the specific orders or even lack of orders you were given in the matter of the abductions of over eighteen hundred Earther females. You know there are strict penalties for such a betrayal of public trust, above all for men in the positions you occupy."

Nivere nodded their behalf. "The defence is aware and ready for your judgment, honoured panel."

"Then hear and submit to our sentence. Dramok Rajhir and Dramok Ospar, you are sentenced to five years of community service each. You will also pay restitution to a fund for the victims of Earth's destruction, said fund administered by the Galactic Council of Planets." Onziv named an astronomical sum that brought gasps echoing in the chamber.

Maf was not so impressed. "Ospar's mines make that in a month. It's barely a slap on the wrist!"

Onziv fixed the red-faced Dramok with a steady gaze. "Do you need to be excused from the court, Councilman Maf?"

Maf said nothing, but he continued to glare.

Onziv returned to the sentencing. "In addition, as these men's silence has violated the Empire's code of transparency and therefore the public's trust, they will both step down from their government positions. Dramok Rajhir and Dramok Ospar, you are both banned from public service for life."

Ospar's only reaction was a tightening of his jaw. However, Rajhir looked stricken, as if dealt a physical blow. His dedication to serving the Empire was well known. Wal felt a stab of sympathy. He could well imagine how he would feel if he was banned from serving as a judge.

Onziv finished quickly, as if to get the unpleasant business done. "The judgment of this honourable panel stands. The two defendants are excused from this court."

Rajhir, Ospar and Nivere all bowed to the judges. Then, as Ospar whispered to the still pale Rajhir, Nivere embraced him. Neither man looked happy as they took their leave to a new tide of muttering.

It was time to hand down Yuder's sentence. Expectant silence descended once more.

Chapter Twenty-Eight

Onziv nodded to Nobek Emro, who was on duty as court official that day. "Bring in Imperial Father Nobek Yuder."

Two Global Security officers and two Royal Guards escorted Yuder into the chambers. He was halfway to the defence counsellor's podium where Nivere waited when a yell sounded from the public gallery.

"Purity for Kalquor! Make the Imperial traitor pay! Death to the oppressors!"

With that, half a dozen men with the fierce visages of Nobeks rushed forward. The Global Security teams stationed at equal intervals along the room's walls mobilised in an instant, racing to intercept the protestors. Within moments, they fought hand to hand. More people joined in the fray while others fell back, getting away from the battle.

Yuder's Royal Guards stayed between him and the fighting while the rest of his security team hustled him back to the door he'd entered through. Nobek Emro and two more guards rushed Nivere out behind him.

Rolat's wide back appeared in front of Wal's podium, the Nobek tense and ready to take on anyone who rushed his Imdiko. Wal moved close to peer over his shoulder. He checked on the Imperial Gallery, worried about Cissy. A wall of Royal Guards had assembled at the entrance to the box. More aimed laser rifles down towards the gallery below, ready to fire through the glass to take out anyone who threatened the Imperial Family. Cissy huddled with the rest of her kin in the middle of the balcony. Her eyes were round as she watched the melee unfold.

Reassured that his Earther love was well protected, Wal checked the council's box to make sure Diltan was all right. Global Security officers had emptied that gallery. Like the Royal Guards across the way, those men had rifles aimed at the floor below, ready to fire if needed.

Well rehearsed for such instances, security had the matter under control. They subdued the rioters, hovercuffing them as a line of officers stood between them and those who had remained in the court. Wal noted that at least a dozen had been arrested.

Onziv's controlled mien crumbled to see his courtroom in chaos. He roared, "Clear this court! Clear the gallery immediately! Court is adjourned until further notice."

There were many angry faces as onlookers were forced out. Rolat glanced back at Wal. "Are you all right, my Imdiko?"

"Yes. I'm relieved that Cissy is so well protected."

"Indeed. The Royal Guards there left me free to take care of you."

The Imperial Family milled about their box, talking excitedly to one another. All but Cissy, who watched Rolat and Wal. Worry filled her face. Rolat and Wal gave her unconvincing smiles to show there was nothing to be afraid of.

"What about Diltan? Did you see him leave?" Wal asked.

"He and Oiteil made the others evacuate immediately, helping Global Security clear the gallery. It was a wise move."

"You think so?"

"Many of the councilmen are clanned to those first Mataras and this protest seemed aimed against that specific issue."

Onziv collected his usual calm demeanour. He called out to the Imperial Gallery, "Apologies, my emperors and empress. I know your nerves are stretched to the breaking point over the disposition of the Imperial Father, but we must guarantee control of the courtroom before the sentence is announced."

Clajak nodded in acknowledgement. His voice muffled by the glass that separated the box from the courtroom, he shouted, "No apology is necessary, honourable judges. Emotions are running too high at the moment. Do as you must to guarantee the safety of all before proceeding."

Onziv bowed and the rest of the panel followed suit. He turned to them. "Let's get out of here and figure out the best way to handle this."

Wal noted Rolat trading scowls with the members of Global Security who had gathered around the judges. His Nobek was intruding on their turf.

"I guess you're safe enough, my Imdiko," Rolat announced. "I'll see to Diltan now."

"Thank you for being here to watch out for us, my Nobek," Wal answered. He glanced up at Cissy again.

Her mouth moved, exaggerating the words he couldn't hear. He was able to make out her message however—*be careful*.

"You too," he mouthed. Royal Guards or not, Wal was scared for them all. His heart pounding, he followed the rest of the panel out of the court.

* * * *

Cissy thought the Empire's collective nerves weren't the only ones that were shot as she waited with the Imperial Clan. Hers were stretched to the breaking point as well. Seeing Diltan, Rolat and Wal was not enough, not by a long shot. She needed to be with them. The desperation made her crazy.

So when a messenger came from the panel of judges that the sentence would not be announced that day after all, her temper boiled. Cissy seethed as Aunt Tara left the Imperial gallery in the company of two Royal Guards to visit Yuder. The rest of the group prepared to leave the court, too, their expressions tight.

She couldn't take it. Her anger burst into the silence. "Terrific. That's just typical of this whole mess. Why does this have to be done this way? Why can't the judges quietly tell us the sentence and get it over with, without it having to be a big circus act? Better yet, why can't you just send Yuder off like you did Tidro?"

In the wake of her outburst, her sister, Lindsey and Jessica smiled wanly. The remaining Royal Guards didn't react at all. The three emperors and Clajak's aide Korkla blinked with apparent shock before recovering their more diplomatic faces.

It was quiet Egilka who answered her. "We can't hear the sentence before the rest of the Empire, cousin."

Clajak nodded. In a heavy voice, he said, "There can be no special treatment. Nothing that speaks of collusion between us and the court."

Bevau gave her an understanding smile. "As for sending Yuder away and keeping him from facing his sentence, that is impossible. Someone has to pay for the crimes of Armageddon. He has taken that responsibility upon himself."

Cissy's anger refused to be tempered. Perhaps it was because she had not voiced the real reason she was upset by the delay. She wanted to be with Clan Diltan again. As long as the case lasted, she couldn't do that.

The frustration wouldn't be contained. Uncomfortable with telling everyone her actual feelings, she ranted about the rest of her concerns instead. "I don't see where a crime has been committed. They have the testimony of all those women saying they were rescued, not abducted. What more evidence could anyone need? This is the craziest mess I've ever seen. I swear, if Wal is a party to Yuder going to prison, I'll never forgive him."

Jessica came close to place a steadying hand on Cissy's shoulder. "He and the rest of the judges have more than just one man's freedom to consider, Cissy. Trust me, the thought of Yuder in a prison camp doesn't sit well with me, either. I'd rather cut off my arm than see it happen. But we may be on the path to civil war if this isn't dealt with right. Yuder has made the sacrifice to keep that from happening. Even Mom understands what's at stake and supports him."

Bevau added, "Don't think for an instant that Honourable Wal isn't aware of all that's at stake. Every last judge on that panel knows. They cannot be swayed by emotion. They have to weigh the good of the Empire against the fate of one man…a man who has proclaimed his guilt."

Besides Tasha, Lindsey was the one person who could get away with outright chastisement of Cissy. She did not mince words. "You can't blame Wal for doing his job. He doesn't deserve your anger."

They were right. Her selfish wish to be back with Wal and the rest of the clan had her acting like an entitled brat. She sagged in defeat.

"I know he doesn't. I can tell just by looking at him how heavy this weighs on him. But I still don't think Yuder should pay as high a price as that Maf or a lot of others seem to think." *Or that I should spend another second without Wal, Diltan and Rolat.*

She tried to get beyond thinking of herself. Cissy considered those who were going to be hurt if Yuder's sentence was severe. She looked at Clajak, the son who had to watch his father's reputation be torn apart—and perhaps lose his father altogether.

She asked him, "If they have no choice but to punish your father, can you step in somehow? Lessen a harsh sentence that will keep him from you and my aunt?"

Clajak's expression was tormented, giving Cissy the answer before he spoke. "Subvert the court by Imperial Decree? That is the surest way to divide the Empire. I think the majority of the people are still on our side right now. That will change if I defend my father. The revolt will gain strength with new accusations of treachery."

Bevau touched Clajak's elbow with a discreet show of support. "Yuder's bravery is Kalquor's saving grace.

His admission of guilt and acceptance of the consequences will keep the Empire whole."

Clajak gave his Nobek a grateful look. "Whatever the sentence is, we must abide by it. It will be hard, but with my clan's strength to keep me steady, I can bear it."

There was something young and vulnerable in the Dramok emperor's eyes at that moment. Cissy knew it ripped Clajak's heart out to leave Yuder to his fate. And yet, just as she could not be selfish in her wants, neither could he. Clajak had an entire kingdom depending on him to do what had to be done.

With his clanmates gathered close around him, Clajak left the gallery. Lindsey followed on their heels. Tasha linked her arm through Cissy's and they brought up the rear, surrounded by Royal Guards.

The chauffeured shuttle that Jessica had provided for Cissy and Tasha's use to travel back and forth between the court and the Matara Complex was in a bay separate from that of the Imperial Clan's. The twins stepped out of the in-house conveyance between two watchful Royal Guards assigned to accompany them to the safety of their apartments.

The polished stone bay was almost empty but for perhaps half a dozen personal shuttles in its cavernous expanse. The booted feet of the guards were silent, leaving only the soft steps of the women to echo. Cissy hardly noticed the near silence since her head was buzzing with all she'd seen in court that day—the violence, the pain in Clajak's eyes and the men she'd give anything to be with right now.

Tasha interrupted her thoughts. "Poor Aunt Tara. I thought she might throw herself right through the gallery's glass when those men went after Yuder. And did you see Clajak's face? Imagine having to watch your father be attacked like that."

Cissy wrung her hands. "They still have to stand aside and watch Yuder be sentenced to who knows what. With the Empire's code of an eye for an eye, what awful things could they be planning—hey!"

The two guards had suddenly wheeled around, shoving her and her sister behind them as they drew percussion blasters. Cissy shouted in horror to see who they pointed their weapons at—Diltan and Rolat, standing just in front of the conveyance system.

Rolat jumped in front of Diltan, his hands held up and open to show he was not armed. "Our apologies, guards. We only wished to speak to our intended, Matara Cecilia."

Seeing that the guards were not backing down, Cissy yelled at the men her legs trembled to run to. "Idiots! What are you two doing sneaking up on Royal Guards like that? Do you want to be killed?"

At the same time, Tasha placed shaking hands on each guard's arm. "It's okay, Nobeks. These men are my sister's lottery picks. That's Councilman Diltan and Head of Penal Colonies Rolat."

The tensed guards began to relax, albeit grudgingly. Cissy glowered over the shoulder of one. Delight to see Diltan and Rolat warred with the horror of their lives being threatened. Tears blurred her vision and made her angry. "It would serve you right if you got shot, you two. After what happened in court, you should know better."

Rolat winced in embarrassment. "Indeed we should. In our haste to catch up with you, we weren't thinking clearly."

He and Diltan bowed to the guards. The armoured men holstered their weapons while continuing to give the pair black stares.

Diltan stepped forward to address the pair. "Once more, we are sorry to have come up on you like that. As Rolat said, we were afraid we'd miss you before you left, Cissy."

It was all she could do to not shove the guard in front of her aside, assuming she could knock a living boulder out of the way. Pretending her heart didn't scream for joy to be so close to Diltan and Rolat, she scowled. "I thought we were to keep clear of each other while this case is going on."

Diltan gave her the smug expression that made her want to simultaneously slap and kiss him. "Except for the Imperial Father's sentencing, the case is over. It may be breaking with propriety but—oh, fuck propriety. We want to be with you. We *have* to be with you."

As Tasha laughed in delight, Rolat gave Diltan an amused look. "'Fuck propriety'? She is rubbing off on you, my Dramok."

"Try not to be so pleased with my defection to the crass side. Cissy?" His smirk vanished, replaced by hopeful eagerness.

Cissy turned her own wishful gaze to her sister. Like Diltan had said, fuck propriety. She'd beg on bended knee to leave with two of her three loves.

Tasha made a shooing gesture. "Go on, get out of here. You need to be with them."

Cissy gave her a loud smooch on the cheek. "Thank you, sis."

One of the guards looked from Rolat and Diltan to Cissy, his expression uncertain. "I have to report to my superior that you insisted on this. You are sure, Matara? And Matara Natasha concurs?"

"Please let her go," Tasha said with exaggerated desperation. "Or we will have to listen to her sob all the way back to the complex. If that happens, it will be up to you to comfort her, Nobek."

The guard's eyes widened at that. He stepped aside to let Cissy pass. "Then you accept responsibility for refusing our protection."

"She has mine," Rolat said, as Cissy hurried to join him and Diltan. "As long as she is with me, nothing will harm her."

The restraint it took to not run to them, to not fling herself into the men's arms, was the worst Cissy had ever had to exercise. Yet she somehow managed it. When she kissed Diltan and Rolat, however, she practically devoured their faces. She ignored Tasha's laughter as they kissed her back, simultaneously dragging her to the conveyance.

Somehow they got on the transport device. Only after the doors closed did the three take a breath.

"Judges' shuttle bay," Diltan told the conveyance. He smiled at Cissy, lighting her whole world. "Wal is waiting for us there. We had a hard time convincing him to do so, but it's well guarded by armed officers. We didn't want his safety left to chance."

Rolat added, "I brought my own transportation, but we'll all ride home together so I can be sure everyone is protected. What a mess this has turned into. I've never seen fighting like that in the high court."

At the reminder that their troubles were far from over, Cissy's joy at being reunited with Clan Diltan muted. She was with the men she loved, but serious trouble remained.

The trio reached the judges' guarded shuttle bay, which was a smaller version of the one Cissy had just left. With the opening to the outside closer, she could feel the warm spring breeze wafting in.

Diltan drew her close while he dug in his waist pouch for identification to show to one of the guards manning the bay. The Nobek sentry gave their vidcards a perfunctory glance. "Honourable Wal's clanmates and not clever disguises, right?"

Rolat chuckled. "Any excitement here, Etz?"

"No, Global Security has all the fun." Etz gave Cissy a polite smile and nod as she brought her identification up on its screen. "Good evening to you, Matara…Cecilia. Cousin to our empress, correct?"

Diltan's expression turned watchful. "Whom we've not been able to see since the trial started. Wal's objectivity—"

"Is impeccable," Etz interrupted, raising his hand in a conciliatory gesture. "Anyone with half a brain knows that about him. Unfortunately, a great many in the Empire seem to possess less than that amount of sense these days. Good luck to you all, Councilman. Ah, there is Honourable Wal waiting rather impatiently."

They all looked towards the mid-size shuttle that the Imdiko emerged from. His face wore its familiar worry, which vanished as he beamed at Cissy.

"Thank the ancestors," Rolat breathed as they headed towards him.

Cissy's heart had renewed its quick thumping. She would soon be able to embrace him. "Did you think someone could get to him in here?"

"I always feel better when I can see my clanmates and am there to protect them, no matter how many precautions have been taken."

Diltan drew a breath that told Cissy he'd been concerned as well. "I am glad to see him, too."

Not content to wait for them by the shuttle, Wal had hurried to meet them halfway. He swept Cissy up in a hug and twirled her around. "Cissy!"

She discovered she was just as relieved as the others to find the Imdiko safe and sound. He'd seemed too exposed in the courtroom when the fighting broke out. She'd come close to cheering when Rolat had jumped between Wal and the gallery.

Cissy planted a kiss on his smiling lips. Then a second. Two more kisses followed before she was able to speak. "That was some show you put on in there."

He chuffed a laugh. "One I hope will not be repeated." He looked to Diltan and Rolat. "Can we go?"

The Nobek pushed the group towards the shuttle. "The sooner, the better."

They got on board. Cissy noted the cabin where six people could lounge in comfort around a table, separate from the front where there was a cockpit for two and a second row of seats behind it. She wondered why Wal needed such an opulent shuttle.

"Luxurious," she said.

The Imdiko let Rolat take the pilot's seat. He took the chair next to the Nobek while Diltan and Cissy settled in the back row. "Sometimes I take my colleagues out to lunch. Sometimes I pick these two buffoons up from work to take them out to a surprise dinner and entertaining. And sometimes we load it up for a few days away on vacation. It's nice to have a larger vehicle for such things."

Rolat didn't seem nearly as delighted as he guided the shuttle out of the court complex. "Most days Diltan or I drop him off at work. I worried with the sentencing that there would be trouble. That's why Wal brought it in today, so we could all travel home together."

"Protective Nobek." Wal's expression was pure affection as he looked at his clanmate. Then he turned his attention back to Cissy, staring at her as if to drink her image in.

She was just as happy to contemplate him and the other two. She was so delirious to be with them that it felt unreal. If anyone said they'd have to spend any more days apart, she'd tear their lips off.

Needing to know that wouldn't happen, she asked Wal, "What's the latest? How long is this delay in the sentencing going to last?"

He twisted in his seat so he could face her. "Court will be in session as usual tomorrow. Onziv is worried that prolonging the announcement will be as detrimental as announcing it could be. Extra precautions will be enacted, however. Everyone will be scanned and searched for weapons before they are allowed in, including blades."

Rolat growled. "I can't say I like it even with the weapons check, my Imdiko. Most Nobeks are trained to kill with their bare hands."

Wal nodded. "That's why containments will be established. There will be a protective field around the judges, the Imperial gallery, the defence counsel's area and the route Imperial Father Yuder will take in and out of the courtroom."

Diltan whooshed out a breath. He slid his arm around Cissy's shoulders, drawing her to his side. She snuggled into his warmth with a happy noise.

He told Wal, "That eases my mind a bit. At least you and Cissy will be well protected. I must say that Global Security and the Royal Guards did a good job today."

Cissy had been watching Wal's face carefully during the conversation. So far, he had not given any hints as to what the panel's decision had been as far as Yuder was concerned.

She prodded him, "The sentence hasn't been announced, but it has been decided."

Wal eyed her, his familiar worried look reasserting itself. "It has, but I cannot discuss it. Head Judge Onziv must declare the sentence to the whole Empire at the same time."

"That's what Clajak said when I pitched a fit about it. Don't worry, Wal. I'm not going to ask you to tell me anything."

Diltan squeezed her shoulders. "You threw a tantrum, huh? I'm not surprised. The pain your family is going through has to be phenomenal."

Cissy said, "That's not why I went off. I blew my stack because I thought the delay would keep us apart. I couldn't handle it, not for another second."

Rolat set the shuttle to follow automatic traffic controls before turning his seat around to face her. The three men looked at her, questioning hope filling their expressions.

In a quiet tone, Rolat said, "It sounds as if you missed us as much as we missed you. For the last two months, all I've thought about is how much I need to be with the woman I love."

Cissy blinked and tears came in a shocking flood. Wal made an upset sound and moved from his seat to sit next to her, squashing her between himself and Diltan.

Feeling them touching her again after so long made her cry harder.

Plus Rolat had said he'd fallen in love with her.

He loved her. What of the other two? How did they feel about her?

Feeling like she'd just glimpsed nirvana and fearful it would be snatched away, Cissy sobbed, "I've missed you all so much! It's been like this huge hole in my body—hell, in my soul without you around. I'm scared that this trial is somehow going to destroy any chance we have of being together. I can't stand the idea of that!"

Now all three men hugged and petted her. As Wal and Rolat tried to dry her tears, Diltan cupped her chin to make her look at him. "Listen to me, Cecilia. Nothing—not the Royal Council, not the Imperial Family, not the High Court, not anything—is going to keep you from us. We are determined to have you."

"It's over," Wal promised. "The whole thing is finished tomorrow. We'll pronounce sentence and it will be done. Though I don't guarantee everyone will be happy with what will happen, at least we can look forward to putting it behind us."

Cissy felt like a frightened child, clinging to any shred of the security she needed. "You promise?"

"Absolutely." Wal smiled. "We're together now, aren't we? And that's the way it's going to stay."

Embarrassed to have crumbled, Cissy rubbed her eyes hard, as if to punish them for crying. "Damn it, I sound like such a wimp and that's not me. I can't stand another day without you three, though. If that's weak, well then, I'll just have to sound weak."

"You, weak? Not for a moment." Diltan chuckled and kissed the tip of her nose. "What you sound like is a woman in love. I hope you are, because we love you, too."

As Cissy tried to absorb that too-wonderful-to-be-true news, the Dramok kissed her. The kiss was slow, it was sensuous and it was thorough. He made love to her through that kiss, making her senses reel. Heat surged throughout her body, bringing her to intense arousal. Cissy had never known a mere kiss could do that.

When Diltan released her, she gazed at him through hazy eyes. His smirk came back, telling her he knew what he did to her. The wonderful, obnoxious bastard.

Sounding way too breathy but unable to control it, Cissy grinned back. "I do love you, you pompous, arrogant jerk. Heaven help me." She looked around to include the rest of the happy clan. "I love all three of you."

Rolat pumped his fists in the air, every ounce the victor. "Yes!" he roared, as if he'd scored a major conquest.

They laughed at his triumphant display. Cissy dared to hope everything would turn out all right for them, if not for the rest of Kalquor.

Chapter Twenty-Nine

As soon as they reached the clan's home, Rolat scooped Cissy up in his arms. She laughed as he carried her into one of the elaborate bathrooms off the clan's sleeping room. There the three men undressed her as fragrant water sluiced from the basin's jets. It was more a pool than a tub, wonderfully decadent in its excess.

Cissy sighed as she was lowered into the bath. It came up to just cover her breasts. The warmth permeated her body, relaxing her muscles. She watched Diltan, Wal and Rolat strip, her eyes delighting in muscled shoulders, wide chests, trim stomachs and thick thighs. Her pussy gave a spasm when she saw the lengths of their dual cocks already erect. Knowing they would be inside her at some point tonight, filling her body, made her eager to skip the foreplay and get right to business.

However, she was determined to welcome them with the same mindfulness as she'd had when they'd said goodbye. If their long separation had taught Cissy anything, it was that she must never take any of the men for granted.

After a quick conference, Rolat fetched a rolling cart with several drawers and brought it to the side of the basin where Cissy sat. Diltan and Wal stepped into the pool and waded close to stand over her. Rolat slid in to join them. Cissy felt small next to the three big Kalquorians, dwarfed by their huge, masculine bodies. The thought of what they could do to her, what they could force her to do for them, turned her on. It didn't matter that Clan Diltan would never push anything on her that she didn't want. It was enough to know they could if they wanted to…and that she was safe from them doing so.

Desiring more of that oh so delicious feeling of vulnerability, Cissy abandoned her usual need to argue for control. Looking up at the clan's leader, she asked, "What do you need me to do?"

Diltan's smile made him almost too devastatingly gorgeous to look at. "Be our good girl. Do as you're told. That's all that is required of you."

"Yes, Dramok. Whatever you want."

"Very good, Cecilia."

They knelt around her. "Turn around, my love," Diltan told her. "We're going to pick you up and lean you over the edge of the basin."

She did as she was told, turning so she faced the side of the pool with her back to the clan. Hands hefted her up, draping her so that her torso rested on the floor and her ass and legs hung over the side. She thought perhaps the festivities would begin with a spanking. That suited her fine. She was in the mood for a little harsh treatment. Maybe it would help bleed out the worry that still wriggled in her mind.

"That's our girl. Spread your legs now."

As she did so, Rolat tugged one of the rolling cabinet's drawers open. From her angle with hair spilling over her eyes, Cissy couldn't tell what he took out.

Hands rubbed over her ass and thighs, massaging to work out the tension she'd carried for too long. Cissy didn't try to contain her groan of appreciation. Maybe that spanking was coming, but until it started she would enjoy this just fine.

The tip of something firm teased her anus. Then the feeling of slickness poured over it. Cissy dived further into relaxation, readying herself for the invasion. It came, a careful insertion of something much smaller than a cock, pressing her open in gradual increments. Cissy smiled. They were taking good care of her. Maybe she didn't want that spanking after all. It was wonderful to be doted on.

The plug wasn't too long and its sweet, slight fullness was inside her in a matter of seconds. Then they tugged on her, pulling her back into the bath.

"Good girl. You'll get a bigger one in a little while if you behave."

"Thank you." Cissy thought good manners might count towards rewards.

"Stand up to be washed."

She did so. The men filled their palms with a cleansing gel from a dispenser. For the next several minutes, they lathered Cissy from chin to her waist. They massaged her with suds, teasing out knots of tension in her shoulders, arms and back. Her breasts and stomach received equal attention, alternating between making her moan with excitement and setting off giggles when ticklish parts were stroked.

Palmfuls of water sluiced over her, rinsing off the suds. Cissy was directed to lean over the edge of the basin again. She did so and the small butt plug was removed. Rolat inserted a larger one, stretching her to about half the girth of a Kalquorian's smaller cock. Cissy shivered, thinking how deliciously full she was going to be when she got the real thing.

"My Nobek, why don't you hold our girl so we can finish washing away these last awful weeks?" Diltan sounded as excited as Cissy felt. Judging from the way his cocks bobbed up against his belly when he moved, his tone was no lie.

"Gladly."

Rolat got behind Cissy. His hands cupped the backs of her knees. "Lean back against my chest," he instructed. She did so and he lifted her, his arms beneath her thighs. She sat above the water, cradled in a chair position.

The lathering resumed. While Rolat held Cissy up, Diltan and Wal each worked on a leg and foot, again massaging free all tightness until she felt like jelly. Cissy thought she might ooze into the water between Rolat's huge arms. She'd never been so relaxed.

She couldn't even summon the strength to tense when Wal's soapy fingers began to cleanse her pussy. All she could do was tremble as his hand worked over her splayed mound. Her head lolled against Rolat's wide chest as she moaned in gratitude for the sweet sensations waking in her core.

His eyes bright with mischief, Wal looked to Diltan. "She needs a thorough rinsing."

The Dramok already had a metallic sprayer in his hand, connected by a tube to one of the many jets that lined the pool. "I would be glad to take care of that."

With a push of a button, a stream of water shot out of the sprayer. Cissy's eyes widened as Diltan brought it towards her pussy. Her hands instinctively shot out to shield herself, but a laughing Wal caught her wrists, making her helpless.

Diltan's evil grin was at odds with the gentle cooing tone he spoke with. "Hold still, little girl. Let me get that soap off."

His aim was deadly accurate. The spray found her clit and Cissy no longer rode gentle swells of arousal. Ecstatic lust burst forth, fully formed and stampeding towards climax.

Had Diltan left the jet of water unmoving, the violent excitement would have swiftly turned to pain. However, he played it over her pussy, letting it stroke the lips and clit and even her plugged ass from different angles. The stream left her shrieking but in rapture. Her body suffused with incredible heat. She damned near crackled with it.

Cissy's sex heaved all at once, the orgasm tearing through as if to escape an intensity it couldn't face. She twisted and jerked in Rolat's arms, her throaty screams turning into high-pitched shrieks. There was no escape. The delicious, insane pleasure continued, forcing brutal climax from her.

Then it was gone, leaving Cissy devastated in its wake. She groaned, her body sagging against the Nobek holding her. Her pussy pulsed with angry surges.

She blinked at the radiant smile beaming from Diltan's face. He held the now quiet sprayer in his hand, pointed away from her. She eyed it as if it were a weapon he might turn on her at any moment. It essentially was.

"Fu-fuck," she wheezed. "Fuck."

"We'll get to that," he answered as the other two laughed. "But first, this."

With his free hand, the Dramok reached to her still convulsing pussy, seizing the red, swollen nubbin at the top. The instant his finger and thumb squeezed, a thunderclap of elation rolled through Cissy again. She yelled at the fresh spasm.

"Don't, Diltan," she begged, her feet kicking arcs of water around the group. "Don't, you're killing me."

"Your word is *sholt,*" he reminded her. He rubbed her clit between finger and thumb, making her arch against the stoic Nobek who held her without straining. "If you want me to stop, it is your only way out."

Cissy gasped as he teased. She couldn't believe that she was tempted to fold because of pleasure. Yet perhaps there could be too much of a good thing. She was crazed from the powerful sensations overloading her wits.

However, the rebellious part of her heard the challenge in Diltan's tone. He believed she was too weak to withstand the gorgeous torment. He didn't think she could take it. Cissy didn't think she could take it, either. In fact, she was sure of it. Yet she couldn't stand to bow to that knowing smirk of his. She might love the man, but she was still ready to argue with him, to make him work to win her over.

Cissy bit her lips together hard, making it hurt, taking what refuge she could from the unbearable bliss.

Diltan's grin spread wide enough to break his face. "There's my stubborn little rebel. Last chance, Cecilia." He pressed the button to turn the jet on again.

A tiny moan of terror escaped Cissy's clenched jaw. She pulled against Wal's grip on her wrists even as she shook her head in refusal to bow.

"As you wish, my love."

He turned the spray on her pussy again. This time her cunt exploded on contact. Every thought was eclipsed by rending passion that tried to tear her body apart.

The jet moved away. Cissy panted, hearing it spatter the surface of the pool. Diltan hadn't turned it off this time. There would be no more invitations to surrender. With Rolat and Wal holding her open and vulnerable to him, he would make her come as often as it pleased the Dramok to do so.

She was lost in a hellish paradise. Cissy welcomed it with all her being.

Once more, thick sprays of thunderous pressure attacked her pussy. Once more, Cissy lost herself in blinding climax. A brief pause. Renewed rapture. Another brief pause. More luscious agony.

She screamed. She writhed. She sobbed. She surrendered over and over to glorious dissolution for her lovers' pleasure. She made their will hers, that they would know she would give them everything for as long as they wanted. Forever, if they would grant it to her.

The spray left again after another frenzied release. Through the roaring in her ears, Cissy heard its liquid whisper silence. She peered with blurred eyes to see Diltan lay it on the side of the basin.

Wal still held her wrists and he brought her clenched fists to his lips to kiss them. "Good girl," he whispered with warmth. His eyes were filled with love as he looked at her. "Beautiful girl."

Rolat moved her so that he cradled her in his arms like a baby. He carried her out of the pool. Diltan and Wal climbed out to gather fluffy towels. They patted her dry as she lay depleted in the Nobek's secure hold.

The touches were as gentle as the orgasms had been brutal. Once again, all the tension bled from her body. She drowsed, enjoying the soft caresses and the tingling coming from her still sensitive sex.

In her relaxed state, she didn't react to the motions of Rolat carrying her away. When he laid her on the cloud-soft sleeping mat in the clan's bedroom, she let herself sink into it. Her eyes closed as she smiled with pleasure. Life was wonderful. Future and past no longer existed for her. Tomorrow was far, far away. The months of being apart were like a distant bad dream. She was content in all ways, happier than she ever remembered being in her entire life.

The clan was quiet as they moved about her. She felt the bedding shift as they brushed against her here and there. Something soft wrapped around her wrists and tightened slightly. Fingers tested for snugness, making sure her circulation wasn't compromised. More silky binds circled her upper thighs. Cissy was too blissful to care what the men were putting on her. She barely noticed for the pleasure that their mere presence gave her.

Even when her legs were bent up, bringing her knees nearly to her shoulders, Cissy didn't rouse from her pleasant dreaming state. The feeling of delicately placed ties that fixed her wrists to her ankles made little impression, as well as the knowledge that a velvet-feeling strap was passed beneath her neck. She heard small clicks and felt motions at the circles around her thighs. A slight pull at the back of her neck told her the strap had been attached there.

It finally occurred to Cissy that she had been trussed up, practically hogtied by the clan. She blinked her eyes open to find the men kneeling around her. She was bound all right, curled on her back with her ass up and splayed wide.

"Look at who woke up," Wal announced in a cheery voice. He knelt between her legs, held open by the thick strap that passed behind her neck, its ends clipped to the thigh bands.

"Just in time," Rolat said. He was on her left side, holding what looked like small alligator clips in one palm. Cissy had gotten in some experience with such clips on her journey to Kalquor. She groaned. Nap time was at an end. The men were far from done with her.

On her right, Diltan held up a red rubber ball. He squeezed it and it squeaked. "In place of saying *sholt* since you will be gagged," he told her as he pressed it into her hand. "Let me hear you use it."

Cissy tried hard not to let him see her shiver as she obeyed. The pliable ball squished easily in her grasp, emitting its squawk.

The Dramok gave her that devilish smirk and held up another ball, this one black, attached to small cushioned straps. "Open your mouth."

The command in his voice had Cissy obeying faster than her mind could work. Diltan put the ball gag between her lips and strapped in place. "Feel free to bite down as needed," he teased.

Still a jerk…but he was her jerk now. Cissy narrowed her eyes in threat.

Wal laughed. "She's awake, all right." His smile was as menacing as his clanmates'. "She may wish otherwise pretty soon."

Rolat bounced the nipple clips in his hand. "I guarantee she will." His threat rang in Cissy's ears.

Wal started by sliding the anal plug out. Cissy had grown used to its presence and missed it terribly. However, seeing the Imdiko lubing up another, larger one let her know she wouldn't miss it for long.

He pressed it in her, filling her almost as well as if he'd used his secondary cock. Cissy's eyes rolled at the wondrous pressure in her nether regions. It felt so good.

Wal wasn't content to let the thick plug nestle inside her, stretching her in its delightful, aching fashion. He pumped it in and out of her, fucking her ass with slow care. Cissy moaned around her gag, thrilling to the sweet violation.

Her view of the Imdiko was blocked by Rolat leaning down to capture a breast in his mouth. He sucked the mound deep in his maw, moving his raspy tongue so that it scraped over her already taut nipple. Glass shards of raw pleasure shivered through Cissy, catching her breath. She arched, offering him more of her flesh.

The Nobek released her tit, sucking hard on it all the way. Her nipple jutted at him, as if to accuse him of abandonment. His tongue peeked out to flick the pebbled round of rosy pink back and forth.

"Lovely," he breathed. Approving of its stiffened state, he pinched it between the padded jaws of one of the clips.

Cissy sucked in a breath. It didn't hurt, not yet, but she was astoundingly sensitive to everything at that moment. The squeezing of the clamp felt profound, sending more darts of excitement through her.

Watching her face with a lazy smile, Rolat tightened the clamp that held her nipple prisoner. The pressure turned to pinching, sending a warm ache through Cissy's breast. Then a lance of pain made her whimper.

"Lovely," Rolat repeated. His eyes were heavy-lidded as he licked his lips and tightened the clamp the slightest increment more. Cissy writhed as the pressure seared. He stopped. "Offer me the other one," he said.

Her eyes stinging with unfallen tears, Cissy arched her chest upward. Rolat seized the second breast as he had the first, sucking hard and abrading it with his rough tongue. The pleasure of that touch swirled headily with the torment of the other. Cissy was tossed in a maelstrom of conflicting sensations.

Too soon, the Nobek had the second clip in place. Red-hot splinters of pain lanced through her breast. His control over her sent arousal to war against the hurt. Cissy couldn't say that she liked the pain so much as being made to surrender to it. The submission was what got her trembling with excitement.

Trembling turned to quaking when Diltan raised a thick wand with the padded bulbous head on the end. He smiled his wicked smile at her as he turned it on. The hum was loud as the rounded end visibly vibrated.

He lowered it towards her pussy. Cissy's bonds left her wide open, her already swollen and sensitive clit exposed. She could only watch as the buzzing instrument homed in on her vulnerable flesh.

Contact sizzled through her pussy, joining with the pleasure of Wal fucking her ass with the plug. Cissy screamed around the gag as elation roiled through her gut. Her body jerked, trying to get away from the too-profound thrill building in strength. Diltan kept up with her twitches, not allowing her to escape.

Wal smacked her ass with a hard hand, adding even more heat to her lower regions. He paddled one ass cheek with his palm and smacked the other cheek with the back of his hand. The spanking underscored her inability to get away from their attentions.

Then Rolat bent down to flick her clamped nipples with his tongue. The raspiness of his touch was the most acute Cissy had ever felt. It should have been painful, but instead it added to the increasing stampede to climax.

Cissy's mind untethered. She could no longer think. All she knew was fire and ecstasy and the helplessness to deny it. She shot straight to the pinnacle of culmination and hovered, climax gathering for one gigantic rush into the heavens.

Then everything stopped. Wal quit spanking and plunging thickness into her ass. Rolat rose from her breast. Diltan pulled the vibrator away.

Cissy hung breathless for another moment, her body on the cusp of succumbing. Then it edged back just a little. Then a little more. Then a little more.

Cissy exhaled on a wail. She quaked in reaction, her body hurting from the denial. Thinking more like an animal in survival mode than a person, she fought her restraints. She tried to bring her legs together so she could at least try to rub free the devouring hunger between them.

The men said nothing. They only watched her desperate struggle with intent gazes, predators sizing up prey.

At last Cissy's thinking mind returned. She stopped fighting to lay gasping and aching. Tears streamed from the corners of her eyes. Her pussy pulsed with raw need, need she feared would not be met for a while.

After a few moments, Wal resumed pumping her ass with the plug. Cissy whimpered. She whimpered again when his hand began that quick cracking against her butt. She uttered a muffled, pleading cry when Diltan powered the vibrator up again. She screamed when it found her clit, shattering her thoughts. She shrieked even louder when Rolat licked her throbbing nipples with his brutal tongue.

Cissy screamed without embarrassment, her mind uncoupled from any notion but that her body must achieve release. She was trapped and orgasm was the only way she could find freedom from the glorious torture she was made to suffer. Cold sweat broke out on her skin as passion reached its zenith, crumbling all she'd ever known into dust.

It stopped again, leaving her suspended on that awful peak where arousal hurt rather than excited. Cissy's cries were that of a tortured animal.

The big man kneeling over her, the one who filled her nipples with enthralling stabs of pain, looked to the one who wielded the humming instrument. "I think her limit has been reached."

"So has mine. We will make the ultimate claim on her body."

Nothing they said made sense to Cissy. All she knew was that she needed relief and these three were her only hope for that. They were also the ones who could withhold it, leaving her grasping forever.

She made a plaintive sound, trying to tell them she would grant them anything they wished. Anything, just to make this awful longing stop.

At first, Cissy thought they were going to walk away. Diltan let the vibrator drop to the floor and Wal pulled the plug out of her ass and tossed it aside. She cried in earnest as the gag was removed from her mouth. Her thoughts were too tattered to allow her speech, however. She wanted to beg, but she couldn't remember how.

The men shifted around her, changing positions and bringing their bodies close. They rolled Cissy on her side. Rolat spooned tight against her back. She felt his slick cocks nestle in between her buttocks. Wal arranged himself so that her face nestled between his shoulder and neck, with her upper leg slung over his hip. Diltan moved up so that he knelt over their heads. He looked down on the rest of them, as if they had gathered there just for him.

Rolat shifted, bringing the tip of his primary cock to her asshole. Cissy's glad cry rang out. They were not abandoning her to suffer unrequited desire. They would fulfil her. They would fulfil themselves through her. She trembled with eagerness, ready to give them everything she possessed in her heart, body and soul.

The Nobek entered her. What should have been a profound ache as his substantial girth spread her ass was pleasure to Cissy. Had she not still been bound, had she been able to move, she would have taken his primary cock even faster. His invasion was steady, but it felt as if an eternity passed before he had filled her with himself.

Cissy moaned in bliss as Rolat pumped his hips, fucking her with sure strokes. Her body was so primed now that she knew she could achieve orgasm this way. Passion built once more, her body making that climb that must end in release this time.

Her cry was strangled when the Nobek abruptly halted with just the tip of his cock encased in her willing flesh. Dismay vanished as Wal moved against her. Hard, wet heat prodded her pussy, guided by his hand. Then astonishing thickness invaded her womanhood. It took several moments before Cissy realised the Imdiko was stuffing *both* his cocks inside her.

The hand he'd used to position himself for the double entry covered her mouth. "Lick my juices off. Taste me," he growled, his eyes alight with excitement.

Cissy obeyed, loving the spicy taste of Kalquorian male as his cocks pushed inside, filling her to her limits. Again, what she thought should have hurt brought only incredible pleasure. She wasn't climbing to orgasm now. She hurtled towards it.

By the time Wal reached his end, Cissy trembled on the verge. She was almost there and she didn't think any force in the universe would keep her from climax this time. As Wal drew himself out, emptying her, Rolat pressed in. Feeling all that pressure from three cocks drove Cissy right to the edge. Nirvana was now inevitable.

From far away, she heard Rolat gasp, "I can feel you through her."

Wal's voice was strained. "Fuck, that's the most wonderful sensation!"

Whatever else the men said was lost to Cissy. The moment of exaltation had arrived.

She soared through a blinding whiteness, her body shattering against a mighty force that seemed to come from inside and out. At last the power that had been denied found its outlet and it streamed in fierce pulses. Cissy hung between worlds, buffeted over and over.

The surges gradually weakened but were not spent. Through the continued pitches and swells, some of the world Cissy knew reasserted itself. She became aware of Rolat and Wal bucking against her, chasing their own pleasures. Diltan's hand appeared to brush the trio's hair back and caress their cheeks. He leaned close, holding his larger, weeping cock. Cissy watched the gorgeous length approach, licking her lips in anticipation.

"Yes, my Matara. Take me. Love me, my beauty. Please—I don't deserve you, but I beg you to make me yours."

He filled her eager mouth. Now the clan possessed her…and she possessed all of them. They were hers now, no matter what. She knew it as sure as she knew her name. It was the most profound moment of Cissy's life.

She was enjoying the last sweet pulses of orgasm when Wal announced his with a cry. Moments later, Rolat's deep groans joined in. They lay gasping and still, their cocks still throbbing inside Cissy when Diltan yelled. His pleasure flooded her mouth, completing the joining.

When the Dramok was depleted, he crawled heavily over the mat's surface to thump down behind Wal. Gasps slowed. Pulses calmed. The four found the strength to cuddle close to one another, sharing warmth in a contented knot.

Little by little, Cissy remembered the world outside the sleeping room, a world that seemed to be less and less secure. *But we aren't,* she assured herself.

To prove it to herself, she said out loud, "Tell me we don't have to be apart again. Tell me this is forever."

Diltan's head appeared over Wal's. He propped his chin on the sleepily smiling Imdiko's shoulder. "You are ours, my love. As soon as decorum allows, I will make the offer to clan you. An offer you will accept."

She chuckled at the order before rolling her eyes at him. "You and appearances. Aren't you the one who said fuck propriety? Well, fuck decorum, too. Decorum sucks."

He grinned but real regret was in his tone. "I agree. However, there is one inescapable fact—you are a member of the Imperial Family. Therefore, certain proprieties will have to be observed as much as we may dislike doing so."

Rolat snickered. "You can't help but vex him in one way or the other, can you, Cissy?"

She sighed. "Even when I play nice with Diltan, I can't play nice with Diltan."

The Dramok reached to stroke her hair, delighting her with his touch. "Have no fear, my love. I will make my intentions known to your family with undue haste."

"And you can be sure I will accept. Heaven help them if they try to stop me."

"That's a bigger threat than any Rolat could offer," Wal observed. "Only a lunatic or Diltan would dare oppose you. But then, the two may be one and the same."

Diltan smacked the Imdiko's ass for that one while Cissy and Rolat laughed.

Happy despite having to wait on naming herself part of Clan Diltan, Cissy said, "I guess that makes us engaged then. Hey, you're ridiculously rich. Where is my ridiculously huge ring with the billion-carat diamond?"

Diltan looked as euphoric as she felt. "I'll buy you rings for every finger, if that will make you happy. Anything your heart desires, my Matara."

She waved off his offer. "I'm not interested in any stupid rocks or jewellery. Just you three. That's all my little old heart wants."

"That will save some money," Wal said, spurring more laughter.

Cissy thought there was no better sound than their mingled joy. That was better than any other declaration of their union.

Chapter Thirty

High expectation and anxiety permeated the court the next morning. The galleries were packed to capacity once more. Cissy was amazed to see the number of Earther women there, all of whom seemed to be surrounded by their clans. The Royal Council's gallery was similarly filled with both councilmen and their clanmates, including Mataras.

It was a gesture of solidarity with Yuder, as well as gratitude. Cissy exchanged hopeful smiles with her sister, aunt, cousins and Jessica's friend Michaela, who had also shown up as a show of support. Could this be a sign that things might go their way? That the revolution faction of Kalquor might be relenting?

If it was, the emperors and their accompanying aides showed no sign of optimism. The men's faces were set in lines of unsmiling stoicism. Clajak in particular sat quite still in his seat.

Tasha leaned in close to Cissy to whisper, "So Wal didn't give you any indication?"

She shook her head, remembering with some embarrassment her combativeness the day before. "It's not proper for him to do so. Plus, I think he's trying to protect everyone from accusations of special treatment."

As usual, Kalquorian hearing won out over whispers. Egilka shifted in his seat to smile at them. "Honourable Wal is a good man and an excellent judge. No matter what, he'll have done things as they should be done."

The Imdiko emperor winced then, as if his words stung him. He glanced worriedly at Clajak, who sat beside him.

The tense set of Clajak's shoulders eased a little. He regarded Egilka. In that look, Cissy saw the respect and trust the Dramok held for his clanmate.

He said, "Indeed Wal will act with the utmost honour. Let me add that no one in his clan has acted improperly when it comes to upholding the Empire." He directed his warm gaze to Cissy. "I hope they make you happy, my cousin. Whatever my father's sentence may be, I can't be more pleased with your choice of a clan."

Cissy was surprised Clajak realised how serious her relationship with Clan Diltan had become. But then, it was his clan's business to know what was going on in the Empire—perhaps they took that responsibility to extended family just as seriously. As everyone else added their smiles, she knew they'd all somehow figured things out...maybe sooner than she had.

Then again, Jessica was Clan Clajak's Matara. Jessica had a habit of sniffing out secrets that affected those she loved.

Cissy was relieved to know her in-laws approved of Clan Diltan. There would be no obstacles to clanning with the men she loved. Even Lindsey, who remained uncertain about the matter after Cissy had told her about Diltan's confession, gave her a thumbs-up to indicate her support.

Cissy turned her attention to Diltan and Rolat, both sitting in the crowded Royal Council gallery. They gave her questioning looks. They had apparently seen something of the exchange. Cissy winked at them with a leer. Then she stuck her tongue out at the pair, being the brat. Rolat grinned and Diltan shook a finger at her. The subdued snickers around Cissy told her that the exchange had been witnessed by her family.

"Those poor men," Tasha sighed.

The courtroom went quiet as the judges walked out onto their platform. All hilarity vanished in an instant. The court officer announced the session had begun.

From his podium, Onziv told the officer, "Bring in Imperial Father Nobek Yuder."

Yuder came out of the door that Cissy had been told was the holding area. This time he was flanked by twice the guards as the day before despite the invisible containment shield between the front area and the public gallery. There were no calls against him. In fact, Cissy could detect only her own breath in the near-absolute silence. Then again, most of the gallery had filled with supporters. Any dissenters would be vastly outnumbered today.

Yuder glanced up at their box, his gaze moving between Clajak and Tara. Then he bowed to Nivere before standing at her side. He faced the judges, standing straight, tall and proud.

He and the judges exchanged nods. Then Onziv spoke.

"Imperial Father Yuder, Nobek of Clan Zarl, you have entered a plea of guilty in the matter of the wilful abductions of Earther Mataras. This action which you confess to resulted in war with Earth, leading to its subsequent destruction. Do you stand by your guilty plea?"

Another slight nod. "I do, Honourable Onziv. I accept the sentence you have deemed just for me."

Onziv took a deep breath. "Very well. Before I pass sentence, I would like the Empire to know that this panel of honourable judges has taken into consideration certain variables. These details include the reasons the defence put forth for Imperial Father Yuder's actions." His direct gaze centred on Yuder. "Your age and the impact your punishment will have on the Imperial Clan, which leads our Empire, has also been considered. The assertions of those Mataras alleged to have been brought against their will to Kalquor and who have come forward to defend you have been weighed."

Onziv's chin lifted. Cissy tensed, knowing the judgment was coming.

The head judge said, "We are satisfied your intentions were for the most part good, striving for the welfare of the Empire. However, we are also unanimous in believing you and then-Emperor Zarl misplaced your concern that our culture be continued through a breeding programme. You wilfully put our culture's continuity ahead of all other more important considerations."

Tasha grabbed Cissy's hand. Cissy squeezed, feeling doom descending.

"Imperial Father, you ignored the warnings from the leadership of Earth that the repercussions of bringing their women here would result in war. In so doing, you cleared the path for Earth's destruction as well as the possible extinction of all species of that planet. For setting us on a course that resulted in Earth's Armageddon, the deaths of billions of its people and placing its indigenous species at risk, justice must be served. You are hereby exiled to the penal colony on the moon of Baldu for a term of fifty years."

The courtroom rang with gasps. Several of the Earther women sobbed, including Michaela. Meanwhile, the emperors and Jessica remained stone-faced, giving no reaction at all. Tara also sat quietly, her expression controlled.

Onziv wasn't done. "In addition to this sentence, this court recommends you be handed over to the Galactic Council of Planets to face that distinguished body's charges. We order that matter to be taken up by the Royal Council and Imperial Clan at their earliest opportunity. Until then, you will be placed in custody to begin serving your sentence at once. This honourable panel's decision is so decreed. Court is adjourned."

The judges filed out. Wal did not look in Cissy's direction. Perhaps he feared what he would see…but Cissy was too shocked to know if she was angry with him or not.

Yuder gazed up at Tara as he was escorted out of the courtroom by his guards. His expression was one of comfort. Tara blew him a kiss, looking braver than Cissy thought possible. Then he went through the door, gone.

Tasha was the first to find her voice. "Fifty years? Auntie Tara—"

Lindsey and Jessica were on their feet, moving to embrace their mother. The men also stood, looking towards her. Even Clajak seemed more concerned for her loss than his own.

Tara's courageous expression never wavered. There was a noticeable tremor in her voice, however. "I'm all right, everyone. After all, we knew it would probably come to this."

Bevau went to her. He bent to press his forehead to hers. "Baldu is a minimum security facility and one that will allow you many visits. It's as easy a penal colony as one could hope for. He will be well treated."

Clajak added, "It's not a work camp, Earth Mom. Yuder's biggest worry there will be boredom." He drew a shuddering breath. "It's a longer sentence than I had hoped for, but in balancing the need for justice, I think the panel did their best."

Tara managed a smile. "Now the rebellion has no leg to stand on, not really. It's what Yuder hoped for. I know he's pleased."

Clajak rubbed his forehead, worry lining his handsome face and ageing it. "I'm more concerned about how he'll fare before the Galactic Council's courts. I do not think they will be so lenient."

Jessica touched his arm, fear lighting in her eyes. "Yuder has already been given a near-life sentence, my Dramok. Do we have to hand him over to them?"

"If we want to keep the Basma's rebellion to an unhappy few, we have no choice. For the Empire's sake, we must vote for Yuder's extradition." Clajak reached to stroke Tara's cheek. "My greatest sorrow is for your loss, Earth Mom. I know how much he means to you. This sacrifice is as much yours as his."

She impatiently scrubbed away the lone tear that streaked from her eye. "It is the way of life, Clajak.

Sorrow and joy, ever trading places forever and always."

Even stoic Egilka was moved to emotion. His voice choked, he told Tara, "Yuder is fortunate to have a mate such as you. We are all lucky in that respect. Your strength bolsters ours."

Cissy silently agreed. Tara had always been a beacon of grace and she shone brighter than ever in the wake of this personal calamity.

Cissy knew she lacked that kind of courage. Now that Clan Diltan was undeniably her future, she would never be able to let them go. Not even for an Empire. Faith and Kalquor be damned—she could not survive such a thing.

She looked to the two men watching her from across the room. Diltan mouthed the words, "I'm sorry."

Cissy nodded. Then she blew them a kiss, much as Tara had to Yuder. However, hers was not a kiss goodbye. She was weak. She would never be able to tell them goodbye.

Cissy sighed, thinking of her belief in reincarnation, the ceaseless cycle of lives until the soul was pure and no longer clung to anything. She'd have to endure many more lifetimes before she'd get things right. There was no way she'd ever be able to give up her clan.

* * * *

Two days passed after Yuder's sentencing. The Royal Council and Imperial Clan assembled to take up the matter of his extradition to Galactic Council space to face their justice. Diltan took his place on the council's seats next to Oiteil.

Kalquor's atmosphere had turned peaceful in the aftermath of conviction and sentencing. Protests had been cancelled and the number of threats against Yuder and the government dwindled. Diltan knew the matter of extradition had potential to incite unrest once more. Though he and Jessica had hoped to change minds through the Earther Mataras' testimony on Yuder's behalf, it had been only partially successful. It was all too obvious that, to keep the Empire from splitting apart, the former emperor would have to face intergalactic justice. Yuder had sent word that he was more than ready to do so.

Diltan looked at Maf, sitting on the bottom tier of the seats. He shifted often, trying to relieve his bent joints. Otherwise, he seemed anticipatory. And why not? He had gotten what he wanted—conviction, sentence and, in a few minutes, if all went well, extradition. Diltan was surprised the man wasn't gloating.

Something else surprised Diltan—Maf's friend and frequent collaborator Councilman Terbal did not sit with him. Diltan looked about, thinking Terbal must be running late. He gaped when he caught sight of the Dramok, sitting on the other end of the tiers in a circle of men.

"What the deuce is that man doing?" Diltan muttered.

"Who?" Oiteil peered in the direction that he stared.

"Terbal. He's sitting with Gamas, Efo and several others who claimed first Earther Mataras."

"That is odd." Oiteil frowned.

Before they could discuss this strange occurrence, Clajak convened the meeting. He did not postpone the unpleasant duty for a second.

Standing before his chair on the dais, he said, "We all know our first business here. Imperial Father Nobek Yuder has been convicted and sentenced for the part he played in the destruction of Earth. This honourable council will now vote to determine whether he will be extradited to the Galactic Council of Planets to face further charges on the interplanetary stage."

"I think not, my emperor."

Diltan was among the many councilmen who gasped and stared in confusion at Terbal. Maf's usual companion had risen to his feet to confront Clajak. The councilman strode to the centre of the floor.

"I speak on behalf of a number of this council, my emperors and empress. Before we throw the Imperial Father to outside interests, we should take a vote on whether he should be pardoned for his so-called crimes."

That brought angry shouts from the public gallery and several members of the council. Diltan exchanged a shocked look with Oiteil. Was Terbal serious?

The Imperial Clan appeared as stunned as Diltan felt. Clajak shook his head as if he thought he was hearing things. As quiet descended in the council chamber once more, he said, "I don't understand, Councilman. Nobek Yuder has admitted his guilt. The Royal Court has handed down its judgment. Why would we subvert its decree?"

"Because it is wrong." Terbal waited for another round of shouting to end before continuing. "I disagree with the assertion of guilt and the sentence, as many of my colleagues do. Yes, Imperial Father Yuder is guilty of a humanitarian effort, one that had unforeseen repercussions. His intentions were pure. He committed this *crime* to save hundreds of Mataras in immediate danger."

Bevau looked at him as if he spoke gibberish. "Earth was destroyed. Billions died. We have bowed before the need for justice, which cannot be denied."

"Justice for what? For what Earth brought upon itself?" Terbal's tone turned derisive, almost disrespectful. "We heard the testimony from our former colleague Dramok Rajhir's mate. We heard and read the accounts of the other women who attested to their lives being saved by Yuder and Zarl's actions. My heart was won by those I once opposed, as were many others'. So I say now, who are we to punish a man for seeing to the rescue of all those poor women? We should be celebrating him and his deceased Dramok as heroes!"

This time a new sound rose to combat the angry mutters. The word *yes* was spoken loudly by as many voices as the dissenters. A large number of heads nodded in support of Terbal.

Diltan's heart pounded. The rift was opening again. He could practically hear it ripping beneath them, threatening to plunge them into the abyss.

Maf rose and lurched out onto the floor to face off with Terbal. "This is ridiculous. Yuder is guilty. He is going to prison. The Galactic Council has demanded justice for Earth and we must surrender to its claim on Yuder. His own son has conceded to this."

Terbal looked at him with sneering distaste. "Since when does the Empire bow to the Galactic Council? They are on no more than a witch-hunt. Since they have not been able to get their hands on the real villain in the war, Earth's Holy Leader Browning Copeland, they are trying to make us their scapegoats. I, for one, will not stand by and sacrifice one of our greatest emperors to such nonsense."

Maf's voice shook with rage. "Are you saying we are above intergalactic law, Councilman? Would you have us ejected from the Galactic Council for one man?"

"I speak for true justice! For an innocent man, for a hero, I spit in the face of the Galactic Council. The Kalquorian Empire, first and foremost!"

The room erupted in yelling, both for and against his cry. Diltan stared at the two men on the council floor, recent friends turned into foes. Two men who were dividing the Empire once more.

Their antagonistic glares were held unblinking. Depending on one's viewpoint, their arguments were equally compelling. To Diltan, they also sounded well-rehearsed.

To his eternal shame, he knew a thing or two about selfish manipulation of others. Toward the end of the battle over Yuder's guilt, Maf had acted like a man determined to put Kalquorians at one another's throats. Diltan had no doubt the man's endgame was still to end the interbreeding of Kalquorian and Earther. Until today, Terbal had seemed entrenched in Maf's corner.

He smelled a setup. Terbal's colours had not changed. He was simply camouflaged now.

Around him, councilmen stood almost to a man, yelling at one another. The gallery above was a bedlam of noise. Shoving had started and Global Security began to clear out the more irate onlookers. The Imperial Clan watched the turmoil build, their dissimilar faces identical in rising horror. They were watching the disintegration they had given so much to disarm.

It was Bevau who slammed his fist on his podium, unleashing a roar that startled everyone to silence. His fangs showed in his dark, feral face, sending a thrill of terror up Diltan's spine. The man might have been half-Imdiko, but that softer side of him had disappeared in his rage.

His voice a blast of thunder, the Nobek emperor shouted, "Quiet in the gallery! Quiet on the floor! This is a council meeting and there will be order if I have to tear every one of your throats out to get it!"

The room was frozen in the glare of his threat. No one dared to breathe for fear the angry monster might come down from the dais to make an example of them. Even bold Jessica, sitting at Bevau's side, stared wide-eyed at her clanmate.

Councilmen's asses sank back to their seats. The gallery kept quiet. Bevau's fangs hinged and his shoulders relaxed. He gave Terbal and Maf a withering stare before sitting down and snarling, "You may resume the debate."

Bowing deeply before speaking, Terbal said, "My emperors, it is within my rights as a concerned lawmaker to call for a vote on the pardoning of Imperial Father Yuder. My motion does not call into question the Royal Court's findings. He remains guilty of this crime some would say he committed." He shot a scowl at Maf before finishing. "I am not one to send a man I and many others call a hero to spend the rest of his life on a penal colony. I beg of you to allow the council to speak."

The four members of the Imperial Clan looked at one another. Clajak, Egilka and Jessica wore worried expressions. Bevau still looked angry, glowering at no one in particular.

Diltan could have screamed. If the vote was for a pardon, then the split that Yuder had sacrificed his honour to keep from happening was still a possibility. After all they had done to stay one step ahead of revolt, Maf had engineered the perfect trap. Through that, the Basma might very well get his war. The Empire would be shaken at the best, shattered at the worst.

Looking sickened, pale as if already mourning the demise of Kalquor, Emperor Egilka gave voice to what the rest seemed incapable of saying. "It is within your rights to call the vote, Councilman Terbal." He rose, steady despite being shaken. "But as you cast your votes, I caution all of you on this council, as duly elected representatives of your territories, to keep in mind the will of your constituents and the welfare of Kalquor. A majority vote, including the votes of the Imperial Clan, determines whether Imperial Father Nobek Yuder will be pardoned."

Terbal turned to the risers where his colleagues sat, their handhelds already poised. With a smile that said he anticipated victory, he called, "Cast your votes, Royal Council."

As much as it pained him on a personal level to do so, Diltan did not hesitate to vote nay to the pardon. Once again, he had no choice but to move against his conscience for what he believed to be the good of the Empire. Then there was nothing to do but wait and watch the votes tally on the large vid that hung over the chamber's floor.

The silence was deafening as the numbers quickly climbed. Knowing that Maf was behind this latest debacle, knowing his influence and how far it spread, Diltan felt no surprise to see that the vote wasn't even close. When the final numbers from the council came in, there was no reason to call for the Imperial Clan's ballots.

Clajak stood. His expression was tragic, nothing like what one would expect from a son whose father would not be serving a prison sentence. As angry mutterings began to climb the register once more, he announced, "The Royal Council has spoken. Nobek Yuder is hereby pardoned for his crime."

Maf glared at everyone, playing the affronted to the hilt. "There is still the matter of handing him over to the Galactic Council. I call for that vote now."

Though he looked angry, Diltan imagined he saw the gleam of triumph in his eyes. Diltan shook all over, thinking how easily they had played into his plans. He fought off the urge to leap from his seat and take Maf by the throat.

Through the buzzing in his ears, he heard Clajak's weary command. "Let the vote commence." Barely a minute later, he announced, "The Royal Council of the Kalquorian Empire has voted against the Galactic Council of Planet's petition to extradite by a margin of two-to-one. There is no reason for the Imperial Clan to vote, though we dissent with this decision."

Fighting broke out in the gallery and Global Security went to work quashing the violence and arresting offenders. The Royal Guards were already mobilised around the Imperial Clan and they held percussion blasters at the ready should anyone threaten the four monarchs...not that Diltan thought even the most enraged protestor would challenge rabid Bevau.

Meanwhile, Maf shouted over the fiercely arguing councilmen. "This is an outrage! We will not be ruled by the tyranny of those looking out for their selfish interests!"

Terbal yelled back, "If Kalquor stands alone, so be it! We will not bow to outside forces!"

Diltan watched the mayhem, knowing the greatest blow was yet to come and knowing there was nothing he could do to stop it. He felt numb in the midst of the surreal scene. Next to him, Oiteil sat with his face in his hands, unable to watch their world fall apart.

Maf's soul, as twisted as his body, shone forth in malignance to Diltan's eyes. The crippled councilman cried, "This empire is a mockery of its once greatness. This council is the greatest mockery! I will not be a party to the wilful ignoring of what our citizens want and deserve." Then, in a mighty bellow, he added, "I resign!"

That brought a chorus of other councilmen shouting their resignations. In a parade of shaking fists and red faces, at least of quarter of the Royal Council walked out of the chamber behind Maf. Nearly half of the remaining council jeered their departure as others cried out pleas for them to come back. As fighting continued in the gallery, the Royal Guards escorted the Imperial Clan out. Jessica openly wept.

Diltan sat in his seat, his legs too numb to let him rise and run away from it all. The grinning Terbal accepted laughing congratulations for putting Maf and the rest of his ilk in their place. He wondered if he had just witnessed the end of Kalquor. He wondered if he was the only sane man left in the Empire.

Chapter Thirty-One

Diltan announced himself at the door of the Imperial Clan's home. Despite having been called in by Clajak, he'd had to present identification to a gauntlet of Royal Guards and submit to half an hour of interrogation by their imposing captain before being allowed through. He wondered what those who hadn't been summoned by the monarchs had to go through to gain admittance.

As soon as he entered the small but elegant greeting room filled with several people, he bowed. He was not surprised to find his former colleague Rajhir and Dramok Ospar there with the Imperial Clan, along with Korkla and Emperor Bevau's aide, Dramok Erybet. Everyone stood, ignoring the many seating options. Their expressions said they were too keyed up to sit for conversation.

Yuder was conspicuously absent. Diltan guessed the Imperial Father was reuniting with Tara McInness.

Diltan centred his attention on the royals. "You called for me, my emperors and my empress."

Clajak nodded. “Your counsel is wanted. We have a huge mess on our hands and are hard-pressed to keep up with events as they happen. But first, how bad did it become in the council after we left?”

Diltan shook his pounding head. “A full quarter of the Royal Council resigned on the spot. More hand in resignations as the hours pass. Some are coming from councilmen who voted to pardon your father.”

“Then it was a plot to destabilise the Empire as we feared,” Clajak said. “I do not doubt Maf is behind this.”

“It would seem so. Many of those who remain, led by Councilman Terbal, voted to expel and block ambassadors from the Galactic Council from Empire space.”

Bevau appeared angry, but he looked more like his usual self than the animal that had turned so threatening in the meeting. “How large was the vote for that?”

“Enough that the Imperial Clan cannot block it, even if Maf’s supporters were there to fight it.”

Rajhir looked as sickened as he had when he’d been barred from serving the government. “It’s more than a setup. This is a conspiracy.”

Diltan realised he was clenching his fists and made himself ease. “I agree. Terbal has been in Maf’s corner for years, along with some of the other councilmen now supporting these insane measures. I think when Imperial Father Yuder pled guilty and they knew they weren’t going to be able to get at their enemies in the council, they concocted this mad scheme.”

Looking lost, Jessica asked, “What are our options now?”

Egilka said, "If we have the luxury of time, we should wait it out a few days and allow cooler heads to prevail. I hear there are protests?"

Diltan said, "Quite a few in all territories."

Erybet folded his arms over his chest. He looked as capable of violence as Bevau as he said, "Global Security is on alert, ready for trouble. They have patrols all over the place, making sure their presence is noted."

Jessica drew a deep breath, gathering her fabled strength. "We accepted the will of the council on the pardon, which was a mistake. It's too late to issue an Imperial Decree overriding that…not that I want my father sent to prison, you understand."

Ospar seized upon her words. "This move to barricade against the Galactic Council can still be repealed, however. My advice is to let the matter sit for a couple of days. What's left of the council will get past the emotional upheaval and see things with different eyes once they acknowledge their constituents are unhappy. They may vote to overturn their own edict."

Rajhir's expression was not hopeful. "That will happen only if the anger doesn't get out of hand in the meantime. Anger can turn to violence quickly and don't think the Basma is going to let this matter settle. His statement is already out decrying the work of 'entitled overlords' taking over our government and the Imperial Clan's unwillingness to stand up against them. He's calling for the oppressed to rise up against those with Earther mates. Our lifebringers are in danger."

Bevau looked to Erybet, who dipped his head, answering an unspoken question. The Nobek Emperor said, "Ground troops are ready to deploy if it comes to it. I sincerely hope not. Military action will only make this matter worse."

Diltan thought about the stories in the weeks leading up to the trial—stories of squads and platoons deserting or, worse still, turning against their officers. How many dissenters remained in the ranks?

He said, "I suggest you release a statement, my emperors and empress. Let the populace know you supported the Royal Court's findings and that you refute the council's move. Hint that an Imperial Decree might be issued if necessary. Urge them to remain peaceful while you work to correct this error in the council's judgment."

Clajak said, "It's all we've got left, isn't it? Words. Weak, paltry words to try and soothe too many shattered nerves. Korkla?"

His unsmiling aide was already working on his handheld. "I will make the arrangements immediately, my emperor."

* * * *

Cissy was reading in her bedroom when Tasha came into her quarters calling her name. There was no mistaking the fear in her twin's voice and Cissy hurried to meet her in the greeting area.

"What's wrong? I thought you were getting ready for a date."

Her hair only half-curled, Tasha looked shaken. "Turn on the news vid. I think this trouble with the Royal Council is getting ugly."

"Vid on, news feed."

The screen came to life. Cissy stared at the huge crowd of shouting Kalquorians clustered outside and on top of the adjacent cliffs that accommodated the Imperial Clan's home and the Government House. The furious mob faced off with thick lines of Global Security officers and Royal Guards.

Cissy tried to follow what the reporter was saying, but her Kalquorian was too weak to keep up with the speed of his natural speech. "Shit. Translation to Earther English mode," she ordered.

The voice disappeared, replaced by electronic speech. "Crowds are demanding that the current council step down and new elections be held. This comes in the wake of the Royal Council's pardon of Imperial Father Nobek Yuder and the vote to refuse the Galactic Council access to him. A statement by the rebel known as the Basma and threats of sanctions issued by the Galactic Council of Planets apparently spurred the protests. Most Kalquorians are saying the Royal Council no longer represents the interests of the Empire."

Tasha's peevish tone couldn't mask her worry. "Great. First the Royal Council goes into mob mentality, now the rest of Kalquor is doing the same thing. Like that will solve anything."

Cissy looked at the cliff where the majority of the protestors had gathered. "I hope Diltan is okay. No one is threatening real violence, are they?"

"Not that I'm aware of. Still, you know how these things go. Security is armed. One little misstep and things get ugly fast."

Cissy shivered. "No kidding. We saw it happen enough times on Earth. The difference was that our government had no problem killing those who didn't agree with it. I don't think Kalquor has the same mindset."

"At least they have that going for them. Are you going to com Diltan to check on him?"

There was nothing Cissy wanted to do more, but she shook her head. "The last thing he needs is me bothering him while he's in the middle of damage control. He's got his hands full enough without having his hysterical girlfriend on the line."

That gave Tasha something to snicker at. "You hysterical. Not likely."

Cissy ordered the vid off, not wanting to look at so many angry faces. "Quite a few of those people aren't exactly enthralled with us Earther gals, either. I think we're better off lying low in our safe little apartments for a while, don't you?"

"I already cancelled tonight's date. Are you going to spend the night with your clan again?"

Cissy shrugged and assumed her best damsel-in-distress look. "I assume so, but I'm not going out there without big, bad Rolat to protect me."

"I'm surprised he's not here now."

Cissy waved her off. "We have plenty of security here at the complex. If I know that protective Nobek, as soon as he gets off work, he'll be with Diltan to keep the bad people away from another 'elitist' councilman. With Diltan doing whatever it is he has to do to calm things down, it could be a while before they show up to fetch me."

Tasha gave her a bright smile. "It's about dinner time. Shall we order from the kitchen or cook?"

Cissy winked. "All that I have in my cooling unit is a little bit of booze, sis."

"That's my girl. I don't have much appetite for food anyway. Screw the grouchy assholes outside and break out the glasses."

They linked arms and headed for the kitchenette. Cissy found herself looking forward to goofing off with Tasha. It felt like the best way to thumb her nose at the tension that pervaded the environment these days.

She said, "You know, even after we're both clanned, we still will have to schedule in plenty of girls' nights."

"No kidding. That's the first thing I warn my prospective harems about. I will get drunk and stupid with my sis on a regular basis."

They laughed and continued to kid each other as if nothing bad could ever happen. As they drank, it even began to feel true. The Empire's problems got further and further away from their consciousness. The apartment rang with their increasingly drunken delight.

* * * *

Diltan commed Rolat and Wal to tell them he was helping the Imperial Clan keep track of the developing protests exploding all over Kalquor and its off-planet colonies. It was difficult to stay ahead of the anger that enveloped the Empire. People marched in support of the decision to pardon Yuder and expel the Galactic Council of Planets' ambassadors. Others surrounded officials' homes and offices, protesting the very same action.

Rolat asked if he and Wal could join Diltan at the Imperial home. He said, "Perhaps we can help monitor the situation. Two extra sets of eyes certainly couldn't hurt." Diltan agreed that they needed the help, but he knew the real reason Rolat offered—the Imperial home could come under siege. With Diltan there, Rolat wanted to be able to protect his Dramok and keep his Imdiko close as well.

Thank goodness there's a full security force at the Matara Complex, Diltan thought. *Otherwise, we'd all be running to check on Cissy and her sister.*

He asked Erybet for permission to have his clanmates join him. Erybet considered. "We've got too many protestors outside right now for it to be safe for your clanmates to pass through. As soon as I feel the situation here is under control, I'll com Rolat to let him know to come."

Diltan thanked him and gave the aide Rolat's contact frequency. He relayed the message to his Nobek, who was none too happy to have to rely on others to keep his Dramok safe.

"I'm in a place surrounded by Royal Guards and Global Security," Diltan reminded him. "Besides, the last place you need to take Wal is through an unruly mob."

"I suppose you're right," Rolat grumbled.

"Have you had a chance to talk to Cissy? I haven't been able to get through."

Mention of their soon-to-be Matara brightened the Nobek's mood. "I spoke to her about fifteen minutes ago. She and Tasha are busy getting drunk since the complex has gone on lockdown for the women's safety. She said she and Tasha had raided the complex's stores for all the bottles they could carry."

"By the ancestors," Diltan snorted. "I hope it's kloq and not bohut this time. We'll have to peel her off the floor."

"We may as well write tonight off as far as tossing the sheets. She'll be passed out by the time we get the all-clear," Rolat agreed. Diltan heard Wal laughing in the background over the matter.

Grinning and shaking his head, Diltan ended the conversation. Trust his rowdy rebel to party while a revolt was in the making. He got to work monitoring the more serious situation of Kalquor's security.

He was assigned to take coms from worried territorial governors, getting their reports and passing along updates. He shared the greeting room with the emperors and Jessica, along with Rajhir and Ospar. Erybet and Korkla set up their own stations in the dining hall. The Imperial Clan's public space had become their ad hoc headquarters.

After an hour of nonstop fielding of information, Diltan was roused from his task by Erybet and Korkla walking into the greeting room. Erybet bowed to Bevau.

"Global Security reports the lockdown of the Government House continues, though about half the crowds are gone. Everyone still inside has to remain until all the protestors disperse, which they are doing at a rather fast rate. It looks like they're ready to go home. We should be able to clear the councilmen and their staff out of the cliff within a couple of hours."

Korkla addressed Clajak. "On an even better note, your message to the Empire has managed to deflect the population's anger from the Imperial Clan. The crowd surrounding this cliff is almost entirely gone."

Erybet glanced at Diltan. "I've already told your Nobek that he and Honourable Wal are cleared to join us here."

"So we're looking good? No threats against the Imperial Clan or Yuder?" Jessica said.

Korkla nodded. "Those protesting today's decisions are placing all the blame on Terbal and his followers in the council."

Egilka shook his head, his frown not easing for a moment. "This situation is still not acceptable. Good sense must prevail and it cannot with this mob mentality. At least it seems some are heeding the call."

Erybet checked his handheld. "We continue to receive reports of growing crowds elsewhere throughout the Empire. There have been clashes. Global Security is calling in a small military force to deal with some problems they're having on the Esofu Continent. Here, however, things are looking better."

"There are still bound to be stragglers, hardliners who will not give up," Bevau said. "Have you sent out the warning that martial law will be enforced if all the protestors do not leave the Government House's location?"

"Yes, my emperor. You're right about the stragglers. A fair number are still choosing to ignore the order to disperse."

Throughout the aides' report, Rajhir and Ospar kept monitoring the news vids. To their irritation, the local feeds had been interrupted from time to time. Technicians had found a short in the receivers of the Imperial House, leaving them to often rely on stations farther away until it had been fixed a few minutes ago. Rajhir and Ospar were playing catch-up on current events.

Rajhir's sudden exclamation got everyone's attention. The Dramok waved them over to join him. "My emperors, you need to see this. The local news vid is replaying a new message from the Basma to the

Empire. It seems to have received this message before the rest of the broadcasters."

The group left their posts, hurrying to join Rajhir and Ospar. The vid was enlarged, though all that there was to see was a still of a bloody boot, the Basma's calling card. The electronic voice issuing from the sound system had been altered to mask the speaker's real voice. Diltan thought it made the Basma sounded utterly inhuman.

"These men who have turned their backs on the Empire—on you, my fellow Kalquorians—they all have one thing in common. Take that thing away and you will reclaim Kalquor. Whether you believe in the foul mixture of Kalquorian and Earther or not, it is the one tool that will bring these despots to their knees. The Earther females are their badge of tyranny. They claimed the first of these women for themselves, guaranteeing their legacies while the average clan goes without. Their lines will live on while yours die out."

Jessica took Egilka's arm. "Oh, I do not like where this is going."

"They know the secret—control the Mataras and you control the Empire. Hold these women hostage and the despots must fall. So what are you waiting for, Kalquorians? Take what you have just as much right to, what these councilmen and the elite have kept for themselves. Take them and do not let them go until the Empire is returned to its people."

Clajak's eyes narrowed. "You said this is a replaying of the message? When did it originally air?"

Rajhir said, "It must have been when the signal went out. The reporter said it first broke into their transmission half an hour ago."

Suspicion filled Bevau's tone. "When did the protestors at the Imperial and Government Houses begin to leave?"

Erybet checked his handheld. "About twenty-five minutes ago." His startled gaze met Bevau's.

The Nobek emperor said, "Erybet, get Nobek Breft from Global Security on the line. Tell him to check on the Matara Complex. I'll com the complex on the Esofu Continent to make sure they're all right."

Erybet moved to a quieter corner as he spoke into his com. Bevau did the same. Diltan's heart froze. When was it he had tried to reach Cissy? Had his com not gone through because of planned interference?

He dug his com out of his pouch and tried her frequency again. "Com failed," the device told him in its bland, disinterested voice. "Wave pattern blocked."

Earlier, it had told him the system was overloaded. Blocked was an entirely different matter.

He looked up to see Jessica watching him from nearby. Her face paled. She knew who he'd just tried to reach.

He told her, "We're too late. They've been cut off."

Bevau's yell came on the heels of his announcement. "Esofu Continent's Matara Complex is under siege. If one complex is under attack—Erybet?"

The Dramok aide nodded, his expression grim. "Breft says he and several squads are on their way there now. They heard the complex was under attack just seconds ago. They can't get a signal through."

Diltan thought his heart might stop. "Cissy. Cissy and Tasha."

Bevau and Erybet had been in ground troop-issued armour the entire time Diltan had been there, the former soldiers ready to go into battle at a moment's notice. Now they moved towards the door. Bevau looked at Jessica and Diltan as they went. "We'll get our cousins and bring them back here."

Jessica had the presence of mind to yell, "Be careful. Oh, what the hell am I saying? You're a Nobek. Erybet, make sure you both come home to your Mataras!"

Erybet sketched a wave as Bevau snorted. "As you command, my empress."

Diltan's frozen body found its way through the shock to chase after the two men. "Wait! I'm going—"

Jessica grabbed his arm as Korkla, Egilka and Clajak moved to stand in his path, blocking him from following the two warriors as the door shut behind them. Ospar and Rajhir took positions in front of the door, also preventing him from leaving.

Jessica said, "No, you are not going. Cissy is one of the few people I'm afraid of having mad at me and she will be mad if you put yourself in harm's way."

Korkla gripped his shoulder, his expression compassionate with understanding. "I know your very being cries out to rescue your beloved. You are not a warrior, however."

Clajak added, "Plus I don't want to face your Nobek if he shows up and discovers we let you go into harm's way. I won't tell you to not worry, because that's an impossibility. Be assured, though, that Bevau and Erybet will get Cissy and Tasha out."

Diltan's fists clenched. A million arguments rose to his lips. His heart screamed that he must run to Cissy now, that he had to snatch her from the jaws of danger. But the men before him would never allow it.

He'd have to wait, at least until Rolat got there. And meanwhile, the clock was ticking against his Cissy, facing who knew what dangers.

* * * *

After the alarms went off, an announcement blared that the complex had been overrun and all Mataras must lock themselves in their rooms. A drunken Tasha grabbed Cissy's arm with one hand, a freshly opened bottle of bohut with the other, and tugged her out of the apartment.

"Let'sh go," she slurred. "We're coushins of Jeshica. We'd make good hoshtaches…hostashes…mustaches."

Cissy smothered a bray of laughter that tried to escape. She lurched unsteadily after her twin, following her to a door that led to service corridors. The complex's staff used the utilitarian back hallways to carry out their work and stay out of the way of the Mataras. Cissy had never been in these areas.

"You know your way aroun' here?" she asked as Tasha navigated turns with staggering confidence.

"Yeah. There are lotsh of good places to have fun with the guards and staff."

Cissy boggled at the knowledge her sister had been carrying on with the complex's personnel rather than her dates. "It's always the quiet ones you have to look out for," she said, feeling the greatness of her wisdom.

Tasha beamed an unrepentant grin and tossed back a swallow of bohut. She made another turn that led to a narrow set of steps. Cissy thought about being cautious, but her sister's confidence made her shove that notion aside. She followed her into an empty hallway that seemed long deserted.

"Whirr are we goin' anyway, you wild, back-hall harlot?"

Tasha took another swig and handed the bottle to Cissy. "There are milesh of tunnels behind—I mean, beneath the complexsh and markesh…marshest…*marketplace*. No one but a few of the higher-up military guys know about 'em. They lead out to the beash. We'll come out practically in Jess' front yard."

Cissy blinked at her twin, impressed. "No shit. Glad you been fucking the right ranking people and not humping the privates of privates."

Tasha adopted a haughty tone. "Only the men with at least four barsh on their uniforms."

She stuck her nose in the air to affect snobbery. With her eyes off the floor, her bare feet tangled together. Cissy grabbed her, barely preventing her from falling. For a few moments they clung tight together, smothering their giggles on each other's shoulders.

When they got going again, Cissy asked, "So what are the tunnels for? Besides naughty getaways, of course."

"In case something like what ish happening happens. If there are riots or terrorists in the marketplace or anywhere underground, the military can rush in and surprise the attackers." Tasha put a finger to her lips in a shushing motion. "It's s'posed to be top secret. If we run into anyone, act super surprised, like we found it by accident."

Cissy raised the bottle to salute her sister. "Well, of course. I'd hate for your pet cocks to get into trouble." She giggled, sipping bohut. "You really are a thug under that sweet smile."

"You have no idea."

They turned a corner and there was another flight of stairs. At the bottom, Tasha stopped. She shoved at a wall panel in such an ungainly manner that Cissy thought her sister had lost her balance again. She gasped and reached for Tasha…then gasped again as a portion of the wall swung out to reveal the circular mouth of a tunnel behind it.

"Shit, thass cool." Cissy squinted at the darkness beyond. "No lights?"

"A few. Come on."

Tasha and Cissy entered the warren of dimly lit passageways dug into the rock. The twilight environs reminded Cissy that Kalquorian eyes were much more sensitive to light than those of Earthers. Little by little she adjusted to the dark.

Tasha led her. She hesitated from time to time when presented with more than one tunnel to travel in.

"You sure you know where we're going?" Cissy asked, taking another drink. She had the vision of someone stumbling across their skeletons a few years from now, both clutching the bottle of bohut. For some reason that struck her as funny and she snorted the alcohol up her nose. She coughed and gagged as her eyes ran with tears at the burn.

"Pretty sure. About another half mile and we'll be—"

Tasha stopped short as they rounded the corner, coming face-to-face with a group of black-uniformed Nobeks. Cissy stared at the percussion blasters pointed at her and her sister. A surge of fright found its way through the muddle of her alcohol-soaked brain.

The tunnel erupted in Kalquorian curses. The blasters lowered and one craggy-faced man came striding forward to confront the women.

"Mataras! What are you doing down here?"

Tasha grabbed the bottle from Cissy and said, "What do you think? We were searching for a place to hide, Nobek. In case you haven't heard, the complesh is under attack."

Cissy peered at the officer's Global Security insignia. She had to lean in so close to see it clearly that her nose brushed the fabric. She straightened to tell her twin, "Only three bars. He's not one of yours, I take it?"

Tasha peered at him and smiled. "Nope. Wish he was, though. I'd lower my sights and panties for a piece of that."

Cissy blinked to clear her gaze as she inspected the seething Nobek. Great body, plenty of muscle, but his weathered face said he was rough around the edges. His nose was big and bent, as if it had been broken half a dozen times. His jaw was too aggressive. She saw a couple of scars on him, too. He was compelling but not a pretty man by any stretch of the imagination.

She looked at her twin in confusion. "Do I know anything about you? Anything at all?"

The commander turned from them, huffing with impatience. He told one of the younger officers, "We can't have them roaming around down here. Take these women to headquarters."

Cissy slapped his bulging shoulder to reclaim his attention. "Actually, you can take us to the Imperial House. We're the cousins of Empress Jessica. Hup, hup, big boy. Let's go."

He glared at her, as if he'd rather put her over his knee and give her the walloping of her life. Cissy thought of Rolat's nice hard hand and sighed. Now that was a Nobek. Worthy of five stars—or bars—at least.

"Rawr," she said, unaware she'd made the sound out loud until Tasha bellowed laughter.

The commander scowled at the bottle in Tasha's hand. "You're both drunk is what you are. If you weren't Mataras, I'd put you in a cell to teach you better sense."

The officer he'd told to escort them away cleared his throat uncomfortably. "Your pardon, Commander, but I recognise them from news vids. They *are* of the Imperial Family. Mataras Cecilia and Natasha, I believe."

The commander shifted his white-hot glare to the young officer. Cissy rolled her eyes. At this rate, Earth would be inhabitable again before she and Tasha got out of here. Shouldn't these men be liberating the Matara Complex instead of arguing over where to put a couple of women?

She shoved the commander's shoulder this time. "The kid is right. So get on with saving the rest of the gals and let us by. Otherwise, it'll be off with your heads." She made chopping motions towards the commander's neck to demonstrate.

Tasha gave her an impatient push, nearly knocking Cissy off her feet. "Oh, for heaven's sake. You are such a bull in a china shop. Try some charm every now and again."

Tasha gave the shocked Nobek a sweet, drunken smile. "Excuse my shister. She has no sense of prospostefy…prefostrophy. *Propriety,* damn it. We keep her chained in a corner most of the time where nobody can see her. It's true!" she continued, as if the man had denied the claim. "Do you know it was only through my efforts that she managed to get engaged to be clanned? Cissy is impossible, but you can see that. Please don't take her lack of good manners personally."

"My lack of manners? You're the one humping everyone but who you should." Cissy swiped to grab the bohut away from Tasha. Her sister held it out of reach while continuing her attempt to sweet-talk the commander.

"Sir, we really are the cousins of Empress Jessica, but wherever you wish us to go, we'll be glad to do so. Thank you. I hope the rest of your day gets better."

The commander looked flummoxed rather than mad now. Cissy thought she detected some of his squad fighting back smiles. She wondered what was so funny.

The officer abruptly bowed to them then turned back to the young Nobek who had affirmed their identity. "Take them straight to the Imperial House. If there is a problem, the Royal Guard can deal with it. The rest of you, let's go!"

He led the men down the tunnel towards the complex. They hurried past Cissy and Tasha. A few dipped their heads in hurried respect, grins lighting their faces. Then they were gone, except for the one officer left to take care of the women.

The young Nobek gave them a bow. "Mataras, this way please."

They fell into step behind him, weaving from side to side in his wake. Cissy grabbed the bottle from Tasha and hissed in her ear, "Little Miss Sweetie-Pie. What a performance. I bet your pussy drips sugar."

Tasha smirked and flipped the hem of her skirt. "That's what they tell me."

The sisters cracked up, hiccupping laughter. Suddenly, the officer went on alert, his blaster coming up as he swung an arm out to keep them back. "Who's there?" he yelled.

A familiar voice called from the darkness ahead. "Ease down, soldier! It's Emperor Bevau and his aide Dramok Erybet!"

"My emperor!" The soldier bowed so deeply that Cissy thought he might break his nose on his knees. "My apologies! I didn't realise—"

Bevau emerged from the gloom, with the too-pretty-to-be-a-man Erybet at his shoulder. The emperor returned the officer's bow.

"Well done, Nobek. No apology is necessary. I appreciate your readiness to defend my cousins and thank you for doing so." His attention moved to the goggling women. "Are you two all right?"

Cissy and Tasha paid no attention to him. Instead, they looked at the officer. The young Nobek was still bent double bowing. His ass stuck up in the air. The women exchanged a glance then shrieked with laughter.

Bevau stepped forward and took the half-full bottle of bohut from Cissy. He handed it to the snickering Erybet. The Nobek put his arms around the sisters, guiding them.

Cissy looked back to see the officer being left behind, his expression confused as they walked away. That made her laugh even harder.

Bevau's rolling chuckles joined in on the merriment. He told Erybet, "At least someone on Kalquor is having a good day. Maybe we should douse the whole Empire in bohut, Erybet."

Cissy said, "I'll drink to that." She would have, too, but Erybet wouldn't give the bottle back.

"You've had enough, young lady."

"Spoilsport. I bet you and Diltan would get along famously."

Chapter Thirty-Two

It was one of those situations that Diltan would have laughed uproariously over had he heard it as someone else's tale. Maybe he'd laugh about it later anyway…but for now, matters were anything but funny.

Rolat and Wal had arrived minutes after Bevau and Erybet's departure. When he got the news, Rolat was determined to head out for the Matara Complex to rescue his Matara and her sister. Diltan opted to go with him. Everyone else protested them going into what the news vids were proclaiming to be a 'tense situation' between converging Global Security squads and a large group of protestors who had overrun the complex's security staff. Even Wal shoved at his clanmates, telling them to not be such macho asses looking to get themselves shot.

Rolat not only swore to storm over, he told Diltan to stay behind. "You've got no fighting experience," he said, dismissing Diltan's insistence on going. "I can't rescue Cissy and keep your ass protected, too."

"Neither of you goes anywhere," Clajak stormed at the pair. "Stop acting like fools and wait for Bevau and Erybet to bring the women here."

"I am responsible for my Matara. I will see to her safety," Rolat growled. "Enough talk. I'm leaving now. If you try to go with me, Diltan, I will beat your ass in front of everyone."

"Oh, save us all from chest-beating men," Jessica said. She spoke into her com. Seconds later, half a dozen armoured Royal Guards filed into the room and lined up in front of the door.

"No one leaves," Jessica told them. "Especially those two idiots." She motioned to Rolat and Diltan.

That was when Rolat lost all patience. He swelled in fury at being challenged, his muscles bunching so that he looked twice his normal size to Diltan. He stepped towards the guards. They tensed into fighting stances.

"Hey!" Wal yelled. He jumped up on Rolat's back, wrapping his arms around the thick, corded neck and his legs around the Nobek's waist. "Just settle down, okay?"

Rolat didn't seem to notice his clanmate clinging to him like a living backpack. He took another step towards the guards. They began to snarl.

Despite Rolat's size and fighting ability, Diltan knew he didn't stand a chance against six battle-trained men. Even though he was more than a little ticked off that Rolat had blatantly thrown off his command, had even threatened him in front of the Imperial Clan, he didn't want to see his Nobek beat down.

"Whoa!" Diltan jumped in front of his advancing clanmate. "Calm down. Take a breath. Think about what you're doing."

"What I'm doing is making people bleed if they don't back the fuck off. Every one of you, get out of my way. I want my Matara now." Rolat sounded nowhere near sensible.

Wal released his neck with one arm to pound his fist against the Nobek's chest. "Stop being a fool! Wake up, you stupid animal!"

Diltan was too busy dancing in front of Rolat to appreciate how ridiculous his high court judge Imdiko looked. Wal perched on the Nobek like a child playing kestarsh-back. Diltan's bouncing and wildly waving of arms was no doubt as indecorous as Wal's behaviour. Most of the other people in the room watched their performance with incredulous expressions.

The clan's outrageous activities were halted by Korkla's shout of, "Global Security has taken the complex! Initial reports are that none of the women were harmed. They all locked themselves in their rooms. The rioters never went into the buildings that house them."

Everyone directed their attention to the news vids. Ospar, who monitored another feed, added, "The same has happened at the other Matara Complex. The mob went after the administration areas, not the women. There was never any sign they wanted to harm the females."

Clajak gave a sigh of relief. "At least the Basma hasn't incited enough madness to hurt our Mataras." He looked at Clan Diltan, still frozen in place. Diltan noted the way the emperor tried to keep his expression neutral…and the grin that wouldn't let him.

Jessica was not so amused. "Are you three asses done now? Cissy and Tasha should be safe. There is no reason to kill each other getting to them. Honestly, I'm not so sure I should give my approval to you clanning my cousin after that ridiculous performance."

Diltan realised his arms were still in the air. He lowered them sheepishly as Wal slid down Rolat's back. The Imdiko was bright red. After he'd gained his feet, he ducked behind the larger Nobek in his embarrassment. Snickers filled the room.

As for Rolat, he stepped back, easing down. He gave Jessica a bow in apology.

"My regrets for being so aggressive, my empress. I lost my head in my fear for Cissy. The thought of standing by while Cissy cowered in that place, under a threat and no doubt frightened—"

The door opened behind the wall of guards. They stepped aside as Cissy and Tasha stumbled their way into the room. Bevau and Erybet followed, smirks stretching their handsome faces. Diltan was sure the half-empty bottle of bohut in Erybet's hand was not his.

Jessica snorted and said, "Yes, Nobek Rolat, my cousin looks utterly traumatised." Eyeing the lurching Cissy, she added, "On second thought, you four do deserve each other. You have my blessing."

Diltan barely heard her. Unable to contain himself, he rushed to Cissy. He and his clanmates surrounded her, kissing her, touching her, reassuring themselves that she was safe and whole. She squealed with delight over the attention, returning the caresses with no inhibitions. Diltan had to clutch her hands to halt her attempt to pull his pants open in front of everyone.

Tasha sounded disgruntled in the midst of all the laughter. "Hey. Where's my kissy face? No fair. I was in danger and needing rescue, too."

Jessica joined in the merriment, enjoying the sight of her drunken cousins. She laughed. "Sorry, Tasha. My clan is off-limits."

Mumbling against Diltan's lips, Cissy said, "Give her one of those Royal Guards. Just make sure he either has a beat-up face or four bars."

Diltan paused the wild welcome, wrinkling his nose at the overpowering odour of alcohol that clouded the air about her. "You are so drunk. In the middle of a riot, no less!"

She laughed. "And you're cute for a pompous ass." She got serious for a moment. "I am so glad you got out of your office okay. All of my guys are safe, it looks like." She smiled all around at the men crowding her then peered around Wal. She beckoned to Erybet. "This calls for a celebration. Hand that bohut over, pretty boy."

Wal snorted. "I think you've celebrated enough, my love."

Clajak asked Bevau, "So you ran into no trouble retrieving our cousins?"

"They'd stumbled on the emergency access tunnels."

Cissy brayed to Tasha, "Yeah, we *stumbled* on them, right, Mata Hari?"

Tasha had found her way to a lounger and sprawled across it, for once every bit as unrefined as her twin. She waved a hand in the air as she said, "Stumbled on them, through them, out of them—"

Rolat glanced from one sister to the other. "By the ancestors, you girls need keepers. Someone find Tasha a clan before she gets herself hurt."

With the Matara Complexes secured, everyone found the ability to relax and laugh at the women's antics. Diltan mooned over the flushed face of his Cissy while she laughed along with them. Even with her eyes bleary, her hair in disarray and stinking of booze, she had never looked so beautiful to him.

She gazed up at him. Defying the love that shone in her eyes, she smarted off, "I guess I've screwed up, huh? All vulgarity, none of your prized décor…decoration…um—"

"Decorum?" Wal suggested.

"That's it! Whatever will you do with me, Dramok Diltan?" She batted her eyes and started to lean against him—and fell hard against his chest instead.

Diltan shook his head and grabbed hold to keep her from splashing to the floor. "If you'll have me and these other two buffoons, I'll clan you right here and now, you mad, messy little Earther."

Cissy gave him wide, delighted eyes. "Yay! He asked me! I'm saying yes! I'm clanned, everyone."

From her lounger, Tasha yelled, "Woohoo! Pass me that bottle! She reeled one—I mean three—in!"

That brought more laughter and cheers from the rest. As Erybet hid the bottle he'd confiscated behind his back, Diltan searched for Clajak. It was good to see the Dramok Emperor, who'd had so little joy lately, cheerful for a change.

Clajak caught his eye and Diltan pretended concern. "My emperor, she is contrary enough to ask to de-clan us later. She'll claim intoxication made her accept my offer."

The emperor came over to clap him on the shoulder. "From what I can see, she's in too much need of supervision to be allowed loose again. She's yours to keep, Clan Diltan. Our congratulations—and best of luck with her!"

Rolat and Wal whooped with triumph. Diltan drank in the beaming face of his new clanmate as congratulations rang in his ears. Yes, Cissy was loud, crass and scruffy. She was also his, now and forever. Diltan had never been happier.

Chapter Thirty-Three

Cissy crept along the halls of her clan's getaway on the moon-based Itahi Colony. Clan Diltan's second of five homes resided within an exclusive resort in a picturesque mountainous region. She sneaked through the sun-spotted corridor.

Not real sun, she reminded herself as she passed one of the vids that simulated a window. The lovely snow-dusted mountain scenery was real enough, being transmitted from just outside the home. Windows were energy wasters, however, so Kalquorians didn't tend to use them in constructed buildings such as this one.

Much as the landscape outside showed, the moon resort was renowned for its hot springs and picturesque beauty. Cissy had nevertheless experienced little of Itahi's pleasures. She'd been too busy indulging in the sensual delights of her clan for the last three days following their clanning ceremony and its subsequent five-day celebration with family and her clanmates' colleagues. Clan Diltan's massive ballroom had gotten its use for the round-the-clock party. Rank had its responsibilities and tending to guests had taken up much of their time during the festivities. Cissy and her men were more than happy to exercise rank's privileges in decadent luxury...and exuberant fucking in the midst of that luxury. Responsibility had taken a distant backseat to pleasure, for at least three out of four of them.

Cissy tiptoed barefoot in a new soaksuit that made the one Wal and Rolat had first seen her in look demure. As usual, she was uncaring of the marble-tiled floors or the expensive rugs that covered them. Ridiculous extravagance, in her opinion. Floors were meant to be walked on, not be dressed up in silks and designs better left hung on walls to be admired. With a hot spring located in the middle of the house, things were bound to get sloppy and wet.

At least it was a small house, compared to the clan's suite back on Kalquor. Diltan had told her it was the smallest of the clan's five homes.

'Five homes? Who the hell needs five homes?' she'd yelled in disbelief. 'That's obscene!'

Diltan gave her a withering look. 'One is within a day's travel of the main prison colony on Jegar, which Rolat sometimes has to spend time at. One is on the moon where Wal's parent clan lives. A third is on the second continent where we enjoy skiing and winter sports for a month or two at a time. Plus some of my investment interests are located there. There are valid reasons for having a residence at each of those places.'

'Valid, huh? Heaven forbid you stay in a hotel or with the parents. No, Dramok Diltan has to have his own house everywhere he parks his entitled ass.'

'Speaking of asses, yours needs a spanking for being so damned impertinent. Come here.'

Thinking of the way his hand had warmed her rear made Cissy wet in a way that had nothing to do with her recent relaxation in the spring. She hurried on her way.

She reached the entertainment room and peeked in the doorway. It wasn't as opulent as their entertainment room in the cliffside home on Kalquor, but it was still luxurious with fine, heavy furniture of the greatest craftsmanship. The loungers and chairs were all custom-made, the fabrics lavish, the cushions plush, the decorating sumptuous. Cissy had made it a point to have ground ronka cheeseburgers shipped in just so she could eat low-class fare in such surroundings. It never failed to make Diltan roll his eyes.

Sure enough, Diltan sat in front of the vid. The sound was turned down low enough that Cissy couldn't hear it. The exuberant sounds of the dance music she increasingly preferred to lemanthev and rimnastin throbbed merrily in the distance. Yet Cissy knew her Dramok watched the news feed coming from Kalquor.

With the Empire managing a tremulous peace these days, the councilman was supposed to ignore current events for the duration of their honeymoon. A host of people back home had promised the worried Dramok that they would inform him immediately if any emergency broke out. Even so, Diltan couldn't help himself. His commitment to the Empire spurred him to sneak off and check in every chance he got. Cissy had to smile at her mate's sense of duty.

There was no denying things were uneasy. In the aftermath of the riots following Yuder's pardon, a third of the Royal Council had resigned in protest. The new elections held to fill those posts were decried by many as being unfair since the only people who ran were those sympathetic to keeping the Earther Mataras on Kalquor. Yet those who identified with Maf and his ilk refused to campaign for the seats. They insisted that fighting the established elite would be pointless.

As Jessica said, anyone with a thought in his head and an eye to see would recognise how ludicrous such arguments were. She sent out a statement begging those opposed to the current politics to run for election, to offer the Empire a balanced voice in the people's representation. For the most part, her plea was hailed. That, plus the Imperial Decree issued by Clan Clajak vetoing the council's vote to expel the Galactic Council's representatives, went a long way towards quieting much of the dissension. Yet Maf and his followers, now comprising a new group called the Foundation for Truth, Honour and Freedom, kept up a volley of partisan broadcasts, seminars and talks that lured others to their call for a pure Empire and the dissolution of the current council. They also criticised the Imperial Clan at every turn, stopping just short of demanding their ouster as well.

Word spread that the Basma's ranks were growing. His broadcasts continued, breaking into programme feeds to exhort Kalquor to revolution, to push out the Earther infestation once and for all. Those broadcasts had increased in frequency after a few military high commanders and admirals disappeared, several of whom were among the Empire's leading experts in encryption measures. The source of the broadcasts could never be traced.

Meanwhile, the new Royal Council continued to push for shutting its borders to the Galactic Council of Planets and any governments not accepting Kalquor's right to be free of outside 'tyranny'. Led by Councilman Terbal, it voted five times within a month to cut off all relations with the Galactic Council. Every time, the Imperial Clan blocked those votes, keeping lines of communication as well as trade open.

Fortunately for Kalquor, the Galactic Council's oversight board was patient. Recognising one of their most influential members was in the midst of a major upheaval, one that could affect a large number of its affiliates, it ceased its efforts to extradite Yuder. It accepted his admission of guilt in absentia and postponed sentencing until 'the current state of unrest in the Kalquorian Empire' found closure.

Protests and demonstrations by both sides continued. However, the threat of real violence only simmered now, waiting to come to a boil…or to be taken off the burner and allowed to cool. Since it was impossible to know which way the Empire's mood would turn, Cissy and her clanmates knew they might have only a short window of time to enjoy their new union.

That was why she, Rolat and Wal had extracted a promise from Diltan that he would concentrate on them and not the state of things back home. A promise he'd been incapable of keeping…and would now pay a price for.

Cissy burst into the room. "Aha! Caught you!"

Diltan jumped with a little scream, having let himself get engrossed in whatever the vid had been showing. He glared at Cissy and uttered a blistering, foul curse before ordering off the vid.

He shook a finger at her, as if she had been the one doing something naughty. Even as he told her off, his eyes widened with appreciation to see her wet and barely clothed. "Damn it, woman, you deserve to have a bell around your neck. You're as sneaky as a Nobek."

She folded her arms over her chest. "Your Nobek will have your hide for breaking our agreement."

"Indeed I will." Rolat and Wal walked in from the room's other door, where they had waited for Cissy's arrival. The Nobek gave Diltan a searing look. "Watching the news vids again, my Dramok? I thought we had a clear understanding that you would not do that."

At his side, Wal wore his judge-ish air. "Reneging on a promise, which is the same as breaking a contract. Our leader is setting a terrible example for his clan."

Cissy couldn't help joining in. "As usual, he is being arrogant and thinking himself above the law. He needs to be punished."

Diltan gave them his patented smirk. "Ah, but we never did come to an agreement as to what penalty my indiscretions would result in. So with no consequences—"

Rolat offered a smirk of his own, a threatening one. "But we did come to an agreement. You just weren't around for the discussion."

The Dramok's sneer dropped off his face in an instant. He took a step back from Rolat. "What? Hey, you can't do that."

"Watch us."

With that, Rolat jumped forward and grabbed Diltan. In an instant, the two men tussled on the fur-scattered floor, rolling all over the place. Cissy laughed at the sight of two full-grown Kalquorians scuffling like boys. Diltan was outmatched, but it was obvious Rolat wasn't looking to hurt him. While Diltan strained to triumph, Rolat's efforts seemed half-hearted.

Wal grinned at her. "It looks like fun. I have to get in on this."

He joined in on the scrap. Cissy cheered Nobek and Imdiko on and jeered at the overwhelmed Dramok. Though Rolat didn't need it, Wal helped him overcome Diltan after a few minutes of struggle.

It ended with Rolat sitting on Diltan's legs, pinning them down. Wal had him by the wrists, leaning his weight to keep his arms held to the floor. Cissy fetched the soft cords they'd hidden in the room as they'd waited for Diltan to be himself.

The Dramok yelled to see the binds in her hands as she approached. His struggles against the other two resumed to no avail. "Hey! Wait just a damned minute!"

Rolat grabbed the ties from Cissy. He moved faster than she could watch, tying Diltan's ankles together then knotting the cord to the leg of the heavy table. He repeated the action with Diltan's wrists, securing them to the leg of a chair. "Oh no," he growled at the clan leader. "You had this coming, you sneaky bastard."

"This too." Wal swept Diltan's hair away from his face and made him face one side. The Imdiko's fangs unhinged. As fast as a rattlesnake's strike, he bit the shouting Diltan's neck.

Cissy peeled off her soaksuit, watching the action with anticipation. Little by little, Diltan's struggles tapered off. His yells drifted into occasional moans. Rolat grinned at Cissy.

"The effect of our venom on each other is different than the effect on Earthers. When we're bitten, we can't answer questions with anything but the truth and we must obey whatever orders we're given. It's impossible to resist."

Cissy was delighted to hear that. "This is going to be so much fun."

Wal straightened, releasing Diltan after licking clean the small trails of blood his bite had brought on. "Dramoks despise not being in control. This is a far better punishment for Diltan than beating him black and blue."

Diltan drew a breath and his upper lip wrinkled back in a snarl. "You are all going to pay for this shit."

Cissy smirked to see him helpless and fuming about it. "Promise?"

He looked at her as she stepped close to stand over him. The fury in his expression died to see her naked. Blatant desire took over. His shorts did an impression of a tent as his cocks swelled. The pungent cinnamon-like scent of Kalquorian desire filled Cissy's nose.

Seeing him like that, aroused for her, made Cissy's nipples peak and her pussy twitch with anticipation. She couldn't wait to have him, her demanding and assured and delicious Dramok.

Wal chuckled as the fight disappeared from his clanmate. With a Diltan-like leer, he told him, "My beautiful Dramok, you will let us enjoy you as we wish. If you behave—"

"For a change," Cissy interrupted.

"We might even allow you to come."

Diltan dragged his gaze from Cissy to appeal to his Imdiko. He jerked on the cords keeping his gorgeous body stretched long. "Isn't tying me up overkill, my clanmates? I'm bitten, so I have no choice but to obey you."

Rolat snorted as he stroked trailing fingers over Diltan's chest. "You are also stubborn and tend to throw off intoxication quicker than most. The binds stay. Now lie there and take what you are given."

Wal winked at Cissy. "Your pleasure, my Matara?"

Cissy put her hands on her hips, feeling like the Queen of the Universe. The mighty Dramok Diltan had fallen and she was going to enjoy every second of his subordination.

"Get those clothes off him. I want to see our prize."

With a hearty laugh, Rolat grabbed the gasping man's shirt collar in both fists. He tore it apart, baring the muscled torso. Diltan groaned at the violence, writhing in response. The Nobek then turned his attention to Diltan's shorts, quickly making confetti out of the fabric to display his rigid cocks. Cissy licked her lips at the sight of the thick, glistening lengths. Diltan shuddered under the weight of her gaze, his eyes filled with want.

They did not treat him with kindness. Soft, feather-tipped fronds were sent over his straining body, teasing him with light touches that heightened growing need. They whispered threats, telling him they would not let him climax, that perhaps they would keep him helpless and hard for the entire honeymoon, using him to placate their own desires.

"Don't, my clanmates," Diltan whimpered. "Please, don't be cruel."

"We can keep biting you, too," Rolat said, tugging on one of the Dramok's nipples. "You'll submit to us in every way, all the time."

Wal gave the clan leader's hip a couple of stinging swats. "No means of control. Your will lost to complete surrender."

Cissy dragged her tongue from the base of Diltan's cock to its weeping tip where Wal's frond circled round and round. "Our pretty plaything, our handsome fuck-toy."

She left off tasting his cock to kiss her way up his body, letting hands and mouth roam all over the swells and dips of his perfectly cut abdomen and chest. His skin was hot as if with a fever, thrilling her as she dragged her lips, tongue and breasts over its surface. Diltan's rapid breath made his flesh rise and fall beneath her.

Cissy suckled on his hard-tipped nipple as Rolat and Wal turned their attention to her. Calloused hands cupped her breasts, squeezing the supple mounds. A gentle touch caressed her pussy, fingertips dipping into the folds to collect the moisture there. They spread her juices to her ass, wetting her for the inflatable butt plug the men often used to prepare her for love.

Cissy kissed her way across Diltan's heaving chest as the plug pressed inside, spreading her open only a little to start with. A thrill transmitted through her loins as it nestled within, a sweet pressure adding to her pleasure.

She flicked the hard button of the Dramok's nipple with her tongue, enjoying his moan of reaction. Fingers plucked at one of her nipples, drawing it into a point. A moment later, there came a hard pinch and a tightening. Cissy shivered as the clamp Rolat placed on her nipple sent slivers of delicious pain and excitement zapping straight to her clit where Wal played.

The Imdiko had the sensitive nub trapped between two fingers, his hand clamped against her pussy. He rubbed back and forth, massaging her folds. Her clit moved within his grip, the friction heady. His other hand delivered the occasional slap to her buttocks when he wasn't reaming her backside with the slowly swelling plug. Her senses swirled with bliss.

Cissy's hand was busy, too, pumping Diltan's slickened cocks in turn to make him cry out with frustrated need. Her moans were a counterpoint to his pleas for mercy as Rolat attached a clamp to her other tit. She nipped the Dramok's flesh to pay him back for some of the gorgeous torment the other two visited on her. He jerked beneath her.

"Would you like to put this on him?" Rolat asked. "It will keep him hard and unable to come for as long as we like."

Cissy straightened to see the rubbery figure-eight-shaped device he held out to her. She recognized the double cock ring that the men had occasionally used on themselves to make their encounters last longer. She'd never considered the option of turning it on any of them.

Over Diltan's desperately repeated no, she accepted the ring. "After all the times he's made me hold out? Hell yes, I want it on him."

Cissy crawled backwards over the trembling body, letting her breasts drag over the suffering Dramok. It brought searing consciousness to her clamped nipples, but the pain was worth it to see the agonised lust on Diltan's face. Making him pay granted big dividends.

She was being made to suffer along with him in ways not of her making. Wal never missed a beat when it came to his handling of her throbbing pussy. The plug continued to glide through increasingly relaxing muscles, opening her more and more for the cocks that would soon claim their rights to her. Cissy found it harder with each passing second to concentrate on Diltan's punishment.

She ended up straddling his corded thighs, her face hovering over his thickly veined cocks. Cissy let her breath waft over them, enjoying how his face twisted in reaction. He hurt, all right. He would hurt more long before they were done with him.

Cissy was grateful for the copious lubrication his penises emitted. It made it easy to slide the tight double cock ring to the bases of his erections. The helpless Dramok watched her with wide, almost terrified eyes.

"Yummy," Cissy said and set to work.

She trusted Rolat to make sure Diltan didn't hurt himself as his head thudded a rapid rhythm against the thick fur between it and the floor. She busied herself with sucking and masturbating his trapped cocks. Hands and mouth delivered torment to the man she had fallen in love with despite herself. Cissy licked Diltan clean of his spicy wetness, swallowing with pleasure. The sweet saltiness of pre-cum was added delight to her tongue. His overwrought cocks quickly replaced everything she devoured, feeding her hungry desire to consume him.

Meanwhile, Diltan had stopped trying to dent the floor with his hard skull. Now his head tossed from side to side, a sign of how hard his body fought for release. "Please," sprang from his lips every few seconds.

Rolat busied himself attaching a metal-link chain to the clamps on her nipples. Had it been a necklace she wore about her neck, Cissy would have never remarked on the weight. However, it felt profound on her breasts, renewing the stinging burn to make her moan around her mouthful of Diltan.

Also making her moan was Wal's wicked tongue teasing her clit as three of his fingers dived in and out of her pussy. Her ass felt swollen with the butt plug, increasing the pressure of the finger-fucking. She thought she'd go cross-eyed from bliss.

Then Rolat gave her breasts a break to concentrate on her vulnerable ass. His huge paddle-size hands delivered quick smacks to both cheeks in rapid succession. None of the spanks on their own were particularly hard, but taken together, Cissy's backside soon sizzled. Even more compelling was where Rolat struck—on the meatiest part of her ass, on either side of her anus. The movement jostled the plug, setting off enthralling sensations throughout her core.

She managed only a few seconds of that before she was nearly out of her skull with arousal. She released Diltan's jerking primary cock with a gasp. "Let me fuck him now."

Wal withdrew his fingers from her clutching pussy and Rolat eased the plug out as well. A second later, Cissy squatted over Diltan's livid cocks, ready to take her pleasure.

She looked down at her prisoner. Diltan's strain showed. Strands of sweat-slick hair clung to his face. His arms, stretched and bound over his head, trembled. His face showed none of the smug expression Cissy had once despised. He looked at her with pleading, with lust, with hopeless love. Seeing the adoration there, as naked and raw as emotion ever got, made Cissy's breath catch.

He loves me with all his heart and soul. He really does.

Her chest feeling like it might burst with joy, Cissy leaned close to place a tender kiss on his lips. When he moaned, she whispered, "Be an obedient boy, now. Behave and give your Matara what she needs. If you do that, my gorgeous, occasionally misguided but deep-down goodhearted Dramok, I'll give you release."

"Anything," Diltan promised. "Anything you want. Everything you ever need. I am yours forever, my Matara."

Cissy kissed him then, kissed him with all the love and passion that were hers to give. The formal vows they'd made during their clanning ceremony couldn't compare with the simple declaration Diltan had just uttered. She kissed him until they both gasped and wept with the strength of their love.

Cissy rose, conqueror and conquered, ready to claim her spoils. Diltan's expression was still one of eager torment, but he smiled up at her.

The tips of his cocks prodded her pussy and anus. Cissy didn't look to see if it was Rolat or Wal or both who positioned them for her. She slid back, sheathing her Dramok with a happy sigh.

Diltan gazed with parted lips and lidded eyes as she rose and fell over him, finding a pace that made her senses sing. Seeing the mighty, muscled body subservient to her needs excited her. Cissy loved being made to surrender most of the time, but she thought she might have to get the men to help her overcome each of them every once in a while. It was heady stuff.

Wal and Rolat watched her fuck the helpless Diltan for a little while, their hands gripping their cocks, stimulating themselves with rapt expressions. Cissy felt their gazes, as scorching hot as the cocks that filled her, caressing her as she performed. She leaned back, propping herself up with her hands on either side of Diltan's thighs, her feet planted beneath his armpits. It gave them all a good view of the Dramok's cocks sliding in and out of her pussy and ass.

Rolat crawled over, his gaze hungrily devouring the sight of her fucking their clanmate. His finger settled on the silver chain between her breasts, tugging on her nipples. He ran his finger over the arc of the chain, moving it back and forth, adding to the weight of its pull. Lightening zapped through her breasts, blistering hot. Cissy's head fell back as she cried out with mingled pain and excitement.

Wal closed in. He took Cissy's mouth in a devouring kiss, plundering, tasting, claiming. His cunning fingers found her clit and closed on it, pinching and rubbing.

Lightning flashed again, this time deep in her belly. Its galvanising force swept her entirety, bellowing up in the form of screams that poured from her throat into Wal's. Her body seized, frozen in time and space as she detonated.

She came back to herself on the swells of depleting bliss to find Wal and Rolat smiling down at her. "You are amazing to watch when you climax," Wal told her.

Diltan spoke between pants. "Come again. Please, my Matara, come again."

"She will," Rolat promised.

Cissy did. She rode Diltan as Wal and Rolat urged her on. Their hands and mouths herded her to culmination again and again as surely as the thick cocks that she thrust into herself. Cissy was granted release wild and raucous, sensual and sublime.

At last there was one last thing that would erase the tiny mote of emptiness that remained in the midst of otherwise incredible lovemaking. "I want your cum filling me," she moaned to Diltan. "I want to taste your cum," she told Wal and Rolat.

"Then that's what you will have, my Matara," Rolat said.

She rose to release the cocks that twitched inside her. Cissy took the utmost care easing the cockring off

Diltan, knowing it wouldn't take much to bring the final push into passion. The Dramok's fists clenched. His teeth ground together as Cissy sleeved him once more.

Once she had settled and Diltan indicated he had some measure of control over himself—"But not much," he gasped—Wal and Rolat stood up. Cissy tilted her head back and opened her mouth.

They brought the tips of their primary cocks to her lips. They stroked themselves as Cissy licked and kissed and sucked them in turn. Their gasps grew louder. Rolat grabbed Cissy's hair in an iron grip that wouldn't allow her to move had she wanted to. She did not, but her excitement increased at his show of power.

She rocked her hips as much as she was able, adding Diltan's moans to those of the other two. Cissy clenched interior muscles to add to his pleasure, massaging his cocks. He tensed beneath her, his denied body realising fulfilment could at last be had.

Diltan's strangled scream was almost musical in its long, trailing note of bliss. When the first peal ended, he cried her name just as ringingly.

That set off Wal. He choked out a grunt that seemed to boil from the deepest pit of him. He pressed the tip of his cock into Cissy's mouth, his grip moving up and down the shaft in a frenzy. He made another choked sound and hot sweet-salty-spiciness poured over her tongue. She swallowed the flood, sucking hard as if the shuddering Imdiko required coaxing to grant her every precious drop.

Rolat managed to hold out just long enough for the last expulsion to leave Wal's body. The Nobek howled, his entire body jerking over Cissy's, splattering her face, breasts and belly. She released Wal to claim the pulsing cock and the remainder of its offering. Rolat's flavour was heavier than the Imdiko's, a delicious counterpoint to Wal's sweeter essence. Cissy savoured it until Wal rubbed her clit, forcing her mouth open to scream as she made one more flight into glory.

Cissy wasn't sure when the lot of them collapsed to the floor around Diltan. A minute or an entire day might have passed by the time she blinked up at the man cuddling her against his side. The Dramok had been untied and he curled against her with Rolat spooning behind him. The Nobek propped up on one arm to grin at her.

"Do you think our Dramok has learned his lesson?"

Cissy snuggled into the warmth of being sandwiched between Diltan and Wal. "Hell no. He'll be up to no good the instant our backs are turned."

"Oh good," Wal said in a happy voice. "While putting people in prison makes me cringe, I do enjoy this form of punishment. When can we catch you watching the news feeds again, Diltan?"

The bastard had his smirk firmly in place. "You won't. I'll be very careful from now on."

Cissy rolled her eyes and told them, "You notice he has no intention of mending his evil ways."

Rolat laughed. "We gave up on that a long time ago."

"I'm a lost cause," Diltan said. His sneer softened to the other smile, the one Cissy liked best. The one that told her how much he loved her. "I'm particularly lost when it comes to you."

"You are a complete rogue who cannot be redeemed," Cissy sighed, her heart melting under that adoring gaze. "I guess that's why I love you, you jerk."

About the Author

Tracy St. John lives in coastal Georgia with her husband and son. You'll often find her haunting train museums with her locomotive-loving son. Besides writing, she has also worked in video production both in front of and behind the camera. She's usually cast as the gun-toting bad gal, getting handcuffed in the end. She has no complaints.

Tracy loves to hear from readers. You can find her contact information, website details and author profile page at http://www.totallybound.com.

TOTALLY
BOUND
Home of Erotic Romance

www.ingramcontent.com/pod-product-compliance
Lightning Source LLC
Chambersburg PA
CBHW070538030726
47505CB00001B/77

* 9 7 8 1 7 8 6 8 6 3 5 8 4 *